A NOVEL

An Epic Journey to the Stars

WILLIAM TYLER

ISBN: 979-8-218-43451-9
ISBN 13:

"If our long-term survival is at stake, we have a basic re-sponsibility to our species to venture into other worlds."

Carl Sagan

# CAST OF CHARACTERS

**Cdr. Jake Merriweather** - Captain of the ISA Starship Endeavor
**Lt. Milo Bridges** - Pilot, Mission Specialists, First Contact Officer
**Lt. Cdr. Donald "Stone" Stoner** - Executive Officer of the ISA Starship Endeavor
**Lt. Catriana "Cat" Cortez** - Pilot, Mission Specialists, Medical Officer (back-up)
**Lt. Javier "Javi" Rodriguez** - Mining Officer, Security Officer
**Lt. Jennifer "Doc" Lee** - Medical Officer
**Lt. Jonathan Mills** - Technical Officer
**CM "Master Chief" Dutch Swenson** - Propulsion Engineer
**Dr. Herbert Mann, "The Professor"** - Exoplanetologist (Planetary Scientist)
**Dr. Paul Girard** - Cryptographer (CNES, ESA)
**Dr. Mike Martin** - Anthropologist
**Dr. Forest Graham** - Botanist
**Zoe Bishop** - Correspondent, Cahill News Organization
**Dakar Zaru Dualla** - Ninth Tal'su (student) of Dualla, First Tal'su of Krei AKA
**Dakar Dualla** - Chief Astronomer of the Quoram (The Science Ministry)
**Yuni** - Tenth Tal`su of Dualla, First Tal`su of Zaru (Young protégé of Dakar Dualla)
**Glyvash** - Assistant to the Chief Astronomer
**Councilor Krei** - Eighth Tal'su of Dualla, First Tal'su of Bentar, Tal'shi (Teacher) of Zaru, Member of the ruling Council of Eleven—the Ben`lei
**The Akan** - Holy Leader of the Ben`lei, Daughter of Xenosta, Goddess of the Sea, Protector of the Faith.
**Wapoe** - Astronomer's apprentice (planet Ulysses)

# CHAPTER 1

*Three billion years in the past, Sagittarius arm of the galaxy*

No sentient life exists on planet Earth and won't for another 2.7 billion years. However, a thriving sentient society does exist on a planet in the Sagittarius arm of the Milky Way Galaxy.

It is on this planet, approximately three billion years ago, that our story begins.

Wapoe pulled the threadbare blanket tighter around his hunched shoulders, leaned forward, and pressed his eye against the telescope's eyepiece. He blinked twice to clear his vision, feeling the discomfort of the cold metal ring pressed against his solitary eye.

His mind might have drifted to the icy winter air whistling through the opening in the great dome above his head. Tonight, however, he was too excited to be concerned with such trivial matters. Tonight, he was on the verge of an important discovery—or so he hoped.

Young and ambitious, Wapoe dreamed of becoming a world-famous scientist, making significant discoveries, and having his portrait enshrined in the prestigious Great Hall of Heroes. Whether it be a new planet, an undiscovered asteroid, or perhaps some unexplained cosmic anomaly, he desired recognition that would etch his name into history.

The thought pleased him greatly.

The first step on his ambitious path was to impress his mentor, the highly respected Chief Astronomer of the State Science Authority. A noteworthy discovery would be just what Wapoe needed to get his master's attention.

Wapoe leaned back on his perch, lifted a warm bowl of broth from a nearby metal stand, and took a sip, careful not to burn his mouth. The pungent aroma filled his nose, or what functioned as a nose for his species. He held the bowl a minute longer, letting the steaming brew warm his hands, before returning it to the small table.

Wapoe was grateful to have his current position, despite the long hours and the bitter cold. Someone born to his station could rarely expect to rise above a life of bare existence. However, Wapoe was cleverer than most. He had done well in his studies, which did not go unnoticed by school administrators. Despite his lack of patronage or family name, the State Science Authority selected Wapoe for their apprentice program. He realized the incredible opportunity he had been given and was intent on succeeding.

Wapoe was especially grateful to have a bowl of hot broth every night. Wrapping his tail around his legs, Wapoe again returned to his search.

"Where are you?" Wapoe mumbled as he fidgeted with the telescope's control wheels. The young apprentice patiently searched for the faint object he had seen the night before—or the smudge, as he had called it. It wasn't much of a smudge, but he was sure he had seen it. At first, he had dismissed the faint apparition as a product of his fatigue, a symptom of eyestrain. It wasn't supposed to be in that stellar region. It was something new. He needed to be sure. Then the clouds had rolled in, thwarting any chance of confirming the sighting.

Tonight, he pointed the telescope toward the predicted coordinates, determined to find the enigmatic object.

"Ah, there you are! You've shifted position," he said, a broad grin on his face. "How did you end up over there?"

He blinked his eye and concentrated his attention on the small patch of sky. Yes. There it was—a small brownish dot with no business being where it was. He was familiar with this grouping of stars and that whatever it was shouldn't be there.

Wapoe now needed to confirm his discovery before he would dare inform his master. Therefore, over the next six nights, bundled against the frigid mountain air and warmed by many bowls of broth, Wapoe diligently recorded more transparencies to document his discovery. Overlaying the transparencies confirmed his suspicions—the object was moving. His calculations also confirmed that the object was much closer than the stars that served as its backdrop.

Unaware of the turmoil his discovery would cause and dreaming of fame and glory, Wapoe reported his findings to his master. His master was skeptical, of course. Such a discovery from someone so young, so inexperienced, was unlikely. The Chief Astronomer, however, was sufficiently intrigued to investigate personally. Thus, he ordered Wapoe to make additional transparencies, supervising the effort himself. After a careful analysis of the new images, the Chief Astronomer came to the undeniable conclusion that Wapoe was right.

The Chief Astronomer hurriedly penned a paper announcing his discovery to the world, disregarding Wapoe's contributions entirely.

Over the coming months, hundreds of astronomers trained their telescopes, great and small, toward the same constellation to view this new visitor. They took their photographs and made their measurements. One by one, each came to the same inescapable conclusion.

It took a year to come to a scientific consensus. The brownish dot was, in fact, a brown dwarf star, and alarmingly, it was on a trajectory that would bring it into Wapoe's home planetary system.

A flurry of scientific papers quickly followed. Some scientists predicted the brown dwarf would pass by harmlessly. Others predicted a fantastic light show in the sky but saw no danger to their home world.

However, a few foresaw an impending catastrophe. They argued that the proximity of a brown dwarf represented a genuine danger to their planet—possibly an extermination event. At first, these scientists were called alarmists. Others disputed, even ridiculed, their findings. On more than one occasion, such claims resulted in outright dismissal.

The media tried to explain the findings to the public. Reporters eagerly described the science of brown dwarfs, using terms like *failed stars or missing links*. They told their readers that, unlike stars, brown dwarfs were too small to sustain nuclear fusion in their cores. The public learned that these hot, dense balls of gas didn't shine as brightly as stars, hence their brownish color. But despite their size, brown dwarfs possessed massive gravity, strong enough to alter the orbit of any planet that wandered too close.

Eventually, as scientists determined the trajectory of the brown dwarf more precisely, the truth of the danger to their home world became apparent. In a broadcast viewed around their world, a well-respected scientist announced in a sobering voice that in a little over three years, the brown dwarf would enter their planetary system, and the effect on their planet would be disastrous.

Nations around the world launched ambitious projects they hoped would prevent the looming catastrophe and save their home world. Government scientists and engineers proposed huge and sometimes outlandish projects that were studied, hotly debated, only to be discarded as impossible.

Some relied on prayers to their deity. Many built underground shelters and began hoarding supplies causing worldwide food shortages. Others decried the whole thing a hoax perpetrated by their leaders or some devious cabal of *others*. Some criticized government scientists for causing the impending disaster.

Massive demonstrations demanding action appeared in every corner of the globe. Some rioted over shortages. Lawlessness prevailed in many countries.

Theirs was not a space-faring society. Other than small satellites hoisted into orbit by unsophisticated rockets, the citizens of this planet had no way of avoiding their fate. Grand schemes to build massive spacecraft were proposed but deemed impossible, yet some governments began hugely funded projects to attempt just that.

As the brown dwarf got closer, most realized their fate was inescapable. When the object finally entered inside the orbit of the system's outermost planet, most governments had fallen.

It took another year before the brown dwarf made its closest approach to their home world. The effect of the massive object was devastating. There were constant quakes. Existing volcanoes erupted, and new volcanoes formed almost overnight. Global temperatures soared. Sulfur dioxide from thousands of erupting volcanoes permeated the air, making it hard to breathe. The elderly, the young, and the frail quickly died. Acid rain fell constantly. Enormous storms ravaged the planet. Food supplies disappeared entirely.

For a while, those who built underground shelters and hoarded provisions survived. However, they eventually succumbed to soaring temperatures, starvation, and toxic air.

Unknown to the dwindling life on the planet, the passing brown dwarf had also exerted its massive gravitational attraction and wrenched the planet from its orbit about its sun.

The dying planet now followed a new trajectory, away from its parent star and out into interstellar space, its oceans steaming and its surface obscured by a toxic mix of volcanic ash, clouds of sulfuric vapor, and acid rain. The most important event in the planet's history had gone unwitnessed and unrecorded. There was no one left to mourn the passing of an entire species. No one would recount its past or plan its future. No one would celebrate its culture or its accomplishments. No one would tell its story.

Every living thing, from the highly developed sentient race with its advanced civilization to the resilient insects that had thrived for millennia, was wiped away by the brown dwarf's powerful gravity.

The brown dwarf had taken more than lives. It had wiped away a vibrant, ethical, diverse, advanced civilization. No other beings in the universe had known of or would ever know of their existence.

Their planet was now a dark, cold, lifeless world, its oceans gone, replaced by a kilometer-thick crust of ice, and its atmosphere stripped away by stellar winds. It would drift through the cosmos for another three billion years before entering the Orion spur of the Milky Way galaxy.

This rogue ice planet wasn't alone. While traversing an asteroid field, it would later gain a moon, a kilometer-wide chunk of rock and iron.

The wandering planet was now on course to intercept an unsuspecting planetary system—a binary star system comprising a yellow star, a red dwarf star, and five planets—one inhabited.

# CHAPTER 2

*2122, Johnson Space Center, Houston, Texas*

Mission Control Center: Launch Director Gene Crenna hunched over his mission book, his eyes flowing down each page in the spiral-bound binder for the hundredth time. Crenna was a man who valued tradition. He could have accessed his mission book on his holo's display but chose not to. Instead, he chose paper, honoring a long line of Launch Directors tracing back 150 years to Chris Kraft and the early Vanguard missions of the 1950s.

Crenna's fingers moved slowly back and forth, tracing the text as if he could absorb their meaning through osmosis. He loved his job and took it seriously. If there was a detail, however innocuous, however innocent looking, that might adversely affect the mission, he was determined to find it. His eyes kept glancing up at the time displayed on his console. Ten minutes, he thought to himself.

To his right sat Vehicle Manager Alice Winters, who was poring over her copy, choosing to read it on her holocom. Winters handled the integration, scheduling, and conduct of vehicle operations. For this mission, she was NASA's liaison with the science team responsible for the vehicle that at this moment was in LEO or Low Earth Orbit. She was speaking over her holo to Dr. Planck, one of the team's scientists.

Sitting at the console to Crenna's right was the Assistant Launch Director and Crenna's best friend, Mike Marshall. Marshall was conversing with the engineers at NASA's Goldstone complex in California. Finally satisfied that Goldstone had resolved a telecommunications glitch, Marshall turned and winked at Crenna.

All three were sitting in the row of consoles closest to the front of the Mission Control Center.

"I'm still not buying it," said Marshall.

"Buying what?" Crenna responded.

"That the damn thing is going to go faster than light. Ole Albert's gonna be doing somersaults in his freaking grave if it does."

"Well, technically, it won't be exceeding FTL, but I get your meaning," laughed Crenna.

"So, you understand the science behind it?" Marshall asked.

Crenna held up his hand with his thumb and forefinger a half inch apart.

"Same here," added Marshall. "I like Samuelson. He seems like a freaking smart dude, but that Plank guy is a dick."

Crenna smiled. "I hear you, buddy. But if this thing works, it will change everything."

"No doubt things will get hectic around here," said Marshall. "I've heard talk that if this works, NASA's budget will triple."

"I think so," said Crenna. "There hasn't been this much excitement around a NASA mission since Europa."

Crenna nodded at the TV cameras lined up against the back wall. "Ever seen so many cameras in here? It's important to NASA, that's for sure. I think the whole freaking world is watching."

Crenna had given much thought to this mission's impact on NASA, science, and humanity. He had visions of interstellar spacecraft making new and exciting discoveries—even the possibility of finding other inhabited planets. What a time to be alive, he thought.

Today's mission was a significant first step. It was a test of a small, unmanned spacecraft launched just a week earlier, currently circling the Earth every ninety minutes in LEO (Low Earth Orbit), just twenty kilometers from the new International Space Station. Code-named Odysseus, the vehicle contained an experimental antimatter reactor, and the new Plank-Samuelson technology NASA hoped would propel the ship faster than the speed of light.

If all went as planned, Odysseus would jump to the vicinity of Saturn, take pictures of the ringed planet, and then jump back into Earth orbit. No one knew exactly how fast the ship would go. This test was to answer that question.

Propelling a spacecraft at speeds faster than light had long been thought impossible. Technically, it still was. However, in 2120, two physicists, Jonas Samuelson, and Conrad Plank, made groundbreaking discoveries that strongly suggested a way to circumvent the light speed barrier. A successful test today would prove Samuelson and Planck correct. A failure would confirm what most physicists believed—there was simply no way around it. As NASA engineers watched from Mission Control, the countdown clock reached zero. For a moment, nothing happened. Then suddenly, Odysseus simply disappeared. An audible gasp filled mission control as engineers and administrators checked their displays. There was no sign of the ship—it was simply gone. Telemetry from the ship ceased. NASA scientists feared the worst but clung to the hope that Odysseus had survived and would eventually reappear.

As the minutes accumulated, almost everyone at Mission Control remained at their posts. Some went for coffee. Others tended to administrative duties. Some tended to their bladders. Some went to the cafeteria to scarf down a bit of lunch before scurrying back. However, few strayed far from Mission Control. If this test succeeded, it would be one of the most difficult and important technological feats ever attempted and completed successfully. Finally, as the clock ticked off four minutes and thirty seconds, Odysseus suddenly reappeared.

There were shouts and much commotion in Mission Control as those who had left their posts scrambled back to their seats.
If Odysseus had successfully completed her programming by flying to Saturn, documenting her arrival by taking pictures, and returning, the proof would be in the telemetry.

All eyes stayed glued to the large displays positioned along the curved walls of the newly redesigned Mission Control, waiting for the first images from Odysseus. As the first hint of Saturn's glorious rings appeared, every engineer, scientist, and administrator stood and cheered. This was proof that Odysseus had indeed voyaged to Saturn. There were hugs, kisses, handshakes, and much backslapping. They had done it. They accomplished the impossible.

An hour and twenty minutes later, the Goldstone Deep Space Communications Complex picked up signals coming from the vicinity of Saturn. Odysseus had called home from Saturn, then raced home to arrive an hour and twenty minutes before her call reached Earth.

Calculations would later show that the craft had traveled at a little over thirty-eight times the speed of light.

At last, the cosmos lay open to exploration. There were parades in all the major capitals around the world. Poets, musicians, and artists celebrated the discovery with new creative works, calling it a new golden age of exploration. Governments around the globe at once began making plans to explore beyond our solar system, looking for new worlds, untapped resources, and possibly intelligent life.

That same year, the space agencies of the United States, the European Union, Canada, Japan, Korea, and China created the International Space Alliance (ISA).

Their number one stated mission was to build a fleet of starships to seek intelligent life and to find new planets where humanity could establish new colonies or find untapped resources.

Construction began almost at once on four starships. They were to represent the best humanity could offer. They would incorporate the new FTL propulsion technology, the fastest computers, the latest advances in materials science, and artificial intelligence.

Problems surfaced shortly after construction began. Construction techniques used for decades on Earth proved more problematic in orbit. New antiproton collectors had to be constructed and launched into orbit around Saturn to harvest sufficient antimatter for the new Plank-Samuelson technology. ISA worked desperately to speed up the construction and testing of their new fleet. Sadly, administrators took shortcuts, which led to expensive errors and missed deadlines.

Congress began investigating the delays, and the charges of mismanagement began circulating in the halls of Congress and the offices of the ISA. Under tremendous pressure from Congress, ISA decided to retrofit an existing spacecraft with the new Plank-Samuelson faster-than-light technology. The task fell to the six-decade old starship Endeavor, then floating in NASA's boneyard of old space vehicles ninety-two-million kilometers from Earth, in an area known as L4.

# CHAPTER 3

*2123, Harbor Steak House, New Annapolis, Maryland*

Jake Merriweather glanced at the weather-worn sign above the restaurant's front door. Although Jake had never dined at the Old Harbor House before, he was aware of its reputation as a first-rate dining establishment. When his old friend Mark Higgins had called to invite him to lunch, he was more than pleased to accept.

Jake grasped the brass door handle and pulled open the heavy wooden door, exposing the restaurant's softly lit interior. A variety of aromas greeted him as he stepped inside. Jake quickly spotted his friend seated at a table near the large front window.

"Mark, sorry I'm late," said Merriweather.

"Hi, Jake. No problem. I just got here myself. I had a meeting this morning at the CBO (Congressional Budget Office), which ran longer than expected." Merriweather glanced at his friend. Higgins had changed little in the last year and a half, thought Merriweather to himself. However, a little gray hair had crept into that blond mop of his.

Higgins had the same thought about his old friend. Merriweather had put on a kilo or two and was now maybe eighty kilos—all of it muscle. Merriweather was a striking figure sporting his usual military-style haircut and dressed in his full dress-white officer's uniform.

As both men took their seats, Merriweather's gaze shifted from his lunch guest to the elegantly faux-wood-paneled restaurant and the picturesque view of the harbor from the large window next to their table. Merriweather appreciated the nautically themed artwork on the walls. *Nice restaurant,* he thought. "How long has this restaurant been around?" he asked.

"There's something on the menu about its history," said Higgins. "Let's see. Oh, year, here it is—since 2045. That's shortly after they moved the Academy to its current location."

"They had to make way for the new *eastern seawall* if I remember correctly," said Merriweather. "It seems a bit dated."

"Like yours truly," joked Higgins.

"Don't get me wrong. I do like it," said Merriweather. "So, tell me, how've you been? It's been what, a year and a half since we've seen each other?"

"Just about that," said Higgins. "Much too long. The last time we got together, I took 200 bucks from you at Congressional. I hope you've thrown that putter away."

"Yeah, don't remind me. I don't think I made a putt all day. We need to get out there again so I can win my money back. How's your family?"

"Glad you asked," said Higgins, as he removed his wallet from his jacket pocket and retrieved a few photographs. "You remember Lisa, my youngest. She's now a freshman at Dartmouth."

"Wow, she's looking more and more like Kathy," said Merriweather, referring to Higgins' wife.

"Smart as a whip, too," said Higgins. Higgins handed Jake a second photo of a young woman standing in front of a whitewashed single-story building surrounded by several dozen children.

"Is that Emma?" asked Jake, referring to Higgins' eldest daughter.

"Yep, that's my Emma. She's on a mission in Ecuador, teaching poor kids how to read and write. She's out to save the world, my Emma, and she's determined to do it herself if she has to."

"I thought Emma might gravitate toward service," said Merriweather. "She's an old soul. You must be proud."

Jake didn't ask about Higgins' son Bo. Bo was a troubled child, in and out of Virginia's correctional system, since he was thirteen. If Mark had wanted to confide in Jake, he would. Otherwise, Jake wouldn't ask.

Merriweather had no photos to show Higgins. A career naval officer, Jake and his wife Leah had decided early on that children were incompatible with the nomadic life of a Navy career. They had planned to adopt once Jake's career was over.

Soon after making that decision, Leah got sick with a rare form of cancer that had no cure. At first, Jake had requested a billet in DC to be closer to his wife. Six months later, Jake retired on his Lieutenant Commander's pension. Leah needed full-time care. He spent the final few months of her life seldom leaving her bedside.

After Leah's death, Jake was despondent, not leaving their home for days. He tried to find comfort in a bottle, but drinking wasn't for him. After a few months, Jake decided that living like a hermit was not what Leah would have wanted for him. He was only fifty.

Mark Higgins finally coaxed Merriweather back into the world. First, there were a few golf outings, followed by invitations to dinner with Mark and his family. Eventually, Jake became part of the Higgins extended family, often going with them on family outings. He was 'Uncle' Jake to the kids.

Higgins had even persuaded Jake to become a NASA astronaut.

"You'd be a natural," Higgins had told him. "With your naval experience as a pilot and your command experience as captain of a Navy destroyer, you're just the guy NASA is looking for."

Jake had reluctantly signed up. Higgins had been right. Merriweather took to space as quickly as he had taken to the air as a combat pilot and to command as a skipper, and soon became one of NASA's best and most experienced astronauts.

Back in the restaurant, Jake continued, "I've wanted to try out this restaurant for a long time. Thanks for recommending it. I assume you've eaten here."

"Certainly," answered Higgins, "whenever I get the chance to eat in Annapolis, this is my first choice. The steaks are to die for, and it's real meat, not that imitation 3-D printed stuff you find in most restaurants. Plus, they have an impressive wine list."

"You still eat meat?" Merriweather asked incredulously.

"I know, I know. I really shouldn't, but this is a special occasion, and I want to treat myself."

"Does Kathy know?"

"Hell, no. She'd kill me."

"Well, just keep it on that side of the table," said Merriweather.

A server arrived and took their orders. Merriweather opted for the risotto with truffles and mushrooms, pairing it with a lightly-oaked Chardonnay. Higgins ordered a New York strip steak and a 2115 Château Petrus, Bordeaux.

While Merriweather ordered, Higgins couldn't help noticing that the server was checking out his friend. Well, why wouldn't she? Jake was a good-looking guy. At almost six feet tall, with blue eyes, chestnut brown hair, a square jaw, an athletic build that defied his age, and widowed, Jake was still a catch. He was old enough to be her father. Still, the attraction was obvious.

"How tall do you figure she is?" Higgins asked, as the young woman disappeared into the kitchen.

Merriweather smiled. He knew Higgins was happily married, but his friend always had a wandering eye.

"I'd say no more than five-five," said Merriweather.

"You mean 165 centimeters?" Higgins asked, smiling.

"Hell no. I'll use metric on everything else, reluctantly, but I'm holding the line when it comes to this."

"You know America is the last holdout. We have to join the rest of the civilized world sometimes."

"You join. I'm happy the way it is. She's five-five. It just doesn't sound right saying she's 165 centimeters."

"You sound like my grandpa," said Higgins. "Can I ask you a technical question?"

"Shoot," answered Merriweather.

"From what I've heard, the problems you guys are having getting those new starships finished—those are all about the materials being used to build them, right? Help me understand the problem," said Higgins.

"It's not so much what, but where. We're using the same materials we've used on some of our older ships. You've heard of nano lattices?" asked Merriweather.

"Sure," answered Higgins. "But remember, you're talking to someone who's not a scientist."

"OK. I'll keep it PG. This new stuff is stronger, more impervious to heat, and has the added benefit of blocking cosmic radiation. So, it's perfect for starships."

"So, what's the issue?"

"Well, there was a yield problem. We were getting a significant amount of defective product from our in-orbit manufacturing processes, but we've licked that problem. The stuff we're getting now looks good."

"Problem solved?" said Higgins.

"That one. But there are still challenges."

"Like?" prompted Higgins.

"The delays we're experiencing now are systemic. Some bozo at ISA decided we should build the new starships in low earth orbit. We've always built our spacecraft on the ground in sections, launched them into orbit with heavy lift vehicles, and assembled them up there. We know how to do that well. While well-intentioned, moving our manufacturing facilities up there has pushed the project back more than anticipated. But we're getting there," said Merriweather.

"So, how long before the new starships are ready to go?" asked Higgins.

"Well, we're just a year into building the ships. First, we had to finish the in-orbit facilities we needed to manufacture them, which took time. In addition, even after we complete the ships, there's an issue regarding getting the fuel to power them."

"How so?" Higgins asked.

"Basically, the issue is getting enough antimatter—specifically antiprotons. The closest natural source of antiprotons in the quantities we require is the radiation belt around Saturn. So, ISA placed over two hundred collectors in orbit around the planet to harvest the antiprotons we need. My guess is that it will be four, maybe five years, before we have enough to fuel all four starships."

"Thanks for getting me up to speed, Jake. I like to at least sound intelligent when I talk about this stuff on the Hill."

"OK, Mark, let's hear it. I assume there's a purpose to this little get-together besides the great food and my technical lectures," said Merriweather.

"Well, I'm hurt that our friendship isn't enough," said Higgins, smiling at his old friend. "However, you're right. I have an agenda. Your boss Admiral Hoskins is testifying before a Congressional subcommittee tomorrow, and I've heard that the Committee Chair, Senator Phil Sanders, plans to call for a cut in ISA's budget. He has been gunning for you people since Materials Science failed to win the starship contract. Of course, Materials Science is in his state and a big contributor to his campaign," said Higgins. "I know you are part of the Admiral's support team, and I thought you should know."

"Well, I appreciate the thought, Mark, but that's hardly news. No one on our side is under any illusion that Sanders is rooting for us. Everyone is aware of his animosity toward ISA. I'm sure that is NOT the reason for this get-together."

"Fine, you're right. I have another motive. It's really about something I heard—about you."

"About me?" Merriweather said. "OK, I'm listening."

"ISA is understandably worried about construction delays. Your starships are over a year behind schedule and over eighty percent over budget. Your management needs to change the discourse. Frankly, they need a win. So, I've heard that they are planning to bring an older spaceship out of retirement and retrofitting it," said Higgins.

"You're talking about Endeavor," said Merriweather.

"You know about Endeavor?" Higgins asked, looking surprised.

"Of course, I know about Endeavor. That's the worst kept secret at ISA. They're planning to move it from L4 in three weeks. Everyone's talking about it."

"OK, explain it to me. What's L4?" asked Higgins, "and keep it simple."

"I should charge tuition," laughed Merriweather. "Endeavor has been sitting up there in L4 for five or six years, if memory serves. The 'L' refers to Lagrange as in Lagrange point. These are locations in space where the gravitational forces of the Sun, the Earth, and the Moon balance each other out. You can park a ship there without having to burn much fuel to keep it from drifting away. We have two mothball fleets, one at L5 and one at L4."

"Interesting. You mean you just park something there, and it stays put?"

"I think I just said that," said Merriweather.

"Cool. Anyway, Command believes they can get a functional starship that way faster. And there's more," said Higgins.

"I imagine it will take about three years," said Merriweather.

"They're planning on two. The whole point is to get something out there in deep space and to do it fast," said Higgins.

"So that's the news?" Merriweather asked.

"Every starship needs a captain," said Higgins, taking a sip of wine.

"Interesting," said Merriweather, drawing out the word. "Who are they thinking about?" Merriweather knew very well what Higgins was getting at. ISA Administrator Neil Spencer had already informed him.

"Kent Simons would be an excellent choice. So would Bob Kain. I imagine that either or both guys would be on the shortlist," said Merriweather.

"Damn, Jake, you'd spoil a wet dream," chided Higgins.

"You're saying they've made a final decision?" asked Merriweather, ignoring his friend's crude remark.

"Jake, you might want to pack your bags," Higgins replied with a huge grin on his face.

"Who, me?" said Merriweather, feigning surprise. "You're not just pulling my leg, are you?"

"Nope, it's a done deal."

"Well, Mark, I think that calls for a toast. What shall we drink too?" Merriweather paused for a moment and tilted his head in thought. "I know. Let's drink to Endeavor, and to Neil Armstrong, to Buzz Aldrin, Captain James frigging Kirk, and anyone else who's ever been to space."

# CHAPTER 4

*Selecting the Crew — Cat Cortez*

Merriweather's friend Mark Higgins had no idea that ISA had already started forming a crew for Endeavor. Merriweather and ISA had distinct visions of the crew for Endeavor's first mission, and their viewpoints didn't always align. Nevertheless, Merriweather, being the captain, had the final say.

Merriweather sat at the desk in his quarters, poring over ISA records, searching for suitable candidates. He preferred individuals with experience, but he also planned on recruiting a few people he knew well—individuals he had served with and trusted.

One candidate unknown to him, however, was Catriana Cortez, a promising young lieutenant currently in her senior year at the Academy. ISA was very high on her and enthusiastically recommended her for the mission.

Although he didn't know her personally, he knew *of* her. What he read in her jacket impressed him. Catriana Cortez was an ISA prodigy. She was top of her class and had shown remarkable abilities in several highly valuable disciplines. In short, she checked all the boxes.

Catriana Cortez would be his first call.

Catriana "Cat" Cortez's journey to the Endeavor began as a young pre-med student at Johns Hopkins University in Baltimore, Maryland. Blessed with a prodigious intellect, an inquiring mind, and an aptitude for languages, Cortez excelled at science in high school and graduated in two years with a perfect 4.0 GPA. She arrived at Johns Hopkins on a full-ride scholarship. It wasn't long before ISA became interested and began following her promising college career, eventually offering her a position in the International Space Academy (jokingly called Star Fleet by those who remembered the old TV program). Although it wasn't the career path she had mapped out for herself, when ISA called, she eagerly jumped at the chance to pursue a career as an astronaut.

During her first year at the Academy, she discovered what was to become the love of her life, piloting high-performance aircraft, including the fleet's newest spacecraft. Cortez seemed to excel at almost any task given to her.

ISA took notice. As did Merriweather.

Cortez hunched over a small desk in her academy dorm room studying for her orbital mechanics class when her holo buzzed.

"Lieutenant Cortez," she said

"Hello, Lieutenant. This is Commander Jake Merriweather. Do you have a moment?"

"Yes, sir." She straightened in her chair when she heard the name. It wasn't every day that someone as famous as Jake Merriweather called. Was she in trouble? Did she do something wrong? She timidly answered. "Of Course, sir."

"Good. I've heard good things about you, Lieutenant. I've been reading up on you. Very impressive, indeed. I think you might be a good fit for a mission ISA is planning."

"Really? I mean—thank you, sir. If I may, what kind of mission, sir?"

"What have you heard about Endeavor?"

Cortez momentarily held her breath as she processed Merriweather's words.

"Oh, my stars! You're the Captain of Endeavor?"

Merriweather chuckled. "Yes, I am, Lieutenant, and I need someone with your skill-set. I need a pilot, and I need a medic. You could potentially fill both requirements. Are you up for a multi-year mission on a starship?"

Cortez couldn't believe what she was hearing. This was beyond her wildest dreams. A commission on a starship and not just any starship but Endeavor. She knew Endeavor was going to be the first to leave the solar system, and Jake frigging Merriweather himself was offering her the chance to be a part of her crew. She took a deep, slow breath to collect her nerves before she answered.

"Yes sir, absolutely. Thank you, sir. When do I report?"

# CHAPTER 5

*March 2123, Kadanoff Center for Theoretical Physics, Chicago*

A booming, disembodied voice filled the auditorium.

"Live in 3, 2, 1."

"Good evening, and welcome to Space-Time. I'm your host, Zoe Bishop."

Bishop acknowledged the audience's applause with a sweep of her hand, smiled at camera one, and then turned to camera two.

"I'm here at the Kadanoff Center for Theoretical Physics at the University of Chicago on a frosty winter night," she said as she grabbed her shoulders and gave a mock shiver. "Tonight, we will talk about the very survival of our species with two of the most influential voices in theoretical physics. We will examine the planned mission of the sixty-year-old Endeavor spacecraft, which will take humans outside our solar system for the first time. We will explore the reasons for the mission and the amazing new technology that will make it possible," said Bishop.

"Now, let me introduce our guests. Joining us here from his office at the University of Houston's Center for Planetary Studies is Exoplanetologist, Dr. Herbert Mann."

As Bishop extended her right arm, a full-color, life-sized hologram of Dr. Mann, standing over six-three, appeared as if by magic. For those sitting in the audience, the image looked as real as Bishop herself.

"Welcome, Dr. Mann."

The audience applauded while Bishop and Mann waited patiently.

"Thank you, Ms. Bishop. Thanks for having me."

At sixty, Dr. Mann looked every bit the distinguished English gentleman he was, from the shock of gray hair that adorned his head, the bushy mustache that covered his upper lip, and the wireframed glasses perched on the bridge of his aquiline nose.

To her audience, Bishop continued. "Dr. Mann is the winner of the David Hellman Prize in astrophysics and author of the book *The Planet Hunter: Finding another Earth*. An amazing book, Dr. Mann. You have a way of making even the most complicated ideas more understandable, and as a layperson, that is much appreciated."

More applause filled the hall.

"Now for our second guest, joining us from his home in Greenbelt, Maryland, is co-winner of this year's Nobel Prize in Physics, Dr. Jonas Samuelson, for his development of the Plank-Samuelson Drive." As Bishop turned to her left, a hologram of Dr. Samuelson materialized.

Samuelson's hologram displayed a much younger man, only thirty-five, of Scandinavian descent, five-eleven, with close-cropped blond hair styled in a crew cut.

"Gentlemen, welcome."

Bishop smiled as the audience applauded.

"Thank you, Zoe, for inviting us," said Samuelson.

"Yes, thank you," echoed Mann. "It is great to be on your show."

Bishop smiled at her guests, turned to the camera, and continued.

"I see we have a packed audience tonight. We have students and faculty of the University of Chicago, plus other brave souls who have ventured out on this chilly March night in Chicago. Thanks to all of you for coming out." Bishop smiled as the audience applauded themselves.

"Although I'm sure many of you are here because the heating system in the hall is better than in your dorm rooms, am I right?"

A mock cheer arose from the seats in the back as students began chanting her name—*Bishop, Bishop, Bishop.*

"Let's start with Dr. Mann. You wrote in your book that our species would cease to exist unless we establish manned colonies outside our own solar system. Some people say that would be a waste of money and that we should concentrate on improving our own world. Why are you right and they're wrong?"

Dr. Mann smiled and rolled his eyes in mock annoyance. "I hear this all the time."

"I guess that's one reason you wrote your book," Bishop said.

"That's right. However, it is a widely held belief."

"OK, what's the answer?"

"Well, some of you may have read in your high school history texts of an asteroid that came within a few thousand kilometers of colliding with Earth."

"2107 or eight, I think. I was twelve or thirteen," said Bishop.

"I was a little older than twelve," said Mann, chuckling. "I was a student

at the university. I remember that there was a lot of concern that the asteroid might actually impact Earth."

"I remember how worried my family was back then," said Bishop.

"There were riots in the streets, even suicides," said Mann. "A direct
hit would have ended all life on this planet. Fortunately, NASA was able to
nudge the asteroid just enough so that it missed us. Thanks to NASA, we
were all spared, but it was a close call. That event opened a lot of eyes, and
it certainly made an impression on one young postgraduate."

"It was one of those 'where were you' moments in history, certainly,"
said Bishop.

"Humanity would have survived," continued Mann, "because of our
Mars colony—but only barely. The colonists were not yet self-sufficient,
and thousands would have succumbed to starvation without supplies from
Earth. Eventually, the population would have stabilized, but they would
have struggled."

"Scary thought," said Bishop. "Doesn't a Mars colony guarantee our survival?"

"Not really," Mann replied. "When stars like our sun begin to run out of
hydrogen fuel, they grow larger. Eventually, our sun will be so large it will
swallow all the inner planets, including Earth and Mars. When that happens,
and astronomers tell us it will eventually, it will be the end of humanity."

"Are you trying to depress us, doctor?"

"No, just stating a fact. Our survival depends on us becoming a multi-planet species. Our Mars colony is the first step, but there is no guarantee. We
need to keep spreading our seed, so to speak."
Bishop noticed some chuckling in the audience.

"All right, simmer down out there," she said.

This resulted in more audience laughter.
Bishop turned back to Dr. Mann.

"When we get out there, in deep space, what are the odds we'll run into
intelligent life forms?"

"Good question," said Mann. "I personally think the odds are not as good
as many have predicted."

"Why not?"

"I understand the arguments predicting abundant, intelligent life. There
are billions of stars and exoplanets, and many do fall within the so-called
Goldilocks zone, so I agree that the opportunities for life are plentiful."

"Goldilocks' zone," interrupted Bishop, "the distance from a star where
the conditions on a planet are suitable for life."

"That's correct," said Mann. "Our Universe is over thirteen billion years
old. The real question is this. How long does it take a species to become
intelligent? It has taken humanity about fifty thousand years to reach that
point."

"Some would argue we're not there yet," said Bishop.

Again, the audience showed their approval by laughing at Bishop's comment.

"Anthropologists call it behavioral modernity," said Mann.

"Behavioral modernity—that's a term I've not heard before," said Bishop.

"Abstract thinking, the development of art, music, a written language, etc. often characterize modern human behavior," replied Mann. "If there are species out there that have reached the same level of development that we have, or close to it, one could assume it took them at least fifty thousand years to do so. Now, considering the age of the Universe, what are the odds that our fifty thousand years overlap their fifty thousand years? We can guess how long it takes for an intelligent civilization to develop because we have ourselves as an example. However, we have no clue how long a society will last."

"I guess we don't really know," said Bishop.

"No, we don't. Civilizations are not necessarily permanent," he continued. "They can die, either by their own hand or by some natural catastrophe like a planet-killing asteroid or solar explosion."

"That's a grim thought," Bishop replied.

"We have a term for it," said Mann. "The Gaian Bottleneck predicts a near universal extinction of species for various reasons, from global warming to gamma-ray burst to nuclear war."

"Therefore, assuming there's anyone left to meet out there," said Bishop. "The aliens we prefer to meet are those species that became sentient about fifty thousand years ago and have become modern societies recently, so we can communicate with them."

"Well," said Mann, "we don't know if fifty thousand years is typical. We could be quick learners, or we could be slower than most. As you said, we just don't know. We could run into many Stone Age species or extinct civilizations that died out long ago or before they developed spaceflight and spread to other planets. I also prefer the term 'sophont' rather than 'sentient.'"

"Sophont? I guess I should know that word, but I confess my ignorance," said Bishop.

"You're not alone," said Mann. "A sophont is a being with the ability to reason roughly equivalent to or maybe greater than humans, whereas a sentient is a being capable of feeling."

"OK, sophont it is. Thanks for educating all of us. I guess the odds that we'll run into a technologically advanced civilization are even slimmer," said Bishop.

"That's correct," said Mann. "After all, most of our technological development has happened within the last five hundred years."

"Let's talk about visitors to this planet," said Bishop. "Dr. Mann, why do you suppose some technologically advanced multi-planet species have not visited us?"

"Who says they haven't?" said Mann. "Zoe, have you ever been on a picnic and seen an ant hill? Did you feel the desire to stop and have a chat with them? Perhaps some advanced space-faring aliens flew by Earth, looked down on us, and didn't see anyone worth talking to. Or maybe we didn't recognize them as life forms or interpreted their message to us as anything but a natural phenomenon."

"So, we're the ants," said Bishop.
This resulted in more laughter from the audience.

"Since they don't seem to want to visit us," she said. "I guess we'll have to visit them, and that is no simple proposition, given the distances involved. Let's bring in our second guest, Dr. Jonas Samuelson."
Once again, the audience showed their enthusiasm with a hearty round of applause.

"Dr. Samuelson, we all want to congratulate you and Dr. Planck for winning this year's Nobel Prize in physics. Thank you again for joining us tonight. Unfortunately, your colleague could not be with us. I understand he had a previous engagement."

"You're right. In fact, Dr. Planck recently got married and is on his honeymoon," said Dr. Samuelson.

"Well, our congratulations go out to Dr. and Ms. Planck," said Bishop. "Hopefully, we'll have Dr. Planck as a guest on a later show."

More applause from the audience.

"Dr. Samuelson, let's talk about Albert Einstein and Relativity, my favorite topics. There are a lot of budding physicists in our audience here in the Kadanoff Center, and I'm sure they know a lot more about relativity than I do, but for those listening from home or in their car, could you take a moment to touch on relativity and why it's important?"

"I'll try," said Samuelson. "It's been two hundred and fifteen years since Einstein published his General Theory of Relativity. Most people know his story. Although he was an unknown in the world of physics, just a clerk in the Swiss Patent Office, his paper on relativity sent shockwaves through the scientific community. His momentous breakthrough taught us that space and time are intertwined. He even coined a term for it. *Space-time*."

"The name of my show," Bishop chirped.

"Indeed," said Samuelson, smiling. "One linchpin of relativity is that nothing with mass can travel faster than the speed of light. To move a particle with mass to light speed would take an infinite amount of energy.

"What does that mean for us?" Samuelson continued. "Well, it certainly makes space travel more challenging. Given the immense scale of the Universe, much of it seems unreachable. For example, using the latest in plasma ion technology, we can only manage about a third of the speed of light. At that speed, it would take about thirty years to reach the closest star."

As Samuelson took a sip of water, Bishop asked, "However, you and Dr.

Planck discovered a way around it?"

"You've heard of quantum entanglement?" asked Samuelson.

"Yes, I have," said Bishop. "We did an entire show on it back in July. Maybe you can give our TV audience a refresher."

"All right." Samuelson paused and took another sip of water. "Einstein, along with Podolsky and Rosen, discovered quantum entanglement in the twentieth century—1935, to be exact. The weird phenomenon Einstein referred to as spooky action at a distance links two quantum particles, even when separated by vast distances. You affect a change to one, and you see a change in the other instantaneously. Research suggested that the communication between the two was much greater than the speed of light. One of our theories was that communications between the particles occurred in a different dimension, or even a different universe."

"Hyperspace," said Bishop.

"Or so we thought. While scientists eventually concluded that entangled particles didn't communicate with each other, the research did stimulate interest in other dimensions. We used to believe these other dimensions or universes were just a convenient way of explaining the mathematics of reality. Astonishingly, it turned out to be real."

"I assume your discoveries and the technology you've created exploits hyperspace to get around the faster-than-light barrier," said Bishop.

"Yes. In lay terms, the Hyperdrive, as we call it, creates an antiproton field around the spacecraft that phases between our universe and hyperspace at approximately thirty trillion gigahertz—the wavelength of a single proton."

"Thirty trillion?" asked Bishop.

"That's three, followed by twenty-two zeros—every second," said Samuelson.

"So, the spacecraft is in both our universe and in this hyperspace at the same time?" Bishop asked.

"Well, almost simultaneously, for all intents and purposes," said Samuelson. "When the ship is in our universe, it is essentially motionless or traveling at whatever sub-light speed it was before it entered hyperspace. However, when it's in hyperspace, it travels approximately forty times the width of a proton before switching back to our universe at the new location. Now, that doesn't sound like a lot, but it switches so fast that the cumulative speed is almost forty times the speed of light."

"And it doesn't violate the speed of light limitation?" Bishop asked.

"No," said Samuelson," because when the ship is in our space-time, it travels at sub-light speed. Technically, it only travels at FTL in Hyperspace—where the rules are different."

"Doesn't this take a lot of energy?"

"Yes, but not as much as, for instance, the Alcubierre drive concept, which required exotic matter. Our design is much more efficient."

"We did a whole segment on the Alcubierre drive last year," said Bishop. "Your method doesn't require exotic matter?"

"No, just antimatter."

"What about the occupants?" Bishop asked. "Do they feel motion or any vibrations?"

"None," said Samuelson. "It's like they're in an ordinary sub-light spacecraft."

"That's so exciting. How much faster can this innovative technology take us?" Bishop asked.

"For Endeavor, and the current iteration of the technology, about forty times light speed, but for the ships under construction at the IOCF, we expect to double that," said Samuelson.

"Impressive," said Bishop. "One last question—Is there a limit?" Bishop asked.

Samuelson chuckled. "Something tells me that the retro sports car you drive isn't just for show."

A scattering of laughter filled the hall.

"Busted," said Bishop.

Laughter, mixed with applause, rolled through the audience.

"Well, to answer your question, it is energy dependent," said Samuelson. "After Endeavor, we are planning on a new generation of reactor-generators we hope to have ready for the new ships under construction. That should give us even more performance."

An hour later, as she exited the Kadanoff Center parking garage in her recently restored sports car, Bishop was still thinking of Samuelson's comment about its performance.

"I wonder what he'd think about this performance," she said as she pressed the accelerator pedal to the floor.

As she sped away, Bishop's thoughts shifted to tonight's broadcast. "Damn," she said under her breath, thinking of several follow-up questions she should have asked. However, one question she had asked was whether Dr. Samuelson was planning to volunteer to go on the first FTL mission. His answer was no, and that worried Bishop. She prayed it wasn't because he was concerned about the technology's safety, because she had already applied to the ISA—and had been accepted.

*Zoe Bishop*

"Are you nuts?"

Zoe Bishop winced at Joe Harrington's outburst as she slumped in one of the plush leather chairs in front of his rather large and imposing desk. Harrington was Vice President of Cahill Publishing's Broadcast Media Division. As a senior executive, he occupied one of the top-floor corner offices at Cahill's downtown Chicago location. Harrington oversaw Cahill's on-air programming. He was also Zoe's boss.

"What were you thinking? You're not planning to accept, are you?"

Zoe squirmed in her seat. She had seen Harrington this animated before, but this was the first time he had directed his intensity toward her. After all, she was his golden girl. He had stumbled upon her science-based podcast one evening driving home from the airport. Zoe impressed him. She was a smart, funny, and eloquent talent with an acerbic wit and impressive intellect. She was flirtatious, but that just added to the appeal. Unable to get her out of his mind, he woke his assistant in the middle of the night and ordered him to track her down and get her into his office ASAP.

The young woman who stood before him that morning was every bit the talent that he had gleaned from her podcast. He also realized she belonged in front of a camera and not behind a microphone. Her radiant smile, quick wit, and intelligence were all qualities that would captivate any audience. Plus, she was cute. Fifty-five kilos, five-seven, blond—no—dirty blond hair. *The camera will eat her up*, he thought.

Zoe's star at Cahill had risen meteorically ever since Harrington had tapped her for his new science-based talk show. Based on her podcast, *Space-Time* achieved almost universal acclaim and was soon the top-rated show in its time slot. She consistently booked A-list guests, including top scientists, relevant politicians, and famous artists.

"I've got to, Mr. Harrington. You know I applied last year. Don't you remember? I sent you a memo."

"Yeah, but I considered that to be PR. I never expected them to select you. Wait, didn't they already announce the crew members?"

"Yes. I was a backup. However, one guy backed out because of a health issue, so, surprise, I'm next in line. I can't say no. It's the chance of a lifetime. I'll get to do what no one else has ever done."

"What about *Space-Time*? It's your show. Are you willing to give it up?"

"I don't think you'll have any problem filling my position. There will be a line out the door. The show is in capable hands. It practically runs itself. Tom is a fantastic producer."

Harrington shook his head. He knew the viewers tuned in to see and hear Zoe Bishop. She was the heart and soul of the show, and viewers loved her. She impressed everyone with her encyclopedic knowledge of science, and she didn't back down from anyone. Her interview with Senator Phil Sanders, who chaired the ISA oversight committee, was legendary. She exposed him to be a petty and vindictive man who lacked knowledge of basic science. After the interview, Sanders immediately fired the assistant who had booked him on her show.

*Space-Time* would suffer without Zoe Bishop as its host.

"How about a raise?"

"I'm sorry, Mr. Harrington. It is not about money. This is something I really want to do. Plus, if you give me a job when I return, think of the stories I can tell."

"If you get back," Harrington replied. "When do you leave?"

"I'm scheduled to begin my training in two months. I have to go through ISA's pilot training program, plus there will be several training flights before we go."

"Well, if there's no changing your mind, I'd better get busy finding your replacement. We'll miss you, Zoe. Be careful out there."

"Thanks, Mr. Harrington, for everything."

Bishop left Harrington's office with some misgivings. Gigs like *Space-Time* didn't grow on trees. Zoe's mind flashed back ten years and what her life was like then. Was she being foolish?

Zoe's life in Chicago had been difficult. She left high school in her junior year and quickly became hooked on methamphetamine. Shoplifting, or boosting as they called it, became a daily way to feed her drug habit. It wasn't long before she found herself standing in front of a judge. A sympathetic court-appointed attorney got her into rehab, avoiding an arrest record.

Six months later, she walked out of the rehab facility drug-free. She moved into a halfway house and took a menial job at a software firm. At age twenty, she received her GED and applied for student aid. Two years later, she had her associate degree in broadcast media.

Unfortunately, having a degree did not guarantee a job, and she was soon living in her car and begging for handouts.

The record-low temperatures of the winter of 2113 drove Zoe from her car and into St. Emanuel's Church to get warm. Shivering alone in the under-heated church and feeling hopeless, she almost didn't hear the voice whisper in her ear. "Would you like my jacket, Miss?"

She almost turned him down. Being the target of unscrupulous men was nearly a daily occurrence. However, something in John Lucas' voice told her she could trust him.

She accepted his jacket, and soon they were laughing over hot chocolate at a nearby restaurant. She probably would have accepted if he had offered to take her home that night. Instead, he gave her money, dropped her off at a local hotel, and made a date for breakfast the next morning.

Over the following few weeks, Zoe fell madly in love with John Lucas. He was too good to be true. He was smart, with a self-effacing style of humor that Zoe much appreciated. While he was twenty years her senior, Zoe sensed in John a kindred spirit. Most of all, he loved her. She thought of him as her savior. He asked her to move in with him, and she accepted.

John Lucas was a physics professor at the University of Chicago who had lost his wife to cancer two years before he met Zoe. Occasionally, Zoe would sense a residual sadness in his eyes, but mostly, he seemed genuinely happy.

After a while, Zoe and John became inseparable. She loved hearing him talk about science because he made complex ideas understandable. One morning, he suggested Zoe sit in on his physics lecture at the university, and she accepted. Soon, she was there every day, soaking in everything he had to teach.

Two years into their relationship, Zoe announced she wanted to go back to school full time. John had awakened a love of knowledge in Zoe that she wanted to fill. She also wanted to meet new people.

John had tightly limited her socializing to his small circle of friends, all older than Zoe. But she wanted more friends her age. She could apply for financial aid, she had told him. She was not asking him to pay for it.

Rather than supporting her wish, John was adamantly opposed. He saw this as a betrayal. He liked the relationship the way it was and saw no reason to change it.

Zoe reluctantly accepted John's decision and let the matter drop. However, the desire for other friends didn't go away. For several weeks, everything returned to normal until she brought the subject up again. Again, John became angry.

Over the following months, John became increasingly suspicious, demanding to know where she was going when she left the apartment and who she was meeting. She even caught him checking messages on her holo.

Zoe didn't like what and who John was becoming.

This was not what she signed up for. He wasn't the man she had first met. He was gentle and caring one moment, angry and even violent the next. Every time she would bring up her desire for friends or wanting more, he would push back. Over time, he became angrier.

The relationship ended badly. Zoe moved out and into a women's shelter. Eventually, she had to get a restraining order. Over time, after a few trips to jail for violating the order, and afraid of losing his job, Lucas had given up. Zoe had suspected that he had found another object for his attention. For whatever reason, he had stopped harassing her.

Zoe's thoughts returned to the present and her upcoming life on Endeavor. Her future was "out there" among the stars, and she was eager for the next chapter in her life to begin.

# CHAPTER 7

*Javier Rodriguez—LaGrange Five—Asteroid Mining Station*

Rodriguez floated into the decontamination shower, twisted his 5 ft. 8 in. frame into position, and slid his feet into the floor restraints. It was no simple task, encased as he was, in his bulky spacesuit. His eighty-kilogram suit, designed for the harsh environment of asteroid mining, added another four inches in height and 76 centimeters (about 2.49 ft) in girth and was not very flexible.

Dust, grit, and fine powder coated his spacesuit, the result of eight long hours commanding and working alongside his eight-person mining crew. Although their supervisor, to Rodriguez, that just meant to be willing to do everything he asked his men to do. His mantra was "lead by doing."
His arms ached, as usual, but it was a feeling he expected and even looked forward to. He was also starving. He planned on getting clean, getting fed, and then getting to bed.

"Decon—begin," said Rodriguez, raising his arms.

Javi heard the telltale sound of pumps spinning up a second before hot water and steam exploded from the myriad of spray nozzles surrounding him.

Rodriguez raised his arms, exposing every inch of his spacesuit to the jets of high-pressure water. Vacuum pumps sucked up the dirty water almost as fast as it flowed into the decontamination shower.

The sixty-second shower was followed by a blast of hot air lasting another minute. A buzzer sounded, signaling the completion of the decontamination process.

It was the first of two showers he would take before he crashed for the night.

Five minutes later, after struggling out of his suit and stripping off his undergarments, Rodriguez returned to the shower, adjusted the control settings, and repeated the process.

Finally clean, Rodriguez pulled on his jumpsuit, the standard outfit for station crewmembers, and retrieved his evening rations from the food locker.

His holo chirped.

"Who's this?" he asked, as he opened a squeeze tube of pureed vegetables.

"Javi, is that you?" asked the caller.

"Yeah. This is Javi Rodriguez. Who's this?"

"It's Jake, Jake Merriweather."

"Jake, is that really you? Jake Merriweather. Hey, man, how are you?"

"Doing well, Javi. It took me a while to track you down. You're a hard man to find."

"I ain't been hiding."

"Yeah, but I never expected to find you floating in L5 (Lagrange five). "What the hell are you doing up there?"

"Ah, you know, drilling holes, blowing stuff up."

"Must be some view."

"When I have time. But you get jaded."

"Still, your view of the Milky Way must be quite something to see."

"It is. We're about four times farther from Earth than the moon, so there's less light pollution."

"I gather you're busy."

"We've laser-blasted a fair number of tunnels into the asteroid, and I spend a lot of time deep inside. So, it's not all floating among the stars—not to get too poetic."

Merriweather chuckled. "Sounds like you. How'd you end up there? Didn't you retire from the agency?"

"For a nanosecond. But I got bored. So, I started my own mining company—Space Rocks, Inc."

"Like the name. So, I take it you're mining asteroids."

"Duh. Nothing gets past you, Jake. But yeah, big ole space rocks."

"In L5?"

"Yes, the current one. We contracted with the Aussies. They took ownership of a deep-space asteroid, and we signed up to extract whatever resources we could from it. They were hoping to find helium 3."

"Find any?"

"Trace amounts, but not the quantity they'd hoped for. They finally settled for all the nickel ore and rare earth elements we could mine."

"Is that profitable?"

"For them or me?"

"For them."

"Oh, yeah. We found a lot of rare earths. They'll recoup all their costs and then some."

"How about you?"

"Well, I ain't complaining. It's a well-paying gig."

"How did you get it to L5?"

"The French have an autonomous spacecraft that bumps into the asteroid often enough and with just the right force to alter its trajectory. It took two years to get it here. It's like bumper cars."

"Yeah, I read about that somewhere. Their spacecraft has a depleted-uranium front end it uses to ram into the asteroid."

"That's the one."

"How long have you been at it?"

"Since it arrived in L5—about eighteen months. We're just wrapping up. We've milked this baby for everything she's got."

"What happens to it now?"

"ISA wants to use it train academy pukes."

"Glad to hear it, Javi."

Merriweather paused a heartbeat before asking the question he had called Rodriguez to ask.

"So, what's your next gig?"

"Not sure yet. I've got a few ideas—a few leads, but nothing in writing. I made enough money on this one, so I can take my time deciding."

"Any desire to get back out there?"

"And by out there, you mean…?"

"Out there. You know. Like way out there. How would you feel about leaving the solar system altogether?"

"Damn. You're talking about Endeavor. Is that yours? I wondered who was going to score that one."

"Yep. I just took command last week."

"Sweet. Faster than light and all that shit."

"Are you interested?"

"Me? Maybe. Who else you got?"

"Well, Dutch Swenson for one, and Don Stoner has signed on, plus a few hot shots ISA plucked from the Academy."

"Sounds like the makings of a first-rate crew?"

"Why not come with us, Javi? ISA's given me some discretion on team members, and I know you'd be perfect for the job."

"What's my assignment?"

"Hell, we don't need a cook, Javi," replied Merriweather. "You'll be Endeavor's Mining Officer, of course."

"Well, if you're sure you don't need a cook. I guess I can do that other thing."

"Damn, that's great news. Welcome aboard."

"When do you need me?"

"As soon as you can get your ass out here. Your stateroom on Endeavor is ready for you."

"I'll wrap things up here and hop the next ore transport home. Two weeks all right?"

"Works for me. And Javi, thanks."

Merriweather clicked off and grinned. *One down and two to go,* he thought as he placed a call to his friend Dutch Swenson.

*2125, ISA Mission Control Center, Houston, Texas*

Crenna glanced at the 3D hologram floating above his head and smiled. Although he had seen this hologram many times before, it always gave him goosebumps.

Gene Crenna, director of ISA's new Mission Control Center in Houston, Texas, took considerable pride in the hologram projection system and his role in acquiring it. He especially enjoyed showing it off to anyone who wandered too close. Currently on display was a large 3D full-color hologram of Earth measuring almost five meters in diameter.

The hologram projector sat in a three-meter-deep pit in the middle of the operations center—an area known as "center stage." Surrounded by engineering consoles, it was used to project a wide range of 3D full-color imagery to the engineers who managed ISA's space missions.

As the hologram of Earth slowly rotated above the heads of the handful of engineers currently on duty and manning their consoles, an avatar representing the new In-Orbit Construction Facility (IOCF) slowly came into view just above the Sea of Japan.

Crenna was currently working on a problem with two members of the telemetry team monitoring the IOCF and several starships under construction nearby. The current situation was a potential hydrazine leak on Endeavor, the oldest of the ships, now station-keeping approximately one hundred kilometers above and trailing the construction facility.

"What do we have, Mike?" Crenna asked as he arrived at Mike Marshall's station.

"Here, let me show you. Alex, show Endeavor," said Marshall.

Alex was the name given to the artificial intelligence that engineers and scientists used to interact with Mission Control's various systems—including the hologram projector.

The hologram of the Earth flickered once, then disappeared, replaced by a realistic projection of the Endeavor spacecraft.

Crenna knew Endeavor very well. He had been the Mission Director on several of Endeavor's epic journeys, and the sight of her always brought back strong feelings. He even had a scale model of the spacecraft sitting on his desk.

Marshall slowly rotated the Endeavor projection from his console using hand gestures until the spacecraft's port side faced the two engineers and Crenna.

"We're detecting a hydrazine leak coming from one of Endeavor's port-side thrusters—right about there," said Marshall, pointing at a spot on the spacecraft's left side. "The problem is we're not seeing any change in Endeavor's attitude."

"So, we can't definitely say it's a leak?"

"Nope."

"Hmmm. OK, where are we with Aries? How long before she de-orbits?" Crenna asked, referring to Aries One, the name of one of Endeavor's two landers (Landing and Ascent Vehicles or LAVs).

"We're coming up on a twenty-minute window."

"Where is she now?"

Again, Marshall spoke to the AI, causing a small 3D image of Endeavor's lander to appear alongside the Endeavor hologram.

"OK, Mike, let's delay Aries' reentry until we check this out," said Crenna. "We might write this off as a sensor problem."

Meanwhile, four-hundred kilometers above the Earth, Lieutenant Milo Bridges had just uncoupled his small landing craft from the Endeavor starship and was station-keeping One-hundred meters off Endeavor's starboard side, preparing for his return to Earth.

Bridges was focusing on his instruments when he heard Mike Marshall's voice in his helmet speaker.

"Aries One, this is Mission Control. Do you copy?"

"We copy, Mission Control," said Bridges.

Bridges was one of Marshall's favorite astronauts, and he smiled when he heard the young lieutenant's voice.

"Milo, we are holding off your de-orbit. We have a minor task we'd like you to perform before we bring you home."

"The window opens in ten minutes, Control."

"Understand, Aries. We'll try to make it as quick as possible."

"OK. Minor tasks are my specialty," said Bridges, "but I charge by the kilometer. I hope this won't take too long. I have a date."

"Copy that, Aries. We are picking up a hydrazine leak from thruster HT-14 just forward of the cage on Endeavor's port side. We'd like you to swing over there and get a visual."

Bridges had just left Endeavor, and he was confident that if there was a leak, he would have heard about it but decided not to argue.

"Will do," Bridges replied. "On my way."

Bridges was more than happy to comply with Mission Control's request. He loved flying the Aries lander. In fact, he loved flying, period. Flying had been a part of his life ever since he got his pilot's license as a teenager in Lawton, Oklahoma. However, flying a spacecraft like Aries was a bit more challenging than piloting his single-engine SkyBird.

Using a combination of short bursts from the thrusters and internal gyroscopes, Bridges directed his twenty-meter-long spacecraft toward the front of the Endeavor starship.

Endeavor was smaller than the newer starships now under construction, but much larger than Aries. The 180-meter-long starship (about twice the length of an American football field) would be Bridges' home for the next two-plus years, and he loved every centimeter of her.

Now pointed directly at the starship, Bridges could see Endeavor from bow to stern in all her glory. *Beautiful*, he thought. Bridges smiled. His mind flashed back to a conversation with shipmate Jonathan Mills when they both reported aboard for duty for the first time. Mills had described Endeavor as a loaf of French bread encircled by three hula hoops and a Frisbee. Bridges laughed when he first heard Mills say it. However, later he did a records search to find out what hula hoops and Frisbees were, but the description stuck.

One of those hula hoops was the *habi*tat ring, a 120-meter diameter torus that surrounded the ship near its midsection. The hab, as it was called, contained the crew's living spaces, where Bridges and his shipmates would spend most of their time during their mission. It was the only place on the ship where the crew would enjoy anything close to normal gravity.

The other two *hula hoops* were the two FTL hyperdrive rings—part of the recent technology that enabled faster-than-light space travel. Each hoop was an imposing 130-meter diameter ring of platinum-coated titanium, anchored to the hull by eight struts. The first ring encircled the ship's bow, while the second surrounded the ship's engines at the stern.

The *Frisbee* was an 80-meter diameter disk that bisected the ship and separated the nuclear reactors at the ship's stern from the forward crew compartments.

The oval shape of the starship's central core and the bronze tint of the radiation and heat-resistant nanotubes that covered it explained Mills' loaf of French bread characterization.

"RHODA, turn on exterior illumination, please," spoke Bridges into his headset's microphone.

All the new starships required AI to manage their complex systems, and Endeavor was no exception. RHODA, or Referential Holographic Online Digital Assistant, was the most powerful AI ever created.

After getting no response, Bridges repeated his command. "RHODA, please turn on exterior illumination."

"Sorry, flyboy, RHODA is offline again."

Bridges smiled, recognizing the voice of Endeavor's other pilot, Lieutenant Catriana 'Cat' Cortez.

"So, what's up with RHODA? She was working fine an hour ago," Bridges added.

"The contractor just installed a software upgrade, which, of course, doesn't work," replied Cortez. "According to them, it's a hardware/software compatibility issue—new software, old hardware. They're working on the problem."

"Well, unless that contractor wants to spend the next two years crammed inside a sardine can with the rest of us, I suggest they get the damn thing fixed," said Bridges.

"Roger that, Milo," chirped Cortez.

"Say, Houston asked me to check out a leaky thruster on HT-14. Do you see that as well?"

"Can't say yes, can't say no," said Cortez. "I've got contractors crawling, uh, make that floating, all over the bridge. They've disassembled half of my instruments, looking for an electrical issue."

"Mind if I look, anyway?"

"Be my guest."

"I will. Can you turn on exterior illumination for me?" asked Bridges.

"Sorry, Milo, no can do. We're having a technical problem with exterior illumination," answered Cortez.

"Seriously? You've got to be kidding me," he replied. "Is there anything on this freaking space barge that is working? You don't have to answer that. It's a rhetorical question," said Bridges with a tinge of frustration. Adopting a more formal protocol, Bridges added, "Bridge, request permission for an inspection flyby."

A second later, "Permission granted, Aries One. Watch the paint job," Cortez replied.

Bridges smiled as he maneuvered his small craft to the front of the larger starship and waved at the array of video cameras that stretched the width of Endeavor's bow.

A heartbeat later, his cockpit holoview snapped on, displaying an image of Cortez, who flashed a smile and waved.

Bridges smiled back. He had been thinking about Cortez a lot lately. The thought of spending the next two or three years with Lieutenant Cortez, confined together in a small starship, was not altogether unpleasant. She was beautiful, intelligent, and perhaps interested in him as well. However,

Bridges was also career driven, and he had to be extra careful in matters of the opposite sex—especially a fellow officer. In addition, he had a history and a reputation he was trying to live down. So, with some difficulty, he put the lovely Ms. Cortez out of his mind.

*Back to matters at hand*, thought Bridges.

With short bursts from Aries' thrusters, Bridges deftly maneuvered his small lander across Endeavor's broad bow to its port side. He had spent many hours examining every aspect of the legendary starship, but it still gave him chills to see it floating there in space, with the Earth providing a glorious backdrop.

NASA's aerospace engineers had designed Endeavor initially to support the exploration of Mars. Various missions over her sixty-five-year lifetime had required further changes. When the growing Mars colony needed a steady flow of colonists and supplies, NASA engineers added new TAMARAK Plasma engines and a dramatic habitat ring. For missions to Mercury and Venus, new materials, resistant to extreme heat and cosmic radiation, were used to reinforce her hull. These changes also made her suitable for missions to the gas giants Saturn and Jupiter.

As Bridges slowly piloted his small craft along the starship's port side, he noted the ship's lack of viewports. Like all modern manned spacecraft, Endeavor relied instead on external video cameras. These cameras transmitted video to displays called holoviews, throughout the ship, which produced images indistinguishable from actual viewports.

After threading his Aries lander between two of the eight struts which anchored the forward hyperdrive ring to the hull, Bridges proceeded rearward toward the imposing habitat ring.

Endeavor's habitat ring didn't connect to the starship's central hull via a rotating hub, as depicted in countless sci-fi movies. Engineers wanted to avoid the weight, complexity, and potential leaks such a design would create. Instead, the connecting spokes attached directly to the spacecraft's central core. This made it necessary to rotate the entire spacecraft to provide artificial gravity for the passengers and crew in the hab.

A rotating ship created one problem, however—how to keep passengers from experiencing motion sickness, especially when looking at the stars spinning by their holoviews. Engineers solved the problem by digitally "stabilizing" the video images, giving the crew a non-spinning view of the cosmos outside even when the ship was rotating.

Currently, Endeavor was not rotating, which made it much easier for Bridges to pilot Aries between two of the habitat ring's three connecting spokes.

Next under the glare of Aries' spotlights was Endeavor's second LAV, currently attached to the starship's port side docking adaptor. Aries Two looked very much like a leech, but with wings that folded upward like a moth.

As Aries One glided alongside the much larger Endeavor, its spotlights reflected off the starship's bronze-tinted surface. Bridges was close enough to see every seam and weld connecting the sections of the starship's 180-meter-long hull.

"You've been through a lot," mumbled Bridges. "Mars, Europa, Titan. I hope you still have more to give."

"I didn't copy that, Aries. Please repeat," said Cortez.

"Oh, sorry, Endeavor. I was just thinking aloud."

"We copy, Aries. Careful with that thinking thing. It could get you into trouble."

Bridges grinned. "Copy that, Endeavor."

Redirecting his spotlights astern, Bridges could see the cage, a maze of titanium girders forming a skeletal structure nearly twenty meters long that divided the starship into two sections—crewed compartments forward—power and propulsion compartments aft. Enclosed within this scaffolding were large spherical tanks containing spacecraft propellant, liquid oxygen, and water for the crew.

Just forward of the cage, Bridges located the hydrazine thruster nozzle with the HT-14 designation stenciled below. Bridges maneuvered Aries as close as he dared to get a good look at the thruster.

"Houston, this is Aries One. Do you copy?" said Bridges.

"This is Houston, Aries. We copy."

"Control, I got up close and personal with your thruster, but I sure as hell don't see any leaks. However, you know that the contractors have half of Endeavor's electrical systems floating all over the bridge? My guess is that they've mis-wired a sensor," Bridges added.

"Thanks, Aries. We've been talking to Endeavor about those issues," said Marshall. "We just needed to get a visual check on the thruster."

"Roger that," said Bridges. "Anything else I can do for you?"

"No, we'll handle it from here. Thanks for your assistance. Your de-orbit window opens in two minutes."

"Roger that," Bridges replied. "Endeavor, this is Aries. Have you been following?"

"Aries, this is Endeavor, yes we have—we copy no visual leak," said Cortez.

"Better to be sure," said Bridges. "I'm going to finish my flyby and then proceed with de-orbit."

"Roger that, Aries."

After passing by the cage and skirting the large disk known as the Frisbee, Bridges adroitly directed his LAV toward the stern of the starship. As he neared the end, he could see the two large bell-shaped nozzles—the business end of Endeavor's main rocket engines.

*I sure hope we won't have to use Bertha*, thought Bridges, referring to the ship's original propulsion system. Bridges knew enough about liquid-fuel rockets to appreciate the dangers in using them. Firing rocket engines that powerful, and that old, was inherently dangerous. If it had been up to him, he would have had them removed, or at least left the fuel tanks empty. But the decision was above his pay grade.

ISA's administrators had wanted to remove Bertha altogether during the retrofit, but NASA veterans argued for keeping her, warning that if the FTL system failed in deep space, Endeavor might need the brute power of the archaic propulsion system to get home. So, despite the risks, they opted to retain Bertha.

Surrounding the rocket engine's nozzles were the eight newly installed TAMARAK plasma ion engines nacelles. The TAMARAKS replaced the decades-old, less powerful VASIMR (Variable Specific Impulse Magneto-plasma Rocket) engines and, although far less powerful than Bertha, were a lot safer. Endeavor would employ TAMARAKs as her primary propulsion system when it was not in FTL mode or was maneuvering close to a planet. Surrounding all of Endeavor's engines was the second of the two large hyperdrive rings.

"I've completed my inspection, Endeavor," radioed Bridges.

"Anything falling off?" asked Cortez.

"Nope. She looks pretty good for her age."

"Hey, never comment on a lady's age, buster."

"Oops, sorry, Cat. Say, I forgot to ask, are you going to the Embarkation ceremony?" asked Bridges.

"Nope, somebody has to mind the store up here," said Cortez. "Plus, it's too damn hot down there in New Annapolis this time of year. I'll stay put and enjoy the ship's air conditioning."

"I didn't see your name on the watch list."

"I swapped with Rodriguez. He has relatives in Maryland."

"Gotcha. OK then, I'll see you in a few days," said Bridges.

"Take pictures," said Cortez.

"Roger that," he replied.

Bridges backed the LAV away from Endeavor and began his reentry checklist. *Just two more nights on Earth before mission launch*, he thought. As Bridges prepared to fire the breaking rockets, he took one more look at Endeavor, now lit from behind by the sudden arc of a new sunrise and silhouetted against the blackness of space.

"See you in a few days," he said.

# CHAPTER 9

*2125, Embarkation Ceremony, Washington, DC, The National Mall*

Jake Merriweather looked at the mass of humanity overflowing the Capital Mall and wondered how he had gotten here. From fighter pilot to ship's captain to astronaut and now…

He had thought his career was over long ago when the Navy drastically cut their manned fighter program and switched to fighter drones, eliminating Merriweather's fighter pilot job.

The Navy, however, had other plans for Jake, and he soon found himself Surface Warfare Officer on a littoral combat ship patrolling the west coast of Africa. It wasn't long before the Navy gave Jake command of his own ship. Once again, Merriweather envisioned a long career as a naval officer.

Then Jake's wife, Leah, got sick. Against her wishes, he retired early. She needed him at home, not far away on some damn ship. *That seemed like just yesterday*, he thought.

"Look at that crowd," whispered ISA Administrator Dr. Neil Spencer, sitting next to him. "They say it's larger than the last Presidential Inauguration—over a million people."

"Don't remind me," said Merriweather. "I'm nervous enough as it is."

"You'll do fine."

Merriweather had his doubts. The largest audience he had ever spoken to before was the eight-hundred students in his high school's graduating class, and he barely got through that. Public speaking wasn't his strong suit. Sit him atop a rocket and blast him into space, and he was fine, but put him behind a podium, and his knees started knocking.

This speech was something else entirely. Humanity was about to leave the solar system for the first time in a spaceship with faster-than-light technology, and the ISA entrusted this mission to him—Jake Merriweather. Jake felt overwhelmed.

Not only was there an enormous crowd stretching all the way to the Washington Monument, but the entire world was watching as well. TV cameras were everywhere—from all the major networks and from every country around the world. More people would watch Merriweather's speech than Armstrong's moon landing or Clark's first steps on Mars.

Merriweather tried to take it all in. He glanced up at the bright blue sky—*a perfect day*, he thought. A steady breeze took the edge off the July heat and humidity that usually invaded Foggy Bottom at this time of year. Flags representing the United States, the European Union, and China bordering the dais produced a steady flap, flap, flapping sound. The fluttering of the patriotic bunting hanging from the dais served as a counterpoint to the constant flapping of the flags.

Sitting on the dais with Merriweather was a contingent of Navy brass headlined by the Secretary of the Navy, all attired in their freshly pressed dress whites, adorned with their colored ribbons, medals, and gold braid. For the umpteenth time, Merriweather fidgeted with his own fruit salad— the medals and ribbons he wore on his dress uniform.

Navy Secretary Bob Neal had just finished his speech and announced the President of the United States. Merriweather took a deep breath. He felt a knot growing in his stomach.

Sound crews had set up large speaker towers at strategic locations all the way out to the Washington Monument. A noticeable delay echoed the speaker's voice back to the dais. Merriweather made a mental note to tune out the echo.

Merriweather glanced at the row of uniforms just below the dais—uniforms worn by the twelve individuals he would lead on this mission of discovery. Twelve incredibly talented, well-trained individuals, willing to risk their lives in service to their—Merriweather almost used the word country. But that wasn't right. They were really risking their lives in service to humanity.

Merriweather felt humbled. Was he the man to lead *them*? Would they risk their lives for *him*?

Merriweather heard the President say his name.

What was he saying? Something about fighter pilots—top of his class at Annapolis?

The audience applauded.

Merriweather tried to focus on his speech. He had been going over it for weeks. The Navy even provided a speech writer to help him craft something befitting the importance of the occasion. Yet he still felt somehow inadequate and unprepared.

*You have to appreciate the irony, don't you?*

Merriweather was suddenly aware of his beloved deceased wife's presence in his thoughts.

*I wondered if you were going to show up,* thought Merriweather. The sound of his wife's voice instantly settled his nerves. It wasn't unusual for his deceased wife to invade his consciousness now and then—especially during momentous occasions such as this.

*What do you think of the old boy now?* Merriweather thought.

*Oh, listen to you. Don't get too full of yourself. You've still a speech to give, and you know how you hate this sort of thing.*

*Don't remind me,* thought Merriweather. *I've been sweating this for a month.*

*It never ceases to amaze me that you could land a fighter jet on the deck of a bobbing carrier and not break a sweat but put you in front of a dozen people, and you get all panicky.*

*Yeah, I can't explain it either,* he replied, *but you know what they say about public speaking.*

*You'll be fine,* she said. *I've been listening when you've been practicing your speech. Sounds good.*

*Hey, could you give me a little privacy?*

*One benefit of being dead, buster. By the way, who is the pretty blond sitting on the stage?*

*Which one? There are several,* thought Merriweather.

*She's sitting with the crew—on the end to the left.*

*Oh, that's the reporter from Cahill. ISA is sending her with us to document our mission.*

*I see. She's cute. I think she has her eye on you.*

*Are you jealous?*

*Not a bit. By the way, they're ready for you.*

*Who's ready? What...*

"They're ready for you," whispered the ISA Administrator, interrupting Jake's thoughts. "The President just announced you."

"Thank you," said Merriweather.

Jake stood and shook the President's hand.

"Thank you, Mr. President."

Merriweather took another deep breath and started speaking. After thanking the President, the President of the European Union, the French Ambassador, the Chinese Ambassador, the Secretary of the Navy, the ISA Director, and a few other dignitaries, Jake launched into his speech.

"I am honored," began Merriweather, "honored to be here with you, the families, the crew, distinguished scientists, and guests. We are here to witness the beginning of yet another historic voyage of the recommissioned ISA Endeavor. Born over sixty-five years ago, Endeavor has forged a distinguished career—a half dozen missions to Mars helping to build the new

Mars colony, a mission to Saturn's moon Europa and the first mission to Titan—a *very* accomplished career indeed.

"Six years ago, after a career that any ship in the fleet would envy, ISA retired Endeavor with full honors and with the gratitude of a grateful nation. But then, four years ago, with the invention of faster-than-light propulsion technology and in consideration of the immense scale of the universe, ISA suddenly found itself with a shortage of viable space vehicles. It was an easy decision to bring Endeavor out of retirement to continue her stellar legacy. No pun intended."

*The audience is laughing. Good, they laughed at my pun,* thought Merriweather. *Or maybe it was just a sympathy laugh.*

"Endeavor is the first spacecraft to be retrofitted with the new Plank-Samuelson faster-than-light technology. We re-commissioned Endeavor ten months ago, and she has now passed her trials with flying colors. She has a well-trained crew, and we're eager to see what she can do out in deep space, and as her commander, so am I."

Commander Merriweather turned toward his officers dressed in their starched and pressed uniforms and introduced them individually. The assembled families and dignitaries applauded after Merriweather introduced each one.

"Joining me on this historic voyage of exploration is Lieutenant Commander Donald Stoner, my First Officer, and a veteran of over fifteen missions to the moon and Mars. Stone and I go way back to my first mission to the new Mars colony. I can think of no one I'd rather have as my second in command than Don Stoner," said Merriweather.

"To Don's right is Mission Specialist Lieutenant Milo Bridges, one of ISA's finest pilots and our First Contact Specialist. For you veterans in the audience, you might not recognize the First Contact Specialist rating. In coordination with ISA, the Navy created the FCS rating three years ago in recognition of the need to have personnel specifically trained in first contact.

"ISA selected twenty individuals from an initial pool of sixteen thousand applicants from all four branches, including ISA. These men and women have demonstrated the intelligence, temperament, resourcefulness, cultural sensitivity, language ability, and character that best exemplified the role we envisioned for First Contact Specialists. After rigorous training and testing, we winnowed that number down to twelve—the best of the best. Endeavor can boast having the top two individuals on her crew, Lieutenant Milo Bridges and Lieutenant Catriana Cortez."

The audience applauded.

"Lieutenant Bridges is here with us today, while Lieutenant Cortez is currently watching us from orbit, overseeing final preparations for our departure."

Again, the audience applauded.

"Next to Lieutenant Bridges is Medical Officer Lieutenant Jennifer Lee.

As many of you know, Lieutenant Lee was a leader in setting up the Mars colony's first full-scale medical facility. One of Jennifer's duties is stasis management—that is, putting our crew into hibernation during much of the mission. Some of our crew will make at least part of the trip in stasis pods, and Jennifer has more experience in the art of stasis sleep than anyone in the space agency. She will also make sure we're all healthy when we return." Merriweather waited until the applause died down before continuing.

"To Jennifer's right is Lieutenant Javier Rodriguez. Javier is our chief mining officer. Javier brings a wealth of experience to Endeavor, having flown over twenty missions throughout our solar system. He wrote the book on how to mine deep-space asteroids for water. Welcome aboard, Javier. We will need your expertise on this trip.

"Next to Javier is Technical Officer Jonathan Mills. Jonathan was the chief architect of the most advanced artificial intelligence computer system ever developed. It is that system that will help guide us during our mission. It's called RHODA—the Referential Hologram Digital Assistant. Ask Jonathan what that means, and he'll talk your ears off."

That brought laughter from the audience.

"Jonathan is also responsible for keeping all of Endeavor's computers and electronics systems working flawlessly—most importantly, our CUBE or Custom Beverage dispenser. There's nothing more important for the crew's well-being than a good cup of coffee."

Jake was pleased by the audience's reaction to his attempted humor.

"Finally, we have Propulsion Engineer Dutch Swenson, who knows more about space propulsion than anyone I know, including yours truly. I have served with Dutch on several interplanetary missions, and there is no one I would rather have in charge of our propulsion systems than Dutch Swenson."

"Also joining us on this mission are four scientists preeminent in their respective fields. We have Exoplanetologist Dr. Herbert Mann, or as we call him, *The Professor*. Dr. Mann and his team have discovered over three thousand potentially habitable planets. He literally wrote the book on planetary science and exoplanets."

"Joining him is a cryptographer and leading expert in exotic languages, Dr. Paul Girard. Paul has written many highly praised books on decryption and famously led the team that finally decrypted the Indus Valley language. We'll need Paul if we find anybody out there that we'd like to talk to. I also want to thank the French Space Agency, CNES, and the European Space Agency, ESA, for loaning Paul to us."

"Next is Anthropologist Dr. Mike Martin. If we find intelligent life out there, Mike will help us understand their culture, which is critical to our ability to communicate. The last thing we'd want to do is insult them. Mike will help us craft our diplomatic efforts if we find intelligent life out there."

"Finally, we have one of the world's leading botanists, Dr. Forest Graham. A primary goal of this mission is to identify planets that can sustain humans, and Dr. Graham's expertise will be vital toward that effort."

"Not with us here today, but currently manning Endeavor in orbit is pilot and backup medical officer Lieutenant Catriana 'Cat' Cortez. Cat is one of the finest pilots in the fleet, and because we all do double and, in her case, triple duty, Cat takes care of our hydroponics bay. That's where we grow our fresh fruits and veggies. Cat will also backup Lieutenant Bridges as First Contact Specialist."

"Zoe Bishop is also joining us for this historic voyage on loan from the Cahill News Organization. I'm sure you all know her from her show, *Space-Time*. Two years ago, I had the pleasure of being a guest on her show. That was quite an experience. Zoe will bring a reporter's eye and instincts to our mission. We are truly fortunate to have her with us."

Pausing for a moment, waiting for the applause to fade, Merriweather gathered himself for his closing remarks.

"Tomorrow, *Endeavor* embarks on her maiden voyage as a deep-space starship. What lies ahead is unknown—perhaps intelligent life, habitable worlds, or wonders beyond anything we've imagined. But as we go, we must remember: we don't represent a single nation or flag. We carry the hopes of an entire planet—of all humankind

"I am reminded that homo sapiens translated means 'wise man.' We haven't been at this very long—the business of space. It was in 1781 that Sir William Herschel discovered the planet Uranus. It was the first planet ever discovered using a telescope. Here we are, just three hundred and forty-four years later, preparing to send our best and brightest out into the cosmos, beyond the limits of our solar system, for the very first time. These are smart people—these brave men and women. However, we must be more than smart. We must remember to be wise.

"I'll close with words that have graced many a vessel as they left safe harbor to venture out into the unknown. God speed Endeavor. May you have fair winds and following seas."

# CHAPTER 10

*Faster than Light*

"Ugh," said Bishop. "This is one hell of a time to have a pimple."
Bishop leaned closer to the camera lens.

"Soften the lighting a bit, Watson."

Watson, a basketball-size robot designed to be a helper for Endeavor's crew, was now performing as camera operator and camera for the Cahill News reporter. Watson could perform various services, including carrying tools or modules, reading instructions, and looking up engineering information. The floating robot could also act as another set of eyes, as in "Watson, read the serial number, please. I can't quite make it out."

"Watson, can you remove the pimple on my chin?"
Bishop watched as the blemish faded from her chin on Watson's built-in video display.

"The wonders of technology," she said to herself. "Follow me, Watson."

Bishop propelled herself toward the center of Endeavor's bridge, followed by the floating robot. "Are you receiving me, Houston?"

"We're receiving you, Endeavor."

"Patch me into my production crew, Houston."

"Roger that, Endeavor."

A second later, Bishop heard the voice of her chief production assistant.

"We're ready to go live down here whenever you are, Ms. Bishop."

"All right, stand by for my mark. OK, everyone," announced Bishop in a voice loud enough to get everyone's attention. "We are going live in five -four -three -two -one."

"Hello, planet Earth. Welcome to this special episode of Space-Time. I am your host, Zoe Bishop."

Bishop had been doing daily reports from Endeavor for the last two weeks and had gotten used to the robot hovering directly in front of her. Her audience had been increasing as well. Today's broadcast would reach an estimated worldwide audience of over one billion people and translated into thirty languages.

If there was ever a moment to feel the pressure of public speaking, this was it. However, Bishop was a professional, and she lived for moments like this one. *x* she thought.

"I am coming to you again from the bridge of the ISA Starship Endeavor, currently four hundred kilometers above New Mexico," said Bishop. "We are traveling at 27,500 kilometers per hour—that's a little over 17000 mph—and circling the Earth every ninety minutes. In the distance is the IOCF. That's the impressive In-Orbit Construction Facility where several more starships are currently under construction.

"I am here with Captain Jake Merriweather as he and his international crew of astronauts and eminent scientists prepare to get underway. In just over two minutes from now, Endeavor and its crew will begin their historic journey; a journey that will take humanity beyond the boundary of our home solar system for the very first time.

"I'm on Endeavor's bridge, the forward-most compartment of this magnificent 180-meter-long starship, enjoying the experience of microgravity. I'm going to propel myself over to the captain's chair to see if I can talk with Endeavor's captain."

Pushing off from an unoccupied gravity seat, Bishop propelled herself toward the captain's chair, followed by her robot assistant, Watson.

"The bridge is a bit more crowded than usual, as you can see. Most of the crew are here getting strapped into their assigned custom molded seats, eagerly awaiting the beginning of this historic event—all but Master Chief *Dutch* Swenson, who is currently at the other end of Endeavor manning the propulsion systems of this magnificent starship.

"Let's listen as the captain readies his ship for departure."

Using a subtle hand gesture, Bishop commanded Watson to turn its camera and microphone toward Merriweather. Watson dutifully complied and was now hovering inches away from Merriweather's face. Merriweather suppressed the instinct to swat the damned thing away. Instead, he checked his instruments as the crew and Bishop, watched his every move. If he was at all nervous or affected by the tremendous importance of the event, he didn't show it. By all outward signs, it was just another day for the captain.

On the inside, however, it was another story. Merriweather always felt the weight of command more intensely when on the bridge. The ship's bridge was a solemn place steeped in tradition, and today, he felt that weight even more. He was acutely aware of the significance of this mission.

For the first time, humanity would travel beyond the boundaries of the solar system. For the first time, Earthlings would set sail for a distant star. It would travel much farther than anyone had ever gone before, and Captain Jake Merriweather was the person chosen to command that mission. He felt the weight of the honor ISA had given him.

"Where are we?" said Merriweather, turning his head toward his executive officer.

"All personnel are at their assigned stations," said the ship's Executive Officer (XO), Lieutenant Commander Don Stoner.

"Very well. RHODA, systems status," said Merriweather, addressing the ship's AI.

"All systems are operating within normal parameters, Captain Merriweather," answered the ship's AI in a feminine voice.

"XO, signal the fleet," said Merriweather.

Using his instruments panel, Stoner sent a short flash-com to the rest of the fleet, signaling Endeavor's imminent departure.

Flash-coms were the twenty-second-century version of the Navy's blinker lights used in WWII. But instead of Morse code, flash-coms were holographic, meaning the ability to transmit not only text, but 3D images.

"We've received acknowledgments from the other ships," stated Stoner seconds later.

Sensing an opportune moment, Bishop positioned herself directly in front of the captain.

"Captain Merriweather, may I have a moment of your time?" asked Bishop.

Merriweather certainly had other, more important matters to attend to this close to departure. Still, given that ISA perceived a public relations benefit of having someone like Zoe Bishop broadcasting from Endeavor, he saw no other option.

"Certainly, Zoe. I'd be happy to," replied Merriweather. "Please strap in there," he said, motioning the Cahill reporter to seat on his left.

"Thank you," said Bishop, doing as directed.

"Did you have time to visit the IOCF, Ms. Bishop?" Merriweather asked.

"No, I didn't. My schedule was just too hectic," she replied.

"Well, that's unfortunate. It's quite impressive. It's larger than the Pentagon, you know. You can see it there," Merriweather said, pointing at the expansive, curved video screen that stretched the entire ten-meter width of the forward bulkhead.

"I wanted to go, and I especially wanted to go aboard one of the new ships under construction," said Bishop.

"The one that's almost completed is the Discovery. You see how they're flashing their running lights. That's for our benefit. They're saying bon voyage."

"Captain, I'm sure many people would like to get your thoughts about the significance of today's event. Have you thought about the importance of this most historic milestone in human history?"

Merriweather paused for a moment before answering.

"I like the word you used—milestone," said Merriweather. "I believe that captures the significance of today's event. It is a milestone. Today, we—humans, Earthlings, our species—are on a mission to explore the stars. We have decided not to be confined to our planet or our solar system." Merriweather turned toward Stoner. "Has the supply shuttle undocked?"

"Yes, sir—twenty minutes ago."

"Cutting it awfully close."

"Yes, sir."

"Is the shuttle clear?"

"All clear, sir."

Merriweather poked a virtual button on the holographic control panel floating in front of him.

"Attention crew—beginning ship's rotation," he announced. A second later, he gave the command. "RHODA, rotate the ship—three rpm."

"Beginning ship's rotation, Captain," responded the AI.

Almost instantly, twelve hydrazine thrusters, positioned around the perimeter of the habitat ring, fired in unison. Sitting in his captain's chair, Merriweather felt the slight shudder he came to expect as his ship began rotating. Others on the bridge watched as the scene outside Endeavor displayed on the giant video screen started moving.

"RHODA, stabilize the primary bridge display," said Merriweather.

A second later, the image on the forward video display ceased spinning.

"Thanks. I was getting queasy," said Bishop. "Question, how much gravity will three rpm produce?" Bishop asked.

Bishop had done her homework and already knew the answer. However, she also knew her audience would appreciate the question.

"Well, the radius of the hab is sixty meters," explained Merriweather, "so three rpm will give us about point six G's—that's inside the hab, of course. It's less here in the ship's central core, where we are—about point zero one G."

"That's sixty percent normal earth's gravity in the habitation ring and one percent here in the core, right?"

"That's correct, Ms. Bishop," said Merriweather.

"I have a few questions from our viewing audience—if I may," said Bishop.

"Fire away," replied Merriweather.

"This first question is from a young viewer from Brazil. She asks: What if you run into God while you're so far from home? What would you say to Him?"

"That is a big question," said Merriweather. "First, I would hope He, or She, would be in the mood to have a conversation. Otherwise….," Merriweather smiled. "I suppose I would thank Him for creating the Universe and, us. I would also thank Him for giving us the intelligence to learn how to travel faster than light. I would also ask Her to point us toward other intelligent beings we might want to meet."

"You used the pronoun Her in that last question. Any reason?" Said Bishop.

"I guess I wanted Her to know that some men can ask for directions," said Merriweather, smiling.

"Funny. Anything else?"

"I guess I would also ask Her to watch over us on our travels—to keep us safe."

"I believe She will. Here's another question," said Bishop, reading off her holoview. "This one is from a woman in Hong Kong. She would like to know if you have a girlfriend?"
Merriweather laughed.

"I think you just might have a fan in Hong Kong, Captain," said Bishop, smiling at the captain's discomfort.

"Well, I, uh, don't have a girlfriend," said Merriweather. "This job keeps me way too busy, and the hours aren't conducive to a healthy relationship."

"Well, Captain, maybe you'll meet someone on this trip," said Bishop.

After an awkward pause, she added. "A good-looking alien, perhaps."

"Not likely, but anything's possible, I suppose."

Bishop ended the broadcast by thanking her production team back in Houston. She also thanked her audience, promising that when she returned, she would share her amazing adventures with them.

"Well, I believe we're ready. Are you ready, Ms. Bishop?"

"Very ready, Captain. The entire world is ready."

"OK then, all hands, prepare for FTL," he announced.

Captain Merriweather glanced once more at the instrument panel and then, looking out at the expanse of stars before him, gave the command.

"RHODA, engage FTL."

A few seconds later, the space around Endeavor began to shimmer. The edges of the spacecraft glowed with a luminous plasma often described as a kind of Saint Elmo's fire. Construction crews watching from the nearby IOCF glimpsed the faint glow of a *bubble* surrounding the Endeavor a split second before it disappeared, leaving no sign of the eighteen-hundred-tonne starship.

Now enveloped in a bubble of rapidly phase-shifting space-time, Endeavor was *slipping* through hyperspace at roughly thirty-nine times the speed of light.

Merriweather checked the readouts graphically displayed on his holoview. "Status, XO."

"Our speed is 38.41C. All systems nominal," replied Stoner.

"All right, gentlemen, the last time Endeavor made this trip took over four years. This time it will take considerably less. In fact, we will make our first stop in about two minutes. Don't stray too far."

# CHAPTER 11

*Antimatter*

To create a bubble phase-shifting space around an eighteen-hundred-tonne starship, one needs a sufficient quantity of anti-protons. Therefore, shortly after the successful Odysseus flight, the newly formed International Space Alliance began looking for natural sources of antiprotons. The new Lorenz Satellite, placed in orbit around Saturn in 2120, had discovered that the gas giant's intense radiation belt produced far more antimatter than previously believed. Beginning in 2122, ISA started an ambitious project to place over two hundred antiproton collectors in orbit around the ringed planet.

It was near Saturn that Endeavor suddenly appeared just two minutes after leaving Earth orbit.

Merriweather noticed the stunned look on everyone's faces as they stared at the glorious sight before them—all of them speechless. No one on Endeavor, excluding the XO Don Stoner, had ever been this close to Saturn and its magnificent rings. Of course, they had seen ultra-high-resolution holograms before, but those paled in comparison. To Merriweather, nothing in the solar system matched the grandeur of Saturn's rings.

Considered by many the *jewel* of the solar system, the sixth planet from the sun was an imposing spectacle—a gas giant with a radius nine times that of Earth and ninety-five times as massive. One hundred and four moons and countless moonlets orbited the ringed planet, including several that were suspected of harboring life in frigid oceans beneath their icy crusts.

What made Saturn unique among the other planets, however, was her incredible ring system. Composed primarily of water-ice and traces of carbon, the massive rings extended outward from Saturn's equator over one hundred and twenty thousand kilometers.

Captain Merriweather reminded himself to breathe.

"What do you think, XO? Change much since the Titan mission you were on?"

"It's even more fucking beautiful than I remember," said Stoner. " I didn't think I'd ever get this close to her again."

"Language, XO," said Merriweather. "There are ladies present."

"Sorry, sir," said Stoner.

"Yeah, watch your fucking mouth," said Doc Lee.

"Nothing I haven't heard before, Captain," said Zoe Bishop.

"Bridge decorum," said Merriweather, glaring at his medical officer. Stoner gestured toward the bridge display and the sight of Saturn and her beautiful icy ring system hanging motionless before them. Closer yet was Saturn's sixth largest moon. "I was referring to that view. It's frigging amazing."

"Yes, I agree. Breathtaking, isn't it?" said Merriweather.

Merriweather waved his hand toward the giant holoview in a sweeping gesture. "Anyone care to play—Name that Moon?"

"It's Enceladus, Captain Merriweather," answered Professor Mann. Endeavor had appeared so close to Enceladus that only a quarter of the moon filled a third of the forward holoview with Saturn and her ring system in the background.

"You should know, professor. RHODA, how many moons are currently visible to us from the forward-facing cameras?" Merriweather asked.

"The moon most visible at this distance and position is Enceladus. Eight moons are currently visible, Captain Merriweather," said the ship's artificial intelligence.

"Eight moons, really? OK, let's see how many we can find and identify," said Merriweather.

The bridge suddenly came alive as Endeavor's crew members tried to outdo each other, calling out as they located the other moons.

Despite being Saturn's sixth largest moon—only a tenth the size of Titan—Enceladus was extraordinarily beautiful. At just over five hundred kilometers in diameter, the icy sphere was still Saturn's brightest moon.

"Ms. Bishop, I want to focus your attention on Enceladus' South Polar Region. What do you see?" asked Merriweather.

"Oh, good. I get to play," chirped Bishop. "Let's see. I see geysers, mostly water vapor and ice. Right?"

"Excellent, Ms. Bishop. I see you have done your homework. Professor, can you tell us more?" said Merriweather, now deferring to the ship's exoplanetologist, Dr. Mann.

"Thank you, Captain," Mann replied is his best professorial voice. "The geysers indicate a moon that is geologically active primarily because of the gravitational interaction with Saturn and proximity with Dione. There. That's Dione in the distance," said Mann, pointing at a nearby moon. "It looks small on the screen, but it's slightly larger than Enceladus. We know Enceladus has liquid water beneath her crust, and we have evidence of a large subsurface ocean beneath her south pole. We think that the immense tidal forces caused by Enceladus' gravitational interaction with Saturn and Dione are the principal cause of her geological activity. I would also add that the water, ice, and debris ejected in those geysers feed Saturn's e-ring."

"RHODA, can you enhance the image on the forward holoview to show the relationship between the plumes coming from Enceladus and Saturn's e-ring?" Merriweather asked.

"Yes, Captain Merriweather," said RHODA.

A second later, the image on the forward holoview changed. Clearly visible now was a wispy trail of vapor swirling off Enceladus, bending in an arc and blending into Saturn's outer ring.

"Magnifique," exclaimed Dr. Girard.

"Do you have an opinion on whether there is life there, Captain?" Bishop asked.

"On Enceladus? Don't know. But where there's liquid water, there's a possibility of life. Unfortunately, Congress defunded a planned expedition to Enceladus, which could have answered that question. Now that we have FTL, however, I am sure they will revisit that decision."

For the next few minutes, no one spoke. Spellbound, the bridge crew gazed in awe at the magnificent sight they were witnessing. Finally, Merriweather broke the silence.

"Well, we have a job to do, gentlemen. We started our voyage with barely enough antimatter for our mission, courtesy of ISA. However, I would like a little cushion in case we need it. I want to locate at least five of the orbiting antiproton collectors and increase our reserves. RHODA, plot our distance from the nearest collector. How far?"

"The nearest antimatter collector is fifty kilometers from our current position, Captain Merriweather."

"Well, kudos to our navigator for popping us out of FTL so close. Thanks RHODA."

"You're welcome, Captain Merriweather," said RHODA.

"OK, let's engage the TAMARAKS to move us to within collection range, RHODA."

"Plasma engines are engaged, and our trajectory computed Captain Merriweather."

Merriweather felt the slight acceleration produced by Endeavor's eight magnetoplasma engines at Endeavor's stern.

"Very good, RHODA. What's our ETA?"

"Our ETA is four hours, Captain Merriweather."

"XO, you coordinate the collecting."

"Ay, Cap'n," said Stoner.

"In the meantime, let's run full diagnostics on the FTL drives," said Merriweather.

Four hours later, the bridge was once again busy as Endeavor neared the first of the antiproton collectors, now visible from Endeavor's forward holoview. The faint glow of the plasma field surrounding the three-hundred-meter-long vehicle distinguished the collector from the panoply of stars beyond it.

The collector was not a single vehicle, but four modules connected by long loop antennas, each over three hundred meters long, creating a large square magnet designed to scoop up and hold antiprotons emanating from the planet's radiation. A small 250kW nuclear battery module powered the collector's plasma field and an antiproton containment vessel needed to transfer the antimatter from the collector to any visiting starship.

Stoner had tapped Milo Bridges to perform the actual transfer.

"Bridges, make sure you position Aries between the planet and yourself. That, plus your suit, should block most of the radiation. But I don't want you outside Aries for longer than about fifteen minutes. So, keep it snappy."

"I plan on it," answered Bridges.

After running through his checklist and getting permission from the XO, Bridges decoupled the Aries LAV from Endeavor's port side docking adapter. Using thrusters, he carefully backed the lander away, putting distance between the tiny LAV and the much larger Endeavor.

Turning Aries toward the collector, Bridges fired his thrusters in short bursts, propelling his ship away from Endeavor. Twenty minutes later, as he neared his target, he engaged his forward thrusters to slow his approach.

"Endeavor, current range to target, three hundred fifty meters and closing ten meters per second," radioed Bridges.

"We copy, Aries. Give us a readout every fifty meters."

"Will do. Range three hundred meters."

Bridges carefully maneuvered his small craft using its hydrazine thrusters and positioning gyroscopes. He had trained extensively in ISA's simulators for just this task and was confident in his ability to perform it successfully. Plus, he was always happy to be at the controls of a spacecraft, aircraft, or any craft he could get his hands on. It is what he lived for.

"Two fifty," he radioed.

Although recently upgraded, Endeavor's communications equipment struggled to overcome the interference generated by Saturn's intense radiation. Bridges' voice was barely discernible above the crackling and hissing emanating from the ship's speakers.

"Two hundred… One fifty… One hundred."

"Slowing to five meters per second."

"Sixty… Fifty… Forty."

"Twenty, slowing to three meters per second."

"OK, Endeavor, I'm holding at ten meters from the collector."

"Copy, Aries. We've sent the command to put the containment vessel into collection mode, and the collector has responded that the payload is ready for pickup."

"Thanks, Endeavor. Please power down the plasma field," Bridges replied.

A second later, the plasma glow abruptly ceased.

"RHODA, hold Aries' current attitude and range to the collector," said Bridges.

"Holding Range and attitude," RHODA replied.

Five minutes later, Bridges had donned the newly improved Personal Maneuvering Unit (PMU) and now stood in the LAV's open access hatch. He had done a few EVAs in his brief career at ISA, but the scene before him took his breath away. It reminded him of the first time he flew an open-cockpit aircraft. He recalled how free he had felt soaring above the clouds. The world was his. Even now, despite the constraints of a spacesuit, he felt totally unfettered. He was master of the Universe yet totally dwarfed by the scale and majesty of this beautiful ringed alien world. He felt unable to take it all in, despite how hard he tried. Although Bridges did not consider himself religious, he thought this was as close as he would ever get to heaven.

"What's the delay, Lieutenant," said Stoner. "Misplace your keys?"

"Damn, they're in my other pants," replied Bridges, "But no worries. I got a spare key."

"The clock's ticking, kid."

"Clocks don't tick anymore, grandpa."

"Watch yourself, Mr. Bridges."

"Aye, grandpa, sir."

Pushing off from the hatch, and using small bursts of gaseous nitrogen from the PMU's maneuvering jets, Bridges slowly moved toward the collector. A few seconds later, he had crossed the short distance separating the LAV and the containment vessel. With difficulty, he turned his attention away from the planet below and to the task at hand.

"OK, I am at the collector and ready to open the access door."
Bridges flashed back to the countless hours he had spent in a simulator performing this task. Simulators had improved over the centuries from the flight simulators produced by companies like Evans and Sutherland back in the twentieth century and the early days of computer graphics, to today's holographic simulators that were so real that even experienced pilots couldn't tell the difference from the real thing. The simulator he had trained on was in low Earth orbit inside the In-Orbit Construction Facility. The microgravity of the IOCF made the experience even more realistic.
Refocusing on the situation, Bridges radioed Endeavor.

"OK, door open. I'm removing the first of the four bolts."

Bridges removed his socket wrench from the tool panel integrated into the PMU. The wrench could supply just the torque needed and could function in the cold vacuum of space. However, except for a slightly longer battery life, its design really hadn't changed all that much in the last hundred years.

Bridges turned the counter ring on the electric socket wrench, selecting the number ten. Next, he positioned the socket over the first bolt and depressed the trigger.

As the socket turned slowly counterclockwise, Bridges counted the revolutions—one -two -three. At the count of ten, the wrench stopped automatically. Bridges lifted the tool, releasing it to float nearby, tethered to the PMU. Bridges extracted the bolt using his fingers and stuck it to a small adhesive plate attached to his suit.

"OK, I'm now removing the second. This is easier than the simulator," Bridges said as he repeated the process he had rehearsed over countless hours. The third bolt was more of a challenge, but nothing his tool couldn't handle.

"On to the fourth bolt," said Bridges. After a few minutes of straining at the stubborn fastener, Bridges reported as much to Endeavor. "I'm having a bit of a problem with the fourth bolt. Trying again."
Bridges checked the bolt for damage, repositioned the wrench, and tried again.

"Damn. Seems to be stuck. I could bang on it with the wrench a bit to loosen it."

The calm yet stern voice of Don Stoner crackled over Bridges' helmet speaker.

"Bridges, you know what happens if the containment vessel fails, don't you?"

Bridges instantly comprehended Stoner's warning.

"Uh, I turn into star stuff?" Bridges replied.

"You, me, and everyone else on Endeavor," said Stoner. "I'd refrain from banging on it if I were you. Try tightening, then loosening it a few times."

"Sounds like a plan."

"Tighten, loosen, tighten, loosen—OK, that did it. It's free now. Thanks for the tip."

"Five minutes elapsed," radioed Stoner.

"Copy that," said Bridges.

Bridges grasped the two small handles that extended from each side of the containment vessel and gave a slight tug.

"OK, the vessel is sliding out now—very smooth. That was easy."

"OK, Bridges, I'm starting the countdown clock at sixty minutes," radioed Stoner.

Bridges knew that the batteries in the portable containment vessel were only good for that long and that he had to get it back to Endeavor before they fully discharged.

"Roger that. Have RHODA watch the box's telemetry and the field stability," said Bridges.

"Thanks for the advice, Lieutenant," replied Stoner, somewhat sarcastically.

Bridges quickly installed the replacement containment vessel he brought from Aries, then gave the installation a thorough check. Satisfied, he headed back to Aries. Thirty minutes later, Bridges and Dutch Swenson uploaded the newly collected antimatter to the primary containment vessel.

Over the next seven days, Endeavor rendezvoused with five more collectors, adding over thirty micrograms of antiprotons to the ship's reserves. The effort wasn't a necessary part of the mission. Endeavor had enough antimatter, thanks to the particle accelerators built by ISA on Earth. Collecting antimatter from Saturn's collectors was to test the viability of in-space antimatter harvesting. Merriweather considered the operation a success even if the quantity of antiprotons harvested was meager.

Over the next two weeks, Merriweather had the crew run every diagnostic on every piece of gear on board and twice on anything involved with the antimatter reactor and the hyperdrive. Twice-daily status reports were required with the crew in eight-on, four-off rotations. Merriweather knew he was driving the crew hard, but he was determined to give the mission its best chance for success.

Finally, convinced that everything was in shipshape, Merriweather gave the order to depart Saturn's orbit. To commemorate the event, Merriweather assembled everyone on the bridge. Addressing the crew, the civilian scientists, and the reporter Bishop, Merriweather compared Endeavor's mission to Christopher Columbus setting sail for the new world.

"Five minutes after we leave Saturn's orbit, we will be farther from Earth than any human has ever traveled. We will encounter unknowns, and we will experience dangers. However, we follow in the footsteps of the great explorers—Columbus, Magellan, Cortez, Glenn, Armstrong, and Clark. They cast aside their fears and pushed the edge of the known world ever outward. We do the same, every one of us. We depart for parts unknown in search of knowledge, not conquest, friendships, not enemies, and we carry with us the hopes of all humanity."

# CHAPTER 12

*Underway, Deep Space, USS Endeavor*

On a small starship like Endeavor, it was hard to keep secrets. Captain Merriweather knew the best way to tamp down gossip or to prevent misinformation from gaining traction was to involve the entire crew in every decision and to keep the lines of communication open and inclusive. Merriweather decided early on to hold regular meetings with the entire crew—meetings he called bull sessions, in the best Navy tradition. Twenty-four hours after departing Saturn's vicinity, Merriweather called his first bull session.

The ship's galley was the only space large enough to hold all thirteen members of Endeavor's crew—other than the bridge. It was the space where the crew ate, relaxed, and socialized.

Merriweather called the first bull session with a simple announcement over his holocom. "Everyone, listen up. This is your captain. Can I get everyone together—in the galley?"

Fifteen minutes later, everyone had gathered, filled their mugs with their unique brew from the bulkhead-mounted Custom Beverage dispenser—called the CUBE—and now waited for Merriweather to begin.

Mann, Girard, Lee, and Bishop took the four seats attached to the one-meter by two-meter table. The others crowded into the remaining space.

"OK, let's get started," said Merriweather as he took a sip from his favorite brew—black coffee.

Merriweather had placed a portable holo-projector in the center of the table before calling the bull session.

"As you know, our destination is a type G2V star system in the constellation Andromeda, about forty-three light years away. RHODA, dim the lights, and display our galaxy. Zoom in on the Orion arm."

As the lights dimmed, a three-dimensional image of the galaxy appeared, floating over the heads of Endeavor's crew.

"I know we've all read the mission briefings. However, it never hurts to refresh our memories. The Webb Four satellite has detected what appears to be an Earth-sized and potentially habitable exoplanet within the Goldilocks zone of its star system. Our mission is to explore the planet and its system and determine its suitability as a deep-space port."

Merriweather adjusted the position of the hologram using hand gestures before continuing.

"While our primary goal is to check out this exoplanet, ISA has also tasked us to check out another issue—some interesting electromagnetic (EM) signals coming from the same general direction. These signals are most likely natural. However, they could indicate a nearby black hole, neutron star, or both. I'll let Dr. Mann give you more info. Professor, care to dazzle us with your brilliance?"

"Thanks, Captain, I'll try. OK, the Armstrong Lunar Radio Telescope (ALeRT) has been studying an FRB, or Fast Radio Burst, emanating from a region of space about eighty light years from Earth. That would be the closest FRB we've ever seen. To compare, the next closest FRB source we have discovered to date, FRB-981114, is approximately one hundred and fifty light years from Earth.

"What ALeRT has detected is a series of highly energetic bursts around 98 Janskys, occurring three or four times per hour over eleven days, followed by eleven days of silence. ALeRT has been following the signal for nine months."

"Janskys?" said Bishop.

"Janskys quantify the flux density of electromagnetic radiation, particularly radio waves."

"Thanks," said Bishop. "You learn something new every day."

"What makes this FRB even more interesting," continued Mann, "is that NASA detected a similar one in this same area of space 200 years ago. They studied that FRB for about a year when it suddenly ceased, and no one knows why.

"Now, as the captain pointed out, these FRBs are typically associated with neutron stars. In addition, the intermittent nature of this FRB could mean that it orbits a black hole, presumably every eleven days. However, we haven't been able to detect signs of either a black hole or a neutron star in that region of space."

"What do you think it is?" asked Bishop.

"I think it's a neutron star orbiting a black hole. It's the best explanation," replied Mann.

"And that's why we brought the Doppler and interferometer gravity-wave detectors?" asked Bishop.

"Exactly. Give Bishop a gold star. On Earth, the instrument was used to detect waves from a binary black hole system. However, out here in space, far from the gravitational systems of Earth, the moon, and the other planets, we should be able to detect the faint waves produced by a system comprising a black hole and a neutron star."

"Thanks, professor," said Merriweather. "ISA hopes we can shed some light on this mystery.

"Our estimated time of arrival (ETA) is three hundred and eighty-five days, depending on how often we drop out of FTL. Our mission plan allows us to explore nearby phenomena we might encounter along the way, so expect the schedule to change if we see anything interesting.

"OK, let's talk about stasis."

This caused an audible groan from the crew.

"I know all of you have had stasis training, so you know what to expect. Because of the long duration of the mission, we need to manage our resources. That means stasis for some of the crew for parts of the trip. You can each expect multiple stints in a stasis pod. Doc Lee will coordinate your requests along with our guest scientists so we can maintain a schedule. I know a schedule already exists, but I want you guys to take one more look at it. It's a quick trip, relatively, so some of you will be exempt. We will drop out of FTL a few times during the trip to drop location buoys, and we will use those occasions to make limited sweeps of the area for potential sources of additional resources. Therefore, expect that our schedule might and probably will change.

"OK," continued Merriweather, "unless there are questions, let's all get back to work."

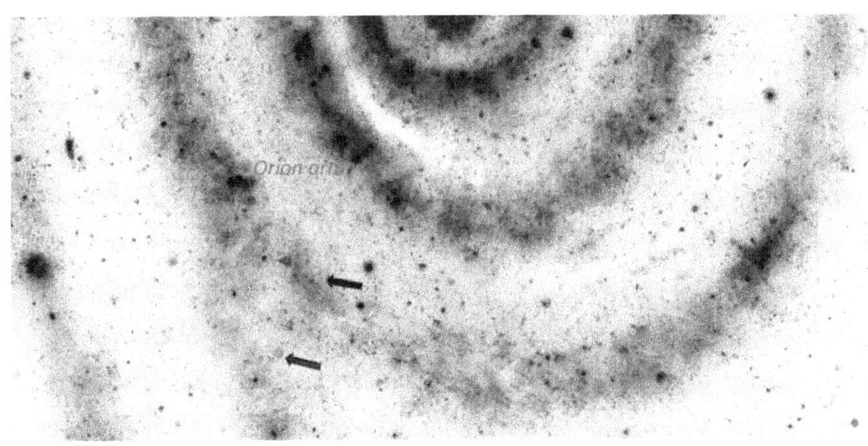

# CHAPTER 13

*Zoe Bishop, personal log, three weeks after embarkation*

Bishop removed the soft moccasin-like booties everyone wore onboard Endeavor, stretched out on her bunk, and asked RHODA to open her personal log. RHODA performed a biometric verification and opened the protected file.

"Personal log entry, July 28, 2125: 16.38," said the AI.

For a moment, Bishop's thoughts turned to RHODA, the ship's omnipresent artificial intelligence, to whom she was about to share her innermost thoughts. Funny, she thought, before her interview with Jonathan Mills tonight, she hadn't given RHODA's technology much thought. It was just a tool, like the CUBE beverage dispenser or her holo—modern marvels to be used and not given another thought. Now, however, she had a newfound appreciation for the technology behind the ubiquitous AI.

Her interview session with Mills was highly informative. Mills was not only brilliant; he could also explain things in a way even a non-scientist could understand. He was also excited to spend as much time talking about his creation as Bishop was willing to sit and listen. Mills was also quite funny, a trait Bishop found quite appealing in some men.

Of course, Mills hadn't noticed he was being interviewed. None of Bishop's shipmates did. Bishop never used the "I" word when speaking with a subject. Over the years, she learned that calling it an interview made people nervous and less willing to open up. Instead, she relied on the innocent question—the feigning of cluelessness—to get her subject to lower their defenses. Bishop had a way of getting people to talk about themselves, forgetting they were talking to a reporter. A Bishop "interview" would usual-ly begin with Bishop asking an innocuous question—as it had earlier with Lieutenant Mills.

"Hey, Jon, what are you up to?" she asked. Bishop found Mills staring at the holoview attached to the bulkhead forward of the ship's galley. At first, she thought he hadn't heard her. But she knew enough not to press, so she waited patiently for Mills to unwind his mind from the depths of the recur-sive code he was focusing on.

After what seemed to Bishop like an eternity but was less than a minute, and without taking his eyes away from the holoview, Mills answered.

"Making a minor improvement to RHODA's code."

"Making it better—wow. I think she's damned impressive already."

"The linguistic disambiguation algorithm has an unnecessary pathway, and I believe I've found a way around it."

"That sounds important," replied Bishop. "What does that do?"

Mills cocked his head as if analyzing her question, then turned to face Bishop. "It's pretty technical. Are you sure you want to hear it?"

Bishop could list a dozen things she would rather do, but this was the opening she'd hoped for.

"Sure, sounds interesting."

From that beginning and over the next hour, Bishop had learned more than she needed to know about artificial intelligence—including disambig-uation linguistics. That segued into the intimate details of Jon's life at Cal Tech, including his first real love interest, a pretty sophomore named Claire. Following that, Bishop expertly steered Mills to his early academic life and the high school math teacher who introduced him to AI. Eventually, Jon opened up about his family life in South Carolina—a disinterested father and an indulgent mother. An intelligent but chubby child, Mills had been bullied, which made him resort to humor as a defensive measure.

Bishop also picked up on those signals girls learn to recognize early on. Mills was interested in her, but a little too shy to turn his feelings into ac-tions. Bishop was likewise interested in Mills. Intelligent men were a turn on for Bishop and she wasn't shy about acting on her feelings. She could picture herself in a relationship with Mills; however, it was a little too early, and this was going to be a long trip.

*How would I describe Mills?* Zoe thought. *Jon is cute but shy, average height, about five-ten, dark hair, maybe eighty kilos. He's thirty—or a trifle younger, I think.*

She dutifully entered those comments, plus other interesting informa-tion about her shipmate, into her personal log.

Bishop smiled. *That's eleven,* she thought. She had now interviewed all of her shipmates. Of course, these weren't the only interviews she would conduct over the next two or three years, but it was a start.

Bishop quickly reviewed her notes to see if she wanted to change or add to what she had recorded for her other shipmates.

Zoe started with Merriweather. He would be the main protagonist of whatever story she would later write. So, she was planning on devoting a great deal of effort to figuring out just what made the captain tick.

Her first impression of Merriweather had been less than favorable. She had approached him on the ship's bridge—apparently at the wrong time— and he had snapped at her. She wasn't used to getting yelled at and left the bridge fuming. Milo Bridges approached her later and tried to calm her down a bit. "Don't get too discouraged," he had said. "Being irascible comes with the captain's job."

The second time she had approached him had gone much better. Zoe found him in the ship's mess and offered to buy him a cup of coffee. "I've only got a few minutes," he had told her, but they chatted for almost an hour. *It's all in the timing*, she thought.

Her second impression of Merriweather was more positive. He came across as thoughtful, aloof, and maybe a little sad. He lost his wife a few years back, and he still thought of her a lot. She broached the subject of his late wife, but he promptly steered the conversation to a book he was reading.

There was still more to know about Endeavor's prickly Captain Merri- weather. Tomorrow, she thought, *I'll take another run at him tomorrow*.

# CHAPTER 14

*Buoy Drop, Thirty days after departure*

"Cap'n on the bridge," shouted Rodriguez as Captain Merriweather floated onto Endeavor's bridge, with Zoe Bishop following close behind. Rodriguez was the only one on the bridge, so his announcement of the captain's arrival was more in keeping with tradition rather than serving any useful purpose.

"Report, Lieutenant," said Merriweather, taking his place in the captain's chair. The captain had already queried RHODA regarding the status of Endeavor's various systems before he left his quarters, so he knew what Rodriguez was about to report, but tradition was tradition.

"All systems are operational, Captain." Rodriguez had also just queried RHODA in anticipation of the captain's arrival on the bridge. He knew Merriweather had also, but this was part of the drill.

"It's a big day, Javi."

"Yes, sir, big day," replied Rodriguez.

Merriweather turned to Zoe Bishop.

"Quite a view out there, isn't it, Ms. Bishop?" Merriweather asked, nodding at the panoply of stars filling the giant video screen that covered the entire forward bulkhead.

"Yes, it is, Captain," she replied. Then, after some introspection, she added: "Can I share something with you?"

"Sure," answered Merriweather, his curiosity piqued.

"It's kind of embarrassing," said Bishop. "But here goes. As a writer, I feel like I should be able to capture in words what I'm seeing and feeling, and my readers expect that from me. I've tried many times to put it into words—the sheer magnitude, the immensity of the universe, what it feels like to be trapped inside this insignificant spacecraft surrounded by the majesty of the cosmos—but so far, I've utterly failed."

Merriweather winced at the term 'insignificant.'

"I think it should be a challenge for any writer," said Merriweather.

"I guess you're right, Captain. You know I come down here often," she continued. "Staring out the window settles my claustrophobia a little." Merriweather chuckled at her use of the term "window" instead of holoview or vidscreen.

"You suffer from claustrophobia?" he asked. "I didn't know that."

"I didn't either. I've never experienced it before. But it's manageable. I'll talk to the Doc if it gets worse," she replied.

"Good. See that you do."

"So, can we talk about your thoughts?" said Bishop.

"Thoughts about what?" asked Merriweather.

"Everything. You know—how you're feeling; the responsibilities of leadership; your place in the history books; the importance of this mission for humanity?"

"Hold on. That's a lot to digest," said Merriweather.

"OK then," said Bishop, "we'll start with something simple. How are you feeling?"

"I'm feeling fine," he answered.

"Not depressed, not feeling overwhelmed, homesick, claustrophobic?"

"Nope, nope, nope, and nope," he said.

"Care to expound on any of that?" Bishop prodded.

"Nope, not really."

"I see. Not a big talker, are you?" said Bishop.

Merriweather responded with a smile. He wondered how much to share. He knew that whatever he said could be shared with the public, and he wasn't sure how he felt about that. However, she was doing her job, and ISA had agreed to this, so reluctantly, he decided to cooperate.

"Well, Zoe, we're leaving behind Earth—everything familiar, everyone we've ever known—so yeah, it rattles the nerves a bit. I imagine it's something like what the first sea captains felt crossing the Atlantic—a sustained surge of adrenaline, mixed with the unknown."

"Anything else?"

"A sense of wonder. No, that sounds too corny. A sense of pride, maybe."

"Pride?"

"Yeah, but not personal pride. We humans have evolved to the point we are now, with the ability to escape from our little cage, overcome our fears, and launch ourselves into the unknown. That is not a minor accomplishment. So, I am proud of humanity. Does that sound corny?"

"A little," she smiled impishly. "OK, here's another question. Do you think we'll find intelligent life out here?"

"Who knows?" said Merriweather. "I watched your show Space-Time, the episode with Dr. Mann, and I agree with the idea it is less likely than we hope. However, I'll defer to biologist Richard Dawkins, who said that the exploration of the universe is important, not whether there's life out there."

"You watched my show? I'm flattered. But thank you, and just to be accurate Captain, Dawkins said that the urge to know more about the universe was irresistible, regardless of whether we find alien life. To characterize his comment to imply that exploring the universe would be *just* as irresistible if we looked for life or not is misstating it a bit, and I don't think Dawkins would agree to that premise."

"Never argue with a writer," laughed Merriweather.

"Or a reader," said Bishop.

Merriweather just smiled at her. "You're a Dawkins fan, then?"

"I've read a bit," said Bishop, smiling. "Someone I knew once was a huge fan, and he had all of Dawkins' books, and I used to borrow them." Something in the way Bishop answered piqued Merriweather's interest.

"Someone you knew—once? A male friend?" he asked.

"Let's just say it was someone I knew," said Bishop.

*Well, that sounds intriguing*, thought Merriweather. For reasons that weren't entirely clear to him, he found it pleasing to see Bishop squirm. So, he pressed ahead.

"Someone you knew—once?" he asked.

"Yes," she said.

"You said 'he.' A boyfriend, then?"

"Why are you so interested?"

Merriweather detected a slight annoyance in Bishop's voice.

"Just curious," he said, smiling.

"Moving forward," said Bishop, "do you think humanity will change if we meet intelligent life out here?"

"That's a big question. I'm just a ship's captain, not a philosopher. What was his name?"

"What? Whose name?"

"Your boyfriend—the Dawkins fan."

"I didn't say boyfriend. Can we drop it, please?"

"OK, if you don't want to talk about him."

"Thank you. So, is there intelligent life out there? Surely you have an opinion."

"Are you sure you want to hear it?"

"I do," said Bishop.

"OK, the public is hungry to discover intelligent life, and they've already accepted the idea of little green men. If we discover primitive civilizations, the public will be fascinated but not shocked or overwhelmed. However, if we stumble upon a civilization much more advanced than we are, it could give us a huge inferiority complex. And some people will be afraid. And there will be a lot of soul searching about our place in the universe."

"Do you think people will begin disbelieving in God?"

"Whoa. You want to go there?"

"Why not? I'm sure you've thought about it."

"Well, I don't think it will affect *my* beliefs."

"Which are?" said Bishop.

"Which *are* none of your business. Let me ask you a question. It's your job to have a sense of what the public thinks, right?"

"Maybe," she said warily.

"So, same question. Do you think people will stop believing in God?" asked Merriweather.

"I ask the questions here," said Bishop, smiling. "So, you expect to find life?"

"Maybe not intelligent life, but I wouldn't be shocked to find microbial life. The universe is just too big and biologically speaking, we're just not that special. I think we'll find life everywhere."

Stoner arrived on the bridge and took the zero-g chair behind the captain.

"Good morning, Cap'n, and you, Ms. Bishop," said Stoner. "Am I interrupting anything?"

"Nope," said Merriweather. "Ms. Bishop was just telling me about her boyfriend. Are we ready?"

"Yes, sir," said Stoner. "This will be a first. I've been looking forward to it all week."

"I guess this will be a first for all of us," said Merriweather.

Merriweather turned to Bishop to explain.

"What I mean by that, Ms. Bishop, is that we've never needed to drop navigation buoys before."

"I can understand that. We've always had the advantage of knowing exactly where we were. We could navigate by locking in on radio signals from Earth or by triangulating on the planets and the sun or even by the stars like old ship captains."

"Excellent, Ms. Bishop. However, the farther we get from our solar system, the less viable those options become."

"I understand the need to drop breadcrumbs," said Bishop. "You don't need to explain."

"Indulge me," said Merriweather. "Pretend I'm the captain."

"Aye, aye, Captain," replied Bishop, saluting and smiling.

"Anyway, as I was saying, the farther we get from earth, the harder it becomes to detect radio signals from Earth and differentiate those from background radiation or radio frequency signals from other, naturally occurring sources," said Merriweather, "and differentiating our sun from all the other stars becomes more and more complex the farther out we get. Even the constellations we've all grown up memorizing look completely different this far out. However, buoys are just one method we've devised to help find our way home."

"Oh? I'm intrigued," said Bishop.

"Well, as you know, the stars you see on the various holoviews throughout the ship are actually..."

"Computer generated. I know all that," interrupted Bishop. "When we're in FTL, we cannot see the actual stars."

Merriweather's expression affirmed his irritation. He wasn't used to being interrupted, but she was a guest and not an actual member of ISA, so he tolerated it.

"Of course, Ms. Bishop, but were you aware that whenever we exit FTL, RHODA compares the simulation with the stars as they appear from our new vantage point? She then adjusts the simulation parameters until there's a perfect match."

"I see. The simulation becomes more accurate," said Bishop.

"Right again," said Merriweather. "That allows us to construct a map we can use to navigate by. But I've saved the best for last."

"I can't wait," she said.

Merriweather couldn't tell if she was being sarcastic, which irritated him even more.

"XO, notify the crew that we are stopping ship's rotation."

After Stoner made the announcement to the crew, Merriweather gave the order to the ship's AI.

"RHODA, cease ship's rotation, discontinue FTL," ordered Merriweather. "RHODA, turn off star field simulation and switch to exterior cameras."

Zoe watched carefully, but couldn't detect a change in the star field on the forward holoview.

"Looks like her simulation matches up pretty well," said Bishop.

"Maybe, but we'll do a thorough analysis before we draw a conclusion," said Merriweather. "RHODA, maximum magnification on the forward holoview," commanded Merriweather.

"What's that pinkish area there in the upper right corner?" Bishop asked. "Oh wait, is that the Heart Nebula?"

"Very good," said Merriweather, "and what do you see right in the middle of the holoview?"

Bishop concentrated on that part of the holoview before answering.

"You mean that ring?" she asked.

"Yes, that one. What can you tell me about it?"

"An Einstein Ring?"

"Right again, Ms. Bishop. I'm impressed."

"I had an astrophysicist on my show who talked about gravitational lensing. So that's what they look like."

"They can," answered Merriweather. "What do you remember about them—from your show?"

"So, I'm being tested," said Zoe, smiling. "OK, here goes. Gravitational lensing occurs when you have a massive object like a star with sufficient gravity to distort space enough to bend light. "

"Very good," said Merriweather, "and an Einstein ring?"

"Right, so that happens when a closer star blocks our view of a more distant one. If the closer star is massive enough, its gravity warps the surrounding space—bending the light from the distant star so it curves around the closer one. When the distant star, the closer star, and the observer line up perfectly, that bent light forms a glowing circle called an Einstein Ring. How did I do?"

"Close enough, Ms. Bishop, except the closer star doesn't have to be a star at all. It just needs to be a massive object. It could be a star. Or it could also be a black hole or a neutron star, anything massive enough to distort space."

"I don't see a star in the middle of the ring. Is it a black hole?"

"We think so," answered Merriweather. "We couldn't get a very good reading on it from Earth or the Webb Four telescope, but we should be able to answer that question soon. The key to using it for navigation is that you only get a complete ring if the source, lens, and observer are in a straight line, as you correctly stated. Otherwise, you just get a partial ring. If we want to use an Einstein ring for navigation, we need to find one near where we want to go, and it has to have a complete and not a partial ring."

"OK, I'm still not getting how it's used for navigation," she said.

"If it's a complete ring, we know we can plot a straight line between the light source, the lens, and our solar system," answered Merriweather. "So, we aim the ship directly at the ringed object until we get close to our destination. When we're ready to come home, we just watch the ring in our rearview mirror, so to speak. If the ring stays complete, we know we're headed toward home. If the ring changes and becomes incomplete, we're off course. It's that simple."

"I see. Ingenious," said Bishop. "So that means we're headed directly at that Einstein Ring in the center of the window."

"The holoview," corrected Merriweather. He couldn't tell if she was using the term 'window' to irritate him or not. "But yes. That is correct. Although it's about a hundred times more distant than our ultimate destination, it's in the same general direction."

Merriweather turned toward his first lieutenant.

"Lieutenant, sound stations for buoy deployment."

"Aye, Cap'n."

"What if we want to go somewhere without an Einstein ring?" Bishop asked.

"Good question."

"I always ask good questions," she said, smiling.

"Can't argue with that," smiled Merriweather. "Do you know what a pulsar is?"

"Sure, do you?" Bishop smiled impishly.

Merriweather smiled again. *Damn, she's annoying*, he thought.

"Basically, a pulsar is a variation of a neutron star."

"And a neutron star is…?"

Merriweather paused for a moment before answering.

"All stars eventually die. If a star is big enough, say four or five times larger than our sun, its death is violent. They die in a massive explosion called a supernova. The explosion blasts most of the dying star's mass into space. However, if the star is large enough, its gravity will hold on to some of its material, creating a small, dense core of protons and electrons. In fact, it doesn't stop there. The collapsing star's gravity is so strong that it fuses the protons and electrons together to make neutrons."

Merriweather underscored his description by squeezing his hands together.

"And pulsars?" Bishop asked.

"Ah yes, pulsars. The process that creates a neutron star also causes it to spin—sometimes hundreds of revolutions a second. It's the same principle that causes an ice skater to spin faster when she pulls in her arms."

"Or *his* arms," said Bishop.

"Yes, or his arms. Some of these neutron stars—and these are the ones we're talking about—have jets of material streaming out of them at nearly the speed of light. As they spin, they flash like a lighthouse."

"How do they help us navigate?" said Bishop.

"We can identify pulsars by their spin rate. So, if we can locate four known pulsars, we can triangulate our position. "

"Ah, ingenious. That makes me feel more—how should I say it—more secure," said Bishop. "I was afraid we might not find our way back home."

"I'm so glad I could help," said Merriweather. Damn. He couldn't tell whether Bishop was sincere or being sarcastic, and his gut told him it was the latter. So why was he attracted to her?

Seconds later, the telltale tone of the ship-wide alert system blared throughout the ship, followed immediately by Stoner's command to man deployment stations.

"How many buoys do we carry?" asked Bishop.

"We have twenty in the cargo hold," said Merriweather. "And we can manufacture more if needed."

"The 3D printer?" said Bishop.

"Right again."

"Stone, give the order to deploy the buoy whenever they're ready," said Merriweather without looking at his XO.

"Yes, sir," said the XO.

"I think I'm going to watch this from the cargo hold," said Bishop.

"Good idea," said Merriweather, watching her depart.

As Bishop floated from the bridge, her thoughts weren't on the buoy drop. Instead, her thoughts were on Captain Merriweather.

He sure is cute when he gets angry.

# CHAPTER 15

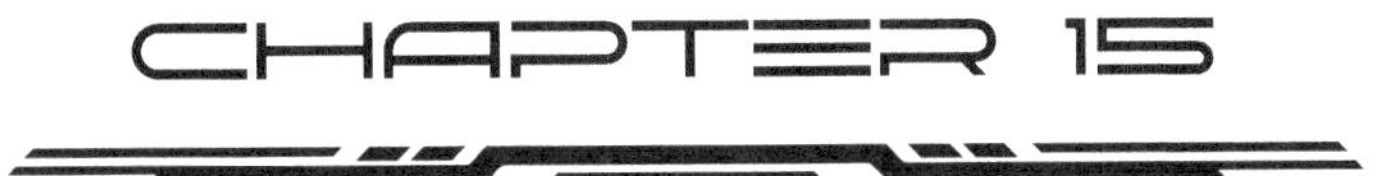

*Stasis—Seven months after embarkation, eighteen light years from Earth*

"Wake up, sleeping beauty."

Bridges' mind grasped for a fast-retreating moment of a delightful dream, only to see it fade away, replaced by a beautiful apparition bearing a striking resemblance to Lieutenant Cortez.

*Hi, sweetheart, are you coming to bed* is what Milo tried to say. What came from his lips, however, was more like…

"heeghh…lo…swee…um…b-bed."

"Didn't quite catch that," Cortez replied.

Bridges slowly raised his hands to his face and felt his lips.

"Muh libs," he slurred.

"Your lips will be swollen for a while. I'll give you some moisturizer."

"Where…? who…?" he asked.

"Stasis… Milo Bridges," she grinned.

"I c-can't… f-feel… muh…. libs," said Bridges.

It took a few minutes before he realized where he was.

"Stasis?" he said.

Cortez watched Bridges as he slowly comprehended his situation.

Bridges was in a coffin-shaped pod, semi-immersed in a rapidly warming fluid designed to keep humans healthy over extended periods of sleep. Bridges shivered.

"D-Damn, it's c-cold. C-Can you w-warm this up any f-faster?" he asked through chattering teeth, somewhat chagrined. "Where's D-Doc Lee?"

"Busy. I'm filling in," Cortez replied.

"Uh, r-right! You're her b-backup. I forgot," said Bridges.

"You forgot?" she said.

"How long?" he asked, changing the subject.

"How long what?"

"How long b-been sleep?"

"Full six months," she answered. "How are you feeling?"

Bridges groaned. "Throat hurts."

"That's a reaction to the feeding tube you had down your throat. The numbness in your limbs is normal as well. It's called paresthesia."

As Bridges' mind cleared, he remembered being put into stasis, but it seemed like it was just a few hours ago, not six months. His mind clawed back memories of his Academy days and the conversation he had with his stasis instructor the first time he was to undergo the procedure. His instructor was a young woman with the bedside manner of a drill sergeant.

> "It's basically hypothermia," she had said. "We lower your core temperature to 32 degrees Celsius, just a few degrees below normal, by having you inhale a coolant through your nose. That will put you into a deep sleep. The process takes about two hours, including inserting a catheter, IV lines, and a feeding tube."
>
> "A catheter! That doesn't sound too appealing," Bridges had said, feigning distress.
>
> "Oh, we give you drugs to make it more comfortable."
>
> "Good drugs or bad drugs?" joked Bridges.
>
> "Adequate drugs," said the instructor brusquely. "We give you a cocktail of drugs that temporarily inactivate two naturally occurring substances, Myostatin and Activin-A, that usually limit the growth of muscle and bone. You'll still experience some loss, but not as much as you would ordinarily. We feed you through a feeding tube. You'll get a nutritional formula with all the glucose, vitamins, and dietary minerals needed to maintain healthy bodily functions."

"Are you with us, Lieutenant?" asked Cortez, interrupting Bridges' trip down memory lane.

Cortez's voice brought Bridges back to the present.

"Wha? Oh, yeah," said Bridges. "I was just remembering my Academy instructor."

Bridges glanced at his crotch, both relieved and somewhat embarrassed to find that someone—likely Cortez—had removed his catheter.

"Let me guess, some cute redhead?" asked Cortez.

Bridges ignored the question.

"I need coffee. Can I get a seventeen from the CUBE?" he asked, referring to his custom blended drink and the custom beverage dispenser.

"What am I, your waitress?" she said, handing him a squeeze bottle.

"Here, drink this—all of it."

Bridges took the container and started drinking, almost gagging halfway through it.

"Tastes like bull semen," he said, making a face. "I think I'm gonna puke."

"You'll be fine," she replied, smiling.

Bridges tilted his head as if a new thought had just entered his mind.

"How long have you been…"

"Two days," said Cortez.

"The others, OK?" Bridges asked.

Cortez slowly helped Bridges from the stasis pod.

"Everyone's fine," she replied. "You'll be a bit unstable for an hour or two. Just take it slow and easy. You'll probably want to shower and dress before you eat anything, and that bull semen you just drank should help you hold everything down."

"I might need help in the shower," said Bridges.

"In your dreams, flyboy," she smiled.

"Well, OK, thanks," Bridges replied as he wobbled away toward one of the self-contained shower units.

Cortez watched him go with more than a passing interest. The form-fitting garment he was wearing left little to the imagination. Although he tried to hide it, she was reasonably sure he was interested in her. Several other crew members had already made their feelings clear in words, sometimes subtle and others not so much, but she had left no room for doubt that she did not share their feelings. Bridges had not crossed that line, making him even more appealing.

She wondered whether she should test the waters with Bridges. ISA's official policy on sex between crew members was that it was none of the agency's business. Neither she nor Bridges were married, nor did either have significant others, at least as far as Cortez knew. She intended to stay celibate for the length of the mission, but her resolve was slowly eroding.

*I've got to get my mind off this*, she thought to herself. *There's too much risk to my career and reputation on the ship.*

Bridges showered slowly, trying to ignore the aches and pains caused by six months of immobility. After getting dressed, he made his way to the ship's galley. He was now eager to catch up on all the ship's news, and Bridges knew you could always find someone in the galley ready and willing to dish out the latest scuttlebutt.

Milo hoped to see more of Cat Cortez. He would have enjoyed spending some time with her. Alas, she wasn't in the galley. Instead, he found the four scientists plus Zoe Bishop playing poker. Poker was the trending leisure activity aboard the spacecraft, and Bishop was its reigning champion. The four players were currently engaged in a lively discussion about evolution and the chances of encountering humanoid life.

"Not buying it, Girard—that whole convergent evolution idea," argued

Dr. Martin. "That dog won't hunt. Given the billions of mutations, the snowflake analogy is more probable—no two alien species will be the same. I'll take two."

Martin tossed two cards onto the pile in the middle of the table.

"I think you've overstated my argument, Doctor," said Dr. Girard, dealing two new cards to Dr. Martin. "I'm not saying we will find humanoid aliens on every habitable planet. I'm only saying that evolution favors certain evolutionary paths. The dealer takes three."

"Can someone explain convergent evolution to me?" asked Bishop, briefly glancing up from her own cards.

"That's your bailiwick, Paul," said Mann.

"Thanks, professor. I'll give it a shot. OK, Zoe, look at our own planet. Almost every species has two eyes and has a symmetrical form—right side, left side—one side, a mirror image of the other. Species with wildly separate evolutionary histories have developed two eyes—one on each side. Look at all the species on Earth that move about on land. Almost all have four limbs—humans, kangaroos, giraffes, and even birds. Nature must see the advantage of having two eyes, a symmetrical form, and four limbs."

"Well, hell, that's because they all evolved from a common ancestor," said Martin. "They evolved from common DNA."

"Are we going to play or are we going to talk?" interjected Mills.

"Keep your shorts on, Jon," said Bishop.

"Perhaps," said Girard, "but it's also true that evolution favors efficient designs. For example, why do most animals have two eyes? Because you need two eyes to perceive depth, which gives you an advantage over a predator that doesn't. Having more than two eyes wouldn't give you any more of an advantage, and it would require the brain to dedicate more of its power to visual processing. So, the most efficient number of eyes seems to be two.

"Then there is brain size," continued Girard. "Our brains have evolved to—how to say? *Plus, ou moins*—more or less the optimal size. In fact, our brains have gotten smaller over the last several hundred thousand years."

"Let's keep politics out of this," said Mills.

"That's a good one," said Martin.

"Amusing," said Girard. "As I was saying, larger brains do not result in faster processing, but they require more energy. Our brains require about twenty percent of our total body energy budget. We're not likely to find a successful, intelligent species with brains much larger or smaller than ours."

"If their brains worked like ours, maybe. They could be completely different. They might have multiple brains like octopuses," countered Martin. If you want to look for the most successful critter on planet Earth, it's the damned cockroach, not humans."

"That's not really true, Mike," said Girard. "The most successful creature, if one measures success by longevity and the diversity of environments where they can survive, is the tardigrade. I'll bet five hundred."

"OK, I have to ask. What's a tardigrade? I'm in," said Mills.

"It is another name for water bear," said Girard.

"Not very helpful," laughed Mills. "What the hell is a water bear?"

"It's a microscopic eight-legged animal found just about everywhere, from Mt. Everest to ocean trenches. They're very hardy, and they've been around forever."

"If you don't count algae or viruses or single-celled organisms or…" began Martin.

"I'm speaking about evolved complex organisms," interrupted Girard.

"What about panspermia?" said Bridges as he entered the ship's galley and took a seat next to Girard. His voice immediately got everyone's attention.

"Oh, hey, look, everyone. It's our ship's backup pilot and doctor of anthropology," announced Girard.

"What? Backup? No, I'm…"

Everyone had a good laugh at Bridges' reaction.

"*Il achète ta poire*" said Girard, ginning.

"What?"

"He said he's pulling your leg, Milo," laughed Bishop.

"All right, funny," said Bridges.

"You speak French?" said Girard.

"*Un petit peu*," replied Bishop.

"What's that mean?" asked Mills.

"A small amount," answered Girard, holding up his hand with his thumb and forefinger a half inch apart.

All the scientists welcomed Bridges to their discussion enthusiastically. Dr. Martin fetched Bridges' favorite drink from the CUBE while the others shook Bridges' hand or slapped him on the back.

"Well, looky who's here? Morning buttercup. Feeling groggy, are we?" asked Martin.

"Yep, still sleepy and sore, but other than that, I feel good. Did I miss anything?" he replied.

"Nothing but a lot of grumpy people complaining about the food," answered Dr. Graham. "I would kill to have a nice steak or even a pork chop now and then, but it seems ISA wants us all to become vegetarians," Graham continued, oblivious to the irony of his statement. "And I don't mean that simulated 3D printer crap," he continued.

"Really," said Girard. "What grumpy people are you referring to? Personally, I think it's rather good, and I can hardly tell the difference."

"Well, you being from France, I'm not surprised," said Graham. "We Iowans know our steak."

"Just where do you suggest we keep the livestock, Dr. Graham?" asked Cat Cortez as she walked into the galley, taking a seat next to Bridges. "Maybe next to your stateroom. I'm sure the smell would remind you of home." Everyone laughed except Graham.

"That will—how you say—teach him a lesson," laughed Girard.

"What's panspermia?" asked Bishop, who was recording the lively conversation.

"If I may," Dr. Mann said, effortlessly slipping into his old professor persona. "Panspermia is the hypothesis that life—or at least DNA—exists throughout the Universe, carried by meteoroids, asteroids, comets, and the like. What Mr. Bridges is suggesting is that the DNA from which we evolved may have arrived on Earth via such a vehicle. If that's the case, then the same genetic material could have seeded life elsewhere, making any extraterrestrial organisms distant relatives of ours. That is your argument, isn't it, Mr. Bridges?"

"I don't know," said Bridges. "I'm just throwing it out there."

"Well, you could be correct, Bridges. After all, life began on Earth shortly after the late heavy bombardment about 3.9 billion years ago. So perhaps some comet brought both water and DNA to Earth," said Mann.

"Hey Bridges, I've got a joke for you," interrupted Mills.

Bridges rolled his eyes.

"A Higgs boson walks into a church, and the priest says, 'we don't allow Higgs bosons here.' The Higgs boson says, 'Hey, without me, how can you have mass?' Get it? Without me, you can't have mass."

"Hilarious. Yeah, I get it. You should tell that one to the captain," said Bridges.

"I'm sure he's heard it already," said Mann.

Dr. Graham leaned close to Dr. Girard and whispered, "I don't get it."

Everyone laughed at Graham's comment.

"Some elementary particles, such as quarks and electrons, get their mass from Higgs bosons," said Girard.

"OK, how about this one?" said Mills. "A neutrino walks into a bar and asks, 'How much for a Martini?' to which the bartender replies..."

Before Mills could finish his sentence, everyone in the galley shouted in unison,

"NO CHARGE," followed by much laughter.

Dr. Girard turned to Dr. Graham to explain the joke. "Because neutrinos are chargeless particles, Forest."

"I knew that," said Dr. Graham indignantly.

More laughter filled the galley.

As the conversation continued, sometimes light-heartedly and sometimes heatedly, Cortez turned to Bridges, "Milo, I might need your help."

"Anything I can do," said Bridges.

"I've been running diagnostics on Aries Two and getting some discrepancies," she said. "Care to take a second look?"

"Sure," he responded.

Taking their leave, Bridges and Cortez made their way to the access hatch connecting Endeavor and Aries Two.

Attached to Endeavor were two smaller spacecraft used for transporting crew and equipment to the surface of whatever planet, moon, or asteroid the situation needed. These landing/ascent vehicles, or LAVs, were marvels of technology. Endeavor's LAVs were the latest design using technology not invented during Endeavor's last commission. LAVs needed to land and take off from planets half again larger than Earth, penetrate dense atmospheres without burning up, and do it repeatedly and reliably.

Approximately twenty meters long, these marvels of technology were extremely light, given the extensive use of ceramic and beryllium nanolattice materials in their construction. LAVs, by necessity, were configurable to support the diverse nature of the missions they might be called upon to perform. One LAV could carry up to a dozen people or twenty metric tonnes of cargo, depending upon the gravity well it was flying into or out of. An LAV could land vertically using four liquid methane-fueled engines in landing nacelles on the four corners of the craft that could swivel a hundred and eighty degrees from front to back. LAVs could also glide horizontally on deployable wings and land on a runway if one existed.

An LAV's two main engines were engineering marvels. Called Atmosphere-Augmented Rocket Engines (AARE), they could augment the onboard liquid oxygen (LOX) oxidizer with oxygen scooped from the atmosphere. This reduced by half the LOX the craft needed to carry and thus its overall weight. The two engines could generate over one hundred thousand foot-pounds (135K newtons) of thrust and burn through fifteen tonnes of propellant in five minutes.

But what made the LAVs particularly well suited for their mission was how configurable they were. If the mission called for a landing on a planet with stronger gravity or on planets with no available O2 in the atmosphere, an auxiliary fuel tank was available. A crew could attach up to four solid rocket motors if more thrust was required.

If a planet's atmosphere was less dense than Earth's, they could swap out an LAV's wings for a longer pair to give it greater lift. If a mission called for longer sustained horizontal flight and a planet's atmosphere contained sufficient oxygen, the crew could attach a pair of small air-breathing jet engines with their own thirty-five-hundred-liter fuel tank.

"RHODA, please pressurize Aries Two and open the access hatch," ordered Cortez.

Cortez and Bridges watched the pressure gauge as they waited.

As the hatch to Aries Two slid open, Cortez grasped the two handholds above and to the sides of the hatch, lifted her feet, and gracefully slid into the opening. That was just one of the many things Bridges admired about Cortez. She moved like a cat—fluid, graceful—but with confidence. Bridges followed but with far less grace, hitting his head on the top of the hatch.

Cortez powered up the spacecraft after Bridges joined her in the cramped cockpit, rubbing the top of his head.

"RHODA, run simulation 'ascent two,'" ordered Cortez.

"Milo, this is a computer simulation of an ascent from the surface under emergency conditions," she said, referring to a cold engine start.

After a few seconds, an emergency tone sounded in the cockpit, and the lighting shifted to red.

"Lieutenant Cortez, I am detecting an anomaly in the flight control computer," RHODA announced.

"RHODA, describe the anomaly," said Cortez.

"Lieutenant Cortez, the flight computer's calculations have produced a thrust vector that is not within acceptable parameters."

"Milo, I ran the numbers on Endeavor's flight control computer and Aries One's computer, and their numbers concur. Then, I had RHODA compare those results with the simulation outcome on Aries Two, and the results are different," said Cortez.

"Wow. That is strange," said Bridges. "I'd suggest purging Aries' flight computer software and reloading it from backup," said Bridges.

"Did that already—no change," said Cortez.

"OK, maybe we could swap out the CPU module," he suggested.

"Did that too," she said.

"OK, then we swap flight computers with Aries One," said Bridges.

"I'll have to get Merriweather's permission, but that sounds like a plan," she agreed.

"Until then, RHODA, run complete hardware and software diagnostics on both Aries One and Aries Two flight computers. Report any discrepancies and or differences between both LAVs," commanded Cortez. "That should take several hours. I'll also get Mills involved; maybe he'll have some ideas."

"That sounds like a plan. Until we've figured this out, I suggest we use Aries One where possible," said Bridges.

"I concur. Thanks for your help, Milo. I'll talk to the captain and let you know what he says."

Milo fumbled for a clever remark, but nothing came. The two sat in a quiet, slightly awkward silence, the air charged with something unspoken.

"Well, I should check in with the captain," he said at last.

"Okay, Milo. If you think of anything else, you know where to find me," she replied with a smile.

Milo climbed out of the pilot's seat and stepped down from the LAV. Cortez watched him go, a bemused expression on her face.

"He'll be back," she murmured.

# CHAPTER 16

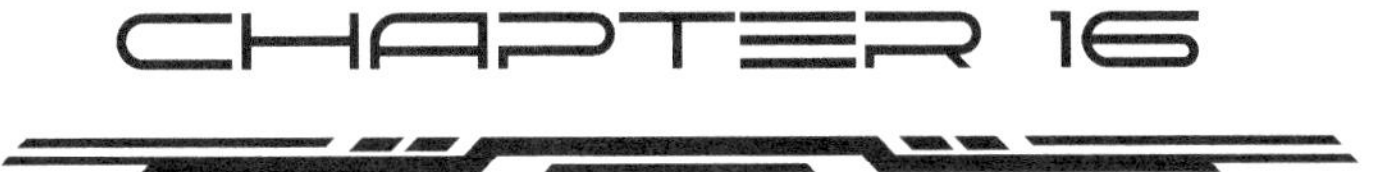

*Spirulina platensis — a few days later*

"Hi, Cat. So, this is where you've been hanging out," announced Bridges as he floated into the minimal gravity environment of the hydroponics bay. Bridges did a slow 360 roll as he examined the jungle of plants lining the walls of the space from floor to ceiling. "I like what you've done with the place."

"I'm usually here this time of day," answered Cortez, without looking up from her close examination of a tank of spirulina platensis.

"I'm glad I found you. I just spoke with the captain, and he declined our request to swap flight computers."

"I expected that," she said. "Did he give a reason?"

"He said he didn't want both LAVs inoperable at the same time—and he didn't want to infect Aries One with whatever Aries Two has."

"Not a problem," replied Cortez. "I got the results of RHODA's diagnostics."

"You did? When?"

"Just before my shift change. I was going to fill you in when I finished here."

"OK, no problem—what did she find?"

"She said there was a thirteen percent probability the error is in the predictive scoring module."

"Not very confident, is she?" said Bridges. "So, what's our next step?"

"I suggest we swap out the module and do some flight testing," she replied.

"Sounds like a plan," said Bridges. "So, what's this?"

"Spirulina platensis," she answered. "It's a type of algae, and did you know algae contains a much higher percentage of nutrients than ordinary vegetables? So, I grow it, and it finds its way into quite a few of our recipes—especially baked goods. We wouldn't want Endeavor to be the first starship with an outbreak of scurvy."

"That explains a lot," said Bridges.

Cortez cast a disapproving look in Bridges' direction before propelling herself to another area of the hydroponics bay.

Bridges and Cortez floated there in awkward silence, each looking for something more to say. "Yes, that certainly makes sense," repeated Bridges.

"Well, I'd better be going," he said. "I gotta get to the bridge. I have the next watch."

"You don't want to see my cricket farm? I can give you a snack to go," Cortez said, smiling impishly.

"Uh, thanks, but no thanks. I enjoyed the tour, though."

"My pleasure," said Cortez.

Cortez watched as Bridges left, wondering if his interest was in hydroponics or her. She was pretty sure it wasn't the algae.

# CHAPTER 17

*Emergency—Eight months after embarkation; twenty-five light years from Earth*

"RHODA, status?" inquired Lieutenant Bridges.

"All systems are operating within normal parameters, Lieutenant Bridges," responded the disembodied voice of the ship's AI.

"Thank you, RHODA," said Bridges reflexively. Although RHODA neither required nor expected a "thank you", it made communications with the ship's AI more natural.

Bridges always felt ill at ease sitting in the captain's seat on the bridge, so instead, he floated in the bridge's microgravity environment.

"Visual mode, RHODA," ordered Bridges.

"Enabling hologram," RHODA replied. A life-size hologram of a young woman appeared near the center of the bridge.

Bridges turned to study the hologram. He wondered who the model for RHODA's avatar had been. Most likely a girlfriend of one of the software programmers or perhaps a programmer herself. She was about five-seven, give or take an inch. She appeared to be in her late twenties, thirty, maybe, with red hair that hung to her shoulders. He wondered if the developers had made her likeness user programmable.

"RHODA, can I adjust the appearance of your hologram?"

"I'm sorry, Lt. Bridges, my appearance cannot be altered."

"Why not?" Bridges asked.

"I do not know," RHODA replied.

Bridges suspected he knew the reason. The programmer hard-coded the image of an old flame and didn't want it messed with.

Milo loved his time on the bridge, especially standing watch. The function of a bridge officer was to monitor the ship's health and to take action in case of an emergency. That usually meant calling the captain, who would then take the action. On a starship like Endeavor, having someone stand a bridge watch was more tradition than a necessity. Milo could control Endeavor from anywhere on the ship, and the ship's AI was monitoring the ship's health twenty-four hours a day. Still, most ships in the fleet held to the tradition that called for a human, usually an officer, standing watch on the bridge.

The bridge watch was a solitary duty station. Others might object to that aspect of standing watch on the bridge, but it appealed to Bridges. He enjoyed being alone with his thoughts. Endeavor might be relatively large as spacecraft go, but it was still just a tiny tin can, sealed off from the vast emptiness surrounding it. Sometimes you couldn't help rubbing shoulders with a fellow crewmember. Bridge-watch time was Milo's escape—his moment of solitude. He loved its history and tradition. It was his place to think.

There was also the sweeping view from the bridge's panoramic holographic display—or as the crew referred to it—the view.

Milo loved the *view*. Looking at the panoply of stars and galaxies was to Milo akin to meditation, and he found it both exhilarating and comforting. Endeavor's bridge stretched the entire width of the starship and measured five meters high from deck to overhead. Embedded in the forward-facing bulkhead was a curved video display spanning its full width and height.

Bridges and other visitors to the bridge saw not a video screen but a giant window to the cosmos that enveloped their starship. There was no discernible barrier between Bridges and the vastness of space and the billions of stars and galaxies before him. He felt he could simply leap through this giant opening and float away into space.

"RHODA, what do you think of the view?" Bridges asked.

Bridges often had one-sided philosophical discussions with the ship's AI.

"Restate the question, Lieutenant Bridges," RHODA replied.

"The view out of the forward holoview, what do you think of it?" repeated Bridges.

"The forward holoview is operating within normal parameters, Lieutenant Bridges," responded RHODA. "Do you wish to make adjustments?"

"No adjustments, thank you. I know the equipment is working, RHODA. I want to know your thoughts or feelings about the view. And call me Milo."

"I understand, Lieutenant Bridges. I will change my standard response. I don't have opinions or feelings, Milo. Restate the question," said RHODA.

"RHODA, when you don't know the answer to a question, respond by saying 'How the hell should I know,'" said Bridges.

"I understand, Milo. I will change my standard response."

Bridges smiled to himself. He had some experience with artificial intelligence software, and this one was the best by far. Mills and his team had really done an excellent job. But Milo aimed to make her more human.

"RHODA, exactly how many habitable planets are there in the universe?" asked Bridges.

"How the hell should I know, Milo?"

*Now we're getting somewhere*, thought Bridges with a smile. With a little more work and she'll have an actual personality.

"Somewhere out there, RHODA is a planet with intelligent life just waiting for a visit from us, and I'm going to be the one who makes first contact. Maybe you'll be the first human AI to contact an alien AI. Would you like that?" asked Bridges.

"How the hell should I know, Milo?"

"RHODA, please deactivate the star field simulation," asked Bridges.

A second later, the view of the cosmos on the forward video screens changed to a soft, bluish glow. Bridges knew that ships at light speed, phasing in and out of hyperspace as Endeavor was now doing, could not see the stars, only the glow from the blue-shifted CMB (Cosmic Microwave Background) radiation as he was now seeing.

"Not much to see, RHODA," said Bridges. "Please activate the star field simulation."

"Much better," he said as a blanket of stars once again painted the forward holoview.

"RHODA, what's the name of that star approaching us on the starboard side?" asked Bridges.

"That star has no official designation," said RHODA.

"How can that be?" said Bridges. "Isn't the star field on the holoview generated from the current star database?"

"That is correct, Milo. Long-range sensors detected the star the last time Endeavor dropped out of FTL, and added it to the ship's copy of the official database. The star does not match any previously known star," answered RHODA.

"Why was it not detected before?" asked Bridges.

"How the hell should I know, Milo?"

"What do you estimate its closest point of approach?" asked Bridges.

"Approximately thirty-two million kilometers," RHODA replied.

*That's pretty damn close*, thought Bridges.

Bridges knew that while Endeavor was phasing between real space and hyperspace, she was in no real danger from the star or any other object in its path. But it would be interesting to catalog the star and get as much information as possible about its planetary system.

"Does that star have a planetary system?" asked Bridges.

"How should I know, Milo."

Bridges considered RHODA's response. This may be a good time to drop out of FTL. But that would not be his call. *Should I wake the captain and ask?* He smiled to himself. Only if he would prefer to be demoted.

"RHODA, if we drop out of FTL and we're still within sensor range of the star, would you collect as much information about its system as possible?" Bridges said.

"I've added your request to my task list, Milo," said RHODA.
A few seconds later, "Milo, I am detecting a problem in the antimatter containment vessel."

That got Bridges' attention.

"What kind of problem, RHODA?"

"The magnetic containment field strength is down 1.943 percent, Milo."

"Is that within safe operating range?"

"Yes, it is, Milo."

"OK, RHODA, can you run a diagnostic?"

"Yes, I can, Milo, but it will require re-entering normal space-time. Do you want me to disengage the FTL drives?"

Bridges thought for a moment. The star was quickly approaching. If he was going to drop out of FTL, he should do it either right now, before the star became too close, or after Endeavor had safely passed. *What would the captain do?* He thought. The decrease in the containment vessel's magnetic field strength could be just a transitory glitch. He needed more data.

"Hold off on that, RHODA."

Bridges removed his holo from his utility belt. "Dutch, are you available?" A few seconds later, Dutch Swenson's gravelly voice sounded over the holo's speakers. "What's up, young Milo?"

"Say, Dutch, RHODA has detected a problem in the antimatter containment vessel. She says the field strength is down a little. Can you go check it out?"

"Down how much?" Dutch Swenson replied in a decidedly more serious tone.

"Almost two percent," said Bridges. "But she says it's still within safe operating parameters."

"Aye, two percent is OK, but I should go have a look. I'm in the wheel right now, so it will take me a few minutes to get back there. I'll call you back." The wheel was a reference to Endeavor's habitat ring.

"Thanks, Dutch, let me know."

"Will do," said Swenson.

*I'm sure it's just a sensor glitch*, thought Bridges, *nothing to worry about*.

A few seconds later, RHODA's voice sounded again in the bridge speakers. "Milo, I am detecting a problem in the antimatter containment vessel."

"I know that RHODA. OK, how bad is it now?" he added.

"The magnetic containment field strength is down 2.611 percent, Milo."

"RHODA, how much more of a safety margin do we have?"

"The safety margin is five percent below optimum field strength."

"OK, RHODA, give me field strength readouts every thirty seconds."

"I will add your request to my task list, Milo," replied RHODA.

Bridges holo'd Swenson again.

"Dutch, RHODA says we're down 2.6 percent."

"Damn. I'm doing what I can, but I can't run a full diagnostic unless we break out of FTL."

"OK, I'm going to wake the captain," said Bridges.

Bridges paused for a moment to organize his thoughts and to plan what he would say to the captain. Waking Merriweather was not something to take lightly.

"Bridge to Captain Merriweather," said Bridges, speaking into his holo.

A few seconds later, a clearly groggy Jake Merriweather answered.

"This better be important," said Merriweather.

"Captain, this is Lieutenant Bridges on the bridge. We have a situation."

"What is it?" asked Merriweather, sensing the urgency in Bridges' voice.

"We're currently tracking a decrease in the magnetic field strength in the antimatter containment vessel," explained Bridges.

"What does Dutch say?" asked Merriweather.

"He's looking into it."

"All right, I'll be there shortly," said Merriweather.

A few seconds later: "Milo, the antimatter containment field strength is down 3.5 percent from optimum," said the ship's artificial intelligence.

The light from the unnamed star was now blindingly bright, casting knife-edged shadows on the bridge. It was now too late to drop out of FTL safely. *We just need a few more minutes*, thought Bridges, *just a few more minutes*. "RHODA, pipe thirty-second readouts into engineering and the bridge, and reduce the brightness level on the forward holoview by twenty percent," commanded Bridges. "I can't see a damned thing."

"Milo, the antimatter containment field strength is down 4.1 percent. Bridge holoview brightness decreased by twenty percent," said RHODA.

It was now clear to Bridges that he could no longer delay the inevitable. He had to deal with the containment issue immediately. He would worry about the star later.

"I'm making the call," Bridges said to himself. "RHODA, disengage the FTL drives. Cease ship's rotation."

A second later, the emergency claxon sounded throughout the ship as Endeavor dropped to sub-light. Bridges noticed a slight flicker on the forward holoview as it switched from a computer-generated depiction of the universe outside to a feed from the forward video camera.

"RHODA, distance to that star?" barked Bridges. Even after adjustments to the bridge display's brightness, Milo still had to hold his hand above his eyes to shield them from the intense glare.

"Approximately thirty-three million kilometers, Milo," RHODA replied. RHODA's designers had smartly given her the ability to provide rounded numbers to her human interrogators in situations she deemed critical. Human beings, it was determined, could comprehend round numbers faster.

"Dutch, tell me something, anything, please," barked Bridges. "We're running out of time."

"I'm not seeing anything, Milo," said a harried Dutch Swenson.

"Milo, I am detecting an increase in hull temperatures," interrupted RHODA.

"No shit," barked Bridges.

"Milo, the antimatter containment field strength is down 5.2 percent. This is below safe limits," said RHODA.

"RHODA, can you put the containment vessel in safe mode?"

"I cannot," RHODA replied.

"Why the hell not?" shouted Bridges.

"The electronics needed to secure the containment vessel are automatically shut down when magnetic containment falls below the minimum threshold," the AI replied.

"Well, that's just fucking great," barked Bridges. "RHODA, what will happen if the antimatter vessel loses containment?" Bridges asked, already knowing the answer.

"The antiprotons will come into contact with the containment vessel walls producing a one point two megaton annihilation event."

"RHODA, what is the probability Endeavor will survive the event?"

"Zero percent probability."

Bridges had expected RHODA's answer. "Damn," he said aloud. A thousand thoughts raced through his head. Everyone on this ship was about to die, and he could do nothing about it. In fact, it was probably his fault. He should have taken the ship out of FTL sooner, giving Dutch more time to diagnose the problem.

*Only one thing to do*, he thought.

"RHODA, what's our velocity relative to the star?"

"Endeavor's relative velocity is forty-four thousand kilometers per hour," she replied.

"Is that enough velocity to escape the star's gravity?"

"Negative," RHODA replied.

"Damn!" Milo shouted. "Is it enough to sustain orbit?"

"Endeavor can sustain three orbits around the star."

"Hallelujah," said Bridges. "At least something hasn't turned to crap."

"RHODA, on my command, I want you to eject the antimatter containment vessel," said Bridges.

"I have added your command to my task list, Milo," said RHODA.

Bridges stared at the holoview on the port side of the bridge and waited. After what seemed an eternity but was only ten seconds, Bridges gave the two-word command. "RHODA, execute."

Just as Captain Merriweather walked onto the bridge, RHODA responded. "Antimatter containment vessel ejected, Milo."

# CHAPTER 18

*Aftermath*

Beneath Endeavor, a series of explosive bolts surrounding a circular hatch detonated silently. The force of the blast caused the hatch to detach from the starship and hurtle off into space, exposing a two-meter diameter opening in the hull. Almost simultaneously, a five-meter-long cylinder launched from the opening, propelled by compressed gases. At a safe distance from the ship, a hypergolic fuel rocket motor ignited, launching the antimatter containment vessel away from Endeavor at a high rate of speed. Fifteen seconds later, the containment vessel was over five kilometers from the ship.

Inside the ship, Lieutenant Bridges was frantic. He racked his brain, trying to remember everything he had learned at the Academy about antimatter and what to do in a situation like this. He knew he was running out of time and had to do something quickly.

"RHODA, fire forward navigation thrusters port side. Fire aft navigation thrusters, starboard side, maximum power," he commanded, almost shouting the order.

All too slowly, the eighteen-hundred-tonne starship began turning while Bridges anxiously watched the star field pan across the forward holoview. "Come on, come on," he shouted. "Move this thing, dammit!"

"Lieutenant, report," said Captain Merriweather as he quickly propelled himself onto the bridge.

"In a moment, Captain. RHODA, can't you turn the ship any faster?"

"Bridges, what's going on?" said Merriweather with a bit more urgency in his voice.

Before Bridges could reply, a blinding white light filled Endeavor's bridge, causing Bridges and Merriweather to shield their eyes.

"Is that the…?" said Merriweather.

"Sorry, captain. The antimatter containment vessel was failing. We couldn't *safe* the reactor, so my only option was to eject the vessel—sir." The words rushed from Bridges' lips at an incredible speed.

"RHODA, status," ordered Merriweather.

"Sensors are recording elevated levels of gamma and beta radiation," replied RHODA.

"RHODA, are we seeing levels consistent with an antimatter explosion?"

"Radiation levels are consistent with a one-megaton antimatter annihilation event," said the AI.

"RHODA, cease thrusters—stabilize ship orientation—report status of life support systems," ordered Merriweather.

"All life support systems are operating within normal parameters," said RHODA.

"You turned the ship—why?" Merriweather asked.

"I had to put the Frisbee between us and the explosion. The gamma rays…" said Bridges, referring to the large radiation shield that bisected the ship's hull.

Merriweather paused for a second, then nodded in acknowledgment.

"Sensors are recording higher than normal temperatures in the hydrogen and oxygen fuel tanks," RHODA announced.

"Fuck," said Merriweather uncharacteristically. "You jettisoned our antimatter?"

"I had to…containment…it was down…it was about to fail," stammered Bridges.

After staring out the forward holoview and remaining silent for what to Bridges seemed like an eternity, Merriweather finally spoke in a voice calmer than expected. "OK, Lieutenant. That was probably the right call. But you know where that leaves us, right?"

"Up shit's creek—sir."

"Exactly, but right now, we have a more pressing problem. That star is heating our ship and the fuel tanks. Any ideas?" said Merriweather.

Bridges thought for a moment. "Dutch!"

"Dutch? What about Dutch?" said Merriweather.

"He was aft of the Frisbee."

"Oh, God," said Merriweather. "Are you sure?"

"I don't think he would have had time to make it through the hatch."

"Damn."

RHODA's voice snapped both Merriweather and Bridges back to the current emergency.

"Sensors are recording higher than normal temperatures in the hydrogen and oxygen fuel tanks," RHODA announced.

"RHODA, have you analyzed the planetary system for that star?" Bridges asked, remembering his earlier order.

"Yes, I have, Milo."

"Have you detected any nearby planets?"

"Sensors have detected five planets. The closest planet is orbiting the star at thirty-six million kilometers," RHODA replied.

Merriweather immediately grasped Bridges' intentions.

"RHODA, project a holo image of the system," he ordered.

A split second later, floating in the center of Endeavor's bridge, a bright yellow sphere appeared approximately ten centimeters in diameter and orbited by several satellites of varied sizes.

"Now show only the innermost planet and add our position."

"OK, good," he added once RHODA had updated the image.

Both Merriweather and Bridges moved inside the image to get a closer look. They could now see a bright blue spot labeled 'Endeavor' hovering inside and slightly above the orbital plane of the nearby planet.

"RHODA, advance the projection forward by four days."

Merriweather watched as the planet moved slowly along its trajectory.

"Finally, some decent news, Bridges," said Merriweather. "It's moving toward us."

"RHODA, display the planet's velocity."

"Forty-four thousand clicks," said Merriweather, reading the annotation below the nearest planet. "That's slower than I expected. RHODA, compute a rendezvous trajectory using a full burn from the TAMARAKS."

"There is no solution using these parameters, Captain Merriweather."

"No solution? We can't rendezvous with the planet using the TAMARAK engines?"

"Affirmative," RHODA replied.

"Maybe we could use Bertha," said Bridges, referring to the ship's older rocket propulsion engines.

"I don't think so," replied Merriweather. "It takes a lot of prep to fire off Bertha."

"But it would relieve pressure in the tanks," said Bridges.

Merriweather fell silent as he thought through the problem. Merriweather glanced at Bridges as if seeing his young lieutenant for the first time. "Use Bertha?" he repeated. "It's crazy, but...," he said, leaving the sentence unfinished.

"RHODA, compute a rendezvous trajectory using a full burn from the TAMARAKS with auxiliary power from the main engines. Update the projection."

A second later, the holo image reflected the results.

"OK, that's better," said Merriweather with relief. "It looks possible—as long as the damn rocket doesn't blow up. RHODA, how much hydrogen fuel do we have to burn to rendezvous?"

"One hundred percent of our hydrogen fuel would be required," she replied.

"All of it? Jesus!" Merriweather exclaimed. "That's cutting it close."

"RHODA, calculate the delta-v for a full burn of the main engines."

"A one hundred percent burn of the main engines would produce a delta-v of approximately twelve thousand kilometers per hour."

"That would drain the tank, Captain," said Bridges.

"I can't think of an alternative," said Merriweather. "We either burn it ourselves or let it blow up and us with it. We can't stay here. RHODA, estimate how long we have before the propellant tanks fail," ordered Merriweather.

"Propellant tanks will fail in approximately twenty minutes," said RHODA.

Merriweather glanced at Bridges and said, "Any better ideas? Last chance—no—then let's go for it."

Merriweather grabbed his holo from his utility belt. "Dutch, this is the captain."

The silence from the captain's holo lasted longer than he had hoped.

"Dutch, come in," repeated Merriweather.

Finally, Dutch's gravelly voice crackled over the holo's speakers.

"I'm here, Cap'n," Dutch replied.

"Dutch, are you alright? Did you make it through the hatch in time?"

"Sorry, Captain," Dutch replied.

"Damn," whispered Merriweather, a look of deep concern on his face.

"How bad is it, Dutch?"

"I'm OK. Nothing I can't handle, Cap'n," Merriweather heard Dutch coughing violently.

"Dutch, I need you to get yourself to sickbay. Pronto. But first, there's something I need you to do."

Merriweather knew there were anti-radiation drugs in sickbay that could help his old friend if he could get there and take them in time. He also knew that the longer it took to get there, the less effective the drugs would be. Dutch knew it too.

However, if they had any chance to save Endeavor, they would have to fire Bertha, and Dutch was the only one who could set up the firing controls in time.

"Dutch, can you give me a status on Bertha?"

"What do you mean?" replied Dutch Swenson, the exhaustion in his voice painfully clear.

"I mean, is she operable?" said Merriweather.

A few seconds went by before Merriweather's holo crackled.

"You mean…you want to use…her? sir, we haven't…fired Bertha since… the shakedown cruise. I'd need a few days."

"Sorry, Dutch, we don't have a few days. We've only got a few minutes. Can we use her?"

"Cap'n, we're…talking about a liquid-fueled rocket engine. She's in good condition…but there's a process…a checklist…before we can start her. It's…not like I can…just flip a switch."

"Dutch, we don't have a week. Can we light her off or not?" said Merriweather.

"Aye, Cap'n, she's…good to go," said Swenson, obviously struggling.

"OK, do what you gotta do. Then set her up for remote fire control—Got that?"

"Aye, Cap'n."

"Then get up to sickbay as fast as you can. I'll get Lee to meet you half-way," said Merriweather.

Merriweather knew what he was asking of Swenson—something no man had a right to ask. However, he saw no alternative.

"Aye, Cap'n, said Swenson."

"Captain Merriweather, I am detecting an anomaly with the ship's hull temperature. I am also detecting a rise in pressure in the liquid hydrogen and liquid oxygen tanks," announced RHODA.

"RHODA, estimate how long before the propellant tanks fail," ordered Merriweather.

"Propellant tanks will fail in approximately seventeen minutes," said RHODA.

Merriweather spoke calmly into his communicator. "Dutch, I'm having RHODA fire the engines in ten minutes and counting. Set the controls and get out."

"RHODA, recompute delta-v and coordinates to the nearest planet. Compute a trajectory for a rendezvous with the planet and set the launch countdown for ten minutes. Pipe the countdown ship-wide."

"I've relayed firing instructions to the main engine fire control computer," responded RHODA.

"I'm sure Dutch will be OK, Milo. The anti-rad drugs are effective if given in time," said Merriweather.

"Let's hope," said Bridges, clearly worried.

Merriweather fell silent for a few minutes, as if he had made peace with his decision.

"RHODA, did the propellant tanks incur any damage from the antimatter explosion?"

"How the hell should I know, Captain?"

Merriweather slowly turned and glared at his young lieutenant.

"Bridges, what the hell?"

"Sorry, sir," said Bridges. "Permission to go check on Dutch?"

"Permission granted. I'll be there shortly."

Merriweather lifted his holo to his lips.

"All hands, we're firing the main engines in just over nine minutes. Prepare the ship."

# CHAPTER 19

*Dutch Swenson, Rashomon, Ten minutes earlier*

Dutch Swenson loved his job. He loved working on his "rockets," whether replacing a fuel pump on Big Bertha or servicing a helicon antenna in a TAMARAK engine. He had even come to enjoy working on the FTL system, although he didn't profess to understand the physics of it completely. Dutch told anyone who would listen that when he was tinkering with his rockets, he was happier than a tick on a bloodhound.

When the call came down from the bridge, he was using the 3D printer to make parts for a new location buoy Endeavor planned to deploy later in the month.

"What's up young Milo?" Dutch asked as he continued working on the buoy.

As Swenson listened, he slowly turned away from the 3D printer, focusing squarely on what he heard in his earpiece.

"Down how much?" he asked as his eyes narrowed.

"Aye, two percent is OK, but I should go have a look. I'm in the wheel now, so it will take me a few minutes to get back there. I'll call you when I get there."

It's probably just a sensor glitch, thought Swenson, although he figured he'd better check it out just to be safe.

"Will do," said Swenson to Bridges' request for urgency.

The antimatter reactor was in the aft part of the ship, a good fifty meters away. Dutch figured it would take him a good four or five minutes to get there, so he'd better hurry.

Dutch Swenson jogged around the hab ring as quickly as he could until he came to the nearest of the three access tubes connecting the habitat ring to the main body of the Endeavor spacecraft. Climbing the ladder attached to the wall of the tube, he quickly reached the microgravity environment of the central core. Then, using his arms, propelled himself aft toward the antimatter reactor. Two minutes later, Swenson reached the point in the ship where the radiation shield bisected the hull. There, he paused briefly in front of the sole access hatch leading to the rear of the ship. On this side of the hatch were the crew compartments. On the other side were the nuclear reactor and the ship's propulsion systems.

Moving as expeditiously as possible, Dutch grabbed the hatch's access handle, yanked it open, and pulled himself through, closing it behind out of habit. Once inside, Dutch scrambled around the maze of piping, pumps, and electronics, which comprised the recycling system.

Once clear of the plumbing, he turned toward the aft bulkhead and the hatch positioned in the center. Moving as quickly as he dared, he opened the hatch to the access tunnel that led aft toward the reactor and engine compartments. The tunnel was barely 1.5 meters in diameter, and twenty meters long—barely enough room for the pipes and wiring bundles that led back to the aft compartments. Endeavor's fuel and water tanks surrounded the tunnel on the outside, supported by the cage. Dutch made this trip multiple times daily, but always at a somewhat leisurely pace. Now, however, under duress, he found it much more challenging to navigate the cramped and claustrophobic tunnel. This was taking much longer than he feared. *What if he couldn't find a solution? What if?* No, he couldn't think that way. He had to stay calm, remain confident and, above all, hurry. Antimatter was nothing to mess with. *That's serious shit*, he thought to himself.

With that scary thought in mind, Dutch redoubled his pace, frantically pulling himself through the tunnel, hand over hand, using the handholds spaced every half meter.

Emerging from the tunnel thirty seconds later with a few new bruises, Dutch found himself in his favorite space on the ship—the reactor compartment. Here were his children—the antimatter and nuclear reactors and the aft control station from which he could operate the engines. Hell, the entire ship, if needed.

Now inside the reactor compartment, Dutch turned his body, his eyes quickly locating the antimatter reactor controls a good ten meters away. Pushing off from the hatch with his legs, Dutch aimed his body at the instrument panel near the antimatter containment vessel. Three seconds later, Dutch grabbed onto the handholds welded to each side of the instrument cluster. Using his arms, he twisted his body, swinging his legs toward the "floor," then slipped his feet into fabric restraining loops on the deck below the instruments.

The containment vessel rested atop a pedestal approximately a meter in diameter and two meters in height. The pedestal was connected to the main reactor block, with the control panel attached to the reactor block next to the pedestal and at eye level.

Dutch checked the panel. All the lights were green except one, now flashing yellow. A digital readout next to the flashing light displayed the strength of the magnetic field that held the antimatter. The magnetic field prevented the antimatter from contacting the vessel walls. Failure of the magnetic field would be disastrous.

Pushing a few buttons, Dutch checked the various parameters of the plasma-electron saturation current, the ion saturation current, the temperature, and density. Everything looked as it should.

Dutch put his hand to his ear as another message came in from the bridge.

"Damn. I'm doing what I can, but I can't run a full diagnostic unless we break out of FTL," he said, replying to the news from the bridge that the containment vessel's field strength was down 2.9 percent.

Dutch was nearly out of options as he frantically checked off his measurements. He needed to shut down the FTL system to run comprehensive diagnostics, but he needed the captain's say-so to do that.

Suddenly, RHODA's voice sounded in his earpiece.

"The antimatter containment field strength is down 4.1 percent of optimum."

"Shit," said Swenson.

Again, Dutch's earpiece rang with an urgent plea from the bridge.

"I'm not seeing anything, Milo," said a frustrated Dutch Swenson.

Abruptly, the lights on the reactor control panel changed, informing Dutch that Endeavor had dropped out of FTL.

"Finally," he said. "Now maybe I can find out what's going on."

"The antimatter containment field strength is down 5.2 percent of optimum. This is below safe limits," intoned the ship's AI.

Dutch was now sweating like a pig in a sausage factory—one of his favorite expressions. He scanned the compartment looking for his toolbox. "There it is," he said as he pushed off from the instrument panel. Ten seconds later, he had fetched his Longmeyer plasma probe and was flying back to the containment vessel. Suddenly, without warning, the containment vessel slid down into the containment housing and disappeared.

"Oh, my God, he's ejected our antimatter," said a stunned Dutch Swenson.

As Dutch floated in the reactor module, he sensed the ship beginning to turn about him. For a moment, he felt disoriented. *What was the boy doing now?* He thought to himself. Dutch had faced emergencies before, but for the first time, he felt totally helpless.

He was about to contact the bridge to get an update when the realization of his situation suddenly dawned on him. He turned his head and looked over his shoulder, a sickening feeling in the pit of his stomach. The access tunnel hatch was only ten meters away—just a few seconds. He knew his only chance was to get through that hatch before...

Dutch twisted his body, raised his legs, and pushed violently against the reactor block, aiming his body toward the hatch. Flying headlong across the ten meters separating the reactor block and the hatch, he quickly realized he would miss his target. Frantically, he stretched out his arm in a desperate attempt to grab onto the hatch, slamming instead into the bulkhead, his flailing body ricocheting back into the compartment. He had missed the hatch and now found himself floating in the middle of the reactor module, unable to grasp onto anything. *What a freaking rookie-move*, he thought. Dutch twisted his body in violent jerks, trying to propel himself to something, anything, he could grab onto. Finally, he hooked his left foot around a cooling pipe. Bending at the waist, Dutch grabbed the pipe, swung his body around, and re-launched himself toward the hatch. This time, his aim was perfect.

As Dutch slammed into the hatch, he grabbed onto the locking lever. If he could just make it inside the access tunnel, the thousands of liters of liquid hydrogen, oxygen, and water surrounding it might protect him. He was almost there. But as he jerked the hatch open, a high-pitched alarm screeched loudly. Dutch recognized the alarm immediately, and it wasn't what he wanted to hear.

"RHODA, locate Lieutenant Swenson," said Bridges.

"Lieutenant Swenson is in the engine compartment," said RHODA.

Bridges quickly propelled himself through Endeavor's core toward the aft end of the ship as fast as he could. He had one goal—to reach his friend Dutch Swenson as quickly as possible.

"Bridges to Lee. Jennifer, meet me just forward of the Frisbee hatch. Bring anti-rad drugs—as fast as you can," said Bridges.

Lee answered within seconds. "I'm on my way, Milo. Who's it for?"

"Dutch," he responded. "Hurry."

Milo knew he had to reach Dutch before the engines fired. The massive G forces would slam anyone floating around Endeavor unsecured into the nearest bulkhead with devastating consequences. Milo wasn't sure what condition his friend was in, but he feared the worst.

"Main engine ignition in nine minutes," announced RHODA.

If Dutch were in the engine compartment, it would take about three minutes to get to him, thought Bridges. If Lee made it down there in time, Milo could take the anti-rad drugs with him through the tunnel and have enough time to administer them before the engines fired. Being in the engine compartment wasn't the ideal place to be when Bertha fired, but it was survivable. Plus, there were bulkhead restraints there.

"Main engine ignition in eight minutes," announced RHODA.

The only thing slowing Milo's progress was the hatches. RHODA had closed all access hatches as a safety measure during engine firing, forcing Milo to stop at each hatch and open it manually.

"Main engine ignition in seven minutes," announced RHODA.

Doc Lee had yet to arrive when Milo finally arrived at the Frisbee and the access hatch to the tunnel leading to the engine compartment.

"Bridges to Lee, what's your ETA, Jennifer?"

"I'm on my way, Milo—I had to find the meds. Stored the damn things in the wrong place. I'm a minute away—maybe a minute and a half."

"Hurry as fast as you can, Jen," said Bridges.

There was nothing Milo could do now but wait.

"Main engine ignition in six minutes," announced RHODA.

Meanwhile, in the galley, Merriweather had arrived to check on his crew. Everyone, except for Bridges, Lee, and Swenson, had already arrived and had strapped themselves into the bulkhead restraint harnesses. Cortez meticulously checked the radiation badges on each crew member's uniform. While Endeavor's officers maintained military discipline and waited for their captain to speak, the civilian scientist did not, erupting in a volley of questions.

Merriweather raised his hand to quiet his crew. "Let's get through the engine firing. I'll explain everything on the other side."

"How's it looking?" said Merriweather as Cortez checked his dosimeter.

"Fine, it looks like the Frisbee did its job. What's going on?" she replied.

"Main engine ignition in five minutes," announced RHODA.

Meanwhile, at the Frisbee hatch, Dr. Lee arrived with the anti-radiation drugs.

"Milo, I got here as fast as I could," said Lee.

"You brought the meds?" asked Bridges.

"Yes. Of course. How was he exposed?"

"He was in the engine compartment. We had to eject our antimatter."

"Thought so. We could all see the flash from the galley holoviews. Poor Dutch."

"There's only room for one in the tunnel, Jen. Give me the meds, and you strap yourself in."

"I should do it," she said.

"No. I can get through the hatch faster," replied Bridges.

"All right. But I'm right behind you."

"Fine." said Bridges as she handed him a small plastic container.

Milo reached through the opened hatch, grabbed a handle inside the access tunnel, and pulled himself in.

"Ceasing ship rotation. Main engine ignition in four minutes," announced RHODA.

While Milo had been through the tunnel frequently, he had always taken his time navigating the narrow confines. Now, however, he was finding it much more difficult. Lee had far less trouble, given her smaller frame.

As they neared the aft end of the tunnel, Lee heard a strange sound emanating from up ahead.

Thump.

"Argh."

"Are you OK?" asked Lee, who was less than a meter behind. "I should have done this myself. You're going too slow. Milo?"

Something was wrong. Bridges had suddenly stopped moving.

"Milo, what's wrong? Milo?"

Lee grabbed Milo's foot and shook it. When he didn't respond, she knew he was unconscious—or dead. Unfortunately, there wasn't enough room in the tunnel to get around him or to reach his head. She searched for a pulse in his posterior tibial (ankle) and dorsalis pedis (foot) areas.

*Pulse is strong*, thought Lee. *He's not dead*. She concluded he had probably bumped his head and knocked himself unconscious.

Indeed, Bridges was unconscious, knocked cold by a protruding metal bracket.

"Main engine ignition in three minutes," announced RHODA.
RHODA's announcement alarmed Lee. She shook Bridges' leg with all her strength while shouting his name.

"Milo, dammit. Wake up. Milo."

"Main engine ignition in two minutes," announced RHODA.

Time's running out, thought Lee. She briefly thought about backing out of the tunnel for the safety of a bulkhead harness, but she knew she'd never make it in time—she couldn't leave Milo and Dutch. She and Bridges were much closer to the aft end of the tunnel, and their only hope was to get through the tunnel with the meds in the next two minutes.

"Milo, wake up, dammit!" she shouted.

"Stop shouting. I can hear you," said Bridges as he slowly regained consciousness. "My head hurts."

"What happened?"

"I hit my head on a cable retainer. I think I lost consciousness for a second."

"Are you OK?"

"I think so—just a bit dazed."

"All right, then get going."

"OK, I'm going," said Bridges.

A minute later, as Bridges and Lee passed through the tunnel's aft hatch, RHODA's voice rang out.

"Main engine ignition in one minute."

They found Dutch unconscious, floating in the engine compartment. Lee checked his pulse.

"Is he alive?"

"Yes. He's got a pulse," replied Lee.

"We don't have much time," shouted Bridges.

"Tell me something I don't know," said Lee. "You get him in his harness, and I'll administer the meds."

Bridges handed Lee the anti-rad meds and then wrangled Dutch's body into a bulkhead restraint, pulling the straps as tight as he could. Lee extracted the injector from the plastic container and jabbed the needle into Dutch's thigh.

RHODA started counting down the last ten seconds.

"Ten -nine -eight..."

Lee and Bridges scrambled to secure themselves in the remaining bulkhead harnesses, tightening the straps two seconds before Endeavor's powerful main engines erupted.

"Hold on. It's going to be bumpy," shouted Bridges.

"Not my first rodeo," shouted Lee in return.

Endeavor last fired her rocket engines during her shakedown cruise and then for only a few seconds. Endeavor was supposed to rely primarily on her hyperdrives and TAMARAKS. Faced with the real danger of injury to her crew, Endeavor now had to resort to her original propulsion system. This meant Bertha—liquid-fuel rocket engines capable of generating over one million Newtons, or three hundred seventy-five thousand foot-pounds of thrust each.

Once again, the crew experienced the sensation of rapid acceleration. The crew heard and felt the rumbling of the engines—the unseen force that required them to brace themselves against a bulkhead or hang on to a support pillar. But unlike the shakedown cruise, this time was different. This time there seemed to be a sense of urgency to that force—a purposefulness not felt during the engine tests months ago. The crew realized this was not a test, but a real and possibly fatal situation.

Endeavor quickly gained speed, running like the racehorse she used to be before the installation of her hyperdrives. The crew felt the power of Bertha's twin liquid-fuel rocket engines as their massive thrust pushed them back into their seats. This was a far cry from the eerie, motionless, noiseless experience of faster-than-light space flight.

Merriweather couldn't wait for the engines to shut down. He needed to know the status of his friend, Dutch Swenson. So, with the crew still waiting for an explanation, Merriweather instead called Bridges.

"Bridges, this is the captain—report."

"We're fine, Captain," said Bridges, shouting over the noise of the rockets. "Lee and I made it back to Engineering just in time, and Jennifer administered the meds."

"How is he?"

"Still unconscious."

"OK. As soon as the engines shut down, get him to sickbay."

Seventeen minutes later, having exhausted nearly ninety-nine percent of her liquid propellant, Endeavor's main rockets went silent, followed a second later by the push of her eight magnetoplasma TAMARAK engines. There was a collective sigh from Endeavor's officers and civilian scientists, who now looked to Merriweather for answers.

Merriweather recognized the concerned look on their faces.

"I owe all of you an explanation," he said, glancing at each crew member. "First, let me assure you that the ship is in no imminent danger. Twenty minutes ago, we experienced a problem with antimatter containment and forced to drop out of FTL. We had to eject the containment vessel. For those of you who have been curious what antimatter annihilation is like, well, now you know. It's a bit anticlimactic—a lot of light but surprisingly little sound and fury. We got a rather large dose of gamma rays, but the Frisbee protected us. Cortez checked your dosimeters, and none of you received significant exposure.

"We also had another problem. When we dropped out of FTL, we found ourselves extremely close to a large and extremely hot star. The heat from the star was raising the pressure in our liquid propellant tanks. So, we had to make a quick decision. Firing our main engines allowed us to reduce the pressure building up in the tanks and launch us toward a planet we dis-covered nearby. Our plasma engines continue to move us toward this new planet. Our ETA is approximately ninety-six hours."

"We heard you mention Dutch," said Mills.

"Right, Dutch. Unfortunately, Dutch was aft of the Frisbee and sustained a large dose of radiation."

"Is he alright?" Girard asked.

"We don't know. Bridges and Lee are with him now. We have given him anti-radiation medication, but it will take some time to see if it was in time."

No one spoke for a moment until Mills raised his hand.

"Captain, you say we don't have FTL?"

"Yes. That's true. Unfortunately, we lost all our antimatter, so no FTL. However, our FTL drives themselves are undamaged."

All four of Endeavor's civilian scientists spoke up simultaneously.

"Hold on," said Merriweather. "Obviously, this is a setback. We can only use sub-light propulsion for now. But our main rocket engines and plasma drives are OK.

I suspect you are calculating how long it would take to get home at sub-light speed. Let me save you the effort. At quarter-light speed, it would take us over seventy-five years to get home.

"Let me emphasize, we will be home well before that. I know that be-cause I know the way ISA works. In about three years, they will wonder where we are. In four years, they will send another starship to track us down. They will stop once a month to drop location beacons and scan the immediate area for any signals from us. When they drop out near where we are now, they will receive signals from the beacons we are leaving in the area. Those signals will contain information about our condition and our plans. At light speed, they should be able to find us quickly."

"How long do you estimate that will be?" asked Dr. Mann.

"I would expect us to be home in five years. Yes, it's longer than we had planned, but we all knew the mission could take longer. We're all professionals.

"While I can't say we're in a great situation, we are in no imminent danger, and we've weathered the initial emergency."

"What do we know about the planet we're heading for?" asked Dr. Mann.

"Not much. But it should provide relief from the star's radiation. I'm planning on sheltering Endeavor in the planet's umbra."
Merriweather cocked his head as if remembering something he might have forgotten.

"RHODA, how much delta-v did we gain from the main engine burn?" Merriweather asked, referring to the ship's change in velocity.

"The main engine burn resulted in a delta-v of 11,016 km/h," replied the AI.

*I hope it's enough*, he thought before leaving the galley.

Merriweather was worried. He had tried to paint the best picture he could of their situation. That was his job. Doing any less would serve no purpose. But he didn't share all his thoughts with his crew. He was expecting a delta-v of twelve thousand clicks, and they didn't get that from Bertha, and there was no more rocket fuel. They were going to have to get there on plasma engines alone.

That wasn't all he was worried about. He wasn't as sure as he had intimated that a rescue was coming. A lot of factors could work against that scenario.

First, there was Senator Phil Sanders, chair of the subcommittee that provided oversight of ISA and America's space exploration program, doing his best to shut down ISA or, at the very least, reduce its funding. That could easily delay any rescue attempt. Second, ISA was still experiencing problems with some new technology going into the starships under construction at the IOCF. The prime example of that was incorporating the new artificial gravity technology.

Until they solved those problems, the new starships would be stuck in low Earth orbit.

There were also the unknowns. Unforeseen events on Earth could cause a delay in a rescue attempt—financial collapse, war, global pandemic, or a major catastrophe. Of course, these were far-fetched, but what Merriweather didn't know concerned him greatly.

The only thing Merriweather could do was to stay positive and continue the mission, which he was determined to do.

But first, he had to go check in on Dutch Swenson.

# CHAPTER 20

*Goodbye*

Sickbay on Endeavor was little more than a converted stateroom. The ship's designers had done a decent job of cramming as much equipment as possible into the confined space, but Doc Lee still complained about needing more space to anyone who would listen. There was room for the patient, the doctor, and little else. Currently, that was Dutch Swenson and Doc Lee. Merriweather and Bridges hovered just outside the stateroom, whispering to each other.

"He's groggy, but you can talk to him for a few minutes," said Lee, exiting sickbay. "Just don't tire him out too much. He needs rest."

"What are his odds?" Bridges whispered.

Lee just shook her head. "There was just too much damage. He absorbed almost eight and a half sieverts. That's more than I've ever seen anyone survive. Do you want to see him?"

"I can't," said Bridges, shaking his head slowly and dropping his gaze. "After you, sir."

Merriweather's heart went out to his young lieutenant. He had lost shipmates before. He knew Milo blamed himself and that only time would heal those wounds. Merriweather nodded glumly and then entered the cramped compartment.

"Hi, Dutch," said Merriweather, trying to keep the worry out of his voice. "Is the Doc keeping you comfortable?"

Swenson slowly turned his head toward his captain and smiled weakly. "Hi, Cap'n. Yeah, Doc's great." Swenson coughed violently; saliva mixed with blood oozed from the corner of his mouth.

Merriweather located and pulled several medical tissues from a container attached to the bulkhead and wiped away the spittle.

"Bertha really came through for us Dutch, and the TAMARAKS are purring like a box of kittens, thanks to you."

Dutch violently coughed.

"Not bad for old tech," said Swenson, coughing after nearly every word. His breathing was both shallow and rapid, which clearly worried Merriweather.

Merriweather glanced at Doc Lee standing just outside the open sickbay door with a concerned look.

Lee answered the unspoken concern with a shrug as if to say, *there's nothing I can do*.

"I'll have Mills babysit your rockets until you get back on your feet, Dutch. The kid's bright," said Merriweather.

"Yeah, he's...smart kid." Swenson's eyes closed as he drifted off to sleep.

"Let him sleep," said Lee, hovering nearby. "I'll call you when he's awake."

"Okay, Doc."

Merriweather took one more look at his fallen comrade, as if trying to commit his face to memory. Then he turned and left for the galley. Lee approached Bridges, who was leaning against the bulkhead.

"Are you all right, Milo?"

"It's my fault," said Bridges, shaking his head. "I sent him back there, and he was totally exposed."

Lee put her hand on his shoulder. "Don't do that to yourself, Milo. Anyone would have done the same thing."

"How much time?" Milo asked.

Lee could see that her words did little to console her shipmate.

"A few hours... maybe longer. I can keep him comfortable, but..." Lee didn't need to finish her words.

"Do what you can for him, Doc," said Bridges. "His last hours shouldn't be painful."

Taking one more look at his friend lying unconscious on the sickbay gurney, Milo turned and slowly walked away, barely able to hold back the tears. Merriweather understood the crew's concern for their fellow crewmate. However, there were still pressing problems that needed to be addressed. Therefore, he convened a meeting in the galley for the entire ship's company, excluding Doc Lee and, of course, Dutch Swenson. Once they were all seated, he began.

"I've known Dutch Swenson for over 30 years. I was a lowly ensign serving my first billet aboard an LCS patrolling the west coast of Africa. We were supporting a UN contingent trying to track down a bunch of armed guerrillas who were terrorizing the locals."

"Sir, what's an LCS?" Mills interrupted.

Merriweather smiled at his junior technology officer.

"LCS stands for 'Littoral Combat Ship.' It was a shallow-draft ship intended for operations close to shore and up larger rivers. It was agile and stealthy, but I don't think that class exists anymore. I was the Surface Warfare Officer (SWO).

"Anyway, Dutch was the chief engineer, in his early twenties, but already shooting up the ranks. We became good friends."

Merriweather paused and bowed his head. No one said a word, as it was clear to the crew that their captain was struggling with his emotions.

Merriweather looked up and took a slow sip of water before continuing. "I know we are all grieving. But Dutch would want us to get on with our responsibilities. He wouldn't put it that way, of course. He'd call us a bunch of knuckle draggers and tell us to get our asses in gear."

This caused everyone to smile. It was classic Dutch.

"I hesitated before calling this meeting," said Merriweather. "But this affects all of us, and I need your help. As you know, we had to empty the tanks to gain enough delta-v to rendezvous with Hypatia-b. We also need full thrust from the TAMARAKS. But here's our situation in a nutshell. It isn't enough. "Our calculations show we will miss our rendezvous by about five thousand kilometers. At that distance, we won't make the planet's L2."

Merriweather looked around the room at the faces of his shipmates as the realization of their situation sank in. Endeavor's officers maintained military discipline and waited for their captain to invite comments. The civilian scientist, however, did not, erupting in a volley of questions lobbed at Merriweather. Merriweather raised his hand.

"Enough."

The sternness in his voice had an immediate impact as the voices in the galley once again fell silent.

"Please let me continue. The bottom line is we need a kick in the ass to close the gap. So, here is what I've decided. Both of our LAVs are still fully fueled—about fifteen tonnes each. We will transfer the fuel from one LAV to the main propellant tanks. RHODA says that would be enough to buy us the delta-v we need."

Merriweather paused to gauge the reaction of his crew. He knew they would follow his orders no matter what. But a good leader listens as well as commands, and he wanted their feedback. The first question came not from an officer but from the reporter, Zoe Bishop.

"Isn't that dangerous to just have one functioning LAV?"

"It's not protocol, Ms. Bishop, and under normal circumstances, I wouldn't do it, but I don't know of a way around it," said Merriweather.

"Is L2 in the planet's umbra?" asked Girard.

"Yes. The umbra stretches out to 135,000 kilometers. L2 is closer—about 128,000 kilometers. We'll stay in L2 until we determine our next course of action. We'll send a few people down to check out the planet. Maybe we'll find something we can use."

"Like antimatter," said Dr. Graham.

"Not likely, Forest. But maybe water."

Merriweather fielded a dozen more questions before ending the meeting.

"All right, that's settled. Stone, you're in charge of the fuel transfer. Cortez, you'll operate Aries One. When you're ready, we'll need to shut down the TAMARAKS. We need to limit the time the TAMARAKS are down to two hours, so make it snappy—but safe," added Merriweather.

Suddenly, Merriweather noticed a change in the posture of everyone at the meeting. They were no longer looking at their captain, but at something behind him. Merriweather turned and saw Doc Lee standing in the open doorway. The look on her face told the whole story.

# CHAPTER 21

*Hypatia-b*

The planned fuel transfer went off without a hitch, taking just over the hour-and-a-half target set by Captain Merriweather. Two hours after the transfer, Endeavor's main engines erupted again, providing the five-minute kick in the ass the ship needed. For the next forty-two hours, the question on everyone's mind was whether there would be water on the dark side of the planet they were fast approaching.

"What have you found out so far, professor?" asked Captain Merriweather.

Merriweather had asked exoplanetologist Dr. Herbert Mann, Javier Rodriguez, and Lieutenant Cortez to join him for coffee and to get their opinions about their current situation.

"Well, Hypatia-b is a lot like Mercury," said Mann. "She's in a tighter orbit, and somewhat hotter, but geologically very similar. Her atmosphere is long gone, stripped away by solar winds.

"Gravitational stresses keep the planet's interior warm, and we see some volcanic activity. Because of her proximity, she's gravitationally locked, one side of the planet always facing the star. Temps on that side are approximately four to five hundred degrees C while on the night side, it's around minus two-eighty. As one might expect, there is more cratering on the dark side, so we can assume comet strikes as well."

"In my experience, that's a recipe for ice," said Rodriguez. "I can almost smell it, down in those deep craters where the sun don't shine."

"I hope you're right," said Merriweather. "Any significant radiation to worry about?"

"None. If we stay within the planet's umbra, we are perfectly safe," said Mann.

"That's what I expected. Have you detected any antiprotons in the star's radiation?" Merriweather asked.

"No, sir. Not in the quantities we would require for FTL."

"That's a shame," said Merriweather. "What's the gravity situation?"

"Well, she's smaller than Mercury, so her gravity will be less. I calculate about thirty percent of that of Earth's."

"OK, how about you, Lieutenant?" Merriweather asked, glancing at Cortez. "Are you up for an away mission?"

"To the planet, of course, sir."

"Good. You go with her, Javi. Round us up some water."

"You got it, Cap'n," said Rodriguez.

"Oh, and the lower gravity means you can take additional storage tanks with you," said Merriweather. "Cuts down on the number of trips to the surface you'll need."

"Yes, sir," said Cortez.

"I'd like to go as well," said Mann.

"Well, I'd be shocked if you didn't," said Merriweather. "Have you ever landed on a planet, moon, or any alien surface before?"

"No. Not until Endeavor. This would be an amazing opportunity for me," said Dr. Mann.

"OK, just follow Lieutenant Cortez's instructions. Her word is gospel—understood?"

"Will do, and thank you, Captain."

"Cat, Rodriguez has a lot of experience, so lean on him. You'll be fine."

"Of course, sir. You can count on me."

The crew's mood was decidedly more relaxed now that Endeavor was safely positioned within the planet's umbra, shielded from the star's intense heat and radiation.

If it wasn't for the body of Dutch Swenson lying in one of the stasis pods, the crew might have expressed their joy openly. However, it was, and so they couldn't. Instead, their discussions and hopes focused on the likelihood of water.

"Captain Merriweather."

"Yes, Ms. Bishop. What can I do for you?"

"Why is water the fuel of choice for ISA's spacecraft?"

Merriweather turned from the report he was reading as he sipped his coffee. It was a simple question, and he knew the answer—hell, any ISA cadet could speak volumes about water as fuel, but he sensed this was a different kind of question.

"Why don't you tell me?" he replied.

"I will," Bishop replied, smiling. "The universe is awash in water."

"I like what you did there," said Merriweather. "Nice play on words."

"Thank you, but I wasn't done," said Bishop. "As I was saying, the universe is awash in water—liquid water, frozen water, water suspended in alien atmospheres and in alien regolith. Water is everywhere. An ISA spacecraft low on fuel might find a source of water to fill its tanks on a moon, or planet, or even a passing comet."

"I see," said Merriweather. "So, Endeavor's rockets burn water?"

"Indirectly," said Bishop. "The molecular components of water are what?" He quickly saw what Bishop was doing. She had reversed the roles on him. She was the teacher, and he was the student. *Okay. I'll play along,* he thought.

"Hydrogen and oxygen?" he said meekly.

"Very good, Captain. To use water as fuel, we have to first split it into its molecular components and then do what, Captain?"

"Freeze them?" he replied.

"Until?"

"They transition from a gas to a liquid?"

"Very good, Captain."

The light-hearted banter between Merriweather and Bishop caught the attention of the crew, who were hanging onto every word.

"Hydrogen has a high specific impulse, which is also why we use it," Bishop said.

"Specific impulse?" Merriweather asked (as if he didn't know exactly what it was).

"It's a measure of how fast reaction-mass is ejected out of the rocket's nozzle. A high ISP means you don't need as much propellant to move the same amount of mass."

"What is reaction-mass?" Merriweather asked.

"Well, Captain, why don't you look it up and get back to me?"

Instantly, the entire crew broke out in laughter, including the captain.

"Well done, Ms. Bishop. Well done."

Merriweather appreciated Bishop's gesture. The crew had been low, and they needed a reason to smile. Bishop had given them just that—something to laugh at, a brief escape from the weight they were all carrying.

The task of searching for water on the planet below would fall on the shoulders of Cat Cortez and Javi Rodriguez—a mission they eagerly accepted. Cortez had piloted an LAV to a landing on Earth's Moon during her Academy training, but this was entirely different. Cortez fought to keep her focus on the job at hand. Her life, the lives of her passengers, and everyone on

Endeavor depended on how well she performed her job. It was an exhilarating, as well as daunting, feeling. While Javi Rodriguez would direct the operations on the planet, it was Cat's show. She was the mission commander. An hour after getting the final go-ahead from Merriweather, Cat Cortez began her first real away mission. She had created a mission profile (MP) after consulting with Dr. Mann and analyzing Endeavor's sensor data collected over the last forty-eight hours. The MP was designed to guide Aries Two down to a spot one thousand meters above a large crater where sensors had detected signs of water-ice. From there, Cortez would take control and manually guide her spacecraft to a controlled vertical landing.

L2 was a region behind the planet where the centrifugal force on an orbiting object (like Endeavor) equaled and canceled out the combined gravitational forces of the planet and the star. Although it was beyond a typical planetary orbit, Endeavor could remain in the planet's shadow with minimal fuel usage.

Therefore, the first part of their journey would require traveling the twenty-five thousand kilometers from L2 to planetary orbit. This meant using another tool in Aries' arsenal, the EX-23 auxiliary booster rocket. Aries needed the EX-23 for longer distance missions.

After going through the standard pre-launch checklist, Cortez detached Aries from Endeavor's port side docking module, officially beginning the mission. Next, she lined up Aries' rear-docking adaptor with the EX-23, currently secured to Endeavor's hull. A few bursts from Aries' forward thrusters propelled the spacecraft rearward until Cortez felt the mating clamps engage, signaling a successful docking.

Aries, now mated with the auxiliary rocket, used its thrusters to move a few hundred meters away from Endeavor and awaited the final go order from the bridge.

"Aries, you are good to go," said Merriweather. "Good luck, Lieutenant."

"Endeavor, we copy, we're a go. Thank you, Captain. See you in a few days."

Sixty seconds later, Aries was rocketing toward its rendezvous with Hypatia-b on a history-making journey for Cat Cortez and her crew of two.

# CHAPTER 22

*The Landing*

Twenty hours later, the tiny Aries lander entered orbit around the alien world just one hundred kilometers above the planet's surface. After decoupling from the EX-23 booster, Cortez contacted Endeavor.

"Endeavor, this is Aries Two. Permission to proceed?"

"Affirmative, you are a go to proceed," came the response a minute later.

"Amazing to be this close," said Dr. Mann.

"Your colleagues will certainly be envious, professor," said Cortez.

"They will, and I can't wait to brag about it when we get home."

*If we get home*, thought Cortez.

"Ready to go down there and check it out?" she said.

"Absolutely."

"OK, then. Let's do it," said Cortez.

"RHODA, execute Cortez-two-seven," said Cortez.

"Executing Cortez-two-seven," answered the ship's AI.

"Brace for engines," exclaimed Cortez, just moments before Aries main erupted, slamming Cortez and her shipmates back into their seats.

"How about more warning?" shouted Rodriguez over the roar.

Aries' main engines fired for just ten seconds before shutting off. However, those ten seconds were all it took to bend the lander's trajectory toward the planet's surface and their target—a deep crater cloaked in perpetual darkness. Cortez radioed the information back to Endeavor.

"Engine cutoff," she said.

As they descended on the dark side of the tidally locked planet, Cortez nervously monitored her craft's progress. They were still too high to make out much detail below, but she was ready to take manual control when and if necessary.

Cortez concentrated on the speed and elevation of her LAV, the numbers clearly visible on her heads-up display. She switched her helmet's visor mode to night vision.

"That's better," she whispered as the night-vision electronics penetrated the darkness below.

With her engines now silenced, Aries was essentially in freefall. The lack of a planetary atmosphere meant a turbulence-free trip for Aries' passengers, who nevertheless, checked and double-checked their seat harnesses. Cortez watched the laser altitude readout spin downward as her small spacecraft plummeted toward the surface. At ten kilometers, the stark mountains, deep canyons, volcanoes, and lava flows were clearly visible.

"Aries to Endeavor, passing ten klicks."

"Copy that, Aries. We've got your feed," replied Endeavor.

As the ship fell past the ten-klick altitude, Cortez braced herself, expecting the four Artemis engines to fire. Instead, RHODA's voice sounded in her helmet speaker.

"Alert: Navigation error. IMU drift detected. Control transfer recommended."

*Damn*, thought Cortez. *Great time for RHODA to flake out. Must be the problem Milo and I found. Guess we didn't fix it after all.*

Cortez had experienced emergencies as a pilot before. She knew the first thing she had to do was to get control of her emotions.

Breathe deeply, exhale slowly, stay calm, and remember your training. You've got this, she thought.

"Endeavor, Aries. RHODA dropped out—manual descent underway. Altitude seven-two-zero-zero. Adjusting heading—debris field ahead. Stand by for burn."

"Copy that, Aries. Manual control."

Passing seven kilometers, Cortez fired the spacecraft's thrusters, reorienting the ship, and pointing its nose skyward. Almost simultaneously, its four powerful Artemis engines roared to life, directing their combined thrusts downward, slamming Cortez and her crewmates back into their seats.

Seconds later, Cortez throttled back the engines.

"Engines throttled to two-five percent. Visuals are poor—terrain rough, but I've got a flat in a shadow basin," she reported.

"Copy Aries."

"Passing five klicks. Standby for burn."

"Copy Aries. Standing by."

Now five kilometers above the surface, Cortez spotted the designated landing zone nestled deep within a massive crater. At 2,500 meters, the engines flared to life again, jolting the passengers as the LAV decelerated sharply. As the ship's altimeter readout passed 1,300 meters, the engines eased back, and the craft showed to a steady hover, now suspended several hundred meters below the crater's rim.

"Throttle at two-five percent. Elevation nine-seven-five meters and holding," said RHODA.

"Copy Aries. You are go for manual set-down."

Cortez sighed noticeably.

Rodriguez smiled at his young crewmate. "That was fun," he said.

Cortez returned his smile, then returned her attention to the ship's instruments and controls. Without the night-vision capability of her helmet, the pitch-black darkness and looming crater walls would have made seeing anything impossible. Even with the enhanced optics, visibility remained a challenge. She switched on Aries' powerful landing light while simultaneously toggling off her helmet's night-vision, then slowly guided the craft toward the planet's surface.

"There it is!" Cortez exclaimed. Sensor data on her cockpit screen revealed water-ice nestled deep within the shadow of the crater's rim. With subtle movements of her hands on the craft's controls, Cortez slowly guided her LAV over the crater floor, scanning the surface for a suitable landing site. Unfortunately, crevasses and ridges crisscrossed the surface and boulders of all sizes were everywhere. Landing wouldn't be easy.

Cortez glanced at her propellant reserves. I've got about ten minutes to search, she thought. *That's plenty of time*. Finally, she spotted a boulder-free patch near the base of the glacier.

"Endeavor, Aries Two, I've located a suitable site. I'm putting her down," she said.

Thirty seconds later, Aries Two settled onto the surface of the alien world, less than twenty meters from the base of an enormous glacier.

"Endeavor, Aries has landed," said Cortez.

"Aries, we read you have landed. Nice job, Lieutenant."

Cortez suddenly realized that she had been holding her breath for the last thirty seconds. It's OK to breathe now, she thought to herself.

"Endeavor, it looks like there's a ginormous glacier right where we expected," said Cortez.

"We copy, Aries. Did your passengers lose their lunch?"

"Nah, they look OK—green, maybe."

"That's good. So, fill up the tanks, and be careful down there."

"Will do. Aries out."

Thirty minutes later, Cortez, Rodriguez, Mann, and Martin donned their extravehicular activity (EVA) suits, exited the ship, and began setting up area work lights and the mining equipment.

Water mining had evolved over the decades and was now almost entirely performed by robotics. However, offloading the mining equipment still entailed manual labor.

Mining Officer Javi Rodriguez was no stranger to manual labor. In fact, he relished it. Although he was on an alien planet, he very much felt at home—facing a huge water-ice glacier with a spacecraft full of robotics at his disposal. To Javi, this was fun.

"Need help, Javi?" asked Cortez.

"I got it. Looks like a good place to take an ice core," he said, pointing to a spot up the glacier.

"OK. I'm on my way up," said Cortez.

Rodriguez threw a mock salute at Cortez as she began her climb up the thirty-degree front face of the glacier. She returned his salute.

"Let's get started," said Rodriguez as he detached the portable control panel from his utility harness. With practiced expertise, Rodriguez commanded the rear cargo bay door to open and the small mobile tractor to motor down the ramp and drive to the forward cargo bay door. There it waited for the forward door to open and the ramp to deploy. Once the forward ramp was fully extended, Rodriguez instructed the tractor to drive up the ramp, connect to the portable hydrogen fuel cell (HFC) power unit, and pull it out of the spacecraft. In swift succession, Rodriguez used the tractor to extract the mining robot, the Proton Exchange Membrane Electrolyzer (PEME) unit, and the refrigeration unit.

While Rodriguez readied the mining equipment, Cortez carefully climbed twenty meters up the sloping face of the glacier and quickly located a promising spot to take a core sample. Next, she unslung the core drill she had carried on her back like a quiver and depressed the start switch.

With no atmosphere to carry the sound, Cortez couldn't hear the whirring of the drill or feel the ice crunching. She instead had to rely on the vibrations in her hands to guide the drill through the ancient ice. After drilling for ten minutes and reaching the desired depth, Cortez disconnected the drill and slid out an ice core approximately forty millimeters in diameter and fifty centimeters long. Satisfied with her first attempt, Cortez removed the bottom six centimeters of the sample for testing. From her equipment bag, Cortez removed a water-ice analyzer, opened the top, and inserted the core sample.

"RHODA, analyze the core sample."

Ten seconds later, RHODA confirmed the sample was suitable for their purposes and free from harmful impurities. Cortez happily notified Endeavor.

Cortez smiled at herself. She could imagine they were singing and dancing on Endeavor right about now. This was good news. Water meant everything.

Cortez notified the rest of her crewmates of the good news, and Rodriquez responded by jumping almost three meters off the ground.

"Show off!" exclaimed Cortez.

Returning to his work, Rodriguez continued connecting the various units with power cables and flexible tubing. After thirty minutes of hard labor, Rodriguez gave the rig one last check before signaling Cortez that everything was ready to go.

"That was fast. It appears you've done this before."

"What can I say?" said Rodriguez. "I got skills."

"So, you've said," said Cortez.

"She's ready to go, Cap'n."

"OK then, what are you waiting for?"

Rodriguez turned his attention to the reason they were on this dark, alien planet—ice mining.

Commanding the robot from below using a wireless control pad, Rodriquez guided the robot up the thirty-degree sloping face of the glacier to a promising spot fifty meters up, then turned the vehicle perpendicular to the glacier's fall line. Satisfied with the robot's orientation, he switched on the device's high-intensity laser. The ancient ice began melting almost immediately. A suction pump in the robot sent meltwater flowing through the heated tubing, dragging behind the robot and into the PEME unit positioned at the foot of the glacier. The PEME unit began splitting the liquid water into oxygen and hydrogen gases. From there, the gases circulated through the cryogenic unit until they cooled enough to phase into their liquid state. Finally, pumps fed the super-cold liquids into the holding tanks that took up most of Aries' cargo hold.

Cortez and Rodriquez watched intently as the robot crisscrossed the glacier, freeing water from the ancient ice. After thirty minutes of close observation of the mining operations, Cortez relaxed and turned her attention to her alien surroundings. Dr. Mann and Dr. Martin huddled in deep concentration over a peculiar outcropping of rock. Rodriguez busied himself checking the hoses, fittings, and gauges. Cortez turned slowly, trying to take in as much of the alien landscape as she could.

RHODA had estimated the age of the planet at about 3.8 billion years. The surrounding walls of the crater were steep and rugged, soaring hundreds of meters above them. *It would be difficult to walk out in an emergency*, she thought. The inside of the crater was not unlike craters she had seen on an Academy training mission to the moon, discounting the giant glacier, of course. Cortez saw huge boulders, fresh impact craters, and a broad, smooth patch on which Aries now stood. This was possibly created by volcanic activity triggered by meteor impacts and eruptions. She was sure that the water found on the planet resulted from comet impacts.

Once the containers were filled with liquid hydrogen and oxygen, Rodriguez topped off Aries' propellant tanks while Cortez readied the LAV for launch. The weight of the cargo was partially offset by leaving the tractor, the PEME and cryogenic units, plus the HFC power module on the surface for later use.

Doctors Mann and Martin reluctantly cut their exploration short, boarded the spacecraft, and strapped themselves into their seats along with Cortez and Rodriguez.

"RHODA, are you tracking the EX-23 booster?" Cortez asked.

"Affirmative, Lieutenant Cortez."

"Good. RHODA, Access mission profile Cortez-zero-one."

"Mission profile accessed," said the AI.

Turning to Rodriguez, Cortez asked, "Are we ready, guys?"

Her three passengers replied in the affirmative.

Cortez confirmed her passengers were strapped in before giving the command.

"RHODA, execute Cortez-zero-one."

The LAV's four Artemis engines fired almost immediately, lifting the small craft off the planet. Rising quickly from the surface, Aries Two ascended straight up as if in an elevator. At a thousand meters, the LAV slowly lifted its nose to the star-filled sky, its engine pods rotating, directing their thrust toward the rear. Finally, at the optimal time, RHODA ignited the two main engines, creating the thrust necessary to propel the craft rapidly toward space and its rendezvous with the EX-23 booster and their day-long journey back to Endeavor.

# CHAPTER 23

*Second trip to the surface*

Twenty-one hours later, Aries' crew transferred the liquid cargo to Endeavor's propellant tanks via special cold-resistant hoses. Afterwards, Cortez and her crewmates enjoyed a hot meal and a debriefing from Merriweather in the galley.

"Good job down there, Lieutenant. How did it feel to be the first human on an alien planet?"

"I've been thinking about that over the last twenty-four hours," said Cortez. "I would say, amazing, thrilling, the proudest moment of my life. It will take me some time to come up with better words."

"Your name will be in the history books, Lieutenant," said Merriweather, "along with those of your crewmates. Enjoy your moment. You deserve it. Are you up for another trip?"

"Any time, Captain. When?"

"Tomorrow is soon enough, and we'll need four more trips to fill our tanks. So, get some rest."

"Will do, sir."

"Oh, I want you to take another passenger?" asked Merriweather.

"Sure. Glad to have you aboard," answered Cortez.

"Oh, not me," said Merriweather. "I want Bridges with you."

Cortez briefly considered asking Merriweather the reason for his order, but decided against it.

"Yes, sir, of course," said Cortez.

Cortez knew better than to question orders. A trip to the planet below might break Bridges out of his depression. She was sure that was it.

"RHODA, connect me to Lieutenant Bridges' holo," instructed Cortez.

A moment later, she heard Milo's voice. "What can I do for you, Lieutenant?"

"The captain wants you on the next trip to the surface—tomorrow morning at 0800," said Cortez.

After what seemed an eternity but was more like five seconds, Bridges responded. "I'll be there."

Twelve hours later, Bridges grabbed his gear and made his way to the LAV, arriving after everyone else had boarded. Cortez was already sitting in the pilot seat, so Bridges squeezed his five-eleven frame into the copilot seat directly behind her.

"Hello, Lieutenant," said Cortez, getting no acknowledgment from Bridges other than a perfunctory grunt.

"RHODA, close the hatch," said Cortez.

"The hatch is secure." RHODA replied.

"Bridge, Aries Two, permission to launch," radioed Cortez.

"Aries, you are good to go," said the bridge officer on watch, Cmdr. Stoner.

"Endeavor, we copy, we're a go," replied Cortez.

"RHODA, release docking clamps."

For the second time in the last sixty hours, Cortez mated her Aries spacecraft with the refueled Ex-23 booster and readied her spacecraft for the arduous journey to Hypatia-b and back.

"Why did the captain want you on this trip?" Cortez asked.

"I have no idea," answered Bridges. "Maybe he just figured I could be of some help."

"We could always use the extra help, Milo," said Cortez.

"He didn't tell me anything. The first I heard of this is when you called me," said Bridges.

Cortez considered this before responding. "Well, I'm glad to have you on the team."

"To tell you the truth, I was going a bit stir-crazy," said Bridges. "Getting off the ship might be just what I need."

"Me, too," said Cortez. "Plus, I'll get to boss you around a little."

Bridges forced a smile.

# CHAPTER 24

*Cortez's Fall*

Twenty-one hours later, Cortez maneuvered Aries Two to a smooth landing within a few meters of the earlier landing spot.

"Nicely done, Lieutenant," said Bridges. "Couldn't have done it better myself."

"Thanks, Lieutenant. OK, everybody, we'll be on the surface just long enough to top off the tanks and tip the attendant, so don't stray too far. I'd hate to leave anyone behind," Cortez announced over the ship's intercom while glancing over her shoulder at Bridges.

Within thirty minutes, the mining robot was again traversing the glacier, liquid water flowing down the tubing toward the PEME's unit. Cortez busied herself running over her LAV checklist, as always before and during a planned mission. Given Javi's long history and abundant experience in water-ice mining, she didn't feel the need to micromanage his operations.

An hour and a half later, Rodriguez stopped the tractor to check the tanks.

After checking levels in the two collection tanks, Rodriguez did some rough calculations in his head before announcing that they needed another thirty minutes.

"Thanks, Javi." Cortez smiled to herself. Everything was going about as well as expected. "Keep up the good work," she shouted. Cortez cautioned herself not to overlook the dangers she and her crew faced. She remembered one of her instructors telling her, "Space wants to kill you. Never take it for granted." That sage advice was about to become very real.

"Lieutenant, we've got a bit of a problem," announced Rodriguez. He pointed up the glacier in the direction of the mining robot. The robot tractor had ceased its traverse across the glacier and was now sitting at an unusual angle, nose down into what appeared from a distance to be a depression in the glacial ice.

"You think it's a crevasse?" asked Cortez.

"More than likely. But whatever it is, I can't get the tractor to go forward or backward from down here, so I'll have to go up there."

"OK, let me know if you need my help."

Another ten minutes passed before Rodriguez reached the tractor, finding it had indeed partially fallen headfirst into a crack in the ice and was now dangling over the two-meter-wide chasm. Rodriguez contacted Cortez on his holo and described what he saw.

"Can you extract it?"

"I think so. I'm going to give it a go, anyway," he said.

After saying a brief prayer, Rodriguez directed the mining robot to back away from the edge, but as he did so, the nose of the tractor tipped further down into the gaping crevasse.

"Oops, Lieutenant, uh, we have a real problem. I think I've made it worse."

"How so?"

"It's tipped down even further and hanging on by a thread."

"OK, I'm on my way up. Maybe the two of us can get it out," said Cortez.

"Maybe bring Bridges, too. It might take more muscle than the two of us," added Rodriguez.

"Bridges is hanging out with Mann and Martin. Let's see if we can do this ourselves."

Ten minutes later, Cortez and Rodriguez stood gazing down into the two-meter crack in the glacier. The mining robot had driven into a crevasse and was now dangling over the edge at a thirty-degree angle, its forward treads hanging precariously to the far side of the chasm. If the tractor's treads were to lose their grip on the ice, the machine would almost assuredly fall in, and the consequences would be dire. Endeavor did not carry two robots, and without a robot, she could not mine for fuel.

"Javi, you grab onto the hose and pull from the rear. I'll work the controls," said Cortez.

Rodriguez dug his crampons into the ice and wrapped his gloves around the fifteen-centimeter diameter hose. Cortez positioned herself near the crevasse to get a good look at the front of the tractor.

"Ready?" she asked.

"Ready as I can be," he answered.

Carefully, Cortez commanded the tractor to move in reverse. At first, it was working. But suddenly, the ice under Rodriguez's crampons gave way, and he fell to the ice. The tractor lurched forward. Another centimeter and the tractor might have disappeared over the edge and been lost forever. Instead, it caught on a thin ledge just a half meter below the surface. The robot was now dangling at a precarious forty-five-degree angle.

"Maybe we need more help," said Rodriguez.

As much as she hated to admit it, Cortez realized that the two of them were not strong enough to extract the tractor.

"Bridges, Dr. Mann, Dr. Martin, I think we're going to need your help up here," radioed Cortez. "Grab some crampons from the ship and come on up."

While she and Rodriguez waited for Bridges and the two scientists to retrieve from the LAV the crampons they would need to climb the glacier, Cortez notified Endeavor of their predicament.

The plan was straightforward. Again, Cortez would work the controls, and the four men would try to haul out the tractor using brute strength. Only the reduced gravity of this tiny planet made this plan even possible.

This time, Cortez positioned herself on the far side of the crevasse to have a better view of the operation. Again, Cortez slowly commanded the tractor to crawl away from the edge. As the tractor treads moved in reverse, Bridges, Rodriguez, Mann, and Martin strained against the weight of the mining robot. Gradually, centimeter by centimeter, the tractor clawed its way out of the crevasse.

Cortez leaned forward to watch the front of the tractor treads climb the crevasse wall. Finally, the tractor leveled out, its treads gaining a purchase on the far side of the crevasse, backing safely away from the edge.

Cortez, however, did not fare as well. As someone trained in space medicine, she understood the effect prolonged exposure to microgravity had on a person's balance. Cortez knew almost instantly that she had leaned too far forward and was about to fall headfirst into the crevasse.

She felt a rush of adrenaline and fear. In a panic, she reached out as far as she could, desperately trying to grab on to something—anything. But the crevasse was too wide, and the tractor was too far away.

"Cat!" Bridges yelled as he saw Cortez disappear over the edge.

Dropping the hose, Bridges bounded to the edge of the crevasse, almost falling in himself.

"Cat," he yelled. At first, he didn't see her. Finally, in the darkness below, he saw the dim light of her EVA suit beacon as it flashed some ten meters down.

"Cat, can you hear me? Are you OK?"

A second later, "Yes, I'm OK. I think I'm OK. But I can't move, and I'm wedged in down here."

"RHODA, check my suit," she said.

"Your EVA suit is functioning normally, Lieutenant Cortez."

"I can't move my helmet, but my feet are free. I think the crevasse widens out below me," said Cortez.

"Can you move your arms?" Bridges asked.

"No, I don't think so," she replied. "The crevasse is just wide enough for my suit. Wait. OK, I can move my helmet maybe ten degrees to each side, and I can move my arms a bit—just to the side but not to the front or back. The walls are pressing against the front and back of my suit, and I'm wedged in pretty good."

"OK, just stay calm. We'll get you out in a bit," said Bridges.

Bridges quickly updated Endeavor on the situation.

"We don't believe she's injured, but she seems wedged in down there. She's about ten meters down."

"Bridges, this is Merriweather. Is there enough room to get someone down there to free her?"

"No, it doesn't look like it. It's too tight."

"So, what's the plan?"

"Give us a moment, Captain," said Bridges.

Bridges joined the others.

"Can we get a rope down there?" he asked.

"That's not going to work, and there's no way of getting it around her," said Dr. Martin.

Rodriguez looked over the edge and then back to the tractor as if making mental calculations.

"OK, here's what I think we need to do," he said. "We use the laser on the tractor to dig a shaft parallel to the crevasse. Then we dig a horizontal shaft and come in just below her. We will have to detach the laser head and the water suction hose and do some other jury-rigging of the pump, but yeah, it should work."

"How much time?" Bridges asked.

"Maybe thirty minutes to jury-rig the laser and another hour to dig the shaft."

"An hour and a half?" Bridges checked his oxygen supply reserves. "RHO-DA, can you check Lieutenant Cortez's oxygen supply? How much time does she have left?"

"Lieutenant Cortez has seventy-eight minutes of oxygen remaining," RHODA replied.

"Then we'd better get started, and we'd better be quick."

"I'll get the tools," said Rodriguez as he turned and, ignoring the dangers to his own safety, began a mad scramble down the face of the glacier. Rodriguez arrived at the LAV minutes later. Bounding up the cargo ramp, Javi made a mental checklist of all the tools he would need to reconfigure the laser and water suction hose. If he forgot a tool or chose the wrong size wrench, it would mean a second trip up and down the glacier—and almost certain death for Cortez.

Bridges relayed the plan to Endeavor. "Is there any way to get her any supplemental oxygen?" Merriweather asked.

"Not enough room. She's wedged in too tightly."

"Damn. OK, keep me informed," said Merriweather.

Two minutes later, Rodriguez emerged from the LAV carrying a bag of tools and a coil of rope. Then he began the strenuous climb back up the glacier.

It took seven more agonizing minutes before Rodriguez rejoined his worried comrades. He jumped to his task immediately.

"What can we do?" asked Dr. Mann.

"Here, take this wrench and begin removing the suction hose. There are four bolts you'll have to remove—there, there, there, and there," he replied, pointing to each bolt.

Turning to Bridges, "Here, Lieutenant. You might want to come up with a plan B. Just in case," he said, handing Bridges an ice axe and the coil of rope. Fifteen minutes later, Rodriguez finished wrapping duct tape around the laser head and suction hose, making a serviceable handheld mining tool. "I'll take the first crack at it," he said.

Stepping off two meters from the edge of the crevasse, Rodriguez pointed to the ice. With his arm extended, Rodriguez drew a circle showing where he intended the shaft to be. "No closer than two meters from the crevasse," he said. "Any closer and the ice might shift or move around the Lieutenant, and she could fall further down."

Meanwhile, Bridges checked his oxygen reserve. Less than an hour left, he thought. He had a sick feeling in his stomach. He hoped Rodriguez could pull off a miracle, but he couldn't take that chance. Bridges moved away from the group and began mapping out the beginnings of a plan in his head. He knew that any plan he came up with would most likely involve climbing into the crevasse—something he didn't relish.

*ISA didn't cover this scenario at the Academy*, he thought.

Bridges had to pick the right spot. He found it ten meters farther up the glacier. There, the crevasse continued to widen as it plunged into the darkness below. There was no narrowing as there was where Cortez had fallen in.

Immediately, Bridges returned to the group, and the now disconnected tractor. Moving gingerly, Bridges retrieved the control pad where Cortez had dropped it. Working the controls, he slowly backed the tractor away from the crevasse and steered it in a line parallel with the yawing chasm and up the sloping glacier. Next, he uncoiled the rope. Finding an end, he fed it through a semicircular bracket that had earlier held the laser assembly. He continued to pull the rope through the bracket until he had reached the halfway point. Next, he tied the two ends together.

Bridges had a mental picture in his head of what he wanted to do, but doing it was proving to be more confusing. He had to focus. Cat's life depended on it. He couldn't just leave it to someone else.

Soon he had the puzzle of the ropes figured out. First, Bridges tossed the now doubled rope down into the crevasse. Next, he stepped in between the two rope halves and pulled them up to his armpits. The next part was proving to be impossible wearing his bulky EVA suit.

"Can I help y'all out, Milo?"

Bridges turned to see Dr. Martin standing behind him.

"Oh, yeah, thanks, Mike. I need to crisscross these two ropes behind me."

Martin grabbed the two ropes and crisscrossed them the way Bridges had described. He handed the crisscrossed ropes back to Milo, one rope under each arm. Bridges brought the two ropes together and stepped over them, so they ran between his legs.

Bridges reached back with his hand. "Hand me both ropes." Bridges pulled the doubled rope up to his groin, then wrapped the ropes around one arm and grasped them with his gloved fist.

The ropes now traced a path from the tractor's laser assembly bracket, crisscrossed behind Bridges' back, wrapped around to his front, then went down through his crotch, under one thigh, and back up to wrap around his arm and finally to his clenched fist. The whole contraption formed a primitive climbing harness and seat. The balance of the doubled rope hung down into the crevasse. Looking down, Bridges convinced himself that the rope was long enough to do the job. He hoped so.

Meanwhile, Rodriguez had given the laser mining tool to Dr. Mann, who was now laboring to cut through the ancient glacial ice. They had managed to dig a shaft approximately five meters down and were a little less than halfway to their goal. A steady cloud of steam and ice particles rose from the shaft, obscuring the workers. Rodriguez had instructed them to leave circular ridges in the shaft to enable them to climb in and out.

Meanwhile, ten meters up the glacier, Bridges and Martin continued with their Plan B.

"Well, here goes nothing," said Bridges as he slowly backed over the edge and lowered himself into the crevasse. Controlling his rate of descent by loosening and tightening his grip on the ropes, Bridges descended deeper into the darkness.

"Mike, I need you to let me know when you think I'm lower down than Cortez."

"Hope you know what you're fixin' to do, Milo."

"So do I, Mike."

Bridges had to know that his oxygen reserves were dwindling and probably even faster than Cortez's, considering his level of exertion. But he pushed that thought from his mind. There was no going back. Either they would both survive, or both would die.

"I reckon you're about thirteen to fifteen meters down, Milo," said Martin.

"OK, now here's what I want you to do. Take the control pad and drive the tractor slowly toward the shaft."

"How in the hell do I drive this thing, Milo? I've never done or even seen it done before today."

"Damn it, Mike. You're a freaking scientist. Figure it out."

"OK, OK. Give me a damned minute. I can do this. OK, yeah, it's this doo-hickey here. OK, why is nothing happening?"

"Did you turn it on?"

"Shit, OK, I've got it now," said Martin as he found the "Start" control.

Slowly, the tractor backed down the glacier toward the point where Lieutenant Cortez had fallen in. The irregularity of the crevasse's icy edge made for a bumpy ride for Bridges. Several times, the ropes would snag on a crack or fissure in the ice, requiring Dr. Martin to stop the tractor to free the rope. Bridges had left the ice axe with Martin, who now used it to chip away at each obstruction.

Meanwhile, Rodriguez, now wielding the laser mining contraption, had finally reached the desired depth, turned the laser inward toward the crevasse, and begun digging a horizontal tunnel. If his calculations were correct, the tunnel would breach the crevasse just below the Lieutenant.

"How are you holding up down there, Cat?" Bridges asked.

"Kind of lonely, Milo. And I think my carbon dioxide level is climbing a bit too. The air's getting stale. I'd ask RHODA, but I don't think I want to know," she added.

"I just asked RHODA, and she says not to worry. You have plenty to spare," lied Bridges.

"That's good. Hate to think you guys are doing all this work for nothing."

"RHODA, check my oxygen reserves," said Bridges.

"You have approximately five minutes of oxygen remaining, Milo."

*Crap*, he thought. Can't think about that. I have to get to Cat. She should have a few minutes more, hopefully.

Bridges was now within a meter of his crewmate. His helmet light gave him a good view of Cortez, about two meters in front of and above his current position. He planned to tie the excess rope below him around her waist. But first, he had to figure out how to raise himself high enough. The trouble was, there was no room. He barely had room to turn his body.

Rodriguez and Martin labored furiously, excavating the rescue tunnel, and quickly depleting their own oxygen reserves in the process. Unlike Cortez and Bridges, however, they could swap out their empty tanks for back-ups.

The laser continued to melt the ice separating the horizontal shaft from the crevasse. They were getting close.

Suddenly Rodriguez felt the ice below him shift. He stopped the laser and turned off the water pump. He leaned his head forward until his helmet contacted the now thin wall between the tunnel and the crevasse. At first, he felt nothing. Then suddenly, a sharp cracking sound filled his helmet as the ice wall between himself and the chasm collapsed.

Simultaneously, a slab of ice wedged between the crevasse wall and Cortez's suit crumbled and fell away. Cat felt herself beginning to fall, along with her hopes that her crewmates would save her.

Rodriguez watched in horror as Cortez suddenly dropped from the icy embrace of the glacier and past the tunnel opening. There was nothing he could do. His hands still held the jury-rigged laser mining tool and there was no way he could drop it in time to reach Cortez as she fell. He knew, as did the others, that this was their only opportunity to save their crewmate. If she fell deeper into the crevasse, there would be no way to rescue her before her oxygen supply ran out.

As Cortez fell past the opening of the cross-tunnel in the ice, she glimpsed her crewmate Rodriguez standing there with eyes widened and a hopeless look on his face. *This is it, she thought. This is how it ends for me.* However, just as suddenly as her fall had begun, just below the shaft dug by her crewmates, she stopped, grabbed by some unknown force or creature inhabiting the crevasse. Rodriguez dropped the laser and fell to his knees. He reached into the crevasse and wrapped his arms around Cortez's helmet.

"Do you have a good grip on her, Javi?"

"Is that you, Milo?" said Rodriguez.

"Milo?" shouted Cortez. "You caught me."

"Who did you expect?" the exertion registering in Bridge's voice. "I'm just below you, Cat. Javi, can you pull her out?"

"I think so," said Rodriguez. "Professor, come here and help!" he shouted.

A few seconds later, with Bridges pushing from below, Mann and Rodriguez pulled Cortez up and into the cross-tunnel opening.

"Are you injured, Lieutenant?" Mann asked.

"No. I don't think so, but it's getting difficult to breathe."

As Javi and Mann helped Cortez up the vertical shaft and onto the glacier's surface, Mike Martin began extracting Bridges from the crevasse. Slowly, Martin commanded the tractor to move back up the glacier where the crevasse was wider. Then, turning the tractor away from the crevasse, they pulled Bridges slowly toward the surface and out of the chasm.

Bridges tried to stand, then sank back to his knees. Struggling to breathe, Bridges mouthed the words "I think I'm out…" before losing consciousness and collapsing back to the icy surface.

"I need help over here," shouted Martin. "Javi, bring an air tank."

Rodriguez rushed to his fallen comrade and, kneeling by his side, quickly disconnected Bridges' depleted air tank and installed a fresh one.

"Are you with me, buddy?" Rodriguez implored.

Bridges didn't answer. Rodriguez leaned over, touching his facemask to Bridges.

"He's breathing, but it's shallow. Let's get him down to the ship—quickly," he shouted.

It was a race against time. Rodriguez and Mann placed Bridges and Cortez on top of the mining tractor and steered it toward the foot of the glacier. Six minutes later, all six entered the LAV. It took another sixty seconds before the cargo door was closed and the LAV re-pressurized.

Rodriguez quickly removed Bridges' helmet, but his shipmate was still unconscious.

Martin, tending to Cortez, helped her remove her helmet. "Are you OK?" he asked.

"I'm OK," she said. Turning her attention to Bridges, she said, "Milo, are you OK? Milo? Wake up, Milo."

Cortez leaned over Bridges' lifeless body and placed her mouth over his. She blew several long steady streams of air, trying to fill his lungs. His fellow crewmates surrounded him, trying to will their shipmate back to life with their thoughts. Finally, Bridges gasped, gulping in air, coughing, his body shaking.

"There he is!" yelled Rodriguez. "He's back."

Tears of joy filled Cat's eyes as she leaned close to Milo's face. "Welcome back," she said.

After his breathing returned to normal, Bridges lifted his arms and placed a gloved hand on each side of Cat's head. Slowly, he pulled her face to his and kissed her. "Thanks for saving my life."

Cortez pulled her head away forcefully.

"That was totally inappropriate, Lieutenant," she said to the laughter that filled the LAV. "But I'll let it go. I think you are still a bit delirious."

An hour later, with fresh air tanks, Rodriguez disconnected the hoses from Aries' propellant tanks while Dr. Mann and Dr. Martin decoupled the crawler from the electrolysis unit. Cortez and Bridges recovered inside the LAV.

"Lieutenant Cortez, are you up to piloting the ship?" asked Dr. Mann.

"Yes, I am. No problem, and that's what I'm here for."

Thirty minutes later, Aries was rocketing from the planet's surface, all safely aboard with tanks filled to the brim with their liquid cargo.

# CHAPTER 25

*Captain's Log, date 10.05.2125, Commander Jake Merriweather*

Captain Merriweather poured a glass of brandy from the bottle he kept in his safe and gazed at an image of his deceased wife displayed on his holoview. He often turned to her when faced with a difficult decision, and it was at times like these that he felt closest to her. Looking at her image, he felt the heavy responsibility to his ship, crew, and old friend—to Dutch Swenson.

"RHODA, open personal log, password sierra–delta–fifteen–oh-seven."

"Hi, Honey. I…"

Merriweather struggled to find the words he wanted to say. It was his twentieth anniversary, and he was missing his wife, Leah.

"Hi, Honey. Happy anniversary."

Merriweather took a sip of brandy before continuing.

"Can you believe it's been twenty years? Seems like yesterday when you favored me with a dance at the officers' club. I'm glad your friend, Melinda, talked you into coming. Otherwise, we might never have met.

"You could probably tell from my reaction or that stupid expression on my face that I was smitten. That was quite a night. Before the night was over, both of us knew. I did, anyway. Maybe you just took pity on a lovesick sailor. Whatever the reason, I'm glad you came around. I can't imagine what my life would have been without you in it. Even with you gone these last ten years, you are still with me. I carry you here, in my heart."

Merriweather sighed deeply and dabbed at the tear forming in the corner of his eye.

"There's something else. You remember my old friend, Dutch Swenson? Well, we lost him. It was a terrible accident, and, well, Dutch was in the wrong place at the wrong time, and now he's gone just like that. We're all mourning him. Sometimes I wonder if I'm cut out for this—this job."

Merriweather downed the brandy and then poured another glass.

"Oh, and did I mention that we're stranded in another freaking solar system? That's an important little detail, isn't it? Lost all our antimatter, and now our FTL drive is useless. So, we're looking at eighty years to get home. How do I lead my men when they know that all their friends and family, hell, everyone they know, will be dead before we get home? I feel like I've failed them.

"I'm sorry, honey. I don't mean to dump all of this on you. I…"

Merriweather drained his glass.

"RHODA, close personal file."

Merriweather placed the brandy bottle and the glass back in his safe. He returned the photo to the shelf above his desk, logged into the official ship's mission file, and began speaking.

Endeavor is station-keeping at L2 (LaGrange point) of an unknown planetary system, approximately thirty-six million kilometers from an unknown star—type G2V—we've named Hypatia. I selected Hypatia from the official ISA name list as per article 3 of the mission requirements. Using IAU convention, the planet's designation is Hypatia-b. We are using the planet to shield us from the star's radiation, giving us time to formulate a plan.

Our FTL drives are down. We had to eject our antimatter, and we do not have the means to generate more. Our options are to find a planet within this star's planetary system that might have the technology or the resources we need or to begin our trip home and hope we can contact a rescue ship. We lost a crewmember when we jettisoned the antimatter. Dutch Swenson was our chief propulsion engineer and a longtime friend. He was in an unprotected compartment and received a lethal dose of gamma rays caused by the failure of the antimatter containment vessel. The crew took it hard but are soldiering on.

We've launched several planetary probes to map this star's planetary system. It's a binary star system with a type G2V (Hypatia) and an orbiting red dwarf we've designated Hypatia-Proxima. We have detected several planets orbiting Hypatia, but none, unfortunately, appears to be within its habitable zone. The red dwarf, however, has its own planet, and Dr. Girard believes it may support life. We've given the planet the official name Hypatia-Proxima-b, but the crew has taken to calling it Sanctuary. Our plasma drives are operational, and we have adequate reserves of liquid argon propellant, enabling us to reach it in about twelve to thirteen months.

That is the option I have taken. We will also launch several beacons that will transmit on emergency frequencies. With any luck, we can meet up with any rescue ships at Sanctuary.

Merriweather dated the audio file and saved it to the official ship's log before signing off.

Given the near catastrophe aboard Endeavor and the mishap on Hypatia-b, Merriweather delayed Endeavor's departure for Sanctuary by two weeks. This gave ample time for Bridges and Cortez to fully recover from their ordeal and to lead several more forays to the planet's surface to collect water and manufacture sufficient quantities of liquid hydrogen and liquid oxygen to fill the tanks on Endeavor and both LAVs.

Merriweather satisfied himself that the crew had fully recovered and that his ship was in top condition, then called his crew together to inform them of his decision.

As the last of the crew entered the ship's galley, Merriweather began.

"OK, I know all of you want to get on with our mission, as do I. Obviously, without our hyperdrive, we have to modify our original mission. But we can still investigate a planet where life may be possible. Therefore, I've asked Lieutenant Cortez to calculate a trajectory that will take us to the planet we've been referring to as Sanctuary—Lieutenant." Merriweather gestured to Cortez to provide the details.

Cortez positioned a small holo-projector in the center of the galley table. She then typed a few commands on her tablet. Instantly, a holo image of the planetary system materialized above their heads.

"As you can see, this is a binary star system. This large object here, designated *Hypatia-Proxima*, is a small red dwarf. The professor calculates its spectral class as M7.5 to M8. It's about 10% the mass and 12% the radius of this system's primary star, Hypatia.

"Orbiting *Hypatia-Proxima* at an average of forty-eight million kilometers is the planet we have been calling Sanctuary—official designation *Hypatia-Proxima-b*. That it's a binary-star system will obviously complicate our trajectory somewhat."

Cortez pointed out Endeavor's current position, station-keeping in the umbra of Hypatia-b, and then the planet Sanctuary, the proposed destination. With a few keystrokes, Cortez created a bright red elliptical line representing the proposed trajectory.

"A second problem we have is that Sanctuary is not at an optimal position in her orbit for a direct Hoffman trajectory. We would have to delay our departure by six months to go there directly. I'm sure everyone here would rather not hang around for another half a year. So, RHODA and I have come up with an alternative plan.

Cortez paused for a moment to sip her coffee before continuing.

"Last week, the professor detected a fast-moving object he first thought was a comet heading away from the star. However, after working with RHODA and measuring the object's size, he realized it was a dwarf planet about the size of Europa. This dwarf planet is in a highly elliptical orbit, sometimes inside Sanctuary's orbit and sometimes far outside."

"Why such an extreme orbit?" Asked Bishop.

"Good question, Zoe. Another planet could have knocked the planet off its orbit. Another possibility is that it is a rogue planet. It may have formed in some distant system and later expelled by a passing black hole or dwarf star. It may have just wandered too close to Hypatia and is now part of its system.

"Either of these events occurred several million years ago—if not more. Dr. Mann discovered the planet, so the honor of naming it fell to him. He's chosen Ulysses, the Greek word for wanderer. The official designation is Hypatia-g."

Cortez reviewed the notes on her tablet before continuing.

"Currently, the planet is at its perihelion or closest to Hypatia. That's perfect for us. If we do a close flyby of Ulysses, we can use its gravity to slingshot us toward Sanctuary. Plus, with a timely engine burn of about sixty seconds at our periapsis, or closest approach—here," she said, pointing to a point on the trajectory, "we can get a delta-v of between five and ten percent. It also puts us in a better attitude with respect to Sanctuary's orbit. Rather than approaching the planet directly and having to use propellant to slow down, we approach it in the same orbit in a chase position. As you can see, I've calculated an orbit that will take us around Ulysses, and then, using our increased speed, we intersect Sanctuary's orbit *here*. A third engine burn puts us into orbit around the red dwarf and in a trailing position two weeks behind Sanctuary. We intercept the orbit of the larger of the two Sanctuary moons—*here*. A fourth correction burn will put us at L2 just outside the moon's orbit, effectively shielding Endeavor from the prying eyes of any potential intelligent life on the planet. Using max engine burn and plasma engines, the trip will take approximately fourteen months. Questions?"

Mills raised his hand. "You said that planet Ulysses ranges far outside Sanctuary's orbit. How far is far?"

"RHODA calculates about 1.9 billion kilometers (about 1.18 billion mi) with an orbital period of about seventeen years."

"Damn fortunate that it's in town when we need it," said Mills.
Lieutenant Cortez looked around at her fellow officers, expecting more questions. However, getting none, she switched off the holo-projector and sat down.

"Thanks, Lieutenant," said Merriweather, "So this is our mission—to approach Sanctuary carefully and unobserved. Once on station, we will execute standard protocols for planetary investigation. I'm excited about this new opportunity, and in no way is it less of a mission than our original one."

Merriweather paused for a minute while the crew waited to be dismissed. Finally, he spoke.

"There's just one more thing we need to do."

# CHAPTER 26

*Saying goodbye to an old friend*

Endeavor's engines again worked flawlessly, powering the spacecraft and its crew from L2 behind Hypatia-b. Under the constant thrust of its eight TAMARAK plasma engines, Endeavor sped toward its planned rendezvous with the wandering planet Ulysses and its gravity-assist toward Sanctuary. Three days later, Captain Merriweather assembled his crew for one last farewell to an old friend.

On the port side of the forward cargo hold, dressed in their dress blues and standing at military attention, were the ISA members of the crew—Stoner, Bridges, Cortez, Mills, Lee, and Rodriguez. On the starboard side stood the civilian members of the crew—Girard, Mann, Graham, Martin, and Bishop. To keep from floating away in the microgravity environment of the spacecraft's core, each anchored themselves to the deck via temporary restraining straps.

Between them stood Captain Merriweather, his right hand resting on a modified navigation buoy shell holding the body of Dutch Swenson.

Merriweather took a moment to look at each person present. No time during the last year was the weight of his responsibility more keenly felt. Losing someone in your command was heartbreaking enough, but losing a friend was devastating. He had lost both, and he didn't know if he would ever completely recover. However, he was the captain. These people depended on him, and he had to be the leader they needed. Slowly and solemnly, he began speaking.

"We have buried sailors at sea for as long as men have sailed the oceans, and it is an ancient and time-honored Naval tradition. Although ISA is not strictly a Naval organization, it has adopted the tradition and command rank of the U.S. Navy, as we do aboard Endeavor.

"In earlier times, they wrapped the body of a deceased sailor in sailcloth and then sent them over the side. After much debate, ISA decided to offer that option to its members in the unlikely event of our…"

Merriweather paused, trying to decide on the right word to use. He decided to call it what it was.

"…of our death. We all signed up for this trip, and we knew the risks. Dutch knew the risks. Dutch was a veteran space traveler. He faced danger before and never shied away from it. He welcomed it. He told me once that dangerous situations made him feel most alive.

"Dutch also loved space. He loved it so much that his decision was easy. We are here to honor that decision—to commit his remains to the cosmos." After a moment of silence, Merriweather spoke again. "I found these words in an old book of poetry.

> *JUST where that star above*
> *Shines with a cold, dispassionate smile —*
> *If in the flesh I'd travel there,*
> *How many, many a mile!*
> *If this, my soul, should be*
> *Unprisoned from its earthly bond,*
> *Time could not count its markless flight*
> *Beyond that star, beyond!*[1]

"Please bow your heads. We, therefore, commit Dutch's body to the vastness of space, to be turned into corruption, looking for the resurrection of the body when the cosmos shall give up her dead and the life of the world to come. … Amen."

Merriweather raised his head and gave the command to deploy the makeshift coffin. Slowly at first, the modified buoy slid along the rails on which it rested, ultimately disappearing through the open breech door of the launch tube. The crew remained at attention as the door closed with a loud metallic clank followed by an audible hiss as the air inside the tube was vented into space. A few seconds later, the crew heard a loud swoosh as the buoy was forcefully ejected into space.

Rodriguez nodded slowly to Merriweather, signaling the successful launch of the buoy.

"Thank you, Lieutenant," said Merriweather. "Dismissed."

His eyes glued to the holoview attached to the bulkhead, Merriweather watched the receding buoy until he could no longer distinguish it from the millions of stars surrounding them.

"Goodbye, old friend," said Merriweather as he gave his old friend one last salute.

# CHAPTER 27

*Club Phoenix, several months later*

Endeavor raced through the blackness of space under the constant thrust of her eight magnetoplasma TAMARACK engines. Although now traveling slightly over fifty thousand kilometers per hour, there was no sensation of acceleration. Only the whisper of the ship's ventilation system and the distant voices from the ship's galley vitiated the eerie silence.

A knock on his door interrupted Merriweather's thoughts.

"Captain, do you have a moment, sir?"

Merriweather closed the book he was reading. He recognized the voice of Milo Bridges.

"Bridges, sure, come on in," said Captain Merriweather, motioning his young lieutenant to an empty chair in his quarters.

"Sorry to disturb you, sir," said Bridges, noting the book in Merriweather's hand. "What are you reading, sir, if you don't mind my asking?"

"Oh, this," said Merriweather, "it's a book my wife gave me for our tenth anniversary. She knew I liked Rudyard Kipling. I was just reading a poem titled 'If.' Are you familiar with it?"

"No, sir," said Bridges.

"You've probably heard parts of it. It starts like this. 'If you can keep your head when all about you are losing theirs and blaming it on you…"

"Oh, sure, I've heard that, but I didn't know where it was from," said Bridges.

"You should familiarize yourself with it. It is all about leadership. I particularly like the second verse."

Merriweather opened the small book and began reading.

*If you can talk with crowds and keep your virtue,*
*Or walk with kings—nor lose the common touch,*
*If neither foes nor loving friends can hurt you,*
*If all men count with you, but none too much;*
*If you can fill the unforgiving minute*
*With sixty seconds' worth of distance run,*
*Yours is the Earth and everything that's in it,*
*And—which is more—you'll be a Man, my son!2*

Merriweather closed the book, paused for a second, and then handed the book to his young lieutenant.

"I'm lending this to you, Milo. I'll eventually want it back."

"Yes, sir, of course, sir," said Bridges, taking the book.

"OK, now what can I do for you?" Merriweather asked.

"Sir, I've been thinking about our situation. I'm partially to blame for where we are now and…"

"Nonsense, Bridges. You did the right thing. I know I would have done the same. If you had hesitated, we would probably be just so much space dust circling that star, and no one would have ever known what happened to us. But your training kicked in, and you made a tough call. I've noted as much in your file."

"Thank you, sir."

Bridges paused for a moment, letting the captain's words wash away the guilt he was carrying.

"So, was there something else, Bridges?"

"Oh, yes, sir. I have an idea that might help us get home sooner, and I wanted your opinion."

"Son, if you can get us home quicker, I'm definitely interested."

"Sir, we have the materials and resources here on Endeavor to build a Bickford collector."

"Like the antimatter collectors orbiting Saturn?"

"Sort of. Bickford Collectors were a very early concept of what we have now."

"OK, go on."

"Sir, a Bickford antiproton collector is just an antimatter containment vessel, about fifteen hundred meters of loop antenna made from any high-temperature superconducting material and an adequate power source of, say, 200 kilowatts. I believe we have all three."

"Keep going," said Merriweather. "You have my full attention."

"I know we ejected our primary antimatter vessel, but we have the last one I removed from the Saturn collectors. We also have two portable hydrogen fuel cell (HFC) power units we use for mining operations. I believe we could sacrifice one without jeopardizing our ability to mine water. We also have the resources to fabricate the antenna stock."

"What do you plan on using for the superconductor?" Merriweather asked.

"The TAMARAK engines use titanium clad magnesium diboride conductors for their RF helical coils, and we have several big spools of the stuff," answered Bridges.

"OK, that makes sense," said Merriweather, "let's assume we can build it. Where do you suggest we find antiprotons?"

"OK, when RHODA analyzed this planetary system, she identified a gas giant outside the orbit of Sanctuary. "

"Hypatia-f," said Merriweather, stating the official name of the planet.

"Right," said Bridges. "I suggest we take a couple of beacons and cannibalize their ion engines. I've had RHODA check trajectories, and she says that if we launch the collector within the next three months, we can put it in orbit around Hypatia-f within fifteen months. If it's anything like Saturn, we could harvest enough antimatter in a year or two to restart our FTL drives and get us home a year after that."

Merriweather thought for a moment.

"OK, I like it. But let's keep this idea to ourselves for the time being. I don't want to give the troops false hope until we've checked out all the numbers. Bring Jonathan into the loop—the professor, too. You'll need him to verify your gas giant is a viable source. I want a plan with all the numbers before we go public. That understood?"

"Yes, sir. And thank you, sir."

"Damn Bridges, if this works, well, let's just say it could positively affect your career at ISA. Make it happen. Remember, not a word to anybody but Mills and Mann."

Eight hours later, everyone on Endeavor knew the idea Bridges had shared with the captain. It's hard to keep secrets on a small starship. Bridges quickly tracked down Jonathan Mills and Dr. Mann and called them together for a coffee in the galley to present his idea for a jury-rigged antiproton collector.

"Let the record show that this is the first meeting of Club Phoenix," announced Bridges.

"Club what—Phoenix. What's this all about, Bridges?" asked Jonathan Mills.

For the next ten minutes, Bridges explained his idea to build a Bickford antiproton collector from parts aboard Endeavor and launch it into orbit around the large gas giant, Hypatia-f.

"Brilliant," said Dr. Mann. "I didn't know you were so well-versed in antimatter theory, Milo."

"Well, I wasn't, but you know what they say about the mother of invention? I've been reading up on the subject every chance I get and stumbled upon this old whitepaper about collector technology. That's when I got the idea. What do you think, Mills? Can you build it?"

"It's ambitious, that's for sure. Yes, we have a lot of the basic elements. But we'd have to create some new electronics and software to integrate everything. It's all tricky stuff. It's antimatter, after all. One mistake and kablooey. Then there's the small problem of testing it. We don't have any antimatter, remember?"

"I don't see a better option that gets us home while we're still young."

"OK, you've convinced me. I'm in," said Dr. Mann.

"So am I," added Mills. "So how do we start?"

Over the next several hours, Club Phoenix teased together a basic outline for the work that would consume them for the next three months. Merriweather considered the project so important that he even excused Bridges from bridge-watch duties and delayed his next scheduled turn in a stasis pod.

In the ensuing weeks, Dr. Girard was drafted into the club for his expertise. He turned out to be a top-notch software coder and highly proficient in using CAD software and the 3D printer, which they would need to fabricate many of the parts required.

The primary concept involved the development of a plasma magnet designed to capture and store antiprotons found in the radiation belt of Hypatia-f, similar to the collectors placed around Saturn. The Phoenix collector planned to use four loop antennas, each with a diameter of two hundred meters, extending outward from the collector like petals on a flower. These "petals" would generate a plasma magnet, effectively capturing the antiprotons and channeling them into the containment vessel.

The remaining components of the Phoenix collector included a specialized electronics module, an HFC power source repurposed from a mining robot, two large tanks holding extra liquid hydrogen and oxygen for the fuel cells, and an ion propulsion engine salvaged from *Endeavor's* emergency beacon reserve.

One difficulty was getting the unwieldy contraption to and into orbit around Hypatia-f. They would have to collapse the design to make it more manageable and then expand it once in orbit. A second problem was keeping the device oriented precisely in Hypatia-f's magnetic and radiation fields.

Mills ultimately solved both problems by designing a mishmash of gears, gyroscopes, and laser rangefinders, plus a dash of engineering magic. Ultimately, everyone on the ship contributed to the effort. Finally completed, three days short of the launch deadline, the ISA Phoenix rested in Endeavor's cargo hold. The loop antennae were coiled tightly around spools and ready to be expanded to full size once in orbit about Hypatia-f.

Mills had tested the software extensively, and the antenna expansion mechanism underwent multiple tests until everyone was confident that the makeshift design would function properly. Finally, Captain Merriweather declared the new ship ready to go.

"Isn't she the most beautiful thing you've ever seen?" Bridges exclaimed to his fellow Phoenix Club members. "You guys should be proud of the work you've put into it. I, for one, can't wait to see her fly."

Captain Merriweather gathered the officers, crew, and guests on the bridge to witness the launch of the newly created antiproton collector, the Phoenix. As befitting the launch of any new ISA ship, Endeavor's crewmembers wore their dress blues to mark the momentous occasion. Merriweather ordered RHODA to shut down the TAMARAK engines and cease ship rotation to facilitate the launch. Milo Bridges and Jonathan Mills, dressed in EVA gear, waited in the depressurized cargo bay, ready to launch the new ship. The cargo bay door fully opened, affording Bridges and Mills a spectacular view of the cosmos. Each held one end of the newly built ship as it floated weightlessly.

Finally getting a signal from the bridge, the two crewmates shoved the four-ton vessel out of the cargo bay and watched as it slowly drifted away from Endeavor.

"Phoenix is away," said Bridges into his helmet communicator.

"We copy," answered Merriweather.

"Attention," barked Stoner.

Immediately, the officers and crew of Endeavor snapped to attention, as did the four civilian scientists.

"Gentlemen and ladies," began Captain Merriweather. "Lieutenant Bridges came to me with this cockamamie idea three months ago. Three months later, thanks to hard work by the entire crew, we are about to launch that cockamamie idea toward another planet. While we fully expect ISA to mount a rescue effort to find us, it is prudent that we try our best to find our own way home.

"So today, by the authority vested in me by the International Space Alliance, I hereby christen the new spacecraft, Phoenix."

"Company, salute!" barked Stoner.

"RHODA, engage ion propulsion on the Phoenix," commanded Merriweather.

Moments later, the telltale blue-green plasma stream appeared behind Phoenix as she briskly accelerated away from Endeavor.

"May she find fair winds and following seas," said Merriweather.

An hour later, the crew and passengers of Endeavor held their first celebration since leaving Earth orbit. Merriweather suspended temporarily ISA's prohibition of alcoholic beverages. Doctors Lee and Martin concocted passable vodka from the ship's store of potatoes, and Cortez created a decent Margarita blend from other ingredients grown in the hydroponics bay. Bridges donated his collection of twentieth-century music and was the first to inquire about a dance partner.

"Lieutenant, may I have this dance?" asked Bridges.

Cortez, momentarily surprised, gladly acquiesced, and a second later, they were trying their best to dance to Tom Jones's "It's Not Unusual." A few seconds later, Captain Merriweather cut in, followed shortly after that by Stoner. Cortez and Doc Lee happily obliged every dance request while Zoe Bishop quietly demurred.

Later, Merriweather pulled Milo Bridges aside for a quiet word.

"Milo, losing our FTL drive was a devastating blow. Some doubted we'd be rescued as quickly as I suggested. I was proud that the crew took the news as well as they did. But I also knew we were one problem away from losing that sense of calm. What you did cannot be overstated. Whether or not it works is not as important as the feeling that we are improving our odds. You just might have saved us all, Milo. For that, you have my sincere thanks."

"Thank you, Captain," was all Bridges could say. "Thank you."

*Flyby, four months after the Phoenix launch*

Led by Dr. Mann, the four scientists aboard Endeavor were busy collecting as much data as possible from the fast-moving dwarf planet Ulysses as it rapidly approached the starship. The exoplanet's extremely elliptical orbit made it a poor candidate for life, at least life as understood by Endeavor's scientists. Endeavor's instruments detected liquid water—a major indicator of the possibility of life. However, Ulysses was a frozen planet during most of its seventeen-year orbit, producing meltwater lakes only during its close approach to the star. Nevertheless, in the interest of science, Merriweather instructed his XO to launch a probe. The small satellite would orbit the planet, collecting and archiving data until some future spacecraft was in range to collect it.

"Endeavor, this is your captain," Merriweather announced on the ship's speakers. "We will begin our flyby maneuver in approximately fifteen minutes. We will reach periapsis, or closest approach, fifteen minutes after that. At that moment, we will fire our main engines for thirty seconds. We expect the planet's gravity, velocity, and engine burn to give us a delta-v of approximately eight thousand km/h. That doesn't sound like a lot, but it will get us where we want to go weeks earlier. So, everyone, take your stations. We will stop the ships' rotation to prepare for firing our engines. So, make the ship ready for zero g, captain out."

After a few nervous comments, the crew silently reflected on the possibility of a pending calamity. The main engines had so far performed flawlessly. But Dutch was no longer in charge, and his knowledge of chemical rocket engines was no longer available to ensure a successful outcome. Was this the time their luck would change?

*Thirty minutes*, thought Merriweather, checking his watch.

Thirty minutes seemed like an eternity to Merriweather. He had put the ship's AI in charge of the entire operation, so the only thing he could do was monitor the time. He knew that at the exact time required, RHODA would fire the engines. The engines would burn for the precise duration needed to achieve the perfect trajectory. Merriweather also knew that NASA and ISA knew much more about the gravitating body in every other flyby they had performed. Years of study compiled vast amounts of knowledge about a planet's structure, composition, and its gravitational properties. Endeavor didn't have that luxury. Instead, RHODA would perform real-time analysis of the planet below and make real-time adjustments to Endeavor's attitude control and the engine burn. He had tremendous faith in RHODA, but that didn't mean Merriweather wasn't worried.

He checked his watch once again. Ten minutes to go. Ulysses was now filling the forward holoview, bulkhead to bulkhead, deck to overhead. Merriweather felt like he could almost reach out and touch the ice mountains that soared above the planet's surface. He also felt a slight change in Endeavor's attitude and heard the firing of the ship's hydrazine thrusters. Ulysses' gravitational attraction was now bending the ship's trajectory, although neither Merriweather nor the crew could feel the change in direction. However, out of an enhanced sense of responsibility for the crew, Merriweather crossed his fingers, lowered his head, and said a silent prayer. Dr. Mann watched the event in the only place on the ship with an actual window, the ship's cupola. The cupola was a transparent dome on the underside of the spacecraft, favored by the scientists for its three-hundred-and-sixty-degree unobstructed view of the cosmos. There Mann sat with his high-resolution handheld camera, waiting for the event like a child waiting for Christmas morning.

Others chose the relative comfort and the six-tenths gravity of the ship's galley and its large video display.

Lieutenants Bridges and Cortez joined Don Stoner and the captain on the bridge to watch the event on its theater-sized forward display.

"Bridges, do you like classical music?" Merriweather asked in that easy, dispassionate manner he often displayed in stressful situations.

It caught his young lieutenant off guard. Bridges thought for a moment before replying. "Well, I guess I like some of it—the well-known pieces everyone knows. But I'm certainly no expert."

"How about you, Cortez?"

Cortez thought for a moment before replying.

"My mom was a classically trained violinist, and classical music always played in our home. But I rebelled against it, so other than a few violin pieces such as Mozart's Violin Concerto Number Three or Korngold's Concerto and Mendelssohn's E Minor Opus—she positively loved that one—I'm not very knowledgeable," she replied.

"Yeah, not very knowledgeable. I see that," laughed Bridges.

"Stone, I hate to ask, but what's your favorite classical piece?"

"Anything by John Philip Sousa," he replied.

"I'm not sure Sousa qualifies, but I'll accept it," said Merriweather, chuckling.

"RHODA, play music from my digital collection—*The Planets*," said Merriweather. "Pipe it ship-wide."

A second later, the stirring opening stanza filled the ship with an immediate reaction from the crew.

"What the," exclaimed Mills, clearly startled.

"I know that piece," said Girard. "It's called, uh, damn, I can't remember."

"*The Planets*," said Martin.

"Very à propos," said Girard.

"Well, look at you," said Lee, talking to Martain. "How'd you get so smart?"

"Clemson University, baby."

"Party school," she replied.

"I think the captain wants to spice up the flyby with some dramatic music," said Girard.

"Well, it's certainly working," said Mills.

"What were you expecting?" said Martin.

"I dunno, maybe some shaking or something. Shouldn't we be feeling some kind of sensation? We're pretty dammed close to that planet down there."

"You were hoping for a little ball rattling, Mills?" said Martin.

"I didn't expect boring," said Mills. "There's no shaking, no heavy gees, no nothing."

Doc Lee turned to Mills and smiled. She could see that he was anxious—his 'boring' comment notwithstanding.

"Jon, I went through multiple flybys when I was part of the Mars medical detail."

"How so?" said Mills.

"I made a few trips on the Aldrin Cycler," Lee replied.

"Ooh, that's cool," said Mills.

"You did that?" said Bishop. "I once had Buzz Aldrin's great-great-grandson on *Space-Time*, and he had just authored a book about his famous ancestor. What was it like—the Aldrin Cycler, I mean?"

Doc Lee smiled. "It was exciting at first. I remember taking a shuttle into orbit to catch it, and it was my first time in space."

"How old were you?" asked Cortez.

"None of your business. Once we got into orbit, we docked with another ship called the SPACER, which stood for Space Rendezvous if I recall. We would then rendezvous with the Cycler as it rounded Earth. The Cycler was a larger spacecraft that would fly back and forth continually between Earth and Mars in a kind of figure-eight pattern. It would use a close flyby of Mars to slingshot it back toward Earth, then a flyby of Earth to return to Mars."

"I heard it was pretty comfortable for a spacecraft back then," said Bishop.

"It was," replied Lee. "Comfortable staterooms, a large communal area, and it rotated like Endeavor to create artificial gravity. It would pick up supplies when it picked up passengers, so it always had fresh food.

"Anyway," she continued, "we took the SPACER into a much higher orbit where we met up with the Cycler as it rounded Earth. We would rendezvous with and transfer into the Mars lander when we got to Mars.

"To come home, we just reversed the process. I took the Cycler three round trips. It was much like a long sea voyage."

"Sounds like—"

"Five minutes to main engine ignition," announced Merriweather, interrupting Mills mid-sentence.

Merriweather's ship-wide announcement focused everyone's attention back to the current situation. Doc Lee could see the anxiety level ratchet up in Mills' eyes. She felt for him in more ways than one. He was cute, funny, and unattached as far as she could determine. If they survived the flyby, she might try to get a bit closer to Endeavor's tech officer.

As the seconds ticked down, Lee glanced at each of her fellow crewmembers riding out the flyby in the ship's galley. Some kept their eyes glued to the large display now filled with giant craggy ice mountains soaring upwards of five kilometers and kilometer-deep crevasses radiating from impact craters on the planet frighteningly close below. Some had their eyes closed as if meditating. A couple mouthed silent prayers.

"Ten … nine … eight …" announced Merriweather, counting down to engine ignition. As the countdown reached zero, Endeavor's main engines roared to life. As in earlier firings of Endeavor's chemical rockets, crew members could feel the tremendous force of the fuel-gulping engines. The rattling and buffeting Mills had expected suddenly became a reality. The ship felt like it was shaking itself apart. Mills gritted his teeth, a low guttural sound forcing its way from his clenched lips. Doc Lee glanced at him with motherly concern, and she wanted to take him into her arms to comfort him. Just then, Dr. Girard let out a loud "Yeee-haw," resulting in a tremendous release of tension and much laughter from the crew—even Mills.

"How do you say that in French, Paul?"

"I believe the proper translation would be 'Yeee-haw,'" laughed Girard.

Dr. Mann was happily snapping pictures in the cupola, blissfully unaware of the tension in the ship's galley.

On the bridge, Cortez grasped Bridges' hand, interlacing her fingers with his. He turned to look at her and smiled, prompting her to smile and lower her head demurely.

For the next twenty seconds, all eyes were on Ulysses as it rotated slowly below them. It seemed to most that time had stopped.

"Ten seconds to MECO," announced Merriweather, referring to Main Engine Cutoff.

Mills reacted as if startled by the sudden announcement, an almost imperceptible yelp escaping his clenched teeth.

"Nine... eight... seven... six..."

As Merriweather's count reached zero, Endeavor's engines became silent, and the vibrations ceased. Instantly, everyone in the ship's galley cheered. Cortez squeezed Bridges' hand, and Merriweather uttered a silent "amen."

After conferring with RHODA, Merriweather would announce to the crew that the flyby had been successful, and that Endeavor was now blazing along at her new velocity of 63,250 kilometers (about 39,301.73 mi) per hour. Endeavor's speed would continue to increase slowly but steadily under the impulse of her plasma engines until she reached Sanctuary's orbit, still months away. The knowledge that they had shortened their journey cheered the crew considerably.

Merriweather knew there were still unknowns and challenges ahead. Still, he and his crew were happy to have survived yet another day and now had their sights on the possibility of making their first contact with an alien civilization.

On the planet Ulysses below, unbeknownst to Endeavor's crew and buried under kilometers of ice, lay the remains of a once-thriving society, including a young astronomer named Wapoe.

# CHAPTER 28

*Time to get up, again*

"Good morning, Lieutenant," whispered Medical Officer Jennifer "Doc" Lee. "Rise and shine."

Milo Bridges slowly opened his eyes. The pain in his temples made him wince. He raised his arm to shield his eyes from the overhead lights and felt a pain in his shoulder. "Ow," he said, grimacing. He tried to speak, but his mouth wouldn't cooperate. He rubbed his lips, trying to say, "Where am I?", but it came out as a confused, "Wham I?"

"Take it easy, Lieutenant," said Lee. "Don't rush it. You're just coming out of stasis."

Lee helped Bridges sit upright and began removing telemetry probes attached to his skin. She had already removed the catheter before waking him, per the standard operating procedure.

He suddenly leaned over to vomit. Lee handed him a bag.

"Don't mess up my med bay," she said.

Bridges took a deep breath. "Damn, w-worst part of space travel—waking up from f-freaking stasis."

"You're a big baby," said Lee.

"What m-month is this?" Bridges asked.

"June," answered Lee. "Why, do you have an appointment somewhere?"

"No, just trying to get my b-bearings. So, I was under, uh damn, how long?"

"Five months," said Lee. "One hundred and fifty-six days, to be precise."

"Shoulder hurts," Bridges said as he tried stretching out the kinks.

"It's not unusual to suffer a few stiff joints, Milo. The pain should go away in a few minutes."

Lee helped Bridges to his feet and steadied him until his balance returned.

"Any news about—Sanctuary?" Bridges asked.

"Captain Merriweather can fill you in on all the juicy details, but we're getting ready to light off the damn engine again, as if my nerves weren't already shot," said Lee.

Bridges grimaced as he rubbed his shoulder, a puzzled look on his face as if Doc Lee was speaking in some foreign language. Finally, he stared at her.

"On the details? What details?" Bridges asked.

"If you must know, we've received some EM (electromagnetic) transmissions coming from that direction," smiled Lee, helping Bridges out of his stasis pod.

"We've made contact?" Bridges asked, clearly agitated.

"Calm down, junior. No one's contacted anyone," answered Lee, "especially me."

Medical Officer Lee studied her tablet, which displayed Bridges' vitals.

"Take a deep breath," she said.

Bridges took a deep breath. "What do you know about the transmissions? Are they radio frequency, x-ray, infrared, any structure that might indicate intelligence?"

The words rushed from Bridges' lips in rapid fire.

"You'll have plenty of time to review the data and listen to the recordings. Right now, you've got to calm down because your blood pressure is through the roof," said Lee. "Drink this." Lee handed Bridges a squeeze bottle with a clear liquid.

"Not that crap again," he replied, grimacing.

Watching him down the liquid, Lee turned her attention back to her tablet.

"OK, you're good to go. Don't exert yourself for the next 24 hours. Don't run any marathons or engage in any strenuous sexual activities." She smiled but didn't look at Bridges, who was lost in thoughts of alien contact and didn't immediately comprehend what she had said.

"What was that?" he shouted as Lee walked away, pretending not to hear him.

Bridges showered slowly and dressed before heading to the galley in search of answers.

As he walked by Dr. Girard's quarters and saw the door open, he raised a fist in the air and pantomimed a knock. "Doc, have you got a minute?"

"*Entrez*, Milo. Come in. Glad to see you up and about," said Girard.

"I feel like crap. Do you hate stasis as much as I do?"

Dr. Girard responded with a quick smile and a chuckle. "Perhaps more. You've heard that rumor already, have you—about the little green man?"

"Doc Lee told me we've received some EM signals," responded Bridges, looking slightly confused.

"Well," continued Girard, "they're radio frequency, but labeling the signals anything but natural is premature. Not sure what they are yet. We let the crew listen to some transmissions, and there was a repetitive noise that maybe had structure, but we have no idea what it means. I would not yet call it intelligent."

"Can I hear them?" asked Bridges.

"Yes, of course. But the entire crew is getting together to talk about it in," looking at his watch, "about thirty minutes. Afterward, we can return to my station and listen to some transmissions. I'd like to get your opinion."

"Thanks, Dr. Girard, I mean Paul. Looking forward to it," said Bridges as he left to find something to fill the hole in his stomach. Thoughts raced around in his head. *This could be first contact*, he thought. *Holy shit. This is what I trained for. Damn.*

His thoughts turned to his grandparents, as they often did during pivotal moments in his life. He wanted to make them proud. "Damn!" he said aloud. "First contact!"

"Thanks, everyone, for coming," said Merriweather. "I know you are all looking forward to getting more information about our mission and who or what is waiting for us in about three months. First, let's address the most important item on the agenda and why you are here—the piss-poor coffee." Mills groaned. Everyone else laughed.

"The CUBE is acting up again. Mills, I thought you fixed it."

"Sorry, captain. I thought I had it fixed, too."

"Take another look at it, Lieutenant," replied Merriweather. "Okay, second on the list is the possibility of alien contact."

"Second on the list?" said Bridges.

Even Mills laughed at this one.

"Well, we have to keep our priorities straight," said Merriweather.

"In all seriousness," continued Merriweather, "I know you have questions. From a navigational standpoint, we are slightly over three months from our target."

Merriweather turned on the holo-projector.

"To achieve orbit around *Hypatia-Proxima*, the red dwarf, we will need to do a burn to reduce our speed to just under a hundred and ten thousand kilometers per hour, so we'll have to use Bertha. What's Bertha's status, Jon?"

"Good to go, Captain."

"Good. I've scheduled the burn for three days from today. This should put us in orbit around *Hypatia-Proxima*, outside the orbit of Sanctuary. RHODA, show *Hypatia-Proxima*."

A second later, a floating 3D image of the dwarf star the size of a grapefruit appeared above their heads.

"RHODA, show Endeavor's projected trajectory after burn one."

The AI complied by encircling the star with a dotted red line showing Endeavor's planned orbit.

"Include Sanctuary's orbit."

A second red line appeared, showing Sanctuary's orbit inside that of Endeavor's.

"As you can see, once we gain orbit, we will be ahead of Sanctuary and in a wider orbit. This means we will need a second transfer orbit burn, which will occur two weeks after the first burn. RHODA, show Endeavor's orbit after burn two."

The red line showing Endeavor's orbit now paralleled Sanctuary's, with Endeavor trailing the planet.

"From this position, it will take about two months to catch up with our destination," continued Merriweather.

"Once we rendezvous with Sanctuary, we plan to position the ship at L2 (Lagrange point two), outside the larger of her two moons, effectively shielding us from detection.

"From that vantage point, we will continue observing the planet and any potential life forms we might find there."

Merriweather paused briefly to sip from his coffee mug.

"Ship's resources are holding, and we don't anticipate rationing. The hydroponics bay is producing adequately, thanks to the valiant efforts of our medical officer and resident nutritionist," he said, glancing at Doc Lee.

"Don't forget Cortez," said Lee. "I know she's in stasis, but she deserves a ton of credit."

"Of course, thanks to Lee and Cortez," corrected Merriweather

"Water supplies," he continued, "and breathable air are at adequate levels as well.

"But I know that is not what you want to talk about. I'll let Dr. Girard fill you in. Paul."

The attention of the crew turned to Paul Girard in anticipation.

"Thank you, Captain," Girard began. "First, let's address the EM transmissions. Many of you have listened to the recordings, and some of you have interpreted the various sounds we've captured—the whistles, clicks, etc.—as an alien language. Let me be clear. We have not determined that what we are hearing is a spoken language from an intelligent being. It is too early to make that call. We are still in the signal-processing phase of our research. Eventually, we will have a clearer understanding of what we are hearing. But we have been cataloging and indexing the sounds, looking for patterns. This is protocol. Eventually, our language processors will ferret out any structure the transmissions might have if, in fact, it is a language.

"Once we have a structure, then we will attempt to apply context. To do that will require direct observation of the source. If it comes from a sophont species, we will need to understand their culture as well. Once that happens, language translation and understanding should progress more rapidly. This isn't easy. Nor is it something that we can accomplish overnight. It takes time."

Dr. Girard paused and waited for a response. Momentarily, a hand went up.

"Yes, Zoe."

"Paul, if it is a spoken language, does that tell us anything about their physiology?"

"That's a question for Dr. Martin. However, since Mike's in stasis, I'll try to answer.

"We don't want to jump to conclusions like assuming they are humanoid or even that they have mouths or vocal cords in the sense we understand the terms. We know that some species on Earth, such as goats and parrots, can make sounds very similar to human-like speech. There is also some historical evidence of now-extinct tribes in sub-Saharan Africa that communicated in a tonal language consisting largely of whistles. We also know that dolphins communicate using whistles and clicks and can mimic human speech. Therefore, we cannot rule out the possibility that what we're hearing is an alien language. However, we all agree that we will need eyes on the subjects before we can answer those questions."

After a few more general questions, Girard looked at the captain, who nodded.

"Before we adjourn, I want to play you a piece of the transmission that I played for the captain before the meeting. But I caution you, we have not thoroughly analyzed the sound yet, so do not draw any conclusions.
"RHODA, play recording Girard-1302, S'il vous plaît."

As the crew listened, a cacophony of whistles, shrieks, and vocalizations emanated from the ship's speakers.

"Sounds like seagulls and crickets," said Bishop.

"Sounds like porpoises to me," added Bridges.

"Keep listening," said Girard, holding his finger to his lips as if to shush his shipmates.

The ship's crew and passengers grew quiet as they concentrated on the sounds they were hearing. Suddenly, mixed in with the alien noises, something sounded familiar.

"Is that what it sounds like?" said Bishop.

"As I said, it's too early to draw a firm conclusion. But, yes, it sounds very much like it to me, too," said Girard. "It sounds like laughter."

# CHAPTER 29

*Bishop and Merriweather*

Endeavor's cupola was quiet, bathed only in the shifting glow of a nebula beyond the ship's transparent observation dome. Captain Merriweather found Zoe Bishop already there, her body pressed inside the glass bubble, coiled like a serpent, holopad tethered to her arm and drifting lazily at her side.

He hesitated. For once, Merriweather, who could command a starship with ease, seemed uncertain of his next move.

Bishop looked up. "Captain. I thought you avoided this place. Too sentimental—wasn't that your line?"

Merriweather drifted closer in the weightless air. "I said it was unnecessary. I stand by that. Staring at glowing clouds doesn't repair engines."

She smirked. "True. But it does wonders for morale. Or are you suggesting morale matters less than your engines?"

"So, you're the morale officer now? Congratulations."

"I do my part," she said. "Or don't you think what I do is important?"

"Sure, I do. Every crew needs a pain in the ass."

Bishop laughed a little too loudly in the stillness. "You're getting better at this—jokes, banter. Almost human."

He tilted his head. "Careful, Bishop. That sounded dangerously close to a compliment."

She crossed her arms, feigning a defensive pose. "Don't get used to it. I'm just... acknowledging progress. From adversary to tolerable company. A shocking trajectory."

Merriweather allowed himself the faintest smile. "And where exactly does that trajectory end?"

The hum of life support filled the pause that followed.

Bishop shifted, turning toward him. "That depends. On whether the captain in question ever learns to stop hiding behind regulations and efficiency reports."

Merriweather's eyes narrowed—not with anger, but with the wary focus of a man stepping onto uncertain ground. "And if he did?"

"Then," Bishop said, her tone edged with mock-cheerfulness, "he might qualify as someone I'd have coffee with. Maybe even a second cup."

Merriweather chuckled. "I'll make a note. Priority mission objective: acquire coffee. Double ration."

Their eyes met, and this time neither looked away. The nebula's colors washed across the deck, painting them both in shifting light.

Bishop broke the silence with a crooked grin. "Well. This is awkward."

Merriweather nodded. "Terribly. Let's schedule another awkward moment tomorrow, same time."

"Don't push your luck, Captain," she said, though her smile lingered.

# CHAPTER 30

*Sanctuary and Erebus*

As Endeavor continued to close on the planet Hypatia-Proxima-b (its official name), the crew got its first close–up view. Sanctuary, the name given to it by the crew, glowed in the indigo-blackness of space. Bright blue-green and tinted slightly pink by its red dwarf parent sun, with swirling cloud formations and polar ice caps, Sanctuary was amazingly like Earth. The undulating blue-green aurorae stretching from pole to pole offered evidence of the planet's strong magnetosphere. Two magnificently beautiful moons floated nearby—one a reddish-brown orb with a thick churning atmosphere, the other a much smaller, brilliantly white moon similar in appearance to the Jovian moon Enceladus.

Darkness was just beginning to creep over the planet as Endeavor's thrusters fell silent.

The crew watched in fascination as a blizzard of lights on the surface presented spectacular evidence of the existence of an alien civilization.

"I guess there is no doubt now," said Merriweather.

"Do you think they know we're here?" asked Bishop.

"Don't know. Hope not," said Merriweather. "I want to say that a meeting of two alien sophont species has never happened before, but that's not necessarily the case. Who's to say other meetings like this haven't occurred throughout the universe? My guess is that it's not uncommon."

"I think you're right, Captain," said Bridges. "We found intelligent life on our first try. That argues for a universe filled with life."

No one said a word for what seemed like an hour, but was only a minute or two. The crew seemed unable to find adequate words to describe the alien planet rotating below them. Or they just wanted to soak it in without the distraction of others' voices.

"Most beautiful goddam thing I've ever seen," said Stoner, breaking the silence.

"More beautiful than Saturn?" asked Bridges.

"Hell, yeah, more beautiful," said Stoner.

"The aurorae are beautiful," said Zoe Bishop.

"That's a consequence of the strong radiation coming from the red dwarf," said Mann.

Bishop rolled her eyes. "Thanks for explaining that to poor little ole me, Doctor," she said.

"Professor, have you thought about what we should name our new discoveries?" Merriweather asked.

"Captain, I think the crew has already named the planet Sanctuary, and I don't think they'd really take to another name, but then again, you're the captain, and by tradition, the choice is yours."

"I'm good with Sanctuary, for now. I was referring to the two moons?"

"Yes, of course," Mann replied. "I was thinking Erebus for the larger moon. Not much light is likely to penetrate that thick atmosphere, and Erebus was the Greek god of darkness and shadow."

"I like it. Erebus it is. What about the smaller moon?" Merriweather asked.

"For the smaller moon, I was thinking Caerus," said Mann, glancing at Merriweather with anticipation.

"Caerus? I'm not familiar with the reference," said Merriweather.

"Caerus is a minor Greek god," replied Mann. "It's the god of good luck and fortune, and we could use all the good luck and fortune we can get," said Mann.

"Can't argue with that," said Merriweather. "I officially christen Sanctuary's smaller moon Caerus. RHODA, note in the records that Captain Jake Merriweather officially designates the moons of Hypatia-Proxima-b, Erebus, and Caerus."

"I will record that information in the ship's log, Captain," said RHODA.

"XO, launch a surveillance satellite and park it at L1. When it's online, pipe the video to all holoviewers. I want the crew to see the planet," said Merriweather, speaking to Don Stoner. "I want a full surveillance package—low altitude reconnaissance satellite and drones once we've chosen proper targets."

Merriweather motioned Bridges over.

"Lieutenant, prepare Aries One for an away mission. Our water and fuel reserves need replenishing."

"Yes, sir," said Bridges.

"The professor says it may be difficult to find liquid water on the surface, so you may have to look for other sources. Fortunately, the daylight side is now facing away from Sanctuary; that should make it easier to look around."

"Erebus?" asked Bridges.

"Affirmative," replied Merriweather.

"Understood," said Bridges.

"I'd like to tag along if I may, Captain," said Dr. Mann. "I may be of some help in finding those alternate sources, and I also have a background in chemistry."

"Very well, Doctor. Bridges, I'd like to get Endeavor's tanks filled immediately in case we have to leave sooner. Also, set up the Sabatier processor. Our methane supply is less than optimal."

"And the Argas extractor," added Stoner. "Our argon tanks are only a quarter full. We're using our TAMARAKS more than we planned."

"Make it so," commanded Merriweather.

"Yes, sir. With your permission, I'll get the gear together and leave as soon as we're ready."

"XO, call Cortez to the bridge," ordered Merriweather.

Don Stoner lifted his holo to his lips and relayed the captain's order.

"Lieutenant Cortez to the bridge."

Five minutes later, Lieutenant Cortez propelled herself headfirst onto the bridge.

"Reporting as ordered, Captain."

"Ah, yes, Cortez, there you are. Hope I didn't pull you away from anything crucial."

"No, sir. I was watching our arrival at L2 from the galley."

Merriweather motioned Cortez to join him near the forward-facing holoview.

"Beautiful, isn't it?" Merriweather said, more a statement than a question.

"Yes, it is," said Cortez. "It looks so much like Earth. I can't wait to get down there."

"In due time, Lieutenant. In the meantime, are you ready for an away mission?"

"Yes, sir, always."

"Good. I want you to set up an observation package on the planet-facing side of Caerus."

"Caerus?"

"Yes, the smaller of the two moons. You can thank Dr. Mann for the name," said Merriweather. "Caerus is tidally locked, so we'll get data twenty-four seven from our instrumentation package," he explained.

"Oh, and by the way, when you compute a trajectory there and back, remember that we want to keep our presence here secret. Keep Caerus between you and the planet as much as possible until you reach orbit. Let me see the plan before you depart," said Merriweather.

"Yes, Captain," said Cortez. "Is there anything else?"

"That's all," said Merriweather, dismissing his junior lieutenant.

Watching Cortez exit the bridge, Merriweather reflected on the lives of those under his command. He had confidence that his officers could execute his orders, but he couldn't help but constantly remind himself that this was a dangerous job. Space was a hostile environment. Once you forget that fact and start taking your safety for granted, that's when the dangers that surround you would leap up and bite you in the ass. The death of his old friend Dutch Swenson was proof.

Merriweather also knew there was danger in being risk averse. This was the job. All his officers knew the risks and readily accepted them. Merriweather took comfort in knowing that he wouldn't ask his crew to do anything he wouldn't do himself, but he also knew that his position as captain of Endeavor required him to delegate. That said, it was hard not to be protective of his junior officers, especially Bridges and Cortez.

In her quarters, Cat Cortez began preparing for her assignment, employing all her training, skill, and experience. Her captain had entrusted this mission to her, and she was eager to justify his confidence in her abilities. Meanwhile, Lieutenant Bridges was already backing his LAV away from Endeavor's port-side docking hatch. A series of thruster bursts and a few moments later, Bridges, Dr. Mann, Javi Rodriguez, and the spaceship Aries One were plunging toward the surface of Erebus.

"Not a bad career you've chosen for yourself," said Mann.

"Truth be told, Doctor, I've been preparing for this mission ever since I graduated from the ISA Academy," replied Bridges.

Sensing an increase in turbulence, Dr. Mann said, "I assume you did a proper atmospheric analysis."

"Of course, well, RHODA did, anyway. RHODA, the professor wants to hear your atmospheric analysis of Erebus."

"Lieutenant Bridges, do you want me to repeat the atmospheric analysis?" RHODA asked.

"I believe I just said that," said Bridges.

"Erebus' atmosphere comprises 64.4% nitrogen, 10.7% methane, 10.5% oxygen, 8.2% carbon dioxide, 3% argon, 2.1% hydrogen, and 1.0% sulfuric acid. There are trace amounts of ethane, acetylene, propane, and hydrogen cyanide. Atmospheric pressure is 45 kilopascals at the surface and approximately 13.6 kilopascals at eight thousand meters."

"Thanks, RHODA," said Bridges. "What do you think, Doctor?"

"The moon seems to have all the resources we need," said Mann. "It's just a matter of locating them."

"Agreed," said Bridges, somewhat distracted. "Our wings won't help much at this altitude—air's too thin. However, they should buy us a lift once we get nearer the surface. We should be aero braking any moment now."

As if on cue, Aries' thrusters fired almost immediately, reorienting the spacecraft, and lifting its nose to the sky.

"Positioned for aero braking," RHODA announced.

Bridges kept his eyes glued to his instruments. Thick clouds had reduced his visibility to zero. He had to rely on his instruments and RHODA to keep from slamming into a mountain, plunging into a sulfuric acid lake, or some other such calamity.

Aries One continued to fall through the rust-red clouds, its instruments aiming at a point on the surface six-hundred kilometers below. It was Bridges' first landing on an alien moon with an atmosphere, and he was pumped. He hoped the others didn't notice the sweat beading on his forehead or hear his heart beating, which to him sounded like bongo drums.

As Aries continued its descent, Bridges could see the reddish glow from the LAV's ceramic-beryllium skin tinting his craft's windows. This wasn't as smooth as landing on a rock stripped of its atmosphere, he thought. This was more intense—like landing on Earth. Moments later, Aries began shaking violently, buffeted by Erebus' thickening atmosphere. Bridges paid close attention to his spacecraft's external surface temperatures, now steadily climbing.

The ship's speed fell slowly as it encountered an even denser atmosphere near the surface. At four kilometers, RHODA engaged the LAV's four powerful Artemis engines. The sudden rapid deceleration forced Bridges back into his pilot's seat. As the spacecraft's velocity decreased, so did the glow from the ionized atmosphere surrounding it.

Finally, at twenty-five hundred meters, Aries broke through the thick, swirling clouds, giving Bridges and his passengers a view of a shadowy and sinister-looking landscape.

"Elevation, two kilometers, velocity, 300 knots," said RHODA.

"Switch to manual control," said Bridges, suddenly feeling the release of automatic flight controls.

"Manual control engaged," said RHODA.

"Deploy wings."

The passengers heard the whirl of gears and motors as Aries' retractable wings appeared on either side. They also felt the spacecraft lurch upward as the wings clawed into the moon's thick atmosphere.

"Wings deployed," RHODA announced.

Bridges banked the LAV left and right as he gauged the responsiveness of the ship's controls. Reaching his gloved hand toward the instrument cluster, Bridges throttled back the Artemis engines while simultaneously powering up the auxiliary methane engines for conventional flight mode. "And now I'm a fighter jet," said Bridges as he felt the engines kick in. "This is fun."

"Are you enjoying the trip so far?" Bridges asked Dr. Mann, seated in the copilot's seat.

"Can I open my eyes now?" Mann replied, his voice cracking slightly from the stress he obviously felt. "I guess you never get used to this, right? It must be old hat to you and the Lieutenant."

"Right, this is my—oh, let me think—oh yeah, this is my second alien world. It's getting somewhat boring," Bridges joked. "RHODA, take radar and spectral scans of the surface."

"Surface scans in progress, Lieutenant Bridges."

"RHODA, report if you find liquid water."

"I have added your request to my task list," said RHODA.

Bridges brought Aries down to a thousand meters and reduced its speed to a hundred and twenty-five knots. "Can't slow her down anymore and stay aloft in this atmosphere," said Bridges, speaking to himself.

"What's the surface temperature out there, Milo?" asked Mann.

"Looks like sixty degrees Celsius. Warmer than I expected," said Bridges.

"From what I'm seeing down there, I'm not sure RHODA will find flowing water," said Dr. Mann.

"Why not? Too warm?"

"Well, for one reason, Erebus looks very much like a planet in the throes of runaway greenhouse gases—like Venus," said Dr. Mann. "My guess is that high levels of methane, $CO_2$, and sulfur in the atmosphere trapped the heat, causing temperatures to rise and…"

"How about just the abbreviated version?" interrupted Bridges.

"Of course," replied Mann. "If we find any liquid on the surface, it will probably be sulfuric acid or hydrochloric acid pools."

"Are you saying we won't find a source of water on Erebus?" Bridges asked.

"Probably not, but if we can find some sodium hydroxide near an HCl pool, we could do a little chemistry and create some acceptable water," said Mann.

"OK, sounds like a plan. RHODA, can you detect liquid pools of hydrochloric acid on the surface?"

"How the hell should I know?" said RHODA.

*I gotta get that fixed before the captain skins me alive*, thought Bridges. "Do you have any idea where we should look, Doctor?"

"Well, I think—"

"Lieutenant Bridges, I have detected liquid on the surface thirty degrees starboard at fifteen hundred meters," RHODA announced. "There is a sixty-three percent probability it is hydrochloric acid."

"Well, that didn't take long. Thank you, RHODA," said Bridges as he banked the craft to the right. Bridges engaged Aries' powerful landing lights and focused his attention on the planet below and directly ahead of his ship. Suddenly, he saw a large flat surface devoid of detail and, most likely, a body of liquid. Bridges swiveled his head to the left and right, looking for a suitable spot to make a landing.

Not finding anything suitable for a landing strip, he announced, "I guess we're going to have to drop in vertically."

Bridges engaged the four Artemis pod rockets while simultaneously shutting down the methane engines Aries used for horizontal flight. The LAV began to slow and settle toward the surface while Bridges watched the numbers decline in his helmet's heads-up display. A few minutes later, amidst a dust cloud rising from the surface, Aries touched down in a flat spot just twenty meters from a small lake. *Piece of cake*, he thought. *I'm getting pretty good at this.*

"Everyone OK?" said Bridges, turning his head toward his passengers in the rear seats.

"Good here," said Rodriguez.

"Same here," said Mann.

"You said that we'd need sodium hydroxide," said Bridges. "Do you have any idea where to look?"

"Well, we're speaking about lye. It will be a white powdery substance normally found where bodies of salt water once existed but have since evaporated."

"OK. That gives us a starting point," said Bridges. "Your spacesuits will protect you from the sulfuric acid in the atmosphere, but try not to fall into the lake."

Thirty minutes later, Bridges, Mann, and Rodriguez, suited up in their EVA gear, exited Aries to begin their exploration.

"Let's try to keep in sight of each other. Captain would kick my ass if I lost one of you," said Bridges.

Bridges turned slowly to take in the topology of their landing site. Aries had landed on a broad flat plain strewn with boulders, some larger than the LAV. The plain was tilted maybe five degrees, with the lake at the lower end and the rim of a substantial impact crater at the other.

Carrying detection gear, the three crewmates fanned out, scanning for any trace of sodium hydroxide. Bridges moved to the lake's nearest edge and knelt to collect a sample, taking care not to fall in.

Reaching into his equipment pouch—a large pocket sewn into the leg of his EVA suit—Bridges removed a small handheld device called an Isotopic Signature Analyzer. The device was essentially a portable mass spectrometer, which explains its nickname—mass-spec. Next, he released a small scoop attached to the device and carefully dipped it into the lake.

Carefully, he poured the five ml sample into the device's collection port, then closed it with the attached rubber stopper.

"RHODA, analyze the test sample."

"The sample liquid contains hydrochloric acid with a concentration of 10.6 molarity per liter," RHODA replied.

"I've got HCl here," announced Bridges into his helmet mic. "Now, all we need is some lye."

Twenty minutes later, he heard Dr. Mann's excited voice in his helmet speakers. "Bridges—Milo—I think I've found what we need."

"I'll be right there, Doctor," said Bridges.

Bridges bounded over to a shallow depression where Dr. Mann was currently kneeling. The lower gravity allowed Bridges to cover the one-hundred-meter distance, taking long, graceful leaps like a gazelle fleeing a cheetah.

"OK, show me," said Bridges, arriving at the site.

Mann instructed RHODA to analyze a few grams of white powder he scooped from the ground and dropped into his mass-spec device.

"The test substance is sodium hydroxide with trace amounts of sulfur," said RHODA.

"Just what the doctor ordered," said Bridges.

After summoning Rodriguez and consulting with Dr. Mann, they devised a simple plan for water distillation. Rodriguez began unloading the mining equipment from Aries and positioning it between the HCl pool and the sodium hydroxide source.

Bridges and Dr. Mann scouted the nearby terrain and found a suitable depression that they promptly began enlarging. An hour later, Bridges and Mann stopped to take stock of their efforts.

"How big would you say that was?" Mann asked.

"I have a better way," said Bridges. "RHODA, estimate the volume of the depression nearest me and the professor."

"Are you referring to Dr. Mann?" asked RHODA.

"Yes. That's what I meant," said Bridges.

"The volume is approximately five thousand liters," said RHODA.

"There you go," said Bridges. "Five thousand liters."

"I think you rely entirely too much on RHODA," laughed Mann.

"That's what she's here for," said Bridges. "Help me get the plastic sheeting from the ship."

After lining the now-deepened depression with the plastic sheeting, Bridges called his team together.

"Professor, I believe you wanted to say something?"

"Thanks Milo. Yes, I do. Before we mix the lye and the HCl, I wanted to warn you all to be very careful. Adding the two is going to produce an exothermic reaction. There will be a lot of heat and a lot of toxic fumes. Our suits should protect us, but if you smell something, please move a safe distance away."

"OK, you heard him, Javi."

Ten minutes later, using his tablet controller, Rodriguez commanded the tracked crawler with its shovel attached to scoop sodium hydroxide and deliver it to the newly enlarged and plastic-lined depression.

Meanwhile, a long hose connected to a pump began delivering HCl from the lake to the same lined holding pond, producing an energetic chemical reaction and a cloud of fumes belching from the surface. Bridges had retrieved a long paddle shovel from the LAV and was now using it to stir the mixture, occasionally measuring the pH level of the resulting liquid.

"OK, I have a pH of seven," announced Bridges after using his mass-spec to examine a sample.

"Got it," said Mann, turning on a second pump.

The three crewmates watched as the pH-balanced liquid flowed from the holding pond into the Proton Exchange Membrane Electrolyzer (PEME). The gases produced were routed into the cryogenics unit, where they condensed into liquid hydrogen and oxygen, then pumped into large storage bladders in *Aries'* cargo hold.

"Well, that's one," Bridges said. "RHODA, what's our current cargo mass?"

"The cargo load is at thirty-three percent of maximum liftoff capacity relative to this moon's gravity," RHODA responded.

"Okay, team, let's fill the pond two more times," Bridges ordered.

Three hours later, the bladders in Aries' cargo hold were packed with over fifteen metric tonnes of super-cooled liquid oxygen and hydrogen—fuel destined for *Bertha's* tanks.

Satisfied with the haul, the crew paused for fifteen minutes, taking in the stark beauty of the barren landscape. Then, at Bridges' command, they returned to Aries, and prepped the LAV for the journey back to their mother ship.

"Job well done, guys. I think we've done all we can do today. We'll come back tomorrow and do it all over again."

"Shouldn't we set up the Sabatier still today?" Mann asked, referring to *Endeavor's* portable distillery that combined atmospheric $CO_2$ with hydrogen from the PEME unit to produce methane propellant.

"Yes," Bridges replied. "Good call—thanks for the reminder While you handle that, I'll get the Argas unit set up."

Forty-five minutes later, the two processes were up and running, one producing the methane propellant used by the two Aries landers and the second extracting argon gas from the atmosphere to be used by Endeavor's plasma ion engines. Satisfied that they had done all they could, the crew hosed down their suits, then boarded Aries for the return trip to Endeavor.

As Aries rose in the dusty atmosphere of Sanctuary's larger moon, Bridges glimpsed the brightly lit moon Caerus, breaking through the ruddy gloom. He thought of Cortez, hoping she was safe as she proceeded with her own mission. Then he remembered a D.H. Lawrence poem he had learned while growing up in Oklahoma when he was just beginning to court his first love, Ellie Walker. He had bravely sent her an anonymous note with the poem written in his barely legible handwriting.

> *Slowly the moon is rising out of the ruddy haze,*
> *Divesting herself of her golden shift, and so*

*Emerging white and exquisite; and I in amaze*
*See in the sky before me, a woman I did not know*
*I loved, but there she goes, and her beauty hurts my heart;*
*I follow her down the night, begging her not to depart.*[3]

Two-and-a-half hours later, Aries was offloading its precious cargo into Endeavor's storage tanks. When it was complete, Bridges radioed the bridge.

"Bridge, offloading complete."

"Well done, Lieutenant," said the current bridge officer, Don Stoner. "That's enough for today. I'll let the captain know, and he'll decide when he wants you to go back down. For now, you boys have earned some down-time."

"Thank you, sir."

Later, as Bridges lay in his bunk trying to get a few minutes of sleep, his mind turned to Cat Cortez. There she was, thousands of kilometers away, separated from the hostile environment of space by the thin walls of her tiny spacecraft, and he had yet to tell her how he felt. That was the question, wasn't it? How did he feel about her? Was it simply lust, or was it something more? He realized his feelings ran deeper concerning his comely shipmate. What to do about it was the real question.

# CHAPTER 31

*I stayed the cold day with a lonely satellite*

Cortez smiled as she backed Aries Two away from Endeavor. Here was another opportunity to shine—to show her superiors she was as capable as any male pilot in the fleet. Not that her male colleagues ever denigrated her qualifications. In fact, she often received praise from Captain Merriweather, Stoner, Bridges, and others. But in a male-dominated profession, she knew very well that there were detractors. She knew she was good, damn good, in fact. But as a woman, she knew she had to prove it every chance she got. She had to be the best. That's why her feelings for Bridges were so damned complicated. If there were a better pilot in the fleet, it would be Bridges, and here she was on the same damn starship. She couldn't help but feel second best. At the very least, it made her defensive, which drove her to distraction like she was now—distracted.

Bridges hadn't returned from his assignment, and Cortez knew his mission was more dangerous than hers. However, she couldn't think about that.

Pushing those thoughts from her mind, Cortez engaged the engines and accelerated Aries Two away from Endeavor toward the minor moon Caerus.

"Might as well sit back and relax, Jon. It's a long week, there and back," said Cortez. "I hope you brought something to read."

"I brought some tech manuals," he replied, waving his holo. "I need to get more familiar with the TAMARAKS. Hey, is there any chance I could take control for a while?" he replied.

Cortez glanced at her traveling companion with a wry smile. "Control of what? Aries? Do you think you're qualified?"

"Would you teach me?"

"Teach you? Teach you what?"

"How to be a pilot," Mills replied.

"OK, you want to be a pilot? I'll teach you. I have some course notes from the academy that you can borrow. After you've demonstrated some basic understanding of the material, and if the captain OK's it, I will take you out personally and give you some hands-on training—but no shortcuts. If I don't think you're taking it seriously, then forget about it. Understood?"

"Absolutely, and thank you, Lieutenant," said Mills. "Oh, I've got a joke for you."

Cortez groaned and rolled her eyes.

"All right, let's hear it."

"All right, here goes. An alien walks into a bar and orders a martini. 'That'll be one hundred dollars,' said the bartender, adding: 'You're the first alien I've seen around here.' The alien replies, 'A hundred dollars a drink, it's no wonder.'"

"Jon, I heard that one in grade school. You need to up your game," said Cortez.

"You're a tough audience, Lieutenant," said Mills.

The four days passed faster than Cortez expected, thanks to a particularly good novel she was reading. Her traveling companion spent most of his time reading about helicon antennae, magnetic field coils, and ion flux to be much company—when he wasn't peppering Cortez with questions.

On day four, as Aries settled into its orbit around Caerus, Cortez emersed herself in her mission profile notes as she prepared her spacecraft, and her passenger, for her first extraterrestrial landing.

"I don't expect we'll have any problems, Jon. As landing profiles go, this mission is pretty basic."

"But it's your first, right?"

"Yeah, but I've had a great deal of simulator training. Don't worry. I've got this."

"I'm not worried," he lied.

Landing on Caerus required a completely different skill-set than landing on Erebus. Caerus was a small rocky moon devoid of an atmosphere or any substantial gravity. Usually, landing on such a moon in daylight would not be exceedingly difficult. However, that was not their mission. They had to land on the planet-facing side of Caerus, currently cloaked in darkness.

"Night vision mode, RHODA."

"Night vision enabled, Lieutenant Cortez."

"Ah, that's better," said Cortez.

Cortez's helmet face shield now presented her with a ghostly view of the planet's surface features quickly approaching from below. It was unlike anything Cortez had seen before—soaring mountains and deep, rugged canyons as far as the eye could see.

"Jon, this will be like landing in the Alps at night. Finding a flat spot large enough is going to be an issue."

"Like I wasn't worried enough," said Mills.

Superimposed on Cortez's view of the jumbled terrain below their spacecraft was mission-critical information painted on her Heads-Up Display (HUD). The spacecraft's trajectory, displayed on her faceplate as a bright red line, received her full attention, as did her craft's velocity and elevation. Also displayed on her HUD was Cortez's biometric data, including her heart rate, blood pressure, and oxygen usage. Those numbers Cortez tried to ignore.

"Prepare for landing, Mills," she said.

Cortez directed her spacecraft down toward a high plateau formed by what appeared to be lava flows from an extinct volcano.

"Okay, Mills, there's a flat spot. I'm looking for a cluster of boulders—if we set up in a boulder field, it'll help camouflage the equipment and make it harder for the locals to spot us. Wish we had some camo netting, though."

"How about that spot over there?" said Mills, pointing at a spot displayed on Aries' holoview.

The forward camera had swiveled downward and was scanning the surface below, relaying a low-light-enhanced image to the lander's holoview. "I see it. Yes, that should do very well."

A moment later, Aries Two settled gently on Caerus, her Artemis engines at their lowest thrust settings. The lander bounced three or four times before settling in a cloud of ejecta.

"Use helmet lights only—no spotlights."

"I've brought everything I could think of—radiometers, photometers, hyperspectral imaging sensors—plus an ultra-high-res camera with telescopic and multispectral capabilities," said Mills.

"Since you brought all that, let's use it all."

"Absolutely," said an enthusiastic Mills.

"OK. Let's do it," said Cortez.

The landscape was chaotic. Giant boulders, some as large as houses, surrounded the tiny spacecraft. Their helmet lights cast razor-sharp shadows, leaving the rest lit only by the planet hanging above their heads. A fine white powder coated everything.

"Damned spooky," said Mills.

"With your grasp of English, Jon, I can't wait to read your after-action reports," laughed Cortez. "But yeah, damned spooky."

Wearing their EVA suits and bouncing around the surface in the reduced gravity environment of the small moon, Cortez and Mills labored in the semi-darkness. After four hours, Mills finally pronounced everything ready.

"This is pretty neat," gushed Mills. "We'll be able to detect anything in the infrared spectrum, as well as microwaves, gamma rays, and ultraviolet rays. That includes emission spectra of various chemicals in the atmosphere."

"What about plain old audio and video?"

"Of course—with a resolution of about ten centimeters per pixel. If they transmit radio or TV, we can grab those too, and we'll know everything they're saying or doing."

"Feels a little creepy," said Cortez. "I mean invading their privacy like this."

"Yeah, does to me too, but those are the orders."

"Yep, let's turn this turkey on."

A few minutes later, signals from the outpost were being received by Endeavor.

"Signals look strong, Aries, job well done," said Merriweather over Cortez's helmet communicator.

"Thank you, sir. We have some camo work to do here, and then we'll knock off for the night. Lift off tomorrow morning."

"Roger that, Aries. We'll see you in four days."

"Copy that," said Cortez.

Work done, Cortez relaxed and finally allowed herself the luxury of taking in her situation. Here she was, standing on a small rock, twenty-five light years from Earth, just two hundred and ten thousand kilometers from this beautiful alien planet hanging in the dark sky above them. It took her breath away just to look at it.

"What do you think, Mills? Do you think there are beings like us up there?"

"I do. It's hard not to. It looks so much like Earth. The oceans are blue, and there are greens and browns like Earth. There is snow at the poles and clouds everywhere. Wouldn't evolution create the same life forms in the same environment?"

"Well, that's what Dr. Girard believes—convergent evolution."

"Are you looking forward to going up there?" Mills asked.

"Meeting a new species and discovering an alien culture? Absolutely. Think of what they might teach us. Think of what we could teach them. Jon, wouldn't you like to be the scientist that tells them about general relativity or gives them the miracle of penicillin?"

"What about the Prime Directive?" Mills asked.

"You are kidding me, right? There is no such thing, and this isn't the movies."

"Yeah, I know what the ISA's stance on it is, but don't you think there should be?"

"I don't know. Jon, imagine finding an alien race suffering from some disease that penicillin would easily cure. Imagine if we had a Prime Directive that prevented us from sharing it. How would you feel?"

"It would be tough," replied Mills.

"Did you know ISA inherited NASA's old *Office of Planetary Protection*?" said Cortez.

"What?" asked a bemused Mills. "That sounds like something out of a bad sci-fi movie."

"Yeah, it does, doesn't it? But there was an actual organization at NASA by that name," said Cortez.

"And now it's at ISA? What do they do?" Mills asked.

"Well, it is not what you might think. They do not have missile batteries to defend us against invading aliens."

"How do you know what I'm thinking?" Mills asked, feigning surprise.

"Mills, I know you. What they are really concerned about is that we might inadvertently contaminate an alien planet or that we might bring back some alien superbug."

"Still a funny name," said Mills.

"I agree, and I also think a limited prime directive would be a good idea."

The two Earthlings remained quiet as they stood there gazing up at Sanctuary. After a while, Cortez mumbled something to himself.

*Ah, Moon—and Star!*
*You are very far—*
*But were no one*
*Farther than you—*
*Do you think I'd stop*
*For a Firmament—*
*Or a Cubit—or so?*[4]

"What's that from?" Mills asked.

"A poem by Emily Dickinson. I learned it when I was a little girl. It was, uh, oh yeah, 'Ah Moon – and Star.'"

"What's it about?" asked Mills.

"Some believe she was bemoaning her distance from a loved one," said Cortez.

"Milo?" asked Mills.

"Oh, shut up," replied Cortez.

"I couldn't resist," said Mills, laughing. "Say, Lieutenant, do you believe in God?"

The question caught Cortez off guard. She was quiet for almost thirty seconds before she answered.

"I used to. Not so much anymore," she replied.

"Why not?"

"It's been a journey. I guess you can say it results from my belief in science."

"Explain."

"I guess it's tempting to explain everything around us by invoking an all-powerful supreme intelligence. And I don't fault those who do. However, I want to know how something works or why things work the way they do. I need to find answers to the important questions. It's too easy to just say God is the answer. And I've never been one to take the easy way out. My parents raised me to question everything. I guess that's why I am where I am.

"Plus, I don't see a need to insert an unknowable force to explain the universe," continued Cortez. "Science can handle that all by itself. We don't know everything, but science is how we answer questions. That doesn't mean that I don't allow for the existence of a god. But I don't see a need for one to explain what we see. And you?"

"I find the idea of God a comfort," Mills replied. "When I look at Sanctuary, I see a miracle that requires a God. I mean, if there's no God, then who do you thank for the opportunity to stand here and look at this fantastic sight?"

"It is impressive, isn't it?" said Cortez. "OK, here's a question. How do aliens fit into your religious beliefs? For example, since I assume none of the aliens on this planet have accepted Jesus, are they all condemned to Hell? Do they have their own Jesus—their own Hell?"

Mills smiled. "I wondered about that myself. When I told my church I was going on this journey, they were excited for me. More than a few asked if I thought we'd find intelligent life out here. Even my pastor took me aside to ask me."

"Was he concerned?"

"Oh, no. Just the opposite. He was excited for me. Turns out he's a big fan of space travel and a voracious reader of science fiction."

"So, he must have had a thought or two about the subject."

"Sure. He said that he'd given it lots of thought," said Mills.

"And?" said Cortez.

"It was a long discussion, so I'll paraphrase. He figures God tailored the Bible for Earthlings. Aliens would have Bibles suited to them."

"And their own Jesus?"

"Their own manifestation of Jesus, maybe. Plus, not all religions accept Jesus as God."

"Were you a regular churchgoer?" asked Cortez.

"Yeah, when I could. This career isn't exactly conducive to regular churchgoing. Plus, being away from Earth for years makes it impossible. As you remember, I tried to start a weekly service on Endeavor, but there were no takers."

"Sorry about that, Jon. So, what do you do—I mean, do you pray?"

"I meditate some. I brought my Bible."

"How do you think it will affect your congregation when they hear of our discovery?"

"Excited, really. For many, the thought of being alone in the universe would be far more unsettling than the possibility that we're not."

"I agree with that. I was more worried that we wouldn't find anyone. Any thoughts about other religions? What do you think the overall reaction will be?"

"I don't think there is one right answer," replied Mills. "Some will have a hard time accepting it, I expect. Some will deny the existence of aliens altogether. Humans are stubborn. After all, there was still a Flat Earth Society as late as 2095."

"Amazing, right?" said Cortez. "We also threw Copernicus in prison when he said the Earth wasn't the center of the universe."

"That too," said Mills. "However, most will rationalize it—aliens, I mean. They'll have to if they want to survive. Some religions have already accepted the idea. The Mormons say the Earth is but one of many inhabited planets." "Yet other religions preach the idea that we're the center of the universe," said Cortez, "and not, as Carl Sagan once said, 'an insignificant planet circling a humdrum star.'"

"I think we've found our sister 'insignificant planet,'" said Mills.

The conversation lulled as Mills and Cortez watched the planet slowly revolve above them, each lost in their thoughts. Finally, Cortez broke the silence.

"You asked who to thank for the chance to be here, Mills, to see this incredible planet with our own eyes. Well, there's a long list of scientists I could credit for making this possible. I could also spend our entire four-day trip home explaining the formation of stars and planets, all the way back to the Big Bang—without ever needing to invoke some superintelligence to make sense of it. But I won't.

"I get it—people often need a bit of spirituality to help them process the world around them. Let's just say, if God does exist, She did one hell of a job creating Earth and Sanctuary, because they could practically be sister planets. Hopefully, we'll find a race of beings up there we can actually relate to.

"Right now, though, I'm wiped. I'm heading back to *Aries*, zipping into my sleeping bag, and drifting off to dreamland."

"Sounds like a great idea. I could use about ten hours of sleep myself," said Mills.

"You're going to have to make do with five," said Cortez.

# CHAPTER 32



Slowly rising above the horizon, two quarter moons and a bright star hung in the dusky sky. The Endeavor spacecraft, hidden from view by the larger moon Erebus, continued its monitoring of the alien planet. Earthlings Cat Cortez and Jonathan Mills celebrated a successful mission, relaxing in their LAV as it coasted between Caerus and Erebus on its way back to Endeavor.

On the planet, a small creature scurried across the stone floor, clearly agitated, unleashing a torrent of clicks, clucks, and whistles—punctuated by a sound not unlike a drowning cat. Its teacher, however, heard something entirely different. "Teacher, teacher, Caerus has a friend, Caerus has a friend," Yuni shouted excitedly.

The young creature raised an appendage that approximated an arm and pointed toward an open window. In the adjoining room, a larger creature responded.

"What are you on about, Yuni?"

Yuni jumped about excitedly, as any six-year-old human child might do. However, this six-year-old was decidedly not human. Less than a meter in height, the diminutive bipedal creature more closely resembled a grasshopper, albeit one that stood erect and wore clothing. The articulation of its legs (or lower limbs) hinted at an evolutionary path more insect than mammal.

"Caerus has a friend. I can see her through my telescope. She is playing 'See me, see me.' Come see," exclaimed Yuni.

"Be serene, Yuni, I am coming. You have completed your lessons, yes?" chided Yuni's teacher/guardian as she arrived to find her young pupil dancing around like a sartu fly.

"I finished them. Come look," said Yuni, relinquishing her place at the open window where her telescope pointed toward the sky.

The larger bipedal creature stood nearly two meters high with cream-colored skin, a larger than human head and two oversized eyes that protruded slightly from her face. Glowing blue frills extended from either side of her neck, with patches of short white hair just above the frills. The creature ambled over to the youngster on spindly legs that appeared to bend the opposite of humans. Carefully, she bent over and peered through the telescope.

"I see it," said the larger creature, much to the delight of her young tal`-su (student). "Caerus does indeed have a new friend. I wonder who she is." Zara Dualla smiled, her neck frills glowing a brilliant blue—a clear sign of pride among her kind. In Heran culture, the teacher-student bond was sacred, one of the greatest honors a citizen could receive. Dualla felt deeply grateful that the council had entrusted her with this spirited young tal'su.

Zara Dualla, or more formally, Dakar Zara, ninth of Dualla, first of Krei, was an especially important citizen. Not only was she a prominent scientist and chief astronomer of the Quoram science ministry, but she was also practically royalty. She could trace her Dualla tal`estry (roots) back nine generations of teacher-student pairings and was herself taught by the noble Krei, eighth of Dualla, a powerful member of the ruling Ben`lei Council. It was widely expected that Krei would rise to the esteemed role of Akan upon the current Akan's passing, with Zaru then stepping in to claim Krei's seat on the Council.

Zaru beamed at Yuni. She remembered fondly how Yuni had taken to science with enthusiasm. She recalled how she had taught Yuni to make a parabolic mirror by spinning a bowl of moki-bush resin until it hardened and then coating it with pulverized poolau scales.

"Hmm. This is very exciting, Yuni. You may have made a great scientific discovery," she said, caressing the top of the child's head. "For someone so young to make such an important discovery is very unusual. I think this requires a reward. Would you like a treat?"

"Oh, yes, teacher," squealed Yuni as she spun herself around, arm appendages spread wide.

Zaru looked again through the child's toy telescope. There was something there near Caerus. She made a mental note to schedule time on the facility's large telescope as soon as she could.

# CHAPTER 33

*Observation*

Having made his second arduous round trip to the surface of Erebus to find water, Lieutenant Bridges was now working hard alongside Dr. Girard and Dr. Mann, cobbling temporary workstations in a corner of the ship's galley. They hoped to finish the sixth and final station before knocking off for the night. They had been working almost nonstop since returning from Erebus and were exhausted.

Understanding the culture and language of the planet's inhabitants required not only the work of the quantum computer that occupied almost a quarter of the Endeavor spacecraft but also constant surveillance by Endeavor's crew. For the next several months, every crew member would spend most of their time surveilling the aliens. To accommodate this effort, more workstations were required. Bridges, Girard, and Mann were hard at work assembling those additional workstations.

"It's damn inconvenient to have Mills and Cortez on an away mission," exclaimed Girard. "Pass me that cable adapter. Isn't Jonathan supposed to oversee the electronics on this ship?"

"We could use Cat too. She's more at ease with this technology stuff than I am," answered Mann, handing Girard the adapter.

"Guys, we're almost done. So, stop the bitching. What she and Jon are doing is important," said Bridges.

"Well, I need a break. How about something to drink, Herbert?" Girard asked. "How about you, Milo?"

"Sure, coffee for me," said Bridges, "with bourbon, if you have any?"

"We ran out of bourbon the second week out. I'd happily accept a glass of Chardonnay. We must plan better if we take another trip like this," said Girard.

"Oh, hey, Captain, come to check on our work?" asked Dr. Girard, noting Captain Merriweather's entrance onto the ship's galley.

Merriweather had just come from the bridge where he had been communicating with Aries Two, now halfway back from Caerus.

"No, I'm just here for some hot cocoa," he answered as he filled his favorite mug.

"The CUBE's still working, thanks to Mills," said Bridges.

"So far, so good," replied Merriweather. "How are the stations coming? Need any help?"

"I think we've got it, Captain. We're just about done," answered Bridges. "We're already getting telemetry from both orbiting satellites and the outpost on Caerus."

Bridges powered up the workstation he had just completed and typed a few commands on the touchpad. A stream of numbers and tables quickly appeared on the holoview display.

"Here's a list of the radio transmission frequencies we've detected coming from the planet," he said, pointing at one group of figures scrolling on the electronics display.

"We're getting a lot of data on the planet, its atmosphere, spectral scans, and gravimetric data," said Bridges. "I can't wait to launch the surveillance drones. Those alone will keep the entire crew busy."

"That is the point, Lieutenant. Oh, and when you schedule watches for the crew, include me. We'll be spying on our neighbors around the clock, and we'll need all hands on deck," said Merriweather.

"Schedule watches, uh, yes sir," said Bridges, not sure whether to be happy with his new assignment.

"How's RHODA doing with the radio intercepts, Dr. Girard?" asked Merriweather.

"So far, so good," replied Girard. She's building a catalog of different vocalizations, classifying them, and creating statistical maps. Once she gets the signal error down to less than one percent, she will begin building statistical syntax structures."

"You mean like subject, verb, predicate, etc.," said Merriweather.

"If those exist," said Girard. "They are aliens, after all, and their language might be completely uh..."

"... alien," said Merriweather.

"Exactly," said Girard. "Once we know the syntax, we will be one step closer to understanding their meaning."

"And for that, you need context," said Merriweather.

"Correct. Without a Rosetta stone, we will have to watch their activities and interactions."

"I read your paper, Paul. You think it will take months?" asked Merriweather.

"Well, computing has improved since I wrote my doctoral thesis, so it could be quicker than that, but I still say between three and six months."

"Well, if that's what it takes, then so be it. Some of you might hope for some time in stasis before this is over," joked Merriweather.

"I'm ready now," said Dr. Mann.

All eyes turned to Zoe Bishop as she entered the galley.

"Ms. Bishop," said Mann, followed by the same from Merriweather, Bridges, and Girard.

"Professor, captain, guys," said Bishop. "You boys having fun without me?" Zoe had a way of making every remark seem sexual.

"Not as much fun as we could have," said Bridges.

"What are you implying, Milo?" said Bishop in an intentionally suggestive voice.

"I uh," stammered Bridges.

Everyone laughed at Milo's obvious discomfort.

"Are we assuming there are multiple languages down there? You know, multiple countries, like on Earth?" she asked Mann while smiling at Milo.

"Yes, I think we have to assume," said Mann. "RHODA will determine that quickly enough using a statistical analysis of the sounds we are hearing and factoring in the planet's geography."

"How do we decide who to contact first?" Bishop asked.

"I'll take that one," said Bridges, still recovering from embarrassment. "First, we determine how many governments there are and how they rank in size and importance before determining who to contact first. One assumption we've made is that to get that deep into the structure of their geopolitics, we would need the help of a willing collaborator."

"We have to get one of them to help us?" Bishop asked.

"Exactly. Think about it. If it takes a year to break the code of one language, how long would it take to understand twenty—thirty? What if an alien spacecraft visiting Earth just happened to pick Swahili as the first language they decoded? That wouldn't be the best choice for first contact, but you might use that contact as a source of information."

"So, how do we go about choosing this alien spy?" Bishop asked.

"Well, to start, we pick a language associated with larger population centers with clear technology usage. After we decode their language, we find a candidate for first contact. Hopefully, we'll be able to use that contact to build a more complete picture of the planet's geopolitical topology," said Bridges.

"We pick someone who lives in a big city?" asked Bishop.

"No, not necessarily," said Bridges. "We want to keep first contact a secret for as long as it takes to understand what we need to know. The optimal scenario is an intelligent alien—a high-ranking individual or a scientist—

who we can access safely. Perhaps someone who lives in a rural setting."

"Makes sense," said Bishop. "I guess that's why all those alien abductions on Earth happen in the boonies. They're playing by the same playbook."

"Could be," laughed Bridges. "Anyway, that's the desired scenario. If we're lucky, we'll find someone willing to work with us in secret."

"OK, I have a question," said Bishop. "What happens if our chosen collaborator runs to the authorities?"

"Hopefully, that won't happen, but if it does and we can't appeal to their scientific curiosity, then we hightail it out of there and hope the authorities don't believe them," said Bridges.

"Well, I wonder how many of those UFO kooks on Earth were actually telling the truth?" laughed Bishop.

"I've asked the same thing myself," said Merriweather, enjoying the dialogue between his junior officer and reporter.

Merriweather paid close attention to his crew's interactions. He was pleased to see a return to the good-natured banter that had disappeared over the last year since Dutch's death. The crew was much more optimistic now and genuinely excited by the opportunity to study this alien race.

As was he, but that wasn't the only thing he was thinking. Unsaid was the possibility that this planet might be their home for a long time—maybe a lifetime.

# CHAPTER 34

*Dakar Zaru, ninth of Dualla, first of Krei*

Dakar Zaru, ninth of Dualla, first of Krei, referred to semi-formally by her colleagues as Dakar Dualla, was more excited than usual as she headed off to work. She loved her job. As an astronomer, science researcher, and teacher, she got to do the two things she loved most: science and interacting with promising young talent. These were exciting times to be an astronomer (more accurately, "seeker of the motion of celestial bodies" in her language). The Quoram of Science had recently completed a new telescope that allowed researchers to see farther and more clearly than ever before. Dualla was planning to spend time on the new resource to check out the strange object she and her young ward Yuni had discovered the night before.

Dualla had her own theories about the object. If she had her way, she would teach a class on the possibilities of alien life on other planets, but as the daughter of a member of the ruling Council, she had to be more circumspect. It was not only her reputation she had to worry about. The entire Dualla tal'estry could suffer if she wasn't careful. Dualla knew the Council did not share her belief in alien life, especially the head of the Council and the leader of the country itself, the Holy Akan.

As a prominent voice in the Quoram of Science, Dualla's ideas were not easily dismissed. Yet whispers about her credibility circulated quietly around the campus. Even so, her lectures remained consistently well attended.

Eager to start her day, Dualla left her tree-shrouded home on the edge of the small village fifteen minutes earlier than was her usual practice. She didn't take her usual leisurely stroll through the picturesque hamlet. Instead, she hurried along the path as it wound through the groves of fancha trees before finally emerging in the town center, covering the distance in record time.

Dualla would typically acknowledge the citizens who would welcome her to the new day, as was their custom . She enjoyed the close-knit feeling of the small community, which was one of the deciding factors in accepting the post of Chief Astronomer at the new Science Quoram. Today, however, she was in a hurry and preoccupied, so she not-so-politely declined all invitations to stop and interact with the locals.

Barely twenty sols old, she carried an expectation of prestige wherever she traveled, and the local Science Quoram counted themselves fortunate to have a Dualla on their faculty.

Dualla quickly made her way up the busy pathway, dodging the various clusters of scientists and townspeople that often clogged the path, and across the crowded plaza in front of the Quoram's center. Climbing the entrance steps, she encountered one of her colleagues, a low-level supervisor by the name of Glyvash.

Glyvash was one of the more respected male scientists but was still subordinate to every female member of the Quoram. Dualla respected the work he did at the Quoram but disliked his constant fawning.

"Supervisor Glyvash," she said, acknowledging her subordinate in her typically perfunctory manner.

"Your Primacy, pray you slept…"

"Yes, yes, let us not waste time, Glyvash. I have an important matter I wish to discuss with you."

"Me? I am honored. What can I do for my esteemed colleague?"
Glyvash liked to imagine himself a colleague of Dakar Dualla even if her royal lineage placed her far above Glyvash in the social structure. Still, they often worked on the same projects, and she treated him with some tolerance, which was the most any male could hope for.

"I require time on the telescope tonight. Arrange it."

"Tonight? The schedule is full and has been approved by the Council for seven cycles. I really don't see—can I ask the reason?"

Dualla glared at Glyvash. *What impertinence*, she thought.

"If you must know, I believe there might be a small moonlet circling Caerus. I saw it through Yuni's toy telescope last night, and it was very well illuminated and very near Caerus."

"Really, your—toy telescope? Do you really think that warrants…?"
"Glyvash, do not debate this with me. I would not require it if I thought it a trivial matter."

Glyvash recognized at once that he had gone too far. Dualla was his superior. She was also female and a member of the Dualla clan—practically royalty.

"Yes, of course, Your Primacy. I meant no disrespect. I have some time scheduled for myself tonight. Please consider it yours."

"Very good." Then she added, "Your cooperation will be noted."

Her words said one thing, but her tone conveyed her displeasure. *What is it about males?* She thought to herself. *Must one explain every little thing?*

Dualla wheeled about and headed off to her class, muttering, her frills glowing bright red. Glyvash felt sick, wondering how much damage he'd done to his future.

# CHAPTER 35

*Caerus's Friend*

Cortez was catching up on her journal. Sometimes during away missions, there was nothing else to do. RHODA was doing much—or rather all—of the piloting, and Mills was taking yet another nap, so she was alone with her thoughts. She had started her journal shortly after they had departed Earth.

Do all men snore? She wrote. I'd be shocked if the aliens didn't hear him. It's difficult to get into the beauty and grandeur of the scene outside my little spacecraft with that droning going on.

Mills is an OK guy. I've always considered him just a nerd, but to be honest, the guy has some other qualities. He's opened up a bit on this trip, and he thinks about other things than just qubits and qubytes. When we were still on Caerus, he asked whether I believed in God. He obviously does, which was a bit of a surprise for me. Of course, I gave him my standard *I'm a scientist* answer, but my beliefs are a tad more complicated. I've always considered myself to be open-minded, but I had closed my mind to the possibility that there is something there that we don't understand. This trip, our *accidental* discovery of another planet populated with living, thinking beings, seems like something other than pure coincidence. Were we directed here? If we were, then why and by whom? Are we just here to say hello, or do we have a larger purpose?

God, I can't believe I'm writing this. Everything that's happened can be explained using logic, science, and reason. But then again...

Cortez gazed out of her small spacecraft's forward viewport. She had oriented the lander to get the best view of the tiny moonlet Caerus as it receded into the distance.

Cortez could easily see beyond Caerus to the planet below, meaning anyone on Sanctuary could see Aries. There was nothing Cortez could do about it other than hope no one was watching.

Cortez continued to be amazed at what she saw below. She was mesmerized by the lights sprinkled about the planet's surface and the ever-present aurora, the ribbons of blue-green light that danced in the atmosphere. She saw what clearly looked like cities and thoroughfares covering the planet. There was a thriving society down there. *Were they like us, or were they completely alien? Did they think like us, feel like us? Would we be able to make ourselves understood? Would we be able to understand them? Were they dangerous? Did we present a danger to them?*

Cortez imagined that of all the significant discoveries made by our species since we first crawled out of the primordial soup, this might just eclipse them all. Imagine that. They could be on the precipice of the next evolutionary leap for humanity.

For a moment, she envied Milo Bridges. As First Contact Mission Specialist, it would be his job to be the first human to meet them. At some point, if all went well, he would fly down to the surface with Captain Merriweather and introduce Earthlings to the aliens of Sanctuary. How thrilling would that be?

But she would eventually get her opportunity to visit. They all would. With any luck, she would hobnob with the aliens below, teach at an alien university, enjoy strange and wonderful cuisine, and even advance their medical science. Her head was swimming in the possibilities. It was both exhilarating and frightening, and she couldn't wait.

*Still have about eight hours before we get behind Erebus, and out of sight of prying telescopes on Sanctuary,* she thought. *Time for a nap.*

# CHAPTER 36

*Quoram of Science, Large Diameter Telescope*

Dakar Dualla sat with Supervisor Glyvash at the primary control station for the Quoram's powerful new telescope. Dualla had toured the construction site many times during the year she had been on the faculty, but this was her first opportunity to use the instrument since the telescope had come fully online just a week earlier.

"I am honored to demonstrate our new telescope, Your Primacy. This is the most powerful optical device ever built. With it, we can see our universe with more clarity than ever before. It truly is an amazing instrument."

"Thank you, Glyvash. I'm sure it's impressive. But right now, I want to look at Caerus. Please prime the telescope, as I have directed." Dualla was in no mood to listen to Glyvash drone on and on about things of which she was already very well aware.

"Yes, of course," he replied meekly.

Without another word, Glyvash turned his attention to the telescope's control panel, his hands deftly manipulating the controls. Dualla glanced upward as the dome rumbled to life, motors humming and gears clattering like an old clockwork giant. Two sections of the roof parted with a heavy groan, revealing the night sky beyond. The dome continued to rotate for fifteen more seconds before halting with a final metallic clank. Glyvash adjusted the declination controls as Dualla watched the massive telescope slowly tilt skyward.

Seated side by side, Dualla and Glyvash focused on the console's display screen. Together, they watched as the stars scrolled down the screen until the irregular shape of the tiny moon Caerus panned into view.

"It's a significant improvement in resolution, Glyvash."

"Yes, thank you, Dakar," said Glyvash, excited to get his supervisor's affirmation. "See there, craters, ridges, see the detail."

"There will be time enough for that, Glyvash. Right now, I'm looking for something. If I'm right, it will be somewhere between Caerus and Erebus. Focus."

Silently, the two colleagues stared at the tiny display. Slowly, Erebus, the larger of the planet's two moons, filled the screen.

"Hmm. Unfortunately, we still can't see the surface. But you can see darker areas. Perhaps vegetation."

"Yes, indeed," said Glyvash, wisely agreeing with his boss. "Look there," he said with some excitement, pointing at a small bright object on the screen, "between Erebus and Caerus, is that the young child's discovery?"

"Yes, Glyvash, that's what I saw, although it seems much smaller now. Perhaps it has moved farther away."

The two scientists watched silently as the small object moved closer and then seemed to merge with Erebus before disappearing.

"The object has moved behind Erebus, or perhaps crashed upon its surface, Your Primacy."

"I think the former, Glyvash. You are recording this?"

"Yes, of course."

"You can magnify a single frame?"

"Yes," he answered.

Dualla watched Glyvash manipulate controls on his console to rewind and then slowly move forward through the video.

"Go faster," said Dualla, clearly impatient with the pace of her male subordinate. "There, magnify and print out that frame."

"Yes, of course. It will require a few seconds."

Slowly, a photo of the mysterious object emerged from a slot in the console.

"For you, Your Primacy," said Glyvash, handing the paper copy to his colleague. "Can you make out what it is?"

Dualla studied the image with her own magnifying glass for some time before finally admitting that she had no clue as to the object's identity.

"Take this to our image analyst and reply as quickly as possible. This is important, and tell them it is from me."

"Yes, of course, Dakar."

Dualla would have to be satisfied, waiting for the analyst to study the image. After one more glance at the video display, Dualla hurried from the control room.

# CHAPTER 37

*The Briefing*

Lieutenant Cortez expertly guided Aries to a perfect docking at Endeavor's port side docking hatch, a loud clank signaling a successful capture.

"Long field trip, Mills. Glad to be home."

"It's interesting that you consider Endeavor home, Lieutenant. I'm not sure I do—yet."

"I see your point. But I'll be glad to sleep in my bunk tonight."

"Welcome home, Aries," squawked the ship's comm system. "Captain wants you in the galley right away." Cortez recognized the voice of Javier Rodriguez.

"I'm on my way, Javi," Cortez answered.

Cortez scrambled out of her pilot seat and up through the access hatch, floating headfirst into Endeavor. After removing and stowing her spacesuit and helping Mills out of his, Cortez thanked her colleague before turning toward the ship's galley. Using handholds positioned along the walls of the ship, Cortez propelled herself quickly through the microgravity environment of Endeavor's central core and into the hub where the three spokes of the habitat ring attached. Selecting the spoke that led to the galley, Cortez launched herself toward the outer ring. As she progressed through the spoke toward the hab and its artificial gravity, she felt the familiar sensation of "downwardness." She felt her weight for the first time since leaving Caerus four days earlier. Although she knew the centrifugal force provided by the rotation of the hab ring supplied only sixty percent of the gravity found on Earth, it would still take a few hours for her body to adapt.

Cortez grasped and squeezed the sides of the ladder to slow her descent through the spoke as she neared the ring, a technique used by all her colleagues. She entered the ring feet first, dropping the last few feet to the deck. It took her several steps to find her footing. Satisfied she wouldn't fall on her face, Cortez hurried past several crew quarters and made her way to the ship's galley, followed closely by her mission mate, Mills. There she found Captain Merriweather and the rest of Endeavor's crew surrounding the small galley table.

The new surveillance stations that Bridges, Mann, and Rodriguez had recently assembled made the galley more crowded than usual. The crew reserved two seats at the table for Cortez and Mills.

"Welcome home, Cat," said Merriweather.

"Thanks, Captain," replied Cortez.

"First-rate job you did on Caerus."

"Mills deserves most of the credit. I just drove the bus."

"Don't be so modest. Take the compliment."

"Thanks, Captain," Cortez replied, admiring the new workstations along the port side bulkhead. "I like what you've done to the place."

"What? Oh, those," said Merriweather. "The guys did all that in forty-eight hours."

"Impressive," she replied.

"Yes, it is," said Merriweather before turning to address the others standing about the mess deck. "OK, everyone, listen up."
Rodrigues placed a large cup of coffee in front of Merriweather before taking his own place behind the captain. Merriweather simply nodded his thanks.

"The professor is about to give us a rundown of our sister planet."
"In that case, I might need a larger cup of coffee," said Cortez, followed by a chorus of chuckles.

"Maybe one with detailed instructions printed on it," added Rodrigues.

"With a molecular diagram for coffee," said Mills.

The entire crew—even Merriweather—laughed except for Dr. Mann, who looked perplexed.

As the laughter died down, Mann asked in a deadpan voice, "I don't get it," which only reignited the laughter.

Merriweather and the crew of the starship Endeavor were now discovering just what kind of planet they had stumbled upon. Satellite sensors placed in orbit transmitted a steady stream of data about the planet—data carefully analyzed by the scientists aboard Endeavor.

"Earth-like" was the term most often used. Merriweather called it an "Earth Doppelgänger." However, neither term adequately described the planet they had found.

Sanctuary was stunningly beautiful. Bright blue oceans covered seventy-five percent of the planet. Vast stretches of verdant forest covered many of the continents. Ice and snow capped both poles. A mountain range as long as the Andes, with majestic, snow-crested peaks as high as Mount Everest, bisected one of the eight continents. Another continent featured a chain of lakes sparkling like diamonds and stretching over three thousand kilometers. Clouds tinted pink by the red dwarf, reminded Merriweather of frosting on a birthday cake.

At night, the planet came alive with arteries of lights converging like the silk threads of a spider's web glistening with dewdrops. Large urban centers supplied ample proof of a thriving society of intelligent beings. There were highways, cities, farms, bridges, and ocean-going vessels—all evidence of an advanced industrial civilization.

The mood on Endeavor couldn't be higher. Everyone was excited to hear what the sensors had revealed.

After the crew settled once again, Mann began his report.

For the next twenty minutes, Mann covered everything Endeavor's telemetry and surveillance instruments had uncovered about the alien planet—its mass, weight, and atmosphere. The professor was the perfect nickname for Mann, thought Cortez. He gave briefings like a college professor lecturing his class. Cortez could imagine him standing in front of a large blackboard, wearing a sweater with elbow patches, his hands covered in chalk dust.

She looked at the briefing notes she had uploaded to her holo, telling herself she'd review them later. However, the important takeaways from Mann's report were that the Earth doppelgänger they had stumbled upon was a bit larger, somewhat heavier, with stronger gravitational attraction than Earth. That last piece of info concerned Cortez. The Aries lander would require configuration changes to overcome the planet's deeper gravity well.

The planet wide aurora, which seemed like a permanent feature, was most likely caused by a spinning molten core appreciably larger than Earth's. The good news was that Sanctuary had a breathable atmosphere—a little light on oxygen, but nothing they couldn't compensate for. Regardless, Cortez couldn't wait to get down there.

Sensors found little evidence of the burning of fossil fuels—no appreciable sulfur in the atmosphere. This suggested that their society was not oil- or coal-based.

Sanctuary appeared to be an environmental Shangri-La.

After Mann concluded his report and answered a half-dozen questions, Mike Martin began his portion of the briefing, which started with a population estimate of one and a half billion sophonts. *Not too crowded for a planet the size of Earth*, thought Cortez. Martin identified fifteen population centers, each with a million or more inhabitants. Eighty percent of the population lived in the northern and southern temperate zones, ranging from twenty degrees latitude to sixty-six degrees latitude, north and south. Sixty percent of the population lived within three hundred kilometers of an ocean or a major body of water. Martin concluded by saying that Sanctuary was spookily similar to Earth.

Girard spoke next, covering the progress he and RHODA had made in deciphering the alien's language. He concluded by saying that someone might have to go down to the planet to find more information. Cortez and Bridges both immediately agreed with that idea.

Finally, Bridges rose to speak about Endeavor's drone-torpedo technology—not so much for ISA crewmembers, who should already know enough about the technology, but for the civilian scientist and Zoe Bishop.

"Thanks, Captain," began Bridges. "Endeavor carries a complement of four segmented drone torpedoes. Each torpedo carries five drones, four slave drones, and a master drone that controls the other four. Each of these drones includes a high-definition video camera and audio sensor.

"We launch from Endeavor—from the cargo bay. After launch, a small methane rocket engine propels the torpedo to the planet—a journey of about four days," continued Bridges. "After the torpedo has successfully survived entry into the planet's atmosphere, the airbrake and spent rocket engine stage are jettisoned, and the torpedo's wings deploy. A small, super-quiet jet engine powers the torpedo to within several kilometers of the target. At that point, the torpedo breaks apart, releasing the five drones. The remaining propellant consumes what's left of the torpedo, turning it into ash before it hits the ground.

"Won't they see the fireball?" Dr. Girard interrupted.

"We will choose an area far from any inhabited areas," answered Bridges. "However, seen from the ground, it will appear like a simple meteor burning up in the atmosphere.

"The five drones will fly in formation to a point near the target. Once the master drone determines that the area is free of observers, it will scout the area for possible nests for the slave drones, which it transmits to Endeavor. Once we've made the final decisions, the master will then command each of the slaves down to its target nest. Each slave is instructed to attach itself to a vertical or horizontal surface with a view of the surrounding area.

"The master drone then finds a hiding spot on the top of a nearby building and establishes communications with each drone and Endeavor," Bridges concluded.

"Sounds like a marvel of engineering," said Mann. "I, for one, can't wait to see the thing in action."

"Well, it's a complicated process, but if everything goes according to plan, it should give us excellent surveillance," said Bridges.

"And that's what we need," said Merriweather. "However, first, we must choose a suitable target collaborator. We are not there yet. So, unless anyone has something to add," said Merriweather, "no? OK, good report. Now let's get back to work."

## Vital Statistics

### Sanctuary

| | | |
|---|---|---|
| Volume (km³) | 1.19 X 10¹² | 110% Earth Volume |
| Weight (tonnes) | 6.8 X 10²¹ | 115% Earth Volume |
| Orbital period (primary) days | 427 | Hypatia |
| Orbital period (secondary) days | 134.9 | Hypatia-Proxima (Red Dwarf) |
| Rotation period (Hours) | 19 | |
| Axial tilt | 19% | (Earth is 23.4%) |
| Surface gravity (m/s²) | 10.786 | 110% Earth Gravity |
| Temperatures (C) | 10 - 32 | mid-latitudes |
| Atmos. Pressure (kPa) | 109.4 | 108% Earth at surface |
| Atmosphere | – 78% nitrogen<br>– 15% oxygen<br>– 0.04% Carbon dioxide<br>– 7% other elements | |

### Erebus

| | | |
|---|---|---|
| Orbital period (days) | 27 | |
| Rotation period | Tidally locked | |
| Mass (kg) | 8.80 x 10²² | |
| Atmosphere | – 64.4% nitrogen<br>– 10.7% methane<br>– 10.5% oxygen<br>– 8.2% carbon dioxide<br>– 3% argon<br>– 2.1% hydrogen<br>– 1.0% sulfuric acid | |

### Caerus

| | | |
|---|---|---|
| Mass (kg) | 1.08 x 10²⁰ | |
| Orbital period (days) | 18 | |
| Rotation period | Tidally locked | |
| Atmosphere | none | |

# CHAPTER 38

*Drone Launch*

Jonathan Mills was approaching the end of his shift and looking forward to a bite to eat and a quick nap. He and the rest of Endeavor's crew were taking four-hour shifts, pouring over video and still-frame images from the various surveillance satellites in orbit around Sanctuary and the high-res optics installed on the tiny moonlit Caerus. Their goal was to find a small hamlet or village suitable for ongoing surveillance using the drone-torpedo strapped down in the ship's cargo bay.

Dr. Martin suggested that a small village would be better than a large city because there would be more opportunities to witness the same inhabitants multiple times as they went about their lives. After some discussion, Merriweather had agreed, and the search continued with those new parameters.

The crew had been at it for a week.

Mills rubbed his eyes. Four hours of staring at a holoview were having a detrimental effect on his vision, as well as his sanity. He had applied the eyedrops Doc Lee had given to him and the crew, but he wasn't sure they were helping much.

Without looking up, he summoned Mike Martin, who was hunched over another holoview not three meters away.

"Mike, can you come and look at this? I think I'm beginning to see things."

"Sure, buddy. Coming over." Martin moved over to Mills' station to see what he had found. Standing behind Mills and leaning over his crewmate's shoulder, he said, "Whatcha got?"

Mills pointed to a large circular structure frozen on his screen. It resembled either a disk or a dome and was surrounded by a cluster of sizable buildings.

"Well, looky here," said Martin.

"You see a dome, right?"

"Sure as shit," replied Martin.

"See that part of the dome? Doesn't that look like an opening, or is that just a shadow?" Mills asked.

"Could be an opening," responded Martin.

"OK, watch when I advance the video," said Mills.

As the image on the holoview advanced frame by frame, the dome-like object appeared to rotate.

"Does that look like what I think it looks like?" Mills asked.

"Well, if you're thinking a damn telescope, then yeah, it does," answered Martin. "Maybe we should call the captain?"

"I think we should," said Mills.

A few minutes later, a small crowd had formed at Mills' station, including Captain Merriweather, who asked Mills to replay the video. Once again, Mills advanced the video frame by frame. Both he and Martin expressed their opinions that the object in question was an observatory, pointing out what appeared to be a telescope extending from an opening in the dome. Rather than state his opinion, Merriweather asked the other crew members to chime in.

"It could be some sort of weapon," said Rodriguez. "That could be a cannon sticking out there."

"Why would it be there?" asked Bridges. "What is it guarding?"

"Maybe it's protecting the town," said Rodriguez.

"I don't think so, Javi. I wouldn't put one there," said Bridges. "It's surrounded by buildings. I don't think it can be anything other than a telescope."

After another twenty minutes of spirited discussion, Merriweather weighed in with his thoughts.

"Well, gentlemen, if that's a telescope, which I fully believe it is, then that might be some sort of science facility there. I think we've found our target."

In the coming days, the crew scrutinized the images and data from the orbiting surveillance satellites and sensors now installed on Caerus, preparing for the next step—launching a drone-torpedo.

Once Merriweather made his final decision, things moved quickly. The launch team, led by the XO and including Bridges and Mills, declared the torpedo flight ready after subjecting it to a battery of pre-flight tests. Stoner had drilled the launch team until he was satisfied each knew their part. The five-hundred-kilogram torpedo was loaded into the port side launch tube and now awaited the launch command from Captain Merriweather.

"Everything good, XO?"

"Right as rain, Captain."

Satisfied all was ready, Merriweather gave the order. "RHODA, deploy torpedo."

A second later, Merriweather heard the loud swoosh of compressed air forcefully expelling the torpedo from the launch tube.

"Torpedo launched successfully, Captain Merriweather."

Small puffs of hydrazine vented from the torpedo's thrusters as RHODA guided it into firing position. Moments later, its methane engine ignited, propelling the craft swiftly away from Endeavor and toward the bluegreen planet. From their vantage point in the open cargo bay, Mills, Rodriguez, and Bridges watched as the main engine cut off and the ion drive came alive with a steady pulse. It would be four days before the torpedo entered Sanctuary's atmosphere and another hour before its drones reached the hamlet below. With nothing more to do, the crew returned to their surveillance feeds, waiting.

# CHAPTER 39

*Suspicion*

Dakar Dualla and Supervisor Glyvash sat together at the new telescope's control panel, intently gazing at the newly enhanced images of the strange object Dualla and her young student Yuni had discovered six days earlier. The image analyst had finally released her report, which impressed neither the chief astronomer nor her assistant.

"This is nonsense," said Dualla, to which Glyvash nodded in agreement. "An optical artifact? A spot on the lens? The analyst fears the Council more than you."

"Perhaps a little fear is not such a bad thing," responded Glyvash. Dualla turned to stare at her assistant.

"Fear is never good for a scientist. We must follow the evidence wherever it leads us."

"Yes, of course, Your Primacy."

"Look again, Chief Assistant Astronomer," she said, pronouncing his formal title with some contempt in her voice. "What does it look like to you?" Glyvash found himself in a precarious position. He knew the opinion of his boss but also the opinion of the Akan, and he was stuck in the middle.

"It looks like it has geometry, regularity, symmetry, Your Primacy, but perhaps that is just my tired old eyes. And you, Your Primacy. What do you see?"

"Yes, Glyvash. This is no natural object."

"Could be the Belorians," said Glyvash.

Glyvash hoped his supervisor would rethink her subversive opinion regarding its origin. Belore was one of this world's largest and most technologically advanced nations, almost as advanced as her own country of Xerelang. Glyvash had heard rumors the Belorians were developing the technology, and the vehicles needed to launch artificial satellites into space. Still, the scientific community of Xerelang had dismissed the talk as so much propaganda.

"I hardly think so, Glyvash," said Dualla. "What if that is a vessel from the stars—another world?"

"Your Primacy, such statements are dangerous. You know how the ruling Council feels about such thoughts. They could accuse you of heresy."

"Be at peace, Glyvash. I am not making such a claim. It is just an interesting possibility. It would be interesting, would it not?"

"Your Primacy, you might survive The Akan's wrath, expressing even the possibility of space creatures, but I would not be so fortunate."

"Well then, we will keep this to ourselves until we can prove it," she added.

"Thank you, Your Primacy."

Dualla had other ideas, however. She had no doubt she had found evidence of an alien race from the stars. But how would she prove it? Glyvash was right about the Council. Despite Dualla's name and exalted position, she could still be in danger if she went public with such a claim without incontrovertible proof. Best to proceed with caution.

# CHAPTER 40

*Eyes on the prize*

"Where's the drone now?" Merriweather asked as he approached the surveillance console now occupied by Milo Bridges.

"The probe entered the atmosphere eight minutes ago, Captain. It's slowed to about 250 meters (about 820.21 ft) per second. We're expecting drogue chute deployment any moment."

"Drogue chute deployment," RHODA announced, interrupting Bridges' thought.

"And there it is," said Bridges.

"Very good," said Merriweather.

Each holoview station on Endeavor featured two deckmounted seats. Bridges occupied the left while Merriweather dropped into the right, his eyes locking on the shifting holoimage before them.

"Have you ever seen one of these deployed, Milo?"

"No, sir. It's a first for me. The closest I've come is the simulator at the Academy."

"Nothing like the real thing, that's for sure," said Merriweather. "Did you know I was part of the development team? I had the pleasure of deploying one over Earth during the testing phase. It's amazing when it works. The problem was, our success rate never got higher than seventy percent. It's a complicated piece of technology."

"Seems so," said Bridges. "Mills has been running simulations on the software for several weeks, and he's made some tweaks he insists will increase the reliability."

"Tweaks? Seriously? Damn it, why wasn't I told? He's not supposed to be—ah, hell."

Bridges didn't know how to respond, so he said nothing.

"What's done is done, I suppose," continued Merriweather. "But I am going to have a talk with that boy. If we've come all this way to have the mission fail because of a typo or one of Mills' so-called improvements, I'll throw him out of the nearest airlock myself. Let's just hope for his sake it doesn't come to that."

Bridges felt for his shipmate. Mills was confident in his abilities as a software engineer and as a scientist—maybe a bit too confident for his own good.

RHODA continued her status announcements as Merriweather and the rest of the crew monitored the drone's progress.

"Velocity one hundred meters per second… ninety… drogue released… winglets deployed… probe now in horizontal flight… seventy meters per second."

"What's our ETA?" Merriweather asked.

"She'll drop her drones in twenty minutes, on site in thirty," answered Bridges.

"So far, so good. Coffee?" Merriweather asked.

"Coming right up, sir," Bridges said, rising halfway from his control seat.

"No, I'm asking you," said Merriweather, placing his hand on Bridges' shoulder. "Do you want some coffee or whatever crap you drink?"

"Uh, yes, sir, seventeen," said Bridges, handing the captain his empty mug.

"Seventeen, got it," said Merriweather.

Merriweather punched seventeen into the galley's CUBE, dialing up Bridges' custom beverage, and waited for it to dribble into the mug. "What the hell is this bilge?"

"Oh, you mean my brew? It's a veggie blend with seaweed. Cat—uh, I mean Lieutenant Cortez—got me hooked on it," Bridges said. "It's not bad."

"You know what they say, Bridges. There's nothing so bad as that which is not so bad."

"Yes, sir."

Returning to the control station, Merriweather placed the mug in front of his junior lieutenant while taking a slow sip from his coffee.

"I remember the first attempt at deploying one of these drones. There were some old, abandoned CIA buildings just north of Goddard Spaceflight Center—that's where we were testing them. We were trying to place the drones on several target buildings. Everything was going great until the master drone took command of the slaves. At that point, we were essentially cut out of the control loop. Suddenly, the drones made an about-face and made a beeline toward downtown DC. Apparently, the code that accessed the GPS system was buggy."

"GPS system?" Bridges interjected.

Merriweather glanced at his junior officer with a mild look of disgust.

"GPS. Global Positioning. Tell me you know what GPS is. Oh, hell. You're making me feel old. Yeah, we had to use the old Global Positioning Satellite system. Self-referential positioning technology didn't exist at the time. Anyway, for some reason, the master drone took a liking to the Old White House. Before you know it, we're listening to private conversations coming from inside the Oval Office. We had some tall explaining to do after that fiasco. But in the end, it proved the concept could work.

"You must be getting pretty excited about all of this, Bridges," continued Merriweather. "First contact with a new intelligent species."

"Yes, sir, I am. I'm blown away by it. You train so long, and you dream about what it will be like, then it happens, and it's greater than you ever expected."

"Drone deployment," announced RHODA. "All drones report successful synch—proceeding to target."

"So far, so good," said Merriweather.

Zoe Bishop, who had been sitting nearby and taking notes in her holo, moved closer.

"Mind if I watch?"

"Take a seat," said Merriweather.

After an awkward few seconds, Bridges realized there was nowhere for Bishop to sit and Merriweather hadn't made a move to offer his.

"Sit here, Zoe." He said, jumping to his feet.

"Thank you, Milo, Captain. Is that your target?" she asked, pointing at the image of the observatory dome.

"The surrounding buildings," he replied.

"We hope to find some good surveillance positions on those buildings."

"What happens next?"

"For now, we just wait. Once the drones get there, that's when it gets exciting."

Ten minutes later, with the crew watching on the galley's holoview screen, the drone fleet closed in on the science facility. Both alien suns were gone below the horizon, leaving only artificial lighting and a shimmering aurora overhead to define the landscape. In the green haze of the master drone's night-vision feed, they watched the four slave drones alight on the roof one by one. The master drone then swung away, its optics searching for suitable nests.

Using its sophisticated AI, the master drone was careful to stay out of any direct lighting and away from anything that looked like it might be alive. It carefully approached several windows lit from within. As it did, it slowly revolved to display the view from each location. Then it moved off to another location and repeated the process.

After ten minutes of scouting, the master drone returned to the roof, landed, and began transmitting video and images of potential nests, and waited for further instructions.

As the imagery streamed in, Bridges fed it to the galley's holoview. Within moments, dozens of potential nests appeared for Merriweather and the crew to review. After a brief debate, Merriweather instructed Bridges to transmit the chosen coordinates to the master drone.

Now directed by the master drone, slave drone number one moved away from the group and flew deliberately toward the first selected nest, a top-floor corner window of the building northwest of the observatory dome. Merriweather considered this location a likely spot for the office of a high-ranking scientist. This nest should provide valuable intel.

As the drone one hovered near the window, a sticky substance oozed from several small holes in the center of the top disk. Positioning itself slightly below and about twenty centimeters from a target spot above the window, the drone accelerated upward, flipped ninety degrees, and slammed against the wall. The sticky substance hardened instantly upon impact, creating a solid bond with the building. Now firmly attached, the rotor blades stopped spinning and withdrew into the drone's body. The upper and lower disks closed together, leaving a barely perceptible seam. After a brief pause, drone one transmitted its first image to the master drone, which corrected the image's orientation before relaying it to Endeavor.

"One down, three to go," said Merriweather.

As the crew aboard Endeavor watched, the remaining slave drones were sent to their chosen nests after each received its target coordinates. Drone two and three performed the flip motion flawlessly and successfully bonded to the side of their chosen target. The final drone, however, was a different story. As drone four made its last maneuver, slamming into the building's side, a chunk of the wall no thicker than a quarter broke away and fell to the ground, taking the drone with it.

"Damn," said Merriweather. "That's unfortunate. Bridges, see if you can recover it?"

"I'll try," said Bridges.

Bridges entered the commands on his touchpad, but nothing seemed to work.

"Sorry, Captain. The drone seems to have landed in some bushes, and I can't get the rotors moving at all."

"Is it transmitting?" asked Merriweather. "Can we get any images?"

"Yes, sir, it is transmitting."

Bridges pulled up the video and displayed it on his holo.

"I can't make out anything in that image," said Merriweather. "Are there any more?"

Bridges pulled up all the images the drone had transmitted, but they were all the same—dark and blurry.

"We could try to send someone down there to retrieve it," said Bridges.

"It's too risky at this point. If it's discovered, there's nothing there that screams aliens from outer space," said Merriweather. "RHODA, can you enhance the images?"

"Well, that's somewhat better," said Bridges. "Kinda looks like vegetation of some sort."

"Great, now we know what the inside of a bush looks like," said Merriweather. "Let's just hope nobody finds it right away. We can hope so, anyway. For now, we wait. Who's got the watch?"

"I do," said Cortez.

"Very well. Bridges, withdraw the rotors on drone four and close it up. Cortez, I'll meet you on the bridge. I want to discuss our food resources—where we stand."

While some of the crew drifted off to their quarters to catch a few hours of sleep, Dr. Girard and Milo Bridges stayed.

"Not sleepy?" asked Bridges.

"Too excited," Girard replied. "More of your seaweed?"

"How about coffee instead?" said Bridges. "I need the caffeine. Doc, can I ask you a question?"

"Sure, Milo, it would be my pleasure."

"OK, you've written extensively on alien language translation. I remember our instructor at the Academy quoting from your book."

"Which one? I've written seven," said Girard.

"To be honest, I don't remember."

"Ah, my books often have the effect of putting their readers to sleep."

"Don't be modest, Doc. Your books are required reading. So, what made you get into translation in the first place?"

"You sure you want to hear my long, boring story?" Girard asked. "Actually, I do."

For the next hour, Bridges and Girard discussed the details of Girard's story and his current plans to translate the alien's language.

"How long do you think it will take?" Bridges asked.

"Could take weeks, months, or even years."

"Jesus. Hopefully not years. I'm ready to go now," smiled Bridges.

"I imagine you are," smiled Girard. "I know I would be."

"Well, thanks, Doc," said Bridges. "I'm off to get a little sack time."

As Bridges made his way back to his quarters, his thoughts drifted to Cortez. Maybe it was just his imagination, but he could've sworn he'd caught a glimmer of interest from her. Plus, he was tired of waiting.

*Maybe tomorrow*, he thought. *Maybe tomorrow.*

# CHAPTER 41

*First Encounter*

After a few hours, Endeavor's crew drifted back into the galley, drawn by the promise of coffee and any whisper of alien sightings. They hoped this would be it—the first glimpse of intelligent life beyond Earth.

The scientists spoke in hushed voices, debating what they expected, or perhaps only hoped, to see.

Bridges sat apart, lost in thought. *How will history remember the first human to contact an alien race?* he wondered. *Would my name stand alongside Columbus, Neil Armstrong, Samuelson, Planck?*

And what of the aliens themselves? Would they be beyond comprehension, something utterly other? Or as familiar as strangers from another country on Earth?

Just a few more hours.

A slight movement on Bridges' holoview interrupted his thoughts and drew his immediate attention. Something was moving down there.

"Guys, look at this," said Bridges.

Immediately, Girard, Mann, Martin, Graham, and Mills crowded around Bridges' station.

"What is that?" Mills exclaimed.

"It's a quadruped. It has hocks like a horse, but it's the size of a small dog or cat," said Graham.

"More like a pig," said Girard. "a hairless creature, maybe a large rodent."

"Intelligent, maybe?" Mills asked.

"A sophont? No, I don't think so. For one thing, it just appeared to urinate on a bush. Plus, it's meandering around the area and not headed in a specific direction."

"And you've never urinated on a bush?" said Dr. Mann, garnering a few laughs from those gathered around the holoview.

Bridges and his crewmates watched the random movements of *whatever it was* for several minutes before it was no longer in view.

"Hopefully, that was not one of our sophonts," said Dr. Mann.

"Maybe they'll be disappointed in us, too," said Bridges.

"True. We might disgust them. I suppose we have to look past aesthetics and keep an open mind. Did they cover that at the Academy?" asked Mann.

"They did. In fact, they stressed it," answered Bridges. "They talked about the extreme diversity of life on Earth and emphasized that it may have been just an evolutionary accident that our species became the alpha dog. So, beings on this planet could be more like reptiles."

"Or insects," added Girard.

"Or pigs," said Bridges. "When is sunrise?"

"An hour and twenty-three minutes," said Dr. Mann, looking at his watch.

Once again, Endeavor's crew withdrew into small groups. A few laid their heads on the large communal table that dominated the ship's galley, hoping to catch a few minutes of sleep before the big reveal. Bridges' thoughts turned to Cat Cortez, who had retired to her bunk an hour earlier. Bridges wished at that moment that he could join her. *Funny*, he thought, *I'm about to witness history, and what am I thinking about? Getting laid. I guess that says something about my priorities. I wonder what she is dreaming about.*

Meanwhile, Cat Cortez lay in her bunk wide awake. No matter how much she tried to sleep, it wouldn't come. Her thoughts were all over the place. She thought of the discoveries waiting for them down there on Sanctuary. She thought about being so far from home—and she thought of Milo Bridges. There was no getting past it. She had feelings for Bridges, and they were getting stronger. The idea of spending the next two years—or more—near Bridges and doing nothing about it would be torture. No, she was going to do something about it. She was only human, after all.

"Mills, take over for me, will you?" Bridges said. "I've had enough coffee to float this ship—I need a quick break."

Bridges made a quick trip to the Universal Waste Management System (UWMS) to relieve himself of his abundance of coffee. Then he furtively walked up to Cat Cortez's personal quarters.

Bridges paused for a second, undecided whether or not to knock. *It's now or never*, he thought as he knocked softly.

"Cat, are you awake?" Bridges leaned close to the door, listening for a reply or any sounds that might indicate she was awake. He wasn't sure he had whispered loud enough and was about to knock again when—

Bridges' voice startled Cortez, and she instantly recognized the voice of her shipmate. She had been thinking about him in a totally inappropriate way for an ISA officer, and his voice made her catch her breath.

"Yes, yes, I'm awake. Is that you, Milo?"

Bridges wondered briefly if he'd made a big mistake. *There's no turning back now*, he thought.

"Yes, it's me. Are you busy?"

Cortez's door opened. "No, I was just resting."

Bridges stared at her. Her mussed hair made her seem even more desirable than usual—if that was even possible. She had obviously been lying on her bunk. She had removed her uniform and was now wearing a loosely fitting tee shirt and a pair of pajama bottoms. *God, she could make anything look sexy*, he thought. He struggled to find something to say.

"We saw our first alien species," he said instantly regretting his lame conversation choice.

"Intelligent?" she asked.

"No, we don't think so. More like a pet or a rodent."

"Oh," she said.

A few awkward moments passed.

"Would you like to come in?" she asked.

Cortez could sense that Bridges' demeanor was different, and she had an inkling that his visit was of a more personal nature.

"Come in?" said Milo. "Uh, OK."

Bridges glanced over his shoulder before entering. Cortez was sitting on her bunk.

"Close the door, please," she said.

*A hopeful sign*, thought Bridges as he did what she asked.

"I like what you've done with the place," he said again, chastising himself for his lack of originality.

"Glad you like it. Would you like to sit?"

Milo glanced at the solo chair in her quarters, which was occupied by a stack of tech manuals. He looked back at her. Cortez patted the bunk space next to her.

He also sensed that something was different. Cortez was softer, less formal. She smiled at him.

Bridges turned and slowly closed her door. He moved to the bunk and sat gently next to his comely shipmate, turning his body to face hers. He was so close he could feel the heat from her body. She returned his gaze. Slowly, Bridges leaned forward, bringing his face inches from hers. He glanced at her mouth, then her eyes, then her mouth again. Slowly, her lips parted. There was longing in her eyes. Their lips came together—at first tenderly— then with passion.

Suddenly, there was a knock at the door.

"Oh my God," she whispered as she pushed Bridges away. "Yes, who's there?" She blurted.

"Sorry to wake you, Lieutenant, but I am looking for Milo. Have you seen him?" asked Dr. Girard.

Cortez's eyes flashed in anger at Bridges. "Did you tell anyone you were coming here?" she whispered.

"No, I didn't," he whispered in reply.

Cortez frowned.

"No, I haven't," she answered in a voice a touch too casual. "Is it important?"

"If you see him, tell him we've seen our first life form."

"Really? OK. I will if I see him."

"You have to go," said Cortez after Girard had left.

"I'm sorry, Cat, but I didn't tell anyone," said Bridges.

"OK, I believe you. But you still have to go."

"I know. Can I come back later?"

"Let me think about it."

"OK, I'll tell them I was checking out the hydroponics bay."

"Whatever. Just keep this our secret."

"OK."

Cortez opened her door slightly to make sure no one was nearby.

"OK, go."

Bridges cupped his hands around her face and kissed her gently. She sighed slowly. He was pleased she offered no resistance. Whatever barrier that had existed between them was now gone. As he stood and exited her quarters, she smiled. She knew the next time he visited, he would stay awhile.

# CHAPTER 42

*Something in the way she moves*

Bridges quickly made his way back to the galley. Expecting to explain where he had been, he was relieved when no one raised the subject.

"Milo, I think we saw one," said Mills.

"Saw what?" said Bridges.

"A sophont."

"When?"

"About 0615."

"Show me," said Bridges.

"You'll have to replay the video."

Mills relinquished his seat to Bridges, who sat and immediately called up the video, starting at 0615. A few seconds passed before a figure appeared on the left side of the screen, moving to the right.

"Is that it?"

"Yep. What do you think?"

Bridges focused intently on the screen, trying to absorb every detail from the scene he could.

"Well, it's obviously bipedal with a humanoid shape," exclaimed Bridges. "Have you notified the captain?"

"Uh, no, I didn't think to notify him," answered Mills. "Should we wake him?"

"Are you kidding, Mills? Yes, go wake him. He'll want to see this himself. Hell, wake everyone."

Mills scurried away to wake the captain while the crew members who were awake at the time crowded around Bridges.

"Guys, give me some room here," said Bridges. "Here, I'll put it on the big screen."

A few seconds later, the large holoview built into the galley's bulkhead mirrored the image on Bridges' workstation.

"Can you run that again, Milo?" asked Dr. Martin.

"Sure," said Bridges as he cued up the video segment showing the alien.

"OK, stop it there. See the way it's swinging its arms? That's very human-like."

"It's also wearing clothes. What does that tell you, Mike?" said Dr. Graham.

"Well, it could mean a couple of things. Like humans, it could show that the species has spread to other temperate zones."

"Or modesty," added Bishop.

"Maybe, but I don't think so," said Martin. "I reckon it was about survival. It allowed migration to colder regions. The evidence tells us that humans started wearing clothes about one hundred and seventy thousand years ago, just after the second-to-last ice age."

"How the hell do they know that?" asked Graham. "What evidence?"

"Which part?" asked Martin.

"The hundred and seventy thousand years ago," said Graham.

"Have you ever had cooties?" asked Martin.

"Bit personal, don't you think?" asked Graham.

"Just humor me," said Martin. "Have you ever had cooties—what we used to call head lice?"

"Head lice, sure. When I was five."

"What about crabs? Ever had them?"

"Next question," said Graham to a smattering of laughter.

"Well," said Martin, "did you know that head lice and crabs are cousins?"

"No, I didn't, but I'm not surprised you do."

This resulted in even more laughter.

"DNA tells us they were the same as late as 170,000 years ago when they split into two species. When humans had thick hair all over their bodies, the lice could wander from head to toe. But after humans lost most of that hair, head lice couldn't freely migrate to the genital area and vice versa. Head lice and genital lice started evolving separately. Losing his body hair exposed man to the elements, so clothing became essential."

"Interesting, in a creepy sort of way," said Graham. "I think I'll wash my hair tonight."

"Maybe it was just vanity," said Captain Merriweather as he arrived on the scene. "Milo, let's see what we've got."

Again, Bridges played the twelve-second video showing a humanoid creature moving through the hamlet square.

"Definitely humanoid. Score one for Dr. Girard and convergent evolution," said Merriweather. Did we get a front view?"

"No frontal view, but he's likely looking in the direction he's walking," said Bridges.

"Maybe," answered Martin, "but let's not get too far ahead of ourselves."

"I agree," said Merriweather as he turned and walked toward the beverage dispenser. "I need coffee."

Everyone was awake now. Their first sighting of an alien was a momentous event. Dr. Martin and Lieutenant Bridges, the two crewmembers with anthropology degrees, led a spirited debate about the meaning of what they had seen. Every detail of the twelve-second video was dissected to glean as much information about this species as possible.

For twenty minutes, there was no movement on the holoview. Then, another alien appeared, moving across the quad in front of the observatory dome. Much like the first, this one was also humanoid and wearing clothes.

"Very humanoid," said Dr. Mann. "Four limbs, symmetrical, walks upright, definitely humanoid. Those look very much like fingers at the ends of his arms. Can't tell how many, but more than one. Something unusual going on with its legs. Is the knee joint backward?"

"Seems to be," said Bridges.

"Its head seems a bit oversized in relation to its body—compared to us," said Mann. "The arms are longer too."

"And thinner. So are the legs. In fact, he looks kind of anorexic," said Bridges. "A lighter frame would be an advantage on a planet with stronger gravity, right?

"He also has feet, and apparently, he's wearing shoes of a sort," said Cortez, who had joined the group minutes earlier. "Very stylish as well."

Bridges noticed Lieutenant Cortez as she floated onto the ship's galley and turned to greet her. "Morning Lieutenant."

"Morning Milo," she replied.

"Good morning, Lieutenant Cortez. Glad you could join our watch party this morning," said Dr. Martin.

Cortez smiled and moved closer to the holoview to get a better view.

"What's he carrying?" Cortez asked, pointing to an object suspended from the figure's hand. "A bag or briefcase, maybe?" she added.

"Possible," said Martin. "Can anyone make out skin texture or type?"

"Just the color...light green...maybe?" said Mills.

"More like cappuccino," said Cortez.

"RHODA, analyze the sophont in the video and report," said Bridges.

"The sophont has a symmetrical, humanoid shape, four limbs, opposable anterior forelimb appendages, binocular vision, biomechanic plantigrade-bipedalism, a height of approximately one point six meters. The sophont's torso is eight to ten percent longer than its lower limbs. The upper limbs are forty to forty-five percent longer than its torso. The sophont's brain case is approximately fourteen hundred cubic centimeters."

"You're assuming the brain is in the sophont's head," said Mills.

"That is correct," RHODA replied. "In most species, the brain is positioned close to the eyes to minimize latency in processing visual data.

"Thank you, RHODA," said Bridges.

"I have a couple of questions," said Bishop, raising her hand. "Opposable anterior forelimb appendages? Does she mean thumbs?"

"Exactly right," said Dr. Mann, wiggling his thumbs.

"OK. How about biomechanic, uh, something?"

"Plantigrade-bipedalism," interrupted Mann. "That just means it can walk upright."

"Why didn't she just say that?" Bishop said. "Is fourteen hundred cubic centimeters large, compared to us, I mean?"

"Not overly large. A typical adult male has a braincase of about twelve hundred."

"So, they could be smarter."

"Not necessarily. Braincase size isn't a definitive indicator," said Mann.

"He's a short little dude," said Mills. "Or a child," he added.

During the next two hours, over thirty additional sightings of aliens kept the crew busy and engaged in debate. The consensus was that these were inhabitants going to work, school, or some other daily activity. Given the opinion that this was a scientific community based around the existence of a large telescope on the grounds, most of Endeavor's crew were even referring to the village's inhabitants as scientists or engineers. Excitement occurred when several inhabitants stopped to chat with their fellow workers. Endeavor's computers were busy gathering video and audio feeds from the hidden surveillance drones, trying to correlate the actions with the sounds.

"Dr. Martin, any thoughts about why the inhabitants are smaller than humans?" asked Mann.

"I reckon it could be diet, the planet's gravity, the lower oxygen level compared to Earth, or something else entirely. Small stature could be more efficient from a resource standpoint. Ain't no way of knowing without getting one of them into our ship's lab for testing," said Martin.

"Are you suggesting we kidnap and dissect one of them?" asked Mann.

"I wonder how they taste," said Dr. Graham. "A little barbecue sauce and..."

"Ignore him," said Mann, shaking his head.

"I'll try," said Martin, laughing. "I'm saying that after we make contact, maybe we invite one to visit the ship, where we turn them into a guinea pig."

"Doesn't that violate the prime directive?" interjected Mills.

"Jonathan, there's no such thing. This ain't science fiction," said Martin.

"Guys, look at this," said a clearly excited Milo Bridges.

Once again, everyone gathered around the large holoview. Moving slowly across the field of view was another creature, similar to but decidedly different from the aliens they had been seeing.

"That's a female," said Cortez. "It's definitely a female!"

"Now, how can you tell that?" asked Bridges.

"There's just something about the way she moves. The way she holds her arms and hands and the way the others react to her; I'd bet anything that she's a female."

"Assuming similar musculoskeletal differences between the genders plus similar cultural influences—all of which are big assumptions," said Dr. Graham. "They might not even have interior skeletons like we do."

"You mean they might have exoskeletons like crustaceans?" Bishop said.

"It's possible. We can't tell that from the video."

"Fine, but until we learn otherwise, I'm calling her a 'she," said Cortez.

"The others seem to defer to her," added Martin. "Look at the way they are moving aside to let her pass. Perhaps she is a high-ranking official or maybe even royalty. Her style of attire also seems more refined," he said.

"She must be half a meter taller than the others," said Bridges, "and very thin. She has a sort of fluidity of movement—very graceful for someone almost two meters tall. RHODA, can we zoom in on the larger figure's face?"

"Magnifique!" exclaimed Dr. Girard.

"You got that right," added Dr. Graham.

The female alien's face filled the holoview—a vision of exotic beauty. Her cappuccino-colored skin carried a faint green undertone, with a yellowish band running from the crown of her bald head down the back of her neck. Her features were almost human, her soft brown eyes slightly larger than human norms, protruding just enough to seem otherworldly yet still graceful. The most striking detail was the pair of frill-like appendages on either side of her neck, vibrant blue and reminiscent of both fish fins and dinosaur crests.

"It certainly is fascinating how human she looks. This brings up a whole new thought. Could we be related?"

"You mean some ancient race of wandering astronauts seeded both our planets?" asked Dr. Mann.

"That would certainly account for the similarities," responded Dr. Martin. "We could be distant cousins."

"What do you make of the neck frills?" Mann asked.

"They're fascinating, that's for sure. Perhaps they're just for show, or they could have a function. They might be vestiges of a distant aquatic ancestor."

As the assembled crewmembers watched the events unfold, they heard repeated vocalizations coming from the smaller sophonts as they seemed to greet the female.

"There's that pattern again," said Bridges. "RHODA, look for repeated vocal patterns whenever the female alien is in the video. Display a list of matching video segments."

RHODA complied, presenting a list of video files. As Bridges played back each video, the pattern was repeated.

"It sure seems consistent to me," said Mann. "That's a greeting, or perhaps the female's name."

"I say we call her Dualla," said Cortez.

"Why Dualla?" Bishop asked.

"I took a course on twenty-first-century media in college, and I discovered and fell in love with an old TV series called *Interspace*. There was a character named Dualla that I really loved and wanted to be—a strong, kick-ass female alien."

"Sounds like dolphins mating," said Bishop. "How are we supposed to understand that?"

"Hopefully, RHODA and the new language interpretation software will give us answers," said Mills. "A lot of Earth's top scientists spent years working on it. That included experts in morphology, language syntax, semantics, phonetics, dialects, and—"

"We understand, Jonathan," interrupted Girard, "So, what you're essentially saying is that if RHODA cannot figure it out, then it's doubtful we will succeed."

"Did I say that?" Mills asked.

"First name or last name?" Bishop asked.

"You mean Dualla? Maybe they only have one name," said Cortez.

"Oh, oh," exclaimed Bridges. "We might just have a problem."

Bridges entered a few commands on his touchpad, directing a new video feed to the large holoview.

# CHAPTER 43

*Strange discovery*

Dafoo was frantic. He was running late for work and, in his haste, let his pet seemoo escape from his small dwelling. It was not the first time Grudu had escaped. Grudu was an escape artist. Any small opening was all it took for Grudu to escape from Dafoo's humble one-room home. To be perfectly honest, seemoos were not suitable pets for city dwellers. Seemoos loved to run. An Earthling would describe a seemoo as a cross between a small piglet, a rat, and a chicken. Running on two legs, its footlong tail flicking for balance, Grudu easily outpaced poor Dafoo.

Dafoo could not afford to be late again. It had taken a recommendation from a well-connected hatchery mate to secure his position at the science facility, and he certainly could not afford to lose it. His boss, Supervisor Glyvash, had already lectured him for being habitually late. "One more time," Supervisor Glyvash had warned poor Dafoo, and he would be seeking a position elsewhere.

*Please help me, Grudu*, thought Dafoo. *Have pity on me. Show yourself*.

Dafoo sprinted across the grass field that bordered the science building, looking in places he had found Grudu before. Others in the area watched Dafoo's frantic searching with much mirth. They had seen this before. Everyone knew Grudu. The small creature would approach anyone for a scratch behind the ear or a belly rub—everyone except Dafoo, that is. Grudu would run from Dafoo, thinking it was a grand game.

Dafoo was about to abandon his search, rush to his cubicle at work and plead for forgiveness when something caught his eye. It wasn't Grudu but a strange object deep inside a moke bush bordering the building's concourse. Careful to avoid the sharp nettles, Dafoo reached into the bush, grasped the strange object, and gently but firmly pulled it into the light.

*What is this?* Dafoo said to himself, turning the object over in his hands. Dafoo was befuddled. *What could it be? What is it doing here?* He looked around to see if the owner of the object was nearby. However, there was no one around but himself.

Dafoo held the dark gray, disk-shaped object close to his face to get a better look. One side had a semi-spherical transparent bubble right in the center, appearing to be a gemstone of some kind. A thin sliver of vistmantu debris was stuck to the opposite side, and no matter how hard Dafoo pulled, it refused to come off.

*It looks like vistmantu*, thought Dafoo. He looked up at the nearby buildings, hoping to see where the strange thing had been before it fell into the moke bush. Dafoo had never seen such an object.

Suddenly, Dafoo had a brilliant idea. He would take this to Supervisor Glyvash, who he hoped would be so interested he would forget or even excuse Dafoo's tardiness. Yes, that is what he would do.

Catching Grudu would just have to wait. Saving his job was more important. Besides, Grudu would probably show up for feeding when Dafoo returned home in the evening.

Dafoo made his way quickly to the science building.

The Science Quoram building was a sleek, modern structure, erected only three sols earlier during the construction of the grand telescope. Its three floors housed the entire Quoram staff: junior scientists and technicians worked in cubicles on the ground floor, middle managers occupied the second, and senior scientists enjoyed spacious offices on the third. In all, about one hundred and fifty occupants worked there.

Vistmantu, a hard greenish-white stone found in the low hills around the area, was used to coat the external surfaces of the building. The stone, mined and finished locally, gave the building a unique appearance that employees and the townspeople admired. The windows were typical of the times, in the shape of a triangle with a flat bottom and curved sides peaking at the top. Each corner of the building had a door leading into the ground floor, while a wide ramp rose to a grand second-floor entryway lined with six adjacent doors.

Dafoo took the ramp to the second floor. Reaching Supervisor Glyvash's office, Dafoo knocked quietly, hoping his superior would be elsewhere. Unfortunately, he wasn't.

"Come in," said Glyvash in a voice alerting Dafoo that his boss was not in a good mood.

"Supervisor Glyvash, it is I, Dafoo, and I have something important to show you."

Glyvash glanced up from his notes and scowled at the clearly frightened subordinate.

"Well, what is it? I haven't all day."

Dafoo's superior sat in his usual place behind a small desk near the large lancet-shaped window overlooking the science center's courtyard. Dafoo approached apprehensively, holding the disk timidly in his outstretched hand.

"I found this just outside, deep inside a moke bush."

"Hand it here," said Glyvash.

Glyvash took the object from Dafoo's hand and examined it like a trained scientist. His displeasure with Dafoo quickly faded as his attention turned to the mysterious object.

Dafoo waited patiently, wondering whether he should stay or retreat to his station. Finally, Supervisor Glyvash put him out of his misery by dismissing him.

"You may return to your duties," was all Glyvash said.

Dafoo quickly left his boss's office, relieved that there was no mention of tardiness or dismissal. *A thank you would have been nice*, thought Dafoo as he retreated.

Despite being a lowly male, Glyvash considered himself highly intelligent. In his opinion, he was every bit as intelligent as the most senior female on staff. However, believing that and allowing others to know what he thought of his intelligence were two entirely different things. He knew of earlier male colleagues who had spoken too freely and were soon left without a position. Females held sway in this society and allowed no challenge to their authority, especially from a man who considered himself equal.

The question now racing through Glyvash's mind was what to do with this discovery. If he withheld it from Dakar Dualla and it turned out to be important, she could accuse him of going behind her back to incur glory for himself. Likewise, if he presented something to her that proved to be inconsequential, she would accuse him of wasting her time. Either path carried significant risk.

He would have to give this decision his utmost attention.

On Endeavor, the crew watched with fascination as the two alien sophonts on the planet below examined the drone. Merriweather and his scientists now had eyes inside a building overlooking the observatory. Here was an excellent opportunity to eavesdrop on the aliens, apply context to their language, and gain vital information about their behavior.

"Great close-up shots of the faces," said Dr. Martin. "Check out the eyes. There's no sclera. The iris expands the entire width of the orbit. Look, did you see that? It has a nictitating eyelid."

"Nictit...what?" Merriweather said.

"A third eyelid—like a snake or crocodile. It moves horizontally across the eye."

"They're focusing their attention on the lens. I guess that makes sense," said Mills.

The crew watched as the alien lifted an egg-shaped object from the desk and spoke several words into it before placing it back in its previous location.

"A communication device of some sort—it seems to be connected to the desk by a wire," said Martin.

"Not very sophisticated," added Mills.

"As far as we know," said Bridges. "Anyone see anything that looks like a computer?"

"I didn't," said Dr. Martin, followed by a chorus of agreement.

The crew watched as the sophont carefully examined the disk from every angle, as a scientist might. He tapped it with his finger and held it close to his head, as if listening for internal sounds that might shed light on the strange object's identity. Pulling something like a ruler from his desk, he measured the disk's width and thickness. He even licked it with his tongue.

"Great shot of his tongue," laughed Martin.

"Tongues," said Bridges. "Looks like two to me."

"Looks like our friend is going somewhere," said Martin.

On the planet below, the alien Glyvash had made a decision. He would take the mysterious object to the materials lab in the science building's basement. Standing and tucking the small disk into his tunic pouch, Glyvash headed for the nearest ramp.

He had not gone far when he encountered Dakar Dualla.

"Your Primacy, it is good to see you," said Glyvash, bowing to his superior.

"Supervisor Glyvash, why are you in such a hurry this morning?"

Glyvash was momentarily silent as he tried to decide how to answer. Should he show her the strange object or wait until he knew what it was? Should he take the risk? Finally, he took the safer course of action.

"Your Primacy, I am hurrying to the materials lab to have this strange object examined. I am unsure of its purpose."

Dualla noticed the brief silence before his answer. Her frills glowed a soft yellow, a color that forewarned mild displeasure. Glyvash took note with some concern.

"One of my junior assistants found it hidden in a moke bush just outside," he replied, gesturing to a nearby window. "I thought it prudent to find out more before I bothered you."

"Nonsense," said Dualla. "Let me see it."

Glyvash humbly handed over the object. "It is probably a common object of no importance," he said.

"Humph. So common that my senior astronomer's assistant is unaware of its purpose? Maybe, but I'll decide what is and what isn't important."

Dualla took a quick look at the object and then, as an afterthought, said, "Good work, Glyvash. Also, convey my thanks to your assistant."

Glyvash again bowed to his superior and scampered away back to his office. Dualla again inspected the object before placing it in her tunic pouch, thinking she would have more time to examine the strange disk later in the evening. Her schedule was much too busy to consider what purpose the thing might have. It was most likely nothing of importance.

On Endeavor, the crew watched the meeting between the male and female aliens. The ship's surveillance systems recorded the meeting, which was analyzed extensively by the ship's AI.

"What will we do about the drone?" asked Bishop. "What if they figure out what it is?"

Merriweather nodded slightly, acknowledging Bishop's question. "Anyone else? OK, if it were just the drone, I would leave it. But we need more information and are nowhere close to deciphering their language. Sending someone to the surface might solve both problems—gather as much information as we can and, if possible, retrieve the drone, if we can do it without revealing our presence. Anyone disagree? OK, that's settled. Bridges, you are going down there."

"Yes, sir. I'll put together a mission plan ASAP. How much time do I have?"

"Let's see if we can launch in twenty-four hours. I don't want to give them too much time to examine it."

"Yes, sir," said Bridges.

On the outside, Bridges' demeanor was calm and professional, befitting a fleet officer. On the inside, however, he was positively giddy.

*Damn. This is it. I'm going to land on a freaking alien planet. The first human ever. I'll be in the history books.*

# CHAPTER 44

*Field trip*

Landing on an Earth-sized planet, let alone one with a stronger gravity well, was a big deal. It would require every bit of power Bridges' Lander and Ascent Vehicle could muster, and even that wasn't quite enough. He would have to resort to auxiliary boosters to lift off the planet and reach escape velocity. The LAV's designers anticipated this scenario and had provided for just such extra capabilities. RHODA calculated that The LAV would need four auxiliary boosters to get off the planet and back to Endeavor. In addition, some of the Aries spacecraft's standard gear would have to be left back on Endeavor. Aries One would go in—as Bridges put it—lean and mean.

The mission sounded simple enough, but carrying it out would be anything but easy. Bridges was to land on the planet undetected. He had to land close enough to hike to the small hamlet the crew had been surveilling for the last three months. Then, he had to locate and break into the alien Dualla's home and find any material or items that might provide clues to their language—perhaps a book or other written text. Bridges also had to find the surveillance drone, if possible. If he succeeded, he would hike back to Aries One, take off undetected, and make his way back to Endeavor. The odds of success were, in RHODA's words, "How the hell should I know?"

Bridges was glad he had spent so much time in the ship's small gym. While the rotation of the habitat ring produced enough gravity to minimize bone loss and muscle atrophy, it wasn't enough to eliminate the effects altogether. The alien planet's gravity was stronger than Earth's, and he would need all his strength and stamina to complete his mission successfully.

Dualla had been a source of fascination among Endeavor's crew from the moment she first appeared in the small hamlet—already nicknamed *Whoville* by the team. She emerged daily at nearly the same time, moving with a quiet grace that drew both attention and deference from the local citizens as she made her way to the largest building near the observatory dome. Each afternoon, she received the same reaction as she returned to her modest home.

Surveillance drones consistently picked up the same cluster of vocalizations whenever she was nearby, suggesting a pattern—or perhaps a ritual—the crew hadn't yet deciphered.

She would make a second trip to the complex every evening—this time visiting the large dome in the center of the complex. From this, Mike Martin had suggested that the female sophont was an astronomer and a viable candidate for first contact, and this turned out to be the consensus opinion. After further discussion, Merriweather agreed that the female alien, named Dualla by Lieutenant Cortez, would be their target for first contact.

Dualla's home lay on the edge of the hamlet, just a fifteen-minute walk from the dome. She shared the dwelling with a second, smaller alien, possibly a juvenile and perhaps Dualla's offspring. Cortez suggested the name "Yuni" after a pet cat she had as a child.

Captain Merriweather knew sending Bridges to the surface was dangerous—but recovering the surveillance drone was worth the risk. It was their only viable option.

"Don't take any unnecessary chances," he'd told Lieutenant Bridges. "Get in, get out. If you can secure the drone, great. If not, we'll survive. Your primary objective is intel—anything that helps us crack their language. No cowboy hero crap. Got it?"

Bridges understood the risk—and the mission's importance. But deep down, he also knew one thing with certainty:

There wasn't a chance in hell he was coming back without that drone.

"Yes, sir," he replied. "I understand."

Before Bridges could leave Endeavor for the planet's surface, he had to take care of two minor items of importance. The first was to check in with the ship's acting chief engineer. He found Mills in Dutch Swenson's old office aft of the cage.

Bridges had avoided this part of the ship since Dutch's death. It was just too painful. But today, he had to put aside those feelings. Arriving at the hatch, he paused momentarily to compose himself before entering the cramped compartment. He was there to visit Jonathan Mills, who was taking over Dutch's assignments.

"Hey, Jon, any problems getting our special project completed?" Bridges asked.

"Nope," Mills replied, "and it's already stowed away in Aries' hold. I hope it's what you wanted."

"I'm sure it is, Jon. Anything I need to know?"

"Well, it was the first time I've built one," said Mills. "But fortunately for you, I found the design in our 3D design database. I just fed it into the 3D printer and an hour later, I had a pile of parts."

"Very cool," said Bridges.

"It took me less than ten hours altogether. Oh, and the battery is fully charged and should give you about four hours of performance."

"Four hours should be plenty, Jon. I owe you big time."

"Top speed is about forty km/h, but your battery will drain faster at that speed."

"How much faster?"

"At forty km/h, you'll only get about two hours," Mills replied. "If I were you, I'd keep it down to about ten to fifteen."

"That's fine. What do I owe you?"

"You can buy me a bottle of single malt when we get back to Earth, and we'll call it even."

"Will do," said Bridges as he turned to leave. At the hatch, he turned and took one last look at Dutch's old office.

"Forget something?" Mills asked.

"No, uh, thank you, Jon. See you when I get back."

Bridges' next appointment was with Doc Lee. Lee had to fit him with a supplemental oxygen pump before they could depart for the surface. He found her in her small clinic, a space no bigger than standard crew quarters.

"Hey Doc. Are we ready to go?" Bridges asked.

"A little nervous, but excited as hell," she replied.

"Same here," he answered truthfully. "But we'll be fine. Don't worry."

"I'm not worried. This isn't my first rodeo."

Mills laughed. "I sometimes forget how long you've been cavorting around the galaxy."

"Before you were born, buster. Well, maybe that's a bit of an exaggeration," she added.

"Alright, tell me about the rig."

"Well, we have two options, EPO or Oxy-Direc. Given the short duration of the mission—"

"What's option two? I'd rather not take the EPO pills."

"Why the hell not?" asked Lee.

"The side effects."

"The side effects are not that serious."

"I've heard they can cause heart attacks or strokes," said Bridges.

"They can, but that's exceedingly rare. You're in perfect health. The odds of you—"

"I understand it's rare, Doc. However, it happens, right?"

"It can."

"So, what is option two? What are the side effects?"

"Minimal side effects for the Oxy-Direc. It can raise your cholesterol levels, but it's temporary."

"OK, you sold me. Let's go with option two, Doc," said Bridges.

"All right. Oxy-Direc it is. I've always wanted to try it anyway," said Lee.

"You haven't used it before?" Bridges asked with a hint of concern.

"You'll be my first," she replied, smiling impishly. "Take off your shirt."

Lee watched as Bridges pulled his uniform tunic over his head in one swift motion, displaying his well-muscled torso. *There are perks to this job*, she thought.

"So, this is how it works. This tank holds enough Oxy-Direc to last you four hours under normal conditions," said Lee, taping a small flat plastic bottle to his left side. "If you exert yourself too much, it could be as little as two hours, so pace yourself."

Next, she inserted a small syringe into an artery in his left wrist. A small tube connected the tank to the syringe. Lee quickly taped the tubing to Bridges' torso and along his left arm.

Bridges ran his fingers along the rig.

"Walk me through the operation," he said.

"This pack," she explained, pointing to a foil packet she had taped to his chest, "holds bacteria called Methylomirabilis Oxyfera that produces oxygen from nitrite. Your body heat activates them. The oxygen feeds into this container of Oxy-Direc which will encapsulate the oxygen molecules with a thin layer of lipids. The oxygenated liquid flows up your arm and into the artery. Finally, the lipids dissipate, and you get oxygen directly into your bloodstream."

"And no side effects."

"As I said, your cholesterol level will increase slightly," replied Lee.

"I can deal with that," said Bridges, slipping on the alien tunic knockoff Lee had provided for him. "Pretty stylish, don't you think?"

"You look like a pimp," said Lee. "We will treat your increased cholesterol when you get back. Like I said, take it easy, pace yourself, and you should have no problems."

"Thanks," said Bridges, making a face. "Do I look like one of them?"

"How should I know, but try not to run into one in the daytime? You don't speak their language, and you're about a foot too tall."

"Maybe I should carry a basketball," joked Bridges.

"Smartass," Lee said.

After removing most of the Oxy-Direc rig and running down a mental checklist in his head, Bridges turned again to Lee. "Meet you at the hatch in ten minutes?"

"I've just got to check my inventory. Ten minutes tops. Meet you there."

"Don't be late," replied Bridges. "Hate to leave you behind."

Bridges decided at the last moment to make one more stop before heading for the LAV. He found Cortez manning one of the surveillance stations, deeply engrossed in a scene playing out on her screen.

"What's so interesting, Cat?"

"I'm just watching what appears to be some sort of sporting contest," she said, returning to the screen. "Some kids playing in a field. I'm trying to decipher the game's rules, but so far, they're eluding me. Are you on your way out?" she asked.

"Yep. I just thought I'd say goodbye. I'm leaving in a few minutes. Care to walk with me?"

"Sure. I'm ready for a break, anyway."

Together, Bridges and Cortez made their way to the port-side LAV. At the access hatch, Bridges turned to her, rested his hands on her shoulders, and gently pulled her close. He kissed her—slowly, tenderly. She didn't pull away.

"Just in case this turns out badly…," he began.

Cortez placed a finger softly on his lips. "You'll be fine, Milo. You're the second-best pilot ISA has—after me, of course," she added, flashing that mischievous smile that never failed to disarm him. "If anyone can pull this off, it's you. Just be careful. There are… things we need to talk about when you get back."

She leaned in and kissed him—this time it was her turn. "Now get going, Rocket Man. Do us proud. I'll be watching from the bridge, along with everyone else."

Bridges smiled at the reference, turned, grasped the two handholds above the hatch, lifted his feet, and slid into the opening. After settling into the pilot's seat, Bridges began the final preparations for launch. A minute later, Doc Lee slid into the copilot's seat.

"Bridge, Aries One, ready for departure," said Bridges, winking at Lee.

"Aries One, we copy."

"It's not too late to change your mind, Doc," said Bridges, looking at Lee.

"I'm good," said Lee, feigning boredom.

After getting authorization from Captain Merriweather, Bridges slowly backed the small spacecraft away from Endeavor, their home for the last two years. With any luck, they would see their shipmates in nine days. *Whatever happens, he thought, it's going to be exciting.*

From Endeavor's position behind the planet's largest moon, it would take four days for the LAV to reach the planet's surface. *It's a big universe,* he thought. It was nice to have Lieutenant Lee's company on the trip.

Landing on a planet the size of Sanctuary, Hypatia-Proxima-b, or whatever the locals called it, was not a trivial matter. Aries had been outfitted with pretty much every add-on capability available to her and would need all of them, including an extra twenty-thousand-liter propellant tank, two attachable air-breathing jet engines for sustained horizontal flight, and four solid-fuel booster rockets—all to escape the planet's deep gravity well.

However, even with the extra fuel and the solid-fuel booster rockets,

Aries could only reach LPO (Low Planetary Orbit) when leaving Sanctuary. To make it back to Endeavor, Aries would need the help of another one of Aries' accessories—the EX-23 booster.

The EX-23 was a reusable, liquid-fueled booster rocket designed for extended missions like the one Bridges and Lee were now undertaking. Endeavor carried two—one near each docking adapter.

After undocking from Endeavor's port side access module, Bridges backed Aries toward the EX-23 booster attached to Endeavor just forward of the cage.

"RHODA, dock with the port side EX-23," said Bridges.

Milo knew the ship's AI was more skilled at docking than any human pilot. Its calculations were flawless, its reactions instantaneous. Even so, he couldn't shake the notion that he was just as capable—that, given the chance, he could execute the maneuver with equal precision. He trusted his hands, his instincts, and the countless hours he'd spent in training. But the captain had been explicit: RHODA was to be used whenever possible. It wasn't a suggestion—it was policy.

Bridges heard the thrusters fire, followed by the telltale clank and whirring of gears that accompanied the LAV docking maneuver.

"Docking complete," RHODA announced.

*I could have done that just as well*, thought Bridges.

Bridges went over the next steps in his mind.

Aries would transport the booster the four days it would take to get to Sanctuary. Once in orbit, Aries would detach from the EX-23 and leave it in orbit while the LAV landed on the planet. After concluding the mission, Aries would power into LPO and rendezvous with the EX-23, waiting for them in orbit. The EX-23 would then power Aries back to Endeavor.

*Piece of cake*, thought Bridges.

Running through a mission plan repeatedly in one's head was a recipe for insanity, and Bridges knew it. Try as he might, he couldn't quite put it out of his mind. He tried to keep his mind occupied by doing other tasks. Bridges and Lee spent their time reading, updating their personal journals, and sleeping—or by playing chess. Currently, Bridges and Lee relaxed over a game of chess.

Lee was good company, Bridges told himself. Nevertheless, he was happy when he finally eased his LAV into LPO four days later and readied his craft for de-orbiting. The first step was separating from the EX-23 booster. Step two was to communicate with Endeavor.

"Endeavor, Aries, do you copy?"

A long ten seconds later, Bridges heard the voice of Captain Merriweather.

"Endeavor here. We copy you, Aries. What's your status?"

"Endeavor, Aries One, all systems are green. We've successfully separated from the EX-23, and we're eager to get down there. Permission to proceed with de-orbit?"

"Aries, Endeavor, permission granted. Good luck, Lieutenant."

"Roger that," Bridges replied. "Ready, Doc?"

"Hell, yeah," said Lee. "I didn't come all this way to twiddle my thumbs."

"Then let's make us some history."

Bridges smiled as he oriented his lander for de-orbiting, waiting only a few seconds before firing the engines.

# CHAPTER 45

*Detection*

This was a busy time of year for Dualla. The new telescope had gone operational just in the last few weeks, and she felt obligated to prove that it warranted the time and effort. A lot was riding on the success of the new telescope. There were major dissenters on the ruling Council, including The Akan herself.

The Akan was First Primacy of the Ben'lei (Eleven), Daughter of Xenosta, Goddess of the Sea, and Protector of the Faith. As First Primacy on the Council, she was the country's absolute ruler.

Dualla's family had put their name and position squarely behind the project and risked their reputation in doing so. Dualla felt the weight of her family's honor and her own reputation resting squarely upon her shoulders. Arriving home, Dualla located her young student playing in her room.

"There you are, my little one. Have you been mindful of your studies? Have you made any more amazing discoveries?"

"Teacher!" exclaimed Yuni. "Look what I have found. It is very mysterious. Do you know its purpose?"

Yuni had in her hand the strange disk Glyvash had given Dualla three days earlier. Dualla had meant to examine it immediately, but had other work to finish and had put off its examination until tonight. "Where did you find it?"

"It was in your room, Teacher. I hope you do not mind."

Yuni's actions might have irritated Dualla, but she preferred to encourage her young protégé's inquisitiveness.

"You should always ask before you remove anything from my room, Yuni."

"I'm sorry, Teacher," said Yuni. "Are you angry?"

"No, young one. I am not angry. You are forgiven. I too am mystified by the object. Its purpose is unknown to me."

"It must be a magic prayer stone. Do you see the crystal in the center? Surely, it has magic in it. But I do not know how to use it."

"Well, you might be right, little one. Right now, you need to continue your schoolwork. I will take the magic rock and see if I can figure out how to make it work."

"Oh, please, Teacher, let me help."

"Do as I instruct, Yuni. Your lessons come first."

"Yes, Teacher," said a dejected Yuni.

Dualla carried the drone to a large table, where she planned to disassemble it. However, before she had a chance, her communicator buzzed. It was Glyvash.

"Yes, Glyvash, what is so important it could not wait until morning?"

"Please excuse me, Your Primacy, but I thought you would want to know that we have detected an object that appears to be on a collision course with Hera."

Dualla's interest level intensified immediately.

"And you have checked your figures carefully?"

"Yes, yes, three times. There is no doubt about it. It should come down no farther away from us than seven kilums (forty kilometers) to the west. I am myself planning to travel there to witness its impact."

"Do you think this might be the object we saw before?" asked Dualla.

"I believe so, yes, the very one. Its brightness matches the other object, but it is much closer. This is so exciting. I expect it to strike Hera in less than three hours."

"Calm yourself, Glyvash. I shall go with you," said Dualla. "Come straight away. You know where I live?"

"Yes, Your Primacy, I do. I will be there quickly."

Dualla glanced at the object in her hand again, wondering if the sighting and this object were related. "We shall find out," she said to herself.

"Yuni, I must go out for a while. Take mind of your bedtime."

"Yes, teacher."

Thirty minutes later, Dualla and Glyvash were speeding toward the west. Glyvash's personal transportation, a two-seat hydrogen-fueled vehicle, and its occupants sped along the winding two-lane road leading west from the tiny hamlet, lit only by the vehicle's two glow lights.

# CHAPTER 46

*Landing*

As Bridges guided his small craft closer to the blue and green planet that reminded him so much of home, he felt homesick. *It looks so much like Earth*, he thought—massive polar icecaps, pink-tinged clouds swirling across the planet, bright blue oceans, land masses of greens, browns, and yellows. If it were not for the intense aurorae twisting and curling from pole to pole, the similarity to Earth would be even more impressive.

He wondered how his grandparents were doing on the farm. They were getting up in age, and farming was still hard work. He worried that something would happen to them while he was light-years away and unable to contact them or provide any help. Was he a good and dutiful grandson? They had raised him to be independent, but he felt selfish pursuing a career that kept him away from them for so long. He felt akin to sailors who once sailed the oceans on Earth, leaving their wives and children alone for years. Were they selfish? Luckily, Bridges wasn't married, but there were people on Earth he cared for—friends and relatives. Did they occasionally think of him—wondering where he was or what wonders of the universe he was exploring? Did they believe he would ever return home? Did anyone care, or was he a forgotten man?

Bridges suddenly felt alone. Even with Doc Lee sitting next to him, he felt more alone than he had been in the two years since Endeavor had left Earth.

"RHODA, open my personal file—include the following."

Bridges whispered a single paragraph to his grandparents, apologizing for his failings as a grandson. He told them he loved them and hoped they would be proud of him. He thought about adding a note to Cortez, but couldn't decide what to say. The message was automatically transmitted to Endeavor and saved in his personal file.

Given the close quarters inside the Aries cockpit, Lieutenant Lee could not help overhearing Bridges.

"That's a good idea," said Lieutenant Lee.

Lee's goodbye note was considerably longer as she dictated messages in both English and Chinese.

"OK, I'm done," she said when she finished.

"Good, just in time. Let's get down there and find the drone."

Ten minutes later, Bridges and Lee felt a slight vibration—the first sign that their LAV had encountered an atmosphere. Bridges watched his instruments, focusing on his craft's attitude and skin temperature. RHODA was piloting at this stage of the flight, following instructions Bridges and Captain Merriweather had given her. The AI would ensure that Aries chose the optimum path of descent and minimum fuel consumption, vital if Bridges hoped to make it off the planet and safely back to Endeavor. Bridges and Lieutenant Lee were just along for the ride, at least until they neared the planet's surface.

The small spacecraft entered the planet's atmosphere with its nose up at a thirty-degree angle, using its flat underside as an airbrake. Bridges' view, if he bothered to look out the forward viewports, was of a vast expanse of stars dominated by Erebus, the larger of the planet's two moons. However, Bridges' attention was currently on the LAV's instrument cluster and small holoviewer. While Bridges was confident in RHODA's abilities, he was ready to take over if he saw anything that made him nervous—more nervous than he already was.

As focused as he was, he couldn't help noticing the light flickering outside the craft. Glancing out the forward viewport, he saw the streams of ionized gas produced by the friction between the LAV and the atmosphere. The ionized gases twisted and danced on the LAV's viewports, glowing in deep magentas, greens, and purples. "Maybe I should put on some Astro Rock," he said, referring to a popular 22nd-century electronic music genre. "It reminds me of my time at Maryland. We had a laser and hologram light show yearly during graduation week."

Lee smiled and then closed her eyes. She always hated reentry. Although space travel was hardly new to her, she knew that from a statistical perspective, it was still the most dangerous part of space travel.

"It's getting bumpy in here, RHODA," he said. "Do you need me to take over?"

"You're kidding, right?" Lee said.

"I cannot recommend that course of action, Lieutenant. Based on the requirement to minimize propellant consumption, precise control of Aries One is required. Do you want me to recalculate de-orbit parameters?" RHODA replied.

"No, no, that's OK. You're doing fine," said Bridges, knowing full well that RHODA could fly circles around any human pilot. "I'll get my chance."

Lee sighed with relief.

Bridges focused on the spacecraft's instruments as the light show continued outside. Two minutes of intense buffeting finally eased. Outside, the light show had also faded. Thrusters fired, putting Aries in a slightly nose-down configuration.

With Aries' nose now pitched down toward the planet, Bridges got his first glimpse of the cloud cover glowing in the bright moonlight.

At the pre-selected altitude, Aries' wings rotated outward and locked into place, and the craft's flight control systems were enabled.

With engines now silent, the only noise Bridges could hear was the rush of air past his spacecraft.

Aries' velocity continued to decline as it fell through the planet's atmosphere. Although Bridges and Lee could not hear the sonic boom produced by Aries as it flew across the alien landscape, they were aware of it. Aries' designers had tweaked the LAV's drag characteristics to minimize the sound, but they could not eliminate it entirely. Bridges and Lee could only hope that any aliens out and about might find it strange, but not enough to cause concern.

Bridges had chosen this area because of the absence of lights or any sign of development for hundreds of miles in any direction. Hopefully, he thought, he had chosen well.

As Aries slowed to 300 knots, Bridges started the two aft-mounted engines, took control of the LAV's flight controls, and dove beneath the partial cloud cover, emerging over a deeply forested terrain barely viewable in the darkening gloom. Bridges could not employ landing or running lights for fear of detection, so instead, he engaged his night vision. Now flying by instruments, Bridges banked his spacecraft and headed toward his eventual target, Whoville, and the last location of the lost surveillance drone.

Bridges let the LAV settle to an elevation of just a hundred meters before engaging Aries' ground-hugging flight control system.

Aries' jet engines were as quiet as technology could make them, but they were still loud. Bridges' hopes of going undetected depended on the quieter engines, the fading light of day, his low-level flying, and the sparse population. He trusted that only someone directly under the path of his LAV could see the speeding spacecraft.

"Endeavor, this is Aries One. Do you copy?"

Even at the speed of light, it took four seconds before his radio transmission reached Endeavor via the relay satellite put in orbit months earlier. Bridges waited impatiently for a response. It took ten seconds, but to Bridges, it felt like an eternity.

"Aries One, this is Endeavor. Glad to hear from you, Lieutenant." Bridges smiled when he heard the voice of Cat Cortez.

"Good to hear your voice too, Lieutenant," said Bridges. "Aries One is currently in PFM (Powered Flight Mode) on final approach—ETA ten minutes. I'll check in again when we're on the deck."

"We copy. Good luck," said Cortez ten seconds later.

Aries's forward-facing high-definition camera fed the cockpit display in crisp, living detail. Bridges studied the screen, searching for a break in the forest canopy—any flat patch he could use. He preferred to set Aries down like an aircraft rather than perform a vertical touchdown; an aerodynamic landing conserved precious rocket propellant by converting forward speed into lift. That method required flat, open terrain at least one hundred meters long. Failing that, he could always switch to a vertical descent, which demanded more fuel but needed far less horizontal room. Either option was vastly preferable to the one thing he couldn't afford: running out of fuel and crashing.

"That looks like a road down there!" exclaimed Doc Lee.

"So, it does," said Bridges, who had been watching the alien road for several minutes.

Below the speeding spacecraft, a road cut through the forest, meandering through the low hills and valleys, sometimes appearing on their left and sometimes on their right.

"It seems to be going in the same general direction we are—toward Whoville," said Bridges.

Below, the road swung from the right side and then turned again when it was directly under their ship. Aries, following the contours of the topology, elevated over a small ridge. At the summit, Bridges could see the lights of a small city—presumably Whoville—in the distance, perhaps fifty kilometers away.

"Damn," said Bridges.

"What?" said Lee.

"I didn't see it coming until the last minute."

"See what?"

"On the road down there—a vehicle, maybe."

"What kind of vehicle?" said Lee.

"I don't know—a car, I guess."

"Did they see us?"

"How could they miss us? We flew directly over them. Oh yeah, they saw us all right. There is nothing we can do about it now but continue with the

mission," said Bridges. "Let's focus on finding a suitable landing area."

Dualla and Glyvash did not hear or see the craft approaching until it was directly overhead. A deafening roar from the sky startled the vehicle's passengers, causing Glyvash to jerk his machine's steering lever as he dove beneath his seat. The vehicle skidded on the gravel roadway and plunged into a mass of thick bushes on the side of the road.

"By her grace, what was that?" shouted a clearly hysterical Glyvash. "Are you all right, Your Primacy?"

Glyvash was distraught. His two-seater motorcar was now entangled in a thicket of thorny vines, nose down in a ditch. He had panicked when the strange object flew over their heads and had lost control of his motorcar.

The vehicle was not his primary concern, however. What concerned him most was the well-being of Dakar Dualla.

"Calm yourself, Glyvash. I am fine," replied Dualla.

"To the glory of Xenosta," said Glyvash.

Glyvash was relieved, indeed. If something happened to Dakar Dualla, he could lose his position at the Science Quoram—or even worse. He shuddered to think about the repercussions.

However, there was no time to think about that now. Glyvash had to get his motorcar out of the ditch. Was it damaged? Glyvash crawled out of his seat, over the hood, and down into the ditch to examine the vehicle's front end. The only damage he could see was the left glow light. The bracket attached to the vehicle was bent at a ninety-degree angle, causing the light to point to the left—a situation Glyvash easily remedied by grasping the light and bending it back into proper alignment.

Of more concern was the vehicle's wooden frame. If that were broken, they would have to walk back to Whoville.

Ignoring the rain and the water flowing down into the ditch, Glyvash crawled under the vehicle.

"The frame and the wheels are undamaged," he shouted over the rain.

Dualla had already left the vehicle and scrambled to the center of the road. "Glyvash, did you see that?" she said, scanning the skies, eyes as wide as a Tarkhan sea devil, hoping to get another view of the strange craft.

"I saw something," he said as he crawled out from under the motorcar. "It was flying. It flew right over us."

Glyvash turned back to look at his motorcar. "Nothing seems to be broken, Your Primacy."

"It was flying," repeated Dualla, oblivious to Glyvash's words.

"Do you think it was the space object?" Glyvash asked, wiping the mud from his hands.

"What else? It had wings like a bird and two glowing lights pointing behind it. This is exciting, and it proves what I've been saying."

"Your Primacy, please be careful. You could get into serious trouble. I could get in trouble," he added.

"Nonsense, Glyvash. Sometimes you worry like an old Sarka fish. Surely the Council will believe the personal accounts of a Dualla, tal`su (student) of a council member, and a scientist."

"But we have no proof."

"We have the object you found—the disk. We have the photos from our telescope, and now we have this sighting. Surely, it's enough."

"I think we need more."

Dualla cast a dismissive glance at Glyvash.

"And why is it important what you think?"

Dualla's harsh comment stung her chief assistant.

"Do you really think it was some sort of creature?" Glyvash asked meekly.

"No, not a creature—a flying machine," said Dualla, excitement welling up in her voice.

"A machine—that can fly?" said Glyvash. "Surely you are wrong. Is it not forbidden to create such a thing? It is blasphemy."

Dualla was about to reprimand her male assistant, but her excitement and sense of wonder made her more charitable.

"Yes, Glyvash, it is forbidden. But do you think a race so advanced it can travel to the stars would not have mastered the ability to create machines that fly in the air? Do you think they would limit themselves to our religious traditions and irrational laws?"

"It is amazing even to contemplate the science involved. Where do you think it was going in such a hurry?"

Dualla pondered this for a moment before responding. Then her eyes widened.

"They want their object back! The one you found, Glyvash! They intend to land their ship and then..."

Dualla's thoughts immediately turned to Yuni, her young tal`su, alone in their home, unaware she might be in danger.

"Glyvash, we must hurry," shouted Dualla, motioning frantically for Glyvash to extricate their vehicle."

The two scientists struggled to free the three-wheeled motorcar from the thick tangle of bushes that had entrapped it. Finally, with Dualla behind the wheel and Glyvash heaving mightily from the front, the machine lurched free.

Minutes later, the two were racing back toward the small hamlet of Whoville as fast as the tiny vehicle could go.

"The weather is getting much worse, Your Primacy. I am worried. The road is getting very slippery," said Glyvash, shouting over the roar of the driving rain.

"There is nothing we can do about that, Glyvash. Just go as fast as you can," shouted a clearly worried Dualla.

"Oh, I wish I had never seen that thing," wailed Glyvash.

# CHAPTER 47

*Milo's Landing*

Bridges was about to give up hope when he spotted a clearing to his left. He slowed Aries as much as he dared and banked to port to get a clear view of the potential landing strip. To Bridges, it appeared to be a dry lakebed.

"RHODA, analyze the clearing off my port side distance, six-hundred meters."

Two seconds later, RHODA's mellifluous voice sounded in his headset.

"The area's surface composition is unknown. It is sparsely covered by a layer of vegetation approximately thirty centimeters in height."

"Is it level?" asked Bridges.

"The surface slopes upward by one point eight degrees from south to north," said RHODA.

"Is it suitable for a horizontal landing?"

"The surface exceeds the minimum criteria for a horizontal landing," replied the ship's AI.

"I think we have our runway," said Bridges as he banked Aries again to port and lined his ship up for his final approach.

Bridges radioed Endeavor to confirm his intention to land, his voice steady but focused. With the transmission sent, he reached for the landing gear controls and engaged them. A low, mechanical hum filled the cockpit, followed by the reassuring thud of metal locking into place. The sound was familiar, almost routine, yet in moments like this it carried extra weight—confirmation that Aries was ready to meet the ground.

"The landing gear is down and locked," said RHODA.

"There is a bit of crosswind, Doc. This could get bumpy," said Bridges as the LAV glided toward the ersatz runway.

At the last moment, Bridges lifted the spacecraft's nose and throttled back its engines. The lightweight LAV settled slowly, bounced twice, and rolled to a stop seventy-five meters later.

"I don't fancy being out in the open like this," said Bridges as he scanned the surrounding terrain. "Let's throttle up and taxi closer to the tree line. Maybe we can find a break in the trees big enough to hide a spaceship." Bridges commanded the LAV to fold its wings and then, with engines at their lowest output, taxied toward the tree line. A minute later, Bridges tucked the small spacecraft between several large trees, making it practically invisible to prying eyes.

"Nice job, Lieutenant. I think we will be safe here," said Lee, "unless we run into hunters or campers—or an eight-legged thoat."

"An Edgar Rice Burrows fan, I presume," laughed Bridges.

"Since I was a tiny calot," said Lee as she unbuckled herself from her co-pilot's seat. "I got hooked on the John Carter of Mars books."

"I can see you as a calot—three rows of teeth and mean."

"That's me," said Lee, "and I bite."

Bridges radioed their status to Endeavor while Lee readied herself for her sample-collection EVA.

After locking her helmet into place with a firm twist and slinging the portable sample-collection kit over her shoulders, Lieutenant Lee stepped into the ship's airlock—a cramped compartment barely large enough for two in full EVA suits. The interior hatch closed behind her with a muted clunk, and the seals engaged, isolating her from the cabin. She worked the release for the LAV's outer hatch; it opened with a faint hiss as the pressure equalized. Without hesitation, she stepped forward and dropped the short half meter to the planet's surface, feeling the subtle shift in gravity beneath her boots.

"That's one small step for a man, one giant leap for a badass Asian doctor lady," Lee joked. "I feel like I weigh a hundred kilos. Remind me to adjust my diet and my training regimen when we get back to Endeavor."

"No more pasta for you," said Bridges. "Just take it slow. Breathe slowly, and don't exert yourself too much. It takes a while to adjust to the higher gravity."

"Uh, mansplain much? I was landing on alien planets when you were still in diapers, junior."

"Ha. Sorry, Doc. Bad habit. I sometimes forget to respect my elders."

"Watch it, rocket boy, or I'll kick your ass," said Lee.

Bridges returned to his pilot's seat, where he could monitor the ship's sensors. He felt quite comfortable that he—or, more accurately, the ship's motion detectors and infrared heat sensors—would detect any potential threats within 500 meters (about 1640 ft). He also kept a close eye on his fellow shipmate, keeping his EVA suit and helmet on so he could react to any emergency.

Outside, Lee did a slow three-sixty-degree turn to get her bearings and scope out the surrounding terrain. *Nothing like Mars*, she thought. But encouragingly similar to Earth.

On one side was the large open flatland Aries had used as a makeshift runway. Parallel lines in the waving grasses traced Aries' landing. On the other side, a forest populated with trees very much like the trees that bordered her family's farm in China, but at the same time, unfamiliar. In between sat the Aries spacecraft.

It suddenly dawned on Lee that she hadn't seen the outside of an LAV since her last training mission. Soot, caused by their fiery reentry through the planet's atmosphere, blackened the bottom of the spacecraft. *Amazing machine*, she thought.

"Aries, this is Lee—com check."

"Read you loud and clear, Doc," replied Bridges.

Lee glanced skyward, amazed at the intensity of the aurora dancing overhead. That would take some getting used to, she thought.

Refocusing on the task at hand, Lee moved a few meters away from the LAV and then, mindful of the planet's gravity, knelt carefully on one knee. Opening her UV/radiation-proof collection container, she extracted a small tool she used to scoop up a small soil sample. After placing the sample in the container, Lee stood and moved toward a nearby thicket. Bridges watched as she examined and then took samples from several strange yet familiar-looking plants. Bridges looked at his watch. They had agreed that thirty minutes was enough for sample collection, and Bridges wanted to hold her to that limit.

"Fifteen minutes left, Doc."

"Don't rush me. I'm almost done. I want to get a scraping from one of those trees."

"Roger that," he replied.

Lee moved slowly toward a grove of large trees approximately ten meters from the LAV. Bridges continued to monitor her vitals, noting a slight rise in her blood pressure and heart rate. *Well within safe limits*, he thought to himself. Given the planet's gravity and her bulky EVA suit, Lee was doing well. Then again, this wasn't her first dance, he thought.

"Aries, this is Endeavor. Come in," squawked the intercom.

"Endeavor, this is Aries. What's up?" Bridges recognized the no-nonsense voice that immediately identified the caller as Don Stoner.

"Aries, we are seeing a weather front moving into your area. It looks heavy, and we see a ton of lightning flashes."

"How far away, Endeavor?"

"Looks like one to two hours—maybe less. Judging by the clouds, we're seeing pretty high winds."

"How high is high?"

"Upwards of fifty knots. Is there any way you will be off the surface before the storm reaches you?"

"Don't think so. Lee is still outside collecting samples. She says it will take maybe an hour to process them once she gets back inside."

"All right. You'll have to ride out the storm on the surface."

"Roger. We will keep you updated on our status and the storm—out."

Bridges turned his attention back to Lee.

"Doctor, it's time to come back in. We have a large storm front approaching. We may have to move up our schedule a bit," radioed Bridges.

"OK, OK. I'm just going to take an air sample. I'll start back in ten," said Lee.

*But I don't want to go back in*, Lee thought to herself. *I want to stay outside and play.*

Lee looked around. How many people have ever had the chance to be the first person to set foot on an inhabited planet in another stellar system? Lee had other accomplishments in her NASA/ISA career. She had lived on Mars for over three years, setting up the colony's health care system. She pioneered several low-gravity surgical procedures and was in the history books for her innovative treatment of muscular atrophy during stasis. But she knew that here, now, would be the crowning accomplishment of her career. When her kids or grandkids asked her what she remembered most about her adventures in space, this would be the one she would tell them about. Maybe she could spend a bit more time on the surface after Bridges returned from his covert mission, she thought.

Returning to the LAV, Lee entered the airlock and sealed the outer hatch. "RHODA, run decontamination protocol," said Lee.

Lee knew the protocol well—after all, she had been on the team that designed it. So, she knew what to expect. First, UV light and low-level radiation bathed her spacesuit in an ethereal glow. Next, a fine mist comprising ethyl-alcohol, formaldehyde, chlorine, iodine, and a phenol-based chemical filled the airlock and dripped from her suit. Finally, water jets rinsed off the remaining chemicals.

A buzzer sounded, letting Lee know that the decontamination process was over, and she could exit the airlock and enter the cargo hold. Moving deliberately, Lee opened the lid of a Class IV biological safety containment (BSC) box where she placed her sample container. Only after she had satisfied herself that the box was hermetically sealed did she feel secure enough to remove her EVA suit.

"Samples secure, Lieutenant," said Lee. "You can come back and watch if you'd like."

"I'll stay up here and monitor our cameras and sensors. Never know when we might get unwanted visitors," he replied.

"Suit yourself," she replied.

Lee inserted her arms and hands into the glove holes of the BSC box and carefully opened the sample bag.

"RHODA, record my observations," Lee said.

"Recording," said the omnipresent AI.

"OK, first, I'm going to prepare the soil sample," said Lee.

For the next thirty-five minutes, Doc Lee prepared sample slides from the various samples she had taken outside the ship. One by one, she inserted them into a microscope inside the BSC. A small display mounted above and outside the BSC displayed a greatly enlarged image of the sample under the microscope. Lee carefully examined each slide and asked RHODA to compare the image with the ship's voluminous database of known pathogens. This would be a lot easier back on Earth, Lee thought. There, the entire process would be automated—samples scanned, analyzed, and cataloged in moments with no need for manual handling. But here, every kilogram counted, and on an LAV, weight restrictions were unforgiving. Heavy, state-of-the-art analyzers were a luxury no one could justify hauling across light-years. Instead, she was left to work with the bare essentials: fragile sample slides, a compact portable microscope, and her own skill. It felt almost archaic, yet it was all she had.

"Endeavor, this is Aries. Are Doctors Martin and Graham present?"

"Aries, this is Endeavor. Yes, Dr. Lee, they are." The reply arrived after the usual ten-second delay.

"Good. I'm examining a biological sample from a plant scraping, and so far, everything looks completely ordinary—not what I expected at all. I'm seeing the usual plant cell structures: rigid cell walls, intact membranes, distinct nuclei, and what appear to be chloroplasts suspended in cytoplasm. The chromosomes are clearly visible as well. Honestly, I'm both impressed by the clarity and slightly disappointed—there's nothing here that looks remotely alien."

"I hear ya," said Dr. Graham. "You are bringing samples back to Endeavor?"

"Well, I had little time to collect samples, but if we have time and Lieutenant Bridges believes it's safe, I will try to get more."

"Animal samples, too," said Martin.

"I didn't see any animals, but there is a small pond twenty meters from the ship. I could collect a sample there."

"Please do," said Martin.

"I'll fill you guys in after I've completed my analysis, but you can monitor the telemetry while I run more tests."

Lee turned her attention back to the BSC box. The next step was to test for DNA. Most scientists, including the ones aboard Endeavor and Doc Lee, believed that for an alien microbe or pathogen to be harmful to humans, it had to contain DNA.

Lee took the first sample plant scraping, prepared it, and then inserted it into a small device.

"What's that?" Bridges asked, watching from the cockpit on the small holoviewer.

"It's called a Nanopore DNA Sequencer. We normally use it to help us diagnose diseases on long-duration missions, but it's also useful in these situations," Lee replied.

Lee's expression gradually changed to a scowl. "Well, that's interesting. Either the device is broken, or there's no DNA in this sample."

"Maybe the battery is dead," suggested Bridges.

"Now, why didn't I think of that?" said Lee with a hint of sarcasm.

"I ran diagnostics before I inserted the sample. Let's try another one," said Lee as she prepared a second sample. Lee carefully inserted the second sample and pressed the sequence button.

"Still no DNA," she said. "Let's try a different test. I'm going to try a PCR test."

"Good idea," said Bridges.

Lee laughed. "Do you know what a PCR test is?"

"Uh, not really," said Bridges.

"PCR stands for Polymerase Chain Reaction. It's used to analyze short sequences of DNA (or RNA) even if a sample contains only a minute quantity. I'm going to use a device called a Thermal Cycler & Analyzer or TCA," she said, removing the device from her portable equipment kit. After powering up the device and running a built-in diagnostic, Lee inserted a short test tube that contained her first sample.

"This will take about ten minutes, Milo, so you might as well relax."

"How can anyone relax in a situation like this?" said Bridges. "Are you relaxed?"

"Not really. So how are things going with you and Cat?"

"What? What do you mean? Cat and I are just friends."

"If you say so, but it's obvious something is going on between you two. Have you sealed the deal yet?"

"There's nothing to seal. Lieutenant Cortez and I are just colleagues. We're friendly, sure, but that's it. What does she say?"

"She's in denial, too. But you two are perfect for each other."

A second later, a short beep from the TCA signaled the completion of the PCR test.

"Damn. I must be doing something wrong. I'm getting a negative for DNA."

"What does that mean?" Bridges asked.

"Just what I said. There is no DNA in any of my samples, and I can clearly see chromosomes under the microscope."

"Maybe it's alien DNA."

Dr. Lee gave Bridges the 'duh' look. "Our understanding of life would surely argue for the existence of something like DNA. There are other tests, but I don't have the necessary chemistry in my kit, so I'll have to wait until we get back to Endeavor," said Lee. "I guess I brought all these other instruments for nothing."

"Why is that?" Bridges asked.

"You sure have a lot of questions," she said. "Well, all our pathogen analysis gear revolves around DNA; without DNA, there's nothing to analyze."

"So, am I good to go?" Bridges asked.

"Not so fast. I can still run my samples through my aptamer library."

"That's a new one. What is an aptamer library?"

"I thought you knew everything, Bridges."

"Well, I do," laughed Bridges. "I just can't quite remember aptamers."

"Let me refresh your memory," said Lee. "Aptamers are short chains of nucleotides."

"Uh, huh," said Bridges, rolling his eyes.

"First, I incubate my field samples with my aptamer. Complex molecules in the samples are more likely to bind with the nucleotides than simple ones.

"Next, I analyze the binding pattern. Then, I sequence the complex molecules that look promising. These are the ones that are most likely to show life as we understand it."

"You're looking for pathogens, right?" Bridges asked.

"Right again, genius."

"Cool. How long will all that take?"

"Just a few minutes. Relax, it's not like you have any place to go, right?"

"Yeah, right," said Bridges.

Bridges watched as Lee placed a minute quantity of each field sample into a small device she had removed from her lab kit. Each test took less than twenty seconds to run, and each result was followed by a shake of Lee's head.

"I didn't find any known pathogens, but there's also one more thing I want to do."

"What's that?"

"I'm going to do a test specific to you," said Lee. "First, I need to take some of your blood and a skin scraping."

"Great," said Bridges, relocating to the aft cargo bay where Lee had set up shop.

After removing a syringe from her bag, Lee located a vein in Bridges' wrist and extracted a small amount of his blood. Then she used a small knife-like tool to scrape a few skin cells from his cheek. Next, she deposited both samples and a few drops of an accelerator agent into a test tube.

The next step was to inject the plant sample into the test tube. Finally, she inserted the test tube into a BSIA (Biological Sample Incubator and Analyzer), which analyzed the mixture for potentially dangerous chemical byproducts, gases, or other signature reactions.

"So far, everything looks reasonably good. The absence of DNA means that life here is so alien that their microbes and pathogens are probably not compatible with our physiology. That's not to say there aren't any dangers out there. I only tested a small area. I also didn't take samples of skin or blood or anything else from an animal or sentient, so until I do, I suggest you keep your distance."

"Great, that's what I wanted to hear," said Bridges. Bridges pressed the button on his communicator. "Endeavor, this is Aries. Do you copy?"

"Aries, this is Endeavor. Go ahead."

"Endeavor, Dr. Lee has finished her analysis of the environment. Results are negative for harmful pathogens. Do I have the go-ahead for the mission?"

After what seemed like an eternity but was just forty-five seconds, Endeavor responded.

"Aries, you are a go. Proceed cautiously."

"Thank you, Endeavor."

Bridges quickly removed his EVA suit with Lee's help. Next, he reached for the bulkhead to unleash the item Jonathan Mills had made for him.

"Is that what it looks like?" Lee asked.

"Isn't she a beauty? It's an electric motorcycle—an electro-cycle," he said, grinning.

"It looks like a child's toy," said Lee.

"The seat and handlebars extend," said Bridges, doing just that. "It should enable me to get to Whoville and back in less than an hour. That should give me approximately thirty minutes at our primary target to find what I'm looking for. Hopefully, that's enough time."

"Don't forget your breathing gear," said Lee.

"I was getting to that," he replied.

In one swift motion, Bridges pulled the alien-looking tunic over his head, revealing his muscular physique. Lee had seen Bridges' bare chest before, but still enjoyed the view. Opening the bag she had stored in the cargo hold, Lee extracted the foil pack, Oxy-Direct container, tubing, plus a roll of medical tape. Two minutes later, Bridges had the gear firmly taped to his chest and the tube of oxygenated liquid attached to the port she had previously installed in a wrist artery.

After verifying everything was working correctly, Lee gave Bridges a thumbs up. "OK, you're ready to go," she said.

"Thanks, Doc," he replied. "Open the cargo bay door, RHODA."

The door swung down, creating a ramp to the surface.

"It's nice not having to wear that bulky EVA gear," he said. "Air smells normal. God, look at that aurora. If they have music and love songs down here, I bet they often reference that aurora. Hey Doc, what rhymes with aurora?"

"There must be a plethora of words that rhyme," said Lee. "But I can't think of any at the moment."

"Funny," laughed Bridges.

"You better get going, Cowboy," said Lee, "or the storms will be here before you get back."

"I'll find a place to ride it out if it gets bad," said Bridges as he straddled his new ride. "Look for me in about two hours. If I don't make it back, RHODA can pilot the ship back to Endeavor."

"And probably better than you," she said.

Bridges adjusted the small speaker behind his ear and tested the miniature microphone clipped to his tunic. Satisfied that all was in working order, Bridges blew Lee a kiss and switched on the cycle's headlight.

"OK, don't screw things up. And don't start a damn war," said Lee as she watched Bridges, mounted on his electro-cycle, motor down the ramp and into the forest.

Bridges kept the speed of his electro-cycle to twenty kilometers per hour, barely faster than he could run. He needed to conserve the bike's battery as much as possible in case he needed to return to Aries in a hurry. The last thing he needed was a dead battery. This planet's gravity added ten kilos to his weight. Bridges didn't want to risk a mad escape back to the ship on foot.

Mills had provided the electro-cycle with a headlamp, but Bridges was undecided if he should use it. If he left it off, he could accidentally drive into a hole or hit a downed tree branch or large rock, potentially injuring himself. If he used the headlamp, any alien in the vicinity might wonder who he was and what he was doing. He finally opted for safety, calculating that a lighted vehicle on the road at night was a less unusual occurrence than an unlighted vehicle. Plus, if he saw someone approaching and had enough time, he could quickly douse the light and dive into the forest. Fortunately, the unpaved road seemed lightly used.

Bridges planned to stay on the narrow, hard-packed dirt road until he got close enough to Whoville to see its lights. He would then hide the electro-cycle in the heavy bushes that lined the roadway and walk the remaining distance, using the forest as cover.

After an hour of solitary motoring, the lights of Whoville appeared in the gloom. Bridges slowed, then stopped. He calculated the lights were less than a kilometer and a half away. Bridges looked around for anything unusual, like a distinctive tree—*they all looked like cartoon trees*, he thought—or a strange rock or something that would help him identify this spot in the road when he returned from exploring his target in Whoville. Seeing nothing, he marked the tree nearest the road.

Five minutes later, Bridges had finished hiding the electro-cycle and carving "Cat + Milo" into the tree large enough to see from the forest or the road if one was looking closely enough.

"What, am I twelve?" said Bridges, laughing. "RHODA, record my location. I am leaving the electro-cycle here for later retrieval."

"Location recorded," said RHODA.

After forcing his way through the dense wall of brush that choked the roadside, Bridges found the forest's interior surprisingly open, the trees spaced far enough apart to allow easy passage. Reaching into his tunic, he pulled out a pair of e-spectacles and settled them over his eyes. Sleek and lightweight, the state-of-the-art devices were standard issue in every pilot's emergency kit. Their low-light amplification circuitry flickered to life, sharpening the shadows and pulling detail from the gloom—exactly what he needed to navigate the forest's dim, green-tinged interior.

*Strange-looking trees, Bridges thought. Where have I seen those before? Oh, right—Madagascar.* He'd never actually been there, but a documentary he'd watched before leaving Earth had left an impression. The towering, swollen trunks and sparse crowns were unmistakable, reminiscent of the island's iconic baobabs. The film had mentioned how climate change was taking a toll on their numbers, a quiet tragedy unfolding half a world away—a world he might never see again.

The trees in this alien forest rose thirty to forty meters high, their massive trunks spanning five to ten meters across at the base. To Milo, they looked almost like something out of a cartoon—perfectly circular, unnaturally smooth, and narrowing steadily as they reached upward, the tops barely a quarter the width of the bottoms. Branches grew only at the very crown, far above his head.

The few fallen branches within reach were more like oversized pine boughs, but instead of soft, flexible needles, these were stiff and dangerously sharp. Each needle was five to ten millimeters wide at the base, tapering to a needlepoint fine enough to pierce skin with ease. The forest floor was carpeted with them. Bridges would have to watch every step if he wanted to avoid an unwelcome puncture.

Bridges also had to remind himself repeatedly to walk and not run. Being an Earthling on an alien planet with substantial gravity was enough to elevate his blood pressure and heart rate. The chance of being discovered didn't help. He knew that Doc Lee and the crew of Endeavor were monitoring his vitals through the various sensors taped to his body. If his numbers got too high, Endeavor might pull the plug on the mission, and that would not be a good thing. *I should stop and do ten minutes of Tai Chi, thought Bridges as he smiled. I wish I had the time.*

Fifteen minutes later, Bridges could see several dwellings.

Bridges noted a change in the weather. The wind kicked up considerably. He felt occasional drops of rain falling on his face, and it was getting colder.

"Endeavor, can you give me a status report on the storm?"

"Hello Milo. This is Cat." Milo smiled at hearing Cortez's voice. "We are tracking the storm closely, but we're at a disadvantage because we don't know if storms react the same way on this planet as they do on Earth. Our best guess is that you have about an hour before the leading edge of the storm reaches you. We're also measuring winds above one hundred and twenty klicks and lots of rain. Flooding could also be an issue."

"Bridges, this is Merriweather. I'm thinking of terminating the mission. I don't want to put you and Lee in any more danger than you already are."

"Understand, Captain. But I'm already in sight of the target, and turning back now, in my opinion, would be a mistake."

Bridges waited patiently for a response. He knew Merriweather was mulling it over and asking others for input. Finally, a full two minutes later, Merriweather's voice sounded in his earpiece.

"OK, I'm deferring to your judgment. But no hero crap. The dammed drone isn't worth your life."

"I understand, Captain. I'll be safe. Bridges out."

Bridges had to get out of the forest fast. Super-sharp needles were raining down on him from the cartoon tree branches waving in the steadily increasing wind. He already had several minor cuts on his hands and probably on his face, but with the blowing mist now wetting his face, it was hard for him to tell.

A sudden gust of wind caused more super-sharp needles to rain down upon him.

"Damn, that hurts!" he screamed. Bridges examined his arms, finding streaks of blood diluted by the rain. He felt his face and found more blood on his hands. He felt something cold and wet under his tunic, but resisted the temptation to strip. Instead, he rushed from the forest out onto the roadway. *Gotta keep to the schedule*, he thought.

"RHODA, do you have my location?" said Bridges.

"Yes, Milo, I have your location."

"OK, I'm facing a line of dwellings running from my left to my right. Please direct me to the target."

"Milo, move forty-five meters to the north. Then move fifty meters to the east."

"Thanks, RHODA."

Ten minutes later, Bridges stood near the back wall of a structure that resembled an old adobe dwelling. The interior was dark, which either meant that it was unoccupied or that the residents were sleeping.

"RHODA, verify that I am standing near the target."

"You are two meters from the target, Milo."

Bridges took a deep breath. He was about to commit a crime. He was about to break into what was probably someone's home, and he was planning on stealing some of their things. Hopefully, no one was home, but he calculated his odds of going undetected were less than fifty percent.

Moving as quietly as he could, Bridges moved around the structure until he found a door. After sweeping the surrounding area, Bridges placed his hand on the door handle and paused for what seemed an eternity. Slowly but firmly, he pushed against the door. Bridges expected a locked door, but was surprised when the door slowly opened.

*They're not much concerned with home security*, Bridges thought to himself.

Bridges turned up the gain on his night-vision-equipped spectacles and then tentatively entered the darkened structure. He slowly scanned the room, looking for any dangers. A sudden chill moved down his spine. He had the definite feeling that he was being watched. Turning to his left, his eyes settled on two glowing lights. Almost instantly, he realized he was looking at eyes staring menacingly back at him.

# CHAPTER 48

*More alien than first thought*

Dr. Lee continued her discussions with Doctors Martin and Graham on the results of her DNA tests and the significance thereof while she waited for Lieutenant Bridges.

"Perhaps it's a question of chirality," suggested Graham.

"That's a fascinating idea," said Martin. "That could account for the negative DNA readings—especially for the enzyme tests you ran, Doc."
Zoe Bishop had joined Graham and Martin and listened intently to their conversation.

"Sorry for my ignorance, Doctors, but I'm unfamiliar with the term."

"Let me see if I can explain. Are you familiar with L-form and D-form amino acids?" Graham asked.

"I'm flashing back to high school chemistry," said Bishop. "Just so you know, I failed high school chemistry."

"I won't hold that against you," laughed Graham. "Let's see if I can explain it. Chirality is the property of asymmetry. Think of the molecular configuration of amino acids and sugars. You remember those stick models we played with in BioChem class?"

"My eyes are glassing over already, Doc," said Bishop.

"No? Well, let me expand a bit. Every amino acid can occur in two isomeric forms," said Graham. "They can form either a left-handed or right-handed configuration around a central carbon atom, by convention called L-form and D-form. "

"Not L-form and R-form?"

"No, pay attention. It's L-form and D-form. Sugars can also exist in mirror image configurations. The D or L designation depends on which form you're talking about, and most naturally occurring sugars are of the D form."

"OK, I'm with you," said Bishop. "I sort of remember a guest on my show discussing creating an alternative to sugar using its mirror image."

"Exactly," added Dr. Martin, listening to the conversation. "Earth-based life always comprises L-form amino acids and D-form sugars. Molecules of opposite chirality have identical chemical properties as their twins, so life-based upon D-form amino acids and L-form sugars could be possible."

"Endeavor, this is Lee. Would that have caused my test results? Do our instruments assume and require the normal Earth-specific forms?"

"Maybe," said Graham, "especially for enzyme tests, but that's just speculation because we've never had the opposite form of DNA to run our standard tests on—until now, that is."

"I reckon pathogens based on this alternate form of DNA would be harmless," added Martin.

"OK, let's hope you're right," said Lee. "Do you agree, Dr. Graham?"

"Yes, I think I do."

"OK, is the captain there?" Lee asked.

"This is Merriweather," said the captain after the expected ten-second delay. "What's up?"

"Captain, everything is pretty quiet around here, and Lieutenant Bridges is a good hour away, so I'm hoping you will give me the go-ahead for another EVA," said Lee.

"What's the weather like at your location?"

"Not that bad. The wind is less than twenty km/h, and there's no appreciable rain. Captain, there's a pond less than twenty meters from the ship that may contain aquatic bio-forms we could study. I also want to take a few more plant samples. I wouldn't be outside the ship for more than half an hour."

"It would help us confirm our chirality theory," said Graham.

"All right. I don't think I'd be able to talk you out of it anyway," said Merriweather. "Just be careful and stay within sight of your ship and in constant contact with RHODA and Endeavor."

"Copy that," answered Lee.

Lieutenant Lee decided not to wear her EVA suit on this excursion. Instead, she opted for an EPO (Erythropoietin) pill, expecting her stay outside Aries to be short.

Lee was out on the planet's surface within ten minutes. Unlike her earlier EVA, it was now much darker. It was also raining harder than Lee had suggested to Merriweather. The cloud cover had obscured what little light there might have been from Sanctuary's two moons and the constant planetary-wide aurorae. Aries' landing lights were dark, per their orders, and Lee had only her handheld flashlight for illumination.

Lee moved cautiously, trying to remain alert to any dangers that might lurk nearby while she looked for interesting biological samples. Approximately ten meters from the LAV, Lee noticed an interesting small flowering plant. She knelt on one knee and removed a collection bag and a small trowel from her kit. Digging carefully around the plant, Lee gently pulled the plant, its roots intact, from the soil and placed it in the collection bag.

"RHODA—record time and location for collection bag z-0234, plant sample," said Lee, speaking into the tiny microphone pinned to her collar.

"Recorded."

Lee stood, scanned the area, and continued her trek toward the pond. Suddenly, it started raining harder. She instantly regretted not wearing her EVA suit. Water flowed over her face and into her eyes, and her handheld flashlight could not penetrate the torrent of water falling on and around her. Disoriented, Lee was afraid to move. She couldn't see well enough to discern ground from water, and she could no longer see Aries.

"RHODA, do you have my location?"

Lee expected a response from Aries' AI. However, when RHODA failed to respond, a twinge of concern invaded Lee's thoughts.

"RHODA, do you have my location?"

Once again, RHODA failed to respond to Lee's hail.

*What the hell?* Lee thought. After a few minutes reviewing what little information she could deduce, she finally realized that the signal from her mic wasn't strong enough to cut through the heavy rain—or maybe the water running down her neck had shorted it out. There was nothing Lee could do but stand there until the storm diminished. Until then, she had no way of discerning direction. If Lee tried to guess the way back to the ship, she could miss it entirely and get lost or walk directly into a ditch, a raging river, or over a cliff. Damn, what she wouldn't give for a simple compass. Lee had no option but to wait out the storm.

Five minutes later, the storm and the rain had increased in intensity.

"RHODA? Endeavor? Bridges? Does anyone copy?"

Once again, there was no response from RHODA or anyone else.

"What do you mean, we've lost them?" asked Merriweather.

"It's the storm, Captain. It's playing havoc with our communications," said Cortez, who was currently manning the comm station. "We're still receiving telemetry from Milo, but he's not answering our hails. We're getting nothing from Doc."

Merriweather wasn't happy. The comm systems were state-of-the-art. They were designed to function in the harshest environments, and yet he could not reach his people because of a little rain?

"It is raining pretty hard down there, Captain," said Zoe Bishop, who was sitting in the chair next to Merriweather.

"Hell, I know that. But they're my people, and I'm responsible for their safety."

"This is a dangerous business, Captain."

"I know, Zoe. But I still worry. By the way, this is off the record."

"Too late," Bishop smiled. "This might be a bad time, but I'd like to accompany you when you go down there yourself—for first contact."

"I don't know about that. It might not be the best time."

"I'll take an umbrella in case it rains like this again."

Merriweather turned to look at his XO seated behind him. "Stone, fix the damn comm system."

Turning back to Bishop, Merriweather smiled. "I'll think about it."

# CHAPTER 49

*Investigating Dualla's Home*

"What have I gotten myself into?" Bridges mumbled under his breath. He was standing just inside the doorway of an alien's home and staring at something that didn't look at all friendly. Bridges adjusted his low-light spectacles, trying to better understand what he was dealing with. He managed only a vague outline of something that seemed very alien. Maybe a small dinosaur or a kangaroo with a pig nose, a large angry mouth, and very sharp-looking teeth. He might have laughed if he were viewing this creature at a zoo with a big fence or moat between them. However, at this very moment, amusement wasn't his primary feeling.

Bridges was also rethinking the "Should we take weapons to first contact?" debate. He had supported the idea that our first contact should be weapons-free. Now, however, faced with potential injury or death, he wished he had something, anything, to defend himself—a taser, stun gun, or even a big stick. But he had nothing.

He couldn't just stand here forever. Bridges looked around slowly, trying to find something he could use as a weapon. Finding nothing, he decided that the most prudent action was to retreat. Ever so slowly, Bridges backed through the front door, keeping the strange creature in sight. Unfortunately, as Bridges took a step, so did this alien watchdog. Step by step, the two played follow the leader. The animal was now standing in the doorway, allowing Bridges to get a much better look at the creature. The thing had a bulldog's muscular body but stood on its hind legs. Its front legs were much smaller, giving the thing a definite T-Rex vibe.

Bridges stopped. He leaned forward—slowly—reaching for the door handle. He intended to close the door, but the alien T-Rex doppelgänger quickly gleaned Bridges' intention and let out a low, guttural, and very menacing hiss *like some goddamn snake*, thought Bridges.

Bridges slowly raised his hands in an "OK, you win" gesture.

*OK, I'm good with animals. Dogs like me*, he thought.

Slowly, Bridges leaned forward and extended his hand, palm up.

"Nice monster. You're a good boy. Yes, you are. You wanna play? How about I let you out, and you can go for a run?"

The creature moved slowly toward Bridges and hissed again. Its tongue flicked out like a lizard. "They don't pay me enough," Bridges muttered.

Bridges was deciding what to do next when, without warning, the creature lunged toward him.

Bridges stumbled backward and raised his arms to protect his head as the creature barreled past, knocking him to the ground. He instantly realized that the creature's intention was not to attack him, but to escape the confines of its owner's home. Regaining his footing, Bridges turned and watched as the animal, running like a panicked cat, disappeared into the night.

Bridges let out a long, low sigh. That was intense. *My heart rate must be through the roof*, he thought. I wonder what they're thinking on Endeavor. Suddenly, the storm announced its presence by unleashing a torrent of heavy rain. Bridges could barely see the structure just two meters from where he stood. Quickly as he could, he entered the dwelling, closing the door behind him.

Bridges paused a good two minutes, listening for any sounds that might signal another alien presence. Satisfied he had not been detected, he began his investigation of the sophont Dualla's home and a search for Endeavor's downed surveillance drone.

The deluge of water falling on the structure's roof produced a steady but subdued roar, hopefully masking whatever noise he was making. Moving slowly but deliberately, he began his search. Removing his holo from a pouch in his tunic and selecting its camera mode, Bridges recorded every object, alien or familiar, that might be of value to their investigation. There were objects affixed to the walls that looked familiar—images of things and sophonts, both individuals and groups. This species had obviously discovered the technology of photography. Some objects reminded Milo of the tools hung on his grandpa's tool-shop walls, although he didn't know what they used these for. He saw items that wouldn't have seemed out of place in the dwelling of an Australian aborigine or a Native American. There were pictures that, in Bridges' mind, looked like nature scenes—a snow-covered mountain range, a beach, and a picturesque forest trail. One picture was of particular interest. It showed an adult female sophont, probably Dualla, with a juvenile alien, possibly female. *Could this be her offspring?* thought

Bridges. He hoped that mother and daughter were out for the evening, but he had to assume they were both at home and awake in one of the adjoining rooms.

Finishing his search of the walls, Bridges began looking for electronic equipment. Not finding any, he turned his attention to furniture with drawers where Dualla might store important documents. After finding none, Bridges slowly moved into an adjacent room to continue his search.

Meanwhile, approximately ten kilometers to the west, Dualla's desperate dash to save her young tal`su from unknown alien intentions had run into the leading edge of the storm. No longer able to see the roadway, Glyvash had reduced his speed to a snail's pace. But even at this reduced speed, the vehicle slid around like a hockey puck on ice. Glyvash furiously worked the steering lever, trying to anticipate the vehicle's motions, yet he still frequently skidded down the roadway sideways and even backwards.

"Glyvash, can't we go any faster?" wailed Dualla. "I must get home."

"I know," said Glyvash. "However, I cannot see the road. If I go any faster, we could crash."

"Please," implored Dualla, "as fast as you can."

Meanwhile, near the Aries spacecraft, Doc Lee crouched in the torrential rain, still unable to communicate with anyone or to see her way back to the safety of the lander. But she was determined to wait out the storm rather than risk getting lost on the alien planet. How long this storm might last was anyone's guess. She knew storms on Jupiter lasted for years, and she only hoped such was not the case on Sanctuary.

The wind had picked up considerably, and Lee kept her body low to the ground to keep from blowing away. She was also worried about getting swept away in a flash flood or mudslide. Should she continue to stand her ground or try to find her way back to Aries?

Torrents of water flowed over her as the rain continued. She was also finding it hard to breathe. She had taken an EPO pill, but it no longer seemed to have much effect.

"Endeavor, RHODA, this is Doc Lee. Do you copy?" she shouted, trying to be heard over the roar of the wind. She heard only static.

On Endeavor, concern for the fate of Aries was growing. There had been no communication with the crew for over an hour. Was it just a technical problem, or were Bridges and Lee injured, captured, or worse?

"I know everyone is concerned," said Merriweather, "but let's not panic just yet. Bridges and Lee know what they're doing. They just have to wait out the storm. Do we have an update on the storm, Mills?"

Mills was currently monitoring the weather data on another console. His holoview displayed a graphical representation of the planet centered on Aries' landing site. Rainfall appeared as bands of color sweeping over the area, with red showing the greatest intensity.

"It looks like a patch of clear sky is moving into their area, Captain," said

Mills. "There's a band of zero precipitation just to the west of the landing site and moving in an easterly direction. It should be over Aries in ten to fifteen minutes."

"Thanks, Mills. Let me know if you see anything concerning."

Merriweather activated the hologram on his holo and selected the Aries avatar. "Aries, this is Endeavor. Do you copy?"

There was still no response from Aries.

Bridges looked at his watch. He was over an hour behind schedule and beginning to worry about Doc Lee. He couldn't assume locals hadn't chanced upon Aries or Doc Lee. There might be hunters or campers swarming the ship at this very moment. The longer he and Lee were on the planet, the greater the risk of discovery. He had to get back as quickly as he could. He was also concerned about the supplemental breathing rig taped to his chest. Was it his imagination, or was it getting harder to breathe? The rainfall had soaked his tunic, and he didn't know how that might affect the rig. If Lee's estimates were correct, the rig could stop working any minute. He knew the rain must have lowered his body temperature, and the rig depended on body heat to work. It was time to leave.

Bridges took one more look around the small dwelling. He had conducted a thorough search of three rooms in the four-room dwelling. A small sleeping alien occupied the fourth room, so Bridges did only a cursory search, taking just a small book he found on a low table and installing a tiny surveillance camera.

As he turned toward the door to leave, Bridges spotted the surveillance drone.

"There you are," he whispered, stuffing it into his canvas collection bag.

Finally satisfied he had done all he could, Bridges stepped outside and into the pouring rain.

Doc Lee was the first to see the trailing edge of the storm. After an hour and a half of crouching in one place, Lee noticed a lessening of the storm's intensity. Turning on her flashlight, Lee scanned her environment. She could make out faint shapes of objects near her—trees, bushes, plants. Visibility was improving. A risk-averse person may have headed immediately back to the safety of their ship. Doc Lee was not that kind of person.

*OK, which way*, she thought to herself. "I think, oh yeah, it's over in that direction," she said as she headed toward the pond she had seen earlier.

Two minutes later, Lee stood at the water's edge, looking for a suitable location to take her samples. She knelt and took a few scoops of the brackish water to take back Aries for testing.

"RHODA, do you hear me?"

"Affirmative, Lieutenant Lee, I can hear you."

"Finally!" Lee said.

Now able to communicate with RHODA, Lee began recording her samples with the ship's AI, including a half liter of pond water and several water plants she carefully extracted from the water-soaked soil. Satisfied with her collection. Lee headed for Aries, moving as fast as she could.
Dualla and Glyvash were next to see the end of the storm.

"Glyvash, I think the storm is ending. Yes, I can clearly see the road. See the large moke bush on the left?"

"Yes, I see it, Your Primacy," said Glyvash.

"Then why are you driving like an old man?"

"Please, Your Primacy, it is still very slippery. I am still having trouble keeping our motorcar on the road," Glyvash said.

"I insist you go faster, Glyvash, or must I take control?"

"Of course, Your Primacy. I will do as you say."

Against his better instincts and giving in to his superior's demands, Glyvash and Dualla were soon speeding back to Whoville with almost complete disregard for their safety or their lives.

Bridges had already left the home of Dakar Dualla, using his internal compass to direct him toward the roadway back to Aries. He was confident that his years as a pilot had given him a built-in sense of direction. But he hadn't gone far before the rainfall diminished, and he realized he was going in the wrong direction. *So much for my fantastic sense of direction*, he thought wryly.

Fortunately, Bridges' unintentional detour might have saved him from detection by Dualla and Glyvash, who had finally arrived back at the village and were now running toward her home. Bridges had luckily avoided the two aliens and was now moving as fast as he could back toward Aries.

"Aries, this is Endeavor."

Endeavor had been sending this message once a minute for the last hour and a half without an answer. Finally …

"Endeavor, this is Aries. Do you copy?"

"Hey, welcome back, Lieutenant Lee. We were getting worried up here," said Captain Merriweather.

Lee could hear Endeavor's crew cheering in the background.

"I was also getting worried. That was one hellacious rainstorm. I've never experienced anything like it. I was outside, about fifty meters from the ship, when the storm hit. Visibility was zero, and I couldn't see a damn thing. I couldn't even see my feet. I had to crouch to keep the wind from blowing me over, hoping I wasn't in danger of a flash flood. The rain soaked my collar mic," said Lee. "I couldn't even contact RHODA, and Aries was, like I said, just fifty meters away."

"Copy that, Aries. We're all glad you're safe. Have you heard from Lieutenant Bridges?"

"Not yet, but he probably got caught in the same storm. I'm not surprised he's running behind schedule," said Lee.

"OK, Doc. Do you have him on ship sensors?" said Merriweather.

"I was about to check. RHODA, do you have a location for Lieutenant Bridges?" Lee asked.

"Lieutenant Bridges is one kilometer southwest of the target, moving in this direction."

"Did you copy that Endeavor?" Lee asked.

"Copy that, Lieutenant. That's good news. Keep us informed."

"Will do," said Lee.

The torrential rainstorm had mostly obliterated the road from Whoville back to the spot where Bridges stashed his electro-cycle. However, Bridges had no choice but to traverse it as best he could. It was more of a crawl than a run or walk. His feet continued to sink into the muck with every step, making it challenging to maintain any reasonable pace. He was finding it difficult to breathe, and he could feel his heart thumping through his chest. Bridges was sure his supplemental oxygen system, taped to his chest, had stopped working. He knew it would be a struggle to make it back to Aries without supplemental oxygen.

Lee monitored Bridges' vitals from Aries, while Cortez did the same from Endeavor. Both could see the worrisome data now populating their holoviews.

"Aries, Endeavor, do you read?" Cortez transmitted.

"Loud and clear," said Lee.

"Doc, are you monitoring Bridges' vitals?"

"Yes, I am. I've been trying to contact him."

"Copy that. Keep trying. We'll listen in."

"Copy that, Endeavor," said Lee.

"Lieutenant Bridges, this is Aries. Do you copy?"

Getting no response from her hail, Lee tried again.

"Lieutenant Bridges, this is Aries. Do you copy?"

After a prolonged silence, Bridges' voice filled her headset. "Yeah...I'm here, Doc."

Lee could tell that Bridges was struggling to get his breath.

"Milo, thank God, we were getting worried. Are you OK? I'm looking at your numbers. Your breathing and heart rate are through the roof."

"Cool, a...new personal best. I'm...covered with mud...hard to walk... keep falling."

"Do you think you can make it to your electro-cycle?"

When Bridges didn't respond, Lee repeated her hail.

"Milo, do you copy?"

"Milo, do you copy?"

"Lieutenant Bridges, do you copy?

"Bridges, this is Aries. Please respond."

"Rhonda, do you have a fix on Lieutenant Bridges' location?" Lee said.

"Yes, Lieutenant Lee, I have a fix on Lieutenant Bridges' location."

"RHODA, how far is Lieutenant Bridges from his electro-cycle?"

"Lieutenant Bridges is five kilometers from his electro-cycle."

"RHODA, please run a diagnosis on Lieutenant Bridges' holocom."

Ten seconds later, RHODA responded. "Lieutenant Bridges' communicator is fully functional."

"Are you getting this, Endeavor?" Lee asked.

"Yes, we are, Doc. I think you'll have to go get him," said Captain Merriweather, who had joined the conversation.

"Who, me? I've never flown an LAV, sir. I'm a damn Doctor, remember?" replied Lee.

"Don't worry. RHODA can fly Aries. She just needs Bridges' location. Just give her the order."

"OK, um, can you do that from Endeavor?"

"I want you to do it. I'm confident you can handle it, Lieutenant."
Lee could tell from the captain's tone that this was an order.

"Yes, sir," she replied.

Lee took a deep breath. "I'm a damn doctor," she mumbled. "I don't make house calls."

"RHODA, is there an open area large enough to land Aries near Lieutenant Bridges' location?"

Lee was counting on RHODA having access to imagery taken from the lunar outpost on Caerus and the two reconnaissance satellites now orbiting Sanctuary.

"Yes, there is an open field adjacent to Lieutenant Bridges' current location," RHODA replied.

"OK, RHODA, compute a flight plan from our current location to the field adjacent to Lieutenant Bridges. Land Aries close to Lieutenant Bridges and safely as possible."

"Mission plan calculated," intoned the AI.

"Well, then execute it, damn it."

Lee barely had time to strap herself in before Aries' engines erupted, lifting the LAV off in a cloud of steam, mud, debris, and fire.

Dualla heard the noise, albeit faintly, from her home in Whoville. She moved to the large window facing the direction she and Glyvash had gone earlier. She suspected the visitors from the stars caused the noise. But stare as she might, she could see no alien flying machine in the darkness.

Meanwhile, with its wings extended and flying just meters over the treetops, Aries sped toward Bridges' last known location. Lee stared intently at the night-vision-enhanced forward holoview and the flight control instruments, hoping she'd find Bridges safe and in good condition.

After what seemed like an eternity but was, in fact, just minutes, Aries slowed. Lee leaned forward, looking for a heat signature that might be Bridges. Seeing nothing, Lee moved instead to Aries' exit hatch, ready to rush to Bridges' aid as soon as the craft touched down.

Lee heard the roar of Aries' engines intensify as the ship settled softly onto the surface. Springing from the now-opened cargo hatch, Lee rushed down the ramp, scanning her immediate surroundings, looking for Bridges, but also keeping a lookout for aliens.

"RHODA, lead me to Bridges' location."

"Advance ten meters to the northeast."

"Northeast? I don't have a damned compass. How am I supposed to ...?"

Lee was desperate. She looked in every direction, trying to find her crewmate.

"RHODA, which way is Aries pointing?"

"Aries is pointing north by northeast."

"Great," said Lee, calculating the direction she needed to go.

Seconds later, Lee found Bridges semi-buried in the thick ooze of a rain-filled depression. Grabbing the portable breather from her bag, she quickly slipped it over Bridges' mouth and nose, then stretched the elastic band over his head.

"Come on, Lieutenant," she implored. "We need to get back to the ship before we're discovered."

Bridges coughed, opened his eyes, and smiled. "What brings you out on a night like this, Doc?" he mumbled.

"I'm making a damn house call against my better judgment. You'll get my bill in the morning," she replied. "Now get your ass up."

"Oh, don't forget my bag there," said Bridges, waving toward a canvas sack stuffed with objects taken from the alien's home.

Lee helped Bridges to his feet before grabbing his bag. Slowly, the two crewmates struggled back to Aries, sliding, and falling several times before reaching their destination. After helping Bridges out of his muddy garments, Lee reported their situation to Endeavor and received orders to depart the planet immediately.

Now more confident in RHODA's piloting abilities, Lee ordered RHODA to compute a mission flight plan to rendezvous with the EX-23 booster stage, waiting for them in orbit. Satisfied, she helped Bridges into his flight seat.

"It's been one helluva mission, right Doc?" said Bridges, still groggy from his ordeal.

"It sure has, Lieutenant," said Lee as she strapped herself in. "RHODA, execute mission plan Lee two."

As darkness engulfed the countryside, Dualla stood at her bedroom window and watched the strange alien object streak into the sky and disappear behind the clouds. "Who or what are you?" she said out loud. "What do you want?"

# CHAPTER 50

*Booty*

Four days later and safely back on Endeavor, Bridges and Lee sat at the communal galley table, recounting their experiences on Sanctuary to a rapt audience.

"This is why your oxygen stopped," said Lee, handing Bridges a foil bag.

"What's this? Oh, it's the breathing rig," he replied, taking the bag from Lee.

"See all those little holes in it? All the Methylomirabilis Oxyfera leaked out."

"I thought I felt something wet under my tunic. It was those damned tree needles. They cut me up pretty badly and must have punctured the bag."

"You're lucky you made it back," said Lee.

"Thanks, Doc. I owe you."

"And don't think I won't collect," Lee replied.

Dr. Graham and Lieutenant Cortez had eagerly taken over the task of analyzing the samples Lee had collected and now huddled over a mass spectrometer awaiting results. Meanwhile, doctors Girard and Martin were almost giddy as they examined the horde of documents and other materials liberated by Lieutenant Bridges.

At first glance, nothing was particularly "alien" about the documents. The sophonts had obviously developed the technology of making paper. However, a chemical analysis of the alien paper revealed that the aliens used seaweed instead of wood pulp.

"Really," said Mills. "I didn't know that was a thing."

"Sure," replied Merriweather. "There is a seaweed paper industry back on Earth. Making paper from seaweed uses less energy than wood pulp and has the added advantage of extracting carbon from the environment. It makes perfect sense that this society would use seaweed."

One document seemed of particular interest to Captain Merriweather. "Paul, look at this."

Girard returned the document he was examining to the pile and moved closer to Merriweather.

"What is this?" said Girard.

"Not sure. Look at this. From the document's layout, it looks like a calendar," said Merriweather. "We know Erebus takes twenty-seven days to orbit Sanctuary, which in turn takes one hundred and thirty-five days to orbit their red sun. My math tells me that might produce a calendar of five months of twenty-seven days each. That's what I see here—five groupings of twenty-seven symbols."

"I think you're right. Look at these symbols. Those look like phases of two different moons," answered Girard.

'Very cool, that gives us a lot of info...," began Merriweather.

"Including the first twenty-seven numbers in their math," finished Girard.

"Damn, look here, Paul. After the first eleven symbols, the pattern repeats but with a horizontal line over the symbol."

"Oh yeah. This could mean they use a base eleven system, and the horizontal line is their zero," said Girard.

"That also tells me they think a lot like we do, at least with logic and math," said Merriweather.

"Well, let's not... how do you say? *Mettre la charrue avant les bœufs*—get ahead of ourselves," said Girard. "We don't know in which direction they read the numbers. It could be right to left, or even vertical—up or down. And those horizontal lines? They could mean something entirely different."

"You're right. We'll scan all this and see what RHODA can make of it."

"Here's something else," said Girard. "The characters above each month might be the name of that month. And look at this—I just noticed the last three symbols of each name are identical. That could be their functional equivalent of our word 'month.'"

Jonathan Mills listened intently to the two senior crewmates before expressing his thoughts. "You guys seem awfully convinced that this is a calendar. This is an alien world, after all. We shouldn't jump to conclusions."

"True," said Dr. Girard, "but it seems like a plausible hypothesis. Look at the history of the calendar on Earth."

"I think we're about to get another Girard lecture," said Mills, rolling his eyes in mock exasperation.

Girard ignored Mills and continued. "Primitive man used the moon's phases to denote the passage of time. As their need for planning evolved, they would have incorporated days. One of the oldest calendars dates back over fifteen thousand years. A Cro-Magnon man painted it on the walls of a cave at Lascaux in France. I have been there.

"The ancient Babylonians had their own calendar incorporating lunar phases, as did the Egyptians, the Assyrians, and the Hittites. Given the similarities we've seen in their civilization, I expect the same evolution on this planet."

"Here, Jon, you can see symbols representing lunar phases. To me, that's extremely convincing," said Merriweather.

Mills considered this for a moment. "Do you know that Alexander the Great had a unique method for telling time?"

"Oh," said Merriweather warily.

"Yes, he had his physician concoct a special solution into which he soaked strips of cloth. His generals would wrap these strips around their wrists. As the strips dried in the sun, they would change color from green to blue and finally red. Alexander used this method to coordinate his army's divisions."

"Interesting, I've never heard of this before, Jon," said Girard.

"Sure, you have, Paul. They called these cloth strips 'Alexander's Rag Time Bands.'"

As Mills finished his story, a broad smile appeared on his face. The reaction was swift and predictable.

Merriweather groaned, as did Martin and Girard. A few crewmembers laughed out loud.

"Jon, you're incorrigible," said Doc Lee, barely controlling her laughter.

"Worst pun of all time," agreed Dr. Graham.

"OK, enough fun and games," chided Merriweather. "Let's see what else we've got."

Girard leaned over and extracted the next document from the pile. Holding it so Merriweather and Mills could see, Girard said, "What do you make of this?"

"Looks like a highway overpass under construction," said Mills.

"Or some sort of board game," added Merriweather.

"You guys are both wrong." Girard looked closely at the document before explaining. "What we have here, gentlemen, is a PTE."

"A what!" said Merriweather?

"A Periodic Table of Elements," replied Girard.

"You're going to have to convince me because that is like no other periodic table I've ever seen."

"I don't see it either," added Mills.

"All right, gentlemen, let me explain. I have some experience in this area. I was on the dissertation committee for a young female doctoral candidate whose thesis examined the origins of the periodic table. History normally credits Dmitri Mendeleev as the father of the periodic table. The young woman, whose name escapes me at the moment, argued that the credit should properly go to Lothar Meyer. It was a fascinating paper. I could go over the various points she made if...."

"That won't be necessary, Doctor. Just tell us why you think this is a PTE," said Merriweather.

"Very well," said Girard. "We are used to seeing the table in a certain way. But in the mid-1800s, chemists and physicists were looking for an elegant way of presenting the information in the best way possible. One could simply order the elements in atomic-number order or combine all the elements with similar properties—metals, gases, etc., or as some were trying to do, show all the connections in one elegant table. That led to some very creative and even bizarre schemes."

"Professor Girard is in his element now," Bridges whispered to Cortez. She smiled and shushed him.

"A young man named Ingo Hackh created one that was very much like this document," continued Girard. "I loved the name. I considered naming my son Ingo."

Girard paused for a second, a faraway look in his eyes as if revisiting a fond memory.

"Professor, you were saying," said Merriweather.

"Ah yes, sorry. These radial lines here are groups of elements with similar properties. The top left quadrant shows the non-metals, and the top right shows light metals. On the bottom, you have heavy metals on the left and radioactive elements and lanthanides on the lower right. These are the noble gases, and these are the halogens. My word helium seems to be missing."

"This planet's strong magnetic field might account for the lack of helium," said Merriweather.

"I believe you are correct," said Girard. "Good thought."

"Just from my limited knowledge, it looks like they are missing quite a few elements," said Merriweather. "But you've convinced me. Does this help us?"

"I don't see symbols where uranium or plutonium should be, so we can be pretty sure they haven't discovered nuclear weapons," said Girard.

"Well, yes, there is that. But I was hoping it might help us understand their culture or help us decipher their language.

"It is possible," said Girard. "I think it will take more time to process the information. It gives me hope that science is important to their culture, and it gives me hope we can communicate with them."

Merriweather was pleased with the documents Bridges had retrieved from the alien's home. With any luck, RHODA would finally make headway on decrypting their language. Merriweather could feel the excitement growing amongst the crew.

# CHAPTER 51

*Sleep and Sex*

Doc Lee would say often and to anyone who would listen that "Sleep is the best medicine. I should know," she would say. "I'm your doctor."
Bridges contemplated this sage advice as he sat alone in the ship's galley around 2:00 AM Earth time. *Earth time, now that's a funny concept*, he thought. Here they were, light years away from their small, insignificant planet, pretending that the passage of Earth's sun in that sky still influenced their sleeping habits. Instead, adjustments to the starship's lighting and ambient temperature helped the crew manage their circadian rhythms.

Bridges glanced at his wristwatch. 2:01 AM.

Sleep was a significant factor in the success or failure of any long-duration space mission. Trapped in a narrow tube and surrounded by the vacuum of space, a ship's crew would invariably come apart without regular, dependable sleep. The human body depended on it, and the human mind depended on it. Explorers knew this when they sailed vessels made of wood and powered by the wind. It was no less true for vessels made from exotic materials traveling in the hostile environment of space.

*I'm tired. Why can't I sleep?* thought Bridges, checking his watch again. 2:02 AM.

ISA considered regular and consistent sleep to be extremely important. They even taught classes at the Academy on sleep and how to manage it. Doc Lee would regularly check up on each crewmember's health, always inquiring first about their sleep. She kept a sleep log for each crew member. Lee had pharmaceuticals ready if needed but would usually counsel other remedies such as physical activity, soothing music, meditation, and even warm (faux) milk, known as sim-milk. She would even advise sexual activity.

ISA's stance on crew member sex was that it was acceptable if kept discreet and did not breach other fraternization policies. That said, ISA quietly advised its crews on the health benefits of sex. "Sleep and sex," Doc Lee would say, are the two best ways to maintain a healthy mind and a healthy body. She even had a tee shirt emblazoned with the words "Sleep and Sex."

Sex on long-duration missions had been a worry early on. It was initially believed that a balanced crew with the same number of males and females was the best approach. That turned out not to be the case. In the early days of interplanetary spaceflight, ISA monitored a crew's interpersonal activities by requiring every captain to keep a "sex" log, noting all effects on the functioning of the spacecraft. Finally, after much study, the doctors and psychiatrists at the agency realized that there was no correlation between gender balance and ship harmony. Either the crew would figure it out, or it wouldn't. The best a captain could do was to keep a tight lid on any overt displays of sexual attraction.

"Keep it to yourselves, and we won't have a problem," the captain would say.

The crew of Endeavor had, for the most part, figured it out. Doc Lee was currently in relationships with both Jonathan Mills and Mike Martin. Dr. Girard and Dr. Mann kept a low-key relationship as secret as they could. Jake Merriweather was still mourning his deceased wife. Don Stoner and Javier Rodriguez were married and held fast to their marriage vows—so far, at least. Zoe Bishop was the wild card. She was smart, attractive and could turn on the sexual appeal whenever it suited her. But she had turned down advances from several members of the crew. More than one crewmember had raised the possibility of a pairing of Bishop and Captain Merriweather. Bishop had heard this, and while denying any interest in the captain, she had entertained the idea.

The only question remaining was whether Milo Bridges and Cat Cortez would ever turn up the heat on their relationship.

Bridges glanced at his watch. 2:03 AM.

The crew of Endeavor had multiple sleep options. They could retire to the microgravity environment of Endeavor's central hull to float in sleeping bags attached to the bulkhead or bunk down in their sleeping quarters in the hab ring with its partial gravity. Most of the crew switched several times during this mission, trying to find a good night's sleep.

"Knock, knock. Yuni wants her book back."

Bridges' head jerked around at the familiar sound of Cat Cortez's voice. When he spotted her standing a few feet away, his expression turned to disbelief. There she was, his fellow crewmate, completely naked.

"Cat, what are you doing?"

"Knock, knock, Milo. Yuni wants her book back," said Cortez.

Bridges stared at his beautiful crewmate, eyes wide open, mouth agape. He wanted to divert his gaze, partly out of respect for his crewmate and partly out of embarrassment, but he couldn't. His eyes examined every inch of her body. She was even more beautiful than he could ever have imagined.

"Knock, knock, Milo. Yuni wants her book back," said Cortez.
Bridges tried to stand. His intent was to find something to cover her. But his legs wouldn't cooperate. He felt paralyzed. "Cat, wake up," he said.

Knock, knock.

Knock, knock.

Suddenly, Bridges found himself back in his quarters, groggy and disoriented. It was just a dream.

Knock, knock

"Milo, are you awake? It's Cat," she whispered.

It took a few more seconds before Bridges' mind cleared, and he realized where he was. He also realized that someone—Cat, no less—was knocking at his door.

"Yes, I'm awake," said Bridges, "Give me a second."

Bridges sat up, checked to ensure he was decent, then opened the door. Cat Cortez stood just outside—her hair tousled as if she had just gotten out of bed. Quickly, she stepped into his quarters and quietly closed the door behind her.

"What's wrong?" asked Bridges. "Are you OK?"

"I'm fine," Cortez replied, slowly sitting beside him on his bunk. "I just came to see you. We have had little time to talk and, well, I think it's time we, you know, talk."

"I see," said Bridges. "What do you want to talk about?"

Bridges felt the heat coming from her body sitting so close. He felt the warmth of her breath as he gazed into her eyes. She wet her lips and moved slightly closer; her head tilted to the right.

"I don't want to talk. Do you want to talk?" she said in a deep, breathy voice. She smiled at him.

Bridges wanted Cortez more than she could know. He put his right arm around her shoulders and pulled her closer. His right hand stroked her cheek, then slid to her neck. Slowly, he pulled her face to his. Their lips came together. It amazed him at how soft they were. The electricity was palpable. He could feel the yearning in her kiss. Her hands moved to his waist, then slid up under his shirt. Bridges stood and pulled his shirt over his head. Cortez grabbed the waistband of his shorts and pulled them down.

"You're out of uniform, Lieutenant," she said. Cortez stood and gracefully removed her own garments. Everything she does, she does gracefully, thought Bridges. She was now as naked as in Bridges' dream. She was even more beautiful, he thought. Cortez pressed her body against his and wrapped her arms around his neck. After a long, passionate embrace and an even longer kiss, Milo lifted Cat and laid her gently on his bunk. *Why had they waited so long?* thought Bridges. She was thinking the same.

# CHAPTER 52

*Breakthrough*

6:00 AM. Bridges was once again wide awake, but the thoughts circulating in his mind were pleasant. Cortez had just left, but he could still smell that distinctive floral scent she always wore. Her unexpected visit convinced him that what he felt for his fellow crewmember was more than desire, a much deeper feeling than simply physical attraction. Bridges was in love, and he wanted to shout it to the world. He was proud that someone like Cat Cortez could love him in return. But she did. She loved him.

The problem was the rule on ISA spaceships that discouraged public displays of affection.

Therefore, Bridges dressed and began his day as usual, working out in the small gym with fellow fitness freaks, Captain Merriweather, and Don Stoner.

"Getting started a little late, Bridges?" Merriweather asked.

"I had difficulty sleeping last night. I didn't get my usual seven hours."

"Is there anything bothering you?"

"No. No. Just eager to begin our first contact protocol, that's all."

"I imagine you would be. Girard tells me you've made some progress."

"A little, but it's taking much longer than we'd hoped."

"Well, just keep at it and have a little patience. I'm confident you guys will get the job done."

"Thanks, Captain." Bridges appreciated the captain's confidence. He hoped that trust wasn't misplaced.

Bridges finished his workout routine, showered in the hab ring's hygiene unit, and headed for the ship's galley. He would typically be concerned mostly with breakfast, but today, he hoped to see Cortez. However, when he got there, she was nowhere to be seen.

"Anyone seen Cat?" he asked.

"No, why?" answered Mike Martin.

"No reason," Bridges replied nonchalantly.

Bridges grabbed a cup of coffee and sat down next to Dr. Girard.

"Say, Paul, are we getting a data feed from the surveillance camera I installed in the juvenile alien's bedroom?"

"I think so. I've watched so much video lately that I might have imagined it."

"Can we sort the video to show only segments that show both the juvenile and her mother?"

"Sure. We can do this. RHODA, search the video for sequences that show both the adult and juvenile aliens together."

RHODA responded with a list of video segments.

"OK, let's watch the first one," said Bridges.

After watching for about two minutes, Bridges said, "Let's try number two."

The two watched the video for another thirty seconds.

"Stop right there. OK, back up ten seconds. Now play."

"Do you see something?" Girard asked.

The image on the holoviewer showed the young child in bed with her book open, the adult sophont beside her.

"Can you see the title of the book?"

"Yes, but I can't translate it," replies Girard.

"OK, look at this." Bridges pulled a book from the box of documents he had taken from the alien's home. "Doesn't this look like the same book?"

"Yes, you're right. Good eye."

"Her mother must have gotten her a new one to replace the one I took."

"You mean the one you stole? Shame on you."

"Yeah, I felt guilty."

Bridges turned the book's pages until it matched the page the young child and mother were reading.

"OK, now play the video from here."

The two watched as the child read from the book she was holding. Then she hesitated and pointed to a word on the page. The mother then made a sound. Then she repeated it.

Bridges and Girard continued to watch the mother-daughter saga play out on screen. Finally, Girard expressed the obvious. "She is helping her daughter read the damn book."

"Ya think? She's teaching us to read at the same time."

# CHAPTER 53

*Translation*

For the three weeks immediately following the return of Bridges and Lee, the crew prepared for an imminent breakthrough. As the crew's chief cryptographer, Dr. Girard oversaw the decryption effort, so he provided regular updates. Every morning, Girard would check RHODA's progress, and then report to the captain, followed by Girard's morning crew update. At first, everyone had attended his meetings. However, after three weeks of "We're almost there, everyone," Girard could sense the excitement wane.

Finally, on day twenty-four, as the crew gathered in the galley, they noted the absence of Dr. Girard. Most attributed this to more bad news. Perhaps he couldn't give the crew yet another positive yet empty promise of an imminent breakthrough. That all changed when the captain, followed closely by Dr. Girard, walked swiftly into the galley.

"People, can I have your attention? Is everyone here?" Merriweather announced.

Immediately, the crew sensed something was different. Was this the moment everyone had hoped for since first hearing the squeaks and squawks emanating from the ship's long-distance sensors?

"I won't prolong the suspense," began Merriweather. "Dr. Girard has been evaluating RHODA's latest numbers, and it looks like we have a verifiable translation of the alien written language."

No sooner had the last syllable escaped Merriweather's lips than the celebration began, including raucous laughter, applause, a few yippees, and high-fives. Merriweather let the commotion continue for several minutes before interrupting.

"I'll let Dr. Girard speak to the details."

"This is a great day," began Girard. We have successfully translated the language of a sophont alien species, marking a historic first for humanity. We are getting a lot of information from the documents Bridges, and Lee brought back from the planet, including insight into their science, culture, and even how they raise their young.

"Two key documents ultimately unlocked the alien language—the book found in the younger alien's bedroom, and a set of technical papers describing the new telescope just completed in Whoville. You may be interested to hear that their optical formulas look a lot like ours.

"This is how you write the word Whoville in their language."

Girard held up his holo, displaying a string of alien characters.

"We do not yet know how to pronounce it, but we have identified the string of characters that represent it. We have also identified the first eleven digits of their number system, which appears to be base eleven.

"Given the trove of scientific papers Bridges retrieved, we now believe that the adult sophont is likely a scientist—potentially even an astronomer. Therefore, Captain Merriweather and I agree this alien is our primary target for first contact.

"Are there any questions?" Girard asked, glancing at Merriweather, hoping he had not overstepped his bounds by making that announcement. Merriweather smiled and nodded in a signal that, no, he wasn't upset.

"How do you handle proper place names?" asked Bishop. "I understand how you might find translations for those weird dolphin sounds they make when it relates to general vocabulary, but when there is no direct correlation with a word in our language, what do you do?"

"Good question, Zoe. There are two answers to your question. First, we've identified discrete sub-patterns in many alien words. You could think of these as phonemes. We have this in most languages. So, we've created—or rather, RHODA has created a phonetic dictionary of sorts—a one-to-one mapping between English and alien phonemes based on frequency and placement."

"Let me get this straight," said Bishop. "You're saying RHODA will substitute any unknown word in the translation with a phonetic rendering of the alien word, using the closest English phonemes that statistically align with the alien ones."

"I couldn't have said it better myself," said Girard. "RHODA can also rearrange the phonemes to make the word easier for us to visualize or pronounce as a word."

"I think I understand," said Bishop. "Oh, you said there were two answers."

"Well, to be honest, sometimes we just make something up, just like we did for Whoville."

"Really. So, we just invent names for the cities and aliens we find down there?"

"When the phonemes don't suffice, that's right."

"Well, count me in. I have a few names I'd like to add," said Bishop.

"We've already assigned a few," said Merriweather. "Besides Whoville, we've given our scientist the name Dualla, at the suggestion of Lieutenant Cortez and the alien's young daughter Yuni, after Cortez's pet cat. Anything else, Paul?"

"Dualla?" asked Bishop, glancing at Cortez.

"From an old TV show I watched as a child," said Cortez.

"What if she doesn't like the name?" said Bishop.

"Doesn't matter," said Merriweather. "The translation will link what we call her to the sounds her language uses to pronounce her actual name. We say 'Dualla' and she hears R2D2, or whatever she calls herself.

"And one other thing," said Merriweather. "I just referred to the younger alien as Dualla's daughter. We're still determining the relationship between the older and younger sophonts. They could be siblings, or there is some other type of relationship we don't yet understand. Paul, do you have anything you'd like to add?"

"That's all I have, Captain," said Girard.

"Thanks, Paul. In the coming weeks, we will learn a great deal about these sophonts we've come to visit. We are representing our planet, so we want to make a good first impression. The more we know about them, the less likely we are to make some egregious mistake or diplomatic gaffe. It's on all of us to ensure the best possible outcome.

"Paul will continue leading the translation efforts assisted by Lieutenant Bridges. But we need to learn much more than just their written language. To understand their culture and their planet, we will require the expertise of our resident scientists, Doctors Martin, Mann, and Graham.

"Mills will help us understand their technology. Doc Lee and Lt. Cortez will help us understand their physiology. And Zoe can help us understand the way they relate to each other. Everyone has a role. This is the most important task in human history. I expect everyone to give me one hundred and ten percent as we push toward the finish line. Deciphering their language is a monumental accomplishment. But it's just the start. So, keep pushing forward. I also have a special project for Graham and Lee. Could you report to my quarters in five? OK, unless anyone has anything else, let's get cracking."

Five minutes later, Dr. Graham, Doc Lee, and Captain Merriweather sat around the small table in the captain's stateroom.

"Just so I understand," began Merriweather, "the chirality of this planet means we can't eat anything grown here. Is that correct?"

"Yes, sir," said Graham. "It would appear so."

"Is there anything we can do about that? Can we process the food to make it edible?"

"No, sir."

"Crap. I want you both to take a hard look at that. I cannot accept that it's impossible. Take a couple of days to research this. Use RHODA."

"Yes, sir," said both Lee and Graham simultaneously.

# CHAPTER 54

A lot happened in the ensuing four weeks. Cortez spent every night in Bridges' sleeping quarters (when he wasn't in hers). RHODA had translated over five thousand words of the alien written language and made serious progress in translating their spoken language. Girard had announced through everyone's holocom that language classes would begin the following day, and anyone interested could participate. The next day, everyone except Lieutenant Rodriguez showed up.

The language was so challenging that everyone except Bridges and Cortez dropped out after the first class.

Finally, Captain Merriweather convened a Post-Detection Protocol committee meeting—more a formality in their situation but a requirement before first contact could continue.

"Good afternoon, gentlemen and ladies," began Merriweather.

Seated before him were Endeavor's ISA crew, plus Zoe Bishop and the four guest scientists who had joined them on this historic voyage. Each had prepared a report, delivered to Captain Merriweather the previous evening, outlining their opinion and the reasons for their conclusion. Merriweather had reviewed their findings and recommendation and was now prepared to render his final decision.

"RHODA, please record that I have called a meeting of the Post-Detection Protocol (PDP) committee as required by the *United Nations Declaration of Principles Concerning Activities Following the Detection of Extraterrestrial Intelligence*.

"Before I begin, I want to change the name of our alien planet. As all of you are aware, the official designation of the planet is Hypatia-Proxima-b. However, as captain, I have the authority to give the planet an alternate designation.

"Our current analysis shows that the governing authorities of the three largest nation-states are led predominantly by females of the species. These are the first three societies we've studied, yet together they account for nearly seventy percent of the planet's total population. It may be reasonable to conclude that female dominance is not an anomaly here, but possibly the prevailing social structure."

"Therefore, after some thought, I've exercised my prerogative as captain to rename this new planet Hera after the Greek Goddess. We can change it later if our understanding of the facts warrants it.

"Now, let's get down to the main reason for this meeting. Do we proceed with first contact or not? In a perfect universe, we could go down the checklist and decide based on the results. But we do not have that luxury. We cannot communicate with the major governments of Earth to get their opinions as required by the principles, nor can we get approval from the UN's Security Council. Some have argued that alone should argue against making first contact. They may be right.

"I've read each of your reports carefully. You've all made convincing arguments. I expected no less from the intelligent and dedicated men and women here today.

"But as you know, the final decision is mine. Either I can accept your recommendations or make a different decision. Fortunately, I don't have to. While each of you carefully examined the pros and cons of first contact, you eventually came to the same conclusion.

"Before we go any further, I want to allow each of you to bring up any concerns that might have occurred to you since submitting your recommendations."

Merriweather scanned the assembly of officers and guests, looking directly at each one. When no one stood or raised his hand, Merriweather smiled.

"To confirm my understanding of your decision, I would like a show of hands. If you want to proceed with first contact and believe that we have abided by the spirit of the principles, please raise your hand."

One by one, each member of the crew raised their hand.

"RHODA, record in the official ship's log that the decision of the captain and crew is to proceed with first contact."

With that announcement, the entire crew erupted in a loud, spontaneous hurrah.

Merriweather stood, beamed, and declared the meeting over.

As those in the meeting drifted away, some going back to their surveillance stations, others to resume other duties, Merriweather motioned to his two pilots.

"Bridges, Cortez, can you join me in my stateroom in five minutes?" Bridges looked at Cortez as if she knew what Merriweather wanted. Had he discovered their new romantic relationship? Were they about to get reprimanded? Bridges was sure he and Cortez had taken adequate precautions to conceal their nightly trysts. Still, it was a small ship, and past relationships between other crewmembers eventually became fodder for gossip. Cortez shrugged, silently signaling she had no idea what Merriweather wanted.

Five minutes later, Bridges and Cortez stood outside the captain's stateroom. Bridges knocked twice.

"Come," said Captain Merriweather. "Close the door." Merriweather paused for a moment before continuing. "I suppose you're both wondering what this is all about, and I won't keep you in suspense. Bridges, Cortez, after much thought, I've decided to send Cortez down to the planet for first contact."

Merriweather watched his young officers intensely, looking for their reaction to his decision—a decision that could change each of their lives. He knew it wasn't news that Bridges would welcome, but hoped he would understand his reasons.

Bridges was stunned. He had heard the words the captain spoke, but was confused. Surely, there was some mistake. He was the FCO. He should be the one making first contact.

Bridges felt as if someone had gut-punched him. He couldn't breathe. He clenched his fists as he tried to maintain his composure.

Merriweather's decision also surprised Cortez. She couldn't believe it. Everyone knew that this was Bridges' assignment. She looked at Milo. She could see the look on his face and immediately felt guilty.

"Yes, sir," said Bridges. "I'm sure you have your reasons, and I know that Cat, I mean Lieutenant Cortez, will do a hell of a job."

Bridges straightened to attention before continuing.

"If that is all, sir, may I be excused?"

Bridges turned to leave and had his hand on the door before Merriweather stopped him.

"Wait, Milo. Let's talk about this."

"That's unnecessary, Captain. I'm sure you had your reasons."

Bridges opened the door and was gone before Merriweather could stop him.

"I'm sure he'll be all right, Captain. I'll talk to him," said Cortez.

"It would have surprised me if he weren't disappointed," said Merriweather. "I chose you, Cortez, because you are as qualified or more qualified as anyone in every important category for first contact. You've also had the same training as Bridges. In my opinion, the population below would be more inclined to respond positively to a female representative from Earth. I've also been told you have a slight edge in learning their language. Cat, this is not a criticism of Milo but a recognition of your abilities and what you bring to the table."

"Thank you, Captain, for your confidence in my abilities. I won't let you down."

"I'm sure you won't," said Merriweather. "Once we've signed off on your language proficiency, you will put together your mission document as per PDP requirements. I'm expecting that will be in the next two weeks sometime?"

"Yes, sir, understood. Is that all, sir?"

"Yes, Cat, enjoy the recognition. You've earned it."

Cortez felt conflicted. She was happy that she was being given such a fantastic opportunity. But it also saddened her. It came at the expense of her...her...what, boyfriend, lover, best friend. She didn't quite know what they were yet. Cat enjoyed their lovemaking. She felt closer to Milo than anyone she had ever known. She couldn't imagine being with anyone else. Was she in love with him? Was he the one? Her head was spinning.

She found Bridges sitting at a surveillance console, watching a video from one of the drone cameras. A cluster of aliens were enjoying the antics of one of their small, domesticated animals.

"Milo, can we talk?" Cortez put her hand on his shoulder.

"Nothing to talk about."

"Do you want to know why?"

"Don't need to. He's the captain, and the decision is his. There is nothing you, I, or anyone can do about it."

"I'm sorry, Milo. I truly am."

"I know. It wasn't your fault. But I'd rather not talk about it, if you don't mind."

"If that's what you want, of course. But I think we should..."

"Not necessary," he interrupted. "But I am happy for you."

# CHAPTER 55

*Transformation—three weeks later*

"I hope you don't mind that I invited Zoe," Cortez announced as she arrived at Doc Lee's small medical bay. "She wanted to witness my Earthling to Heran transformation."

Lee glanced up from her computer to see Cortez, followed closely by Zoe Bishop. The two crewmates had become fast friends during the mission and spent much of their off time together (especially since the relationship between Cortez and Bridges had cooled).

"Right on time," said Lee. "There's not a lot of room, but I think we can squeeze you in, Bishop. Take the table. We're short on chairs."

Lee wore her favorite tee shirt with the words "Space Bitch" emblazoned across the front. It was a gift from the staff of doctors and nurses who worked for her while she was stationed on Mars, and Lee wore it like a badge of honor.

"Thanks," Bishop replied as she hopped onto the med bay's narrow treatment table. "I'm ready to be entertained."

"I'll do my best," said Lee, motioning Cortez to the only vacant chair available. Cortez took the seat facing a small mirror affixed to the wall just below the med-bay's holoview.

"Are you excited? This is your big day," said Lee.

"Trying to stay calm," answered Cortez. "Hopefully, I won't run into a storm like you and Milo did."

"Don't remind me," said Lee. "I've told no one, but I can't swim."

"Hope it doesn't come to that," said Cortez.

"You girls are spending a lot of time together. People are talking," said Lee.

"We're trying to start a rumor," said Bishop.

"The more scandalous, the better," said Cortez.

"I'll get right on that," smirked Lee, turning to the holoview. "OK, using the data we've received from the drones on the surface, RHODA has created a pretty decent 3D image of our target female Heran," said Lee, pointing to the holoview. "As you can see, the figure is humanoid, with facial features roughly comparable to humans. I suppose we're lucky they don't resemble earthworms or jellyfish, right, Lieutenant?"

"I draw the line at earthworms," laughed Cortez.

"But you're OK being a jellyfish, said Bishop?"

"At least they're pretty, and they can deliver a healthy sting to those who piss her off," said Cortez, staring at Bishop mischievously.

"Let's get on with it, please," said Lee. Speaking more to Bishop than Cortez, she began, "Fortunately for us, ISA has created various tools we can use to develop disguises for spying on aliens.

"We'll start by making minor alterations to the Lieutenant's face using injections of a neurotoxin produced by the bacterium Clostridium botulinum. This will smooth her skin and make her facial muscles move differently to mimic those of the alien.

"Then I'll inject a synthetic compound above her eyes and chin. This will make her face appear longer, and her eyes will protrude, mimicking our target. It also prevents bruising or infections."

"Ouch. Is it supposed to hurt?" said Cortez.

"Don't be such a baby," said Lee.

"How long does it last?" said Cortez, rubbing her newly protruding chin.

"About a week," Lee replied. "After about six days, you'll see a twenty percent reduction in size. The last eighty percent should disappear within the last 24 hours."

"It's every girl's dream to have bulging eyes," said Cortez.
Ignoring the comment, Lee continued.

"Next, we have some special contact lenses we've created to mimic the eyes of our alien target," said Lee, handing Cortez a lens case and a small bottle of saline. Cortez removed the lenses from the small plastic case, rinsed them with saline, and carefully inserted them into her eyes. Blinking them into place, she turned to Bishop. "What do you think?"

"They look like cow eyes," said Bishop. "But cute cow eyes, I must say."

"Thank you, I must say," said Cortez.

"Moving on," Lee continued. "Next, we will apply a prosthetic over her nose and secure it with adhesive."

Lee handed the prosthetic to Cortez, who inspected it before giving it to Bishop.

"Nice," said Bishop. "Can I get one?"

"Sure, but it will have to be larger for you."

Bishop feigned an indignant expression and then stuck her tongue out at Cortez.

Applying the prosthetic was more difficult than Cortez expected. Lee spent almost twenty minutes fussing over the fake appendage, removing and reapplying it several times before she was completely satisfied.

Finally, happy with Cat's appearance, Lee turned her attention to the Lieutenant's skin, retrieving a small plastic box from a bulkhead storage locker. "Next, we need to adjust Cortez's skin tone. For that, we have drugs called Mekatonz that cause a temporary change in skin tone and color," said Lee as she removed two small, shrink-wrapped syringes from the box.

"How temporary?" Bishop asked milliseconds before Cortez.

"Up to her," Lee replied. "Mekatonz works in partnership with oral doses of $B_{12}$. Taking a daily $B_{12}$ tablet prolongs the change. Otherwise, the skin will revert to normal within twenty-four hours.

"There is an issue with Mekatonz and the EPO, which you'll take to supplement your oxygen intake. In combination, they tend to drive down your iron levels, and if you're not careful, they could cause anemia. To combat that, you'll take these iron tablets—with food."
Lee handed Cortez a small bottle of pills.

"I'd like a tan," said Cortez. "Space travel isn't conducive to good-looking skin."

"Got that right," chimed in Bishop. "I'll sign up for the tan, too."

"I'll make a note," said Lee sarcastically as she injected the drug. "Now we'll tackle the most prominent feature of our female alien, the glowing neck frills. Mills 3-D printed some prosthetics that look remarkably realistic. The subject's frills produce a blue glow. For that, I've inserted a light and battery. A small switch in the back turns them on. We'll attach them with the same adhesive."

"How am I supposed to hear?" Cortez asked after noticing that the frills covered her ears.

"This part of the prosthetic is perforated with thousands of little holes—like pores. You should be able to hear fine."

"How do the aliens hear?" Bishop asked.

"We're not sure. We don't see any ears," answered Lee. Could be the frills.

"What every girl should wear to first contact," said Bishop, examining the frills.

"Don't forget the nose," said Cortez.

"Our target has some fun markings on the sides of her head running down her neck," continued Lee, pointing to the image on the holoview. "We'll replicate those by using a pattern painter. I've loaded the tool with a mixture of ink colors matched to the image and programmed the device with the pattern we see on her neck. All I have to do is slowly glide the painter down along the skin as it paints the programmed pattern. The trick is to keep a uniform speed."

"Fascinating," said Bishop as she and Cortez watched Lee perform the procedure.

"The tattoo is temporary. You can remove it with alcohol."

"You drink the alcohol, I hope," Bishop said.

"No, sorry," Lee replied. "Let's keep going. I have other things to do. Hair is a tricky issue. There is not much body hair on our alien—maybe a bit of peach fuzz on her head and some patches of white fur on the sides of her neck. I can apply a mild depilatory on your arms and face, which should do the job. The question is, what to do with the hair on your head? Are you willing to shave your head?"

"If I have to," said Cortez, "but are there any other options?"

"Maybe," said Lee. "We could employ a latex cap. It's not as realistic, but it's an option. What do you think, Bishop?"

"I like the bald look. If it were me, I'd shave my head."

"Well, I'm not you," said Cortez.

"Fortunately, all the images of our principal alien show her wearing a garment with an attached hood. Therefore, the latex cap would work. However, we'll have to cut your hair short."

"OK, let's do that," said Cortez.

"I think Milo might like the bald look," said Lee.

"Milo? What's he got to do with anything?" said Cortez, turning red.

"Oh, nothing," said Lee, giving an exaggerated wink to Bishop.

"What do you have planned for my traveling companion, Lieutenant Rodriguez?" Cortez inquired.

"The same," answered Lee. "His appointment is right after yours."

"Can't wait to see that," Cortez laughed.

"How are you going to hide my knees?" asked Cortez.

"Other than surgery, there's not much we can do," answered Lee.

"Surgery is definitely out," said Cortez.

"Fortunately, the Heran females we've seen were wearing long robes," said Lee. "That will have to suffice.

"We're good with your look, but looking like an alien is only half the problem. We also want to make sure you can communicate with them. So, you will wear a translator."

"I thought Cat learned their language," said Bishop.

"Tried too, but it's too difficult a language to master in the time we had. Having to speak it can be painful," said Cortez before Lee could respond. "It's quite difficult to replicate some of their sounds. Plus, our alien vocabulary is woefully incomplete."

"So, what's the solution?" Bishop asked.

"Let me answer that," said Cortez.

"Be my guest," said Lee, handing Cortez a small device about the size of a deck of cards plus a smaller plastic box.

"As part of my Academy training, I had to show proficiency with a translator and the vocalizer," said Cortez. "They had me wearing the damned thing for two weeks and as a result I suffered from mouth blisters for a month."

"This is the translator," said Cortez, holding up a small device. "RHODA has downloaded everything we know about the Heran language—vocabulary, grammar, structure, idioms, anything, and everything she knows. In addition, if RHODA is in range, she's continually adding to it."

Next, Cortez opened the plastic box and removed a small, curved device.

"This is the neural interface. It detects signals from the part of the brain that controls my speech—tongue, larynx, and other parts of the vocal tract. It's like when you're lip-synching. You speak without actually speaking. Those signals are the ones it detects."

"The left inferior frontal gyrus," said Lee.

"Right, the gyrus," laughed Cortez. "It also communicates with the translator—"

"Which she'll wear in a pouch on the inside of her cloak," said Lee, finishing Cortez's sentence.

"The neural interface will fit in a pouch in Cortez's left-side neck frill," said Lee. "This sensor," she continued, displaying a wire extending from the neural interface, "is attached to her head with adhesive and hidden by her latex cap.

"This microphone goes inside the right-side frill. It's got a range of about ten meters. Working with the translator, it produces an English translation of everything it hears. It also communicates with a wireless earbud."

"That all makes sense, but how do you speak alien?" asked Bishop.

"That's where this second item comes in," said Cortez, removing another device from the plastic box. "This is the vocalizer. It's worn inside the mouth, rests against the upper palate, and clips to your molars."

"Sounds uncomfortable," said Bishop.

"It's torture, but you get used to it. When I want to say something, all I do is mouth the words like I'm lip-synching. The neural interface detects the signals from my brain, sends the English to the translator, which does its thing, and sends the translated sentence to the vocalizer, which produces the sounds. I just form the words with my mouth, and the vocalizer speaks Heran."

"What if you want to say something in English?"

"There's a soft spot on the vocalizer I can press with my tongue. Pressing it turns the vocalizer on or off."

"So, if I can summarize," began Bishop, "you think in English, the neural interface reads your mind and sends your thoughts to the translator, which converts it to Heran. Then the translator sends the Heran to the vocalizer, which produces the sounds, and the Heran comes out of your mouth."

"Right," said Cortez.

"And anything they say to you is picked up by the mic over your right ear, translated to English by the translator, and relayed to your earbud."

"Right again," said Cortez.

"What if the translator doesn't recognize a word?" Bishop asked.

"If it's a word RHODA doesn't know, she will whisper in my ear. I can assign an English word on the spot," said Cortez.

"How do you do that?"

"There are silent commands I can make simply by thinking them. For instance, to add a new correlation, I think the words—'*RHODA, assign the word donkey to the last unassigned pattern.*' I just need to be careful not to mouth the words when I'm thinking of them. The next time I say donkey, the vocalizer produces the correct Heran."

"Nice," Bishop replied.

"However, the best silent function is its ability to function as a basic communicator."

"How does that work?"

"As I mentioned, RHODA can update the database if the translator is in range—about five kilometers. If I think the command '*RHODA, transmit the following,*' anything I think after that is transmitted as is instead of translated."

"So, if you need rescuing, you just think it?"

"Yep."

"Very cool. Can you demonstrate it?" Bishop asked.

"Very cool?" Cortez said, laughing at her friend. "You sound like my great-grandmother?"

"Funny," said Bishop.

Cortez turned on the translator and pressed the vocalizer against the roof of her mouth, producing an audible click.

For a second, she said nothing. Then she looked at Bishop and spoke. A stream of dolphin-like sounds emanated from her mouth.

"Whoa, that was incredible. What did you say?" Bishop asked.

"I asked, 'When you were going to make a move on the captain?'"

"Hilarious," said Bishop, as Cortez and Lee laughed.

Forty-five minutes later and transformed into a Heran female, Cortez exited the medical bay. As she left, she passed Rodriguez, who was about to get his own alien transformation.

# CHAPTER 56

*Attitude Adjustment*

"There you are," said Stoner as he floated onto the bridge. "I've been looking for you."

The XO found Milo Bridges sitting in the captain's chair, reading something on a handheld holoview. Bridges turned to face the XO.

"I'm not that hard to find. It's a small ship," said Bridges before returning his gaze to his holoview.

"All right, listen up, Lieutenant."

"I'm listening," said Bridges, still looking at the screen in his hands.

"I'd appreciate it if you would give me the respect of paying attention, Lieutenant."

Stoner pronounced the word *lieutenant* as if Bridges' rank was in question.

Bridges sighed, then pressed the portable screen onto the touch fastener affixed to the side of the chair before turning toward Stoner. "Sorry, Commander. What's up?"

"What's up indeed," said Stoner. "Are you a freaking idiot?"

Bridges was momentarily startled. Everyone knew the XO could be harsh, but what was this?

"Sorry, sir. What did I do now?"

Stoner glared at him. "Two things. First, it's your attitude."

"My attitude? What's wrong with my attitude?"

Stoner moved closer to Bridges until their faces were just inches apart.

"Are you or are you not an officer in the ISA?"

"Yes, I am."

"Yes, I am, what?" Stoner repeated as a question.

"Yes, I am—SIR," Bridges said, emphasizing the word sir.

"So, is it your belief that when your captain gives an order you don't like, your best course of action is to mope around the ship like somebody stole your pacifier?"

"I'm not moping...."

"You damn straight are," shouted Stoner, interrupting his young officer. "It's obvious to everyone. You've turned your back on the rest of the crew. You stopped playing cards, you're taking your meals in your quarters, you don't spend any time socializing with the rest of the crew, and you're acting like a freaking dumbass."

"It's complicated," Bridges replied, stung by Stoner's remarks.

"Get your head out of your ass. It's simple. The captain gave an order. You don't like it. Too freaking bad. Accept it and move on. There will be other missions. So, knock it off, and that's an order."

"Yes, sir," said Bridges.

"And that brings me to number two, this thing between you and Cortez." Bridges turned back toward his holoview. "That's personal," said Bridges.

"Too freaking bad. Like I said, you're an idiot. That girl is crazy about you. I sure don't get it because you're a moron. But for some reason, that's hard to explain, she likes you. Frankly, you don't deserve her. She's way above your class, buddy. So, if you keep screwing around, you will lose possibly the best thing in your life. You get me?"

"Yes, sir."

"All right then. I don't want to have to talk about this again. Grow a pair. And talk to Cortez."

Bridges watched as the XO left the bridge. He hadn't had a chewing out like that since high school when his grandpa grounded him over that airplane stunt. Maybe Stoner was right. Perhaps he was taking this too personally. Maybe he needed to adjust his attitude.

"Yeah, I am a dumbass," Bridges said to himself.

# CHAPTER 57

*Mission Cortez Begins*

Despite the cooling of their relationship, Cortez still had feelings for Bridges. *I can't leave without saying goodbye*, she thought. She found Bridges standing watch on the bridge, a mostly ceremonial duty but one Merriweather and Stoner insisted on.

"Hi, Milo."

"Hey," he replied. Bridges, seated in the captain's chair, swiveled to face Cortez

"Wow! I knew you were getting ready to go, but—Wow! That's quite a realistic-looking alien disguise."

"You like the look?"

"Very much. It's quite a transformation."

"I'll be leaving in thirty minutes. I wanted to let you know in case something goes wrong."

"Don't put that thought in your head. You'll be fine," he interrupted. "You've flown dangerous missions before."

"I know. But it is an alien planet, and our understanding of Heran is still very…."

"You've got a good team. Javi will protect you."

"I'm not really worried about my safety, Milo. I just worry about screwing up."

Bridges could hear the concern in her voice. This was a genuine concern and not just something one says. She was seriously having doubts about her ability to perform the mission. She exposed to him a side of herself he had not seen before. Her vulnerability smashed through the wall he had constructed around his feelings. He realized now that he had sacrificed someone who had meant so much to him for perceived glory. He felt ashamed of his actions. Echoes of Don Stoner's admonishment still reverberated in his mind.

"Look, Cat, no one on this ship is more qualified, including me," he said. "The captain was absolutely right in selecting you. It's taken me a long time to realize that, and I'm sorry for how I reacted."

"Milo, I never asked for this."

Cortez floated over to Milo and put her arms around his neck. He put his arm under her and lifted her onto his lap. She buried her face in his neck.

"I know," he replied, tears welling in his eyes. "We'll have a long talk when you get back."

Bridges gave Cortez a long, tender kiss.

"Do you think Buzz Aldrin gave Neil Armstrong a kiss before he stepped on the moon?" Cortez asked.

"Well, since I'm not going down to the surface with you, technically, I'm Mike Collins in this scenario," laughed Bridges.

"I suppose. I'm looking forward to that talk. Let's talk every day," she said.

"Of course," he replied.

Cortez gave him one last hug and kissed him on his cheek before turning and propelling herself through the bridge access hatch.

Milo watched her go with a mix of guilt, envy, worry, and longing.

Five minutes later, Cortez met up with Don Stoner and Javi Rodriguez at the docking port for Aries One.

"Hey, guys, ready to make history?" Cortez asked, while wiping a tear from her cheek.

"Let's do it," said Stoner.

"I can't wait," added Rodriguez.

Minutes later, the three crewmates busied themselves in the LAV, reviewing the departure checklist. Cortez had already created a mission profile that would take them down to the planet and to the same open field used by Bridges on his earlier visit. Now, she was going through the normal pre-launch procedures, eager to get start her mission.

After fifteen minutes and finally getting the go-ahead from Captain Merriweather, Cortez flipped the sequence of switches that opened the LAV's docking clamps. Deftly using Aries' hydrazine thrusters, she slowly backed the small craft away from the larger mother ship. Next, Cortez repositioned Aries, lining up its rear-docking adaptor with the recently refueled EX-23 booster latched to Endeavor's port side. Slowly, Cortez backed her spacecraft until she felt the mating clamps engage, signaling a successful docking. "OK, we have all greens," said Cortez. "We're ready for booster extraction." Again, using her LAV's thrusters, Cortez eased the booster rocket from

Endeavor's port side docking ring, in a procedure she had practiced in a simulator a hundred times. The EX-23 booster was critical to their mission. Without it, Aries would not have the fuel or engine power to complete its mission.

"Nice job, Lieutenant," said Stoner. "Are you ready to go?"

"Yes sir," replied Cortez. "With your permission."

"Go ahead. It's your show, "answered Stoner.

Cortez once again scanned her instruments before contacting Endeavor.

"Bridge, this is Aries One. Request permission to proceed with booster-engine burn."

"Permission granted, Lieutenant. Stay safe," said Merriweather. Merriweather could have added some flowery language or reminded Cortez of the importance to humanity of her mission. He decided instead that she did not need the reminder or the added pressure. He had the ultimate confidence in his young lieutenant, and she would make a great representative of her species and her planet.

"We copy," said Cortez. "See you on the other side."

Minutes later, the EX-23 booster rocket engine fired, propelling the small ship and its three occupants toward its moment in history.

For the next four days, the Earthlings sped toward the blue-green world that floated before them in the blackness of space. Each crew member had their duties, but there was ample downtime for them to think about what was about to happen on the planet below. Stoner contemplated his place in the history books and planned on writing one. Of course, he would be the protagonist of the story.

Rodriguez was a consummate professional. Although he had no security officer background, he took his orders seriously. He had a security plan, which he was constantly revising. The safety of the mission was in his hands, and he would allow nothing to happen to his team.

Cortez reflected on her place in history, what it meant to her personally and professionally, how she got here, on this tiny spacecraft, light years from that pale blue dot she called home. If everything went as planned— and really, how often does that happen, she thought—two separate intelligent species would finally meet. Was she up to the moment? *Time will tell*, she thought. There was nothing she could do but rely on her training and push forward.

Four days later, Aries One and her crew of three settled into orbit and waited for the planet revolving below them to be in the correct position. After reporting their status and receiving permission from Endeavor, Cortez detached Aries from the EX-23 booster and oriented the LAV for the critical de-orbit burn.

"RHODA, please execute MP three point zero."

"Executing Mission Plan three point zero, Lieutenant Cortez," RHODA replied.

Aries' main engines instantly ignited, slamming the three humans back in their seats.

"Here we go, gentlemen," said Cortez. "Enjoy the ride."

Cortez had gone through re-entry many times on Earth on training missions, but this was Earth on steroids. The atmosphere was deeper and thicker, and the planet's gravity stronger—all adding to a longer, hotter, and bumpier ride. Cortez focused on her ship's instruments while listening to RHODA calling out elevation in her helmet's built-in speakers.

*Did they know we were coming?* She thought. Could they see the trail of ionized vapor streaming behind their spacecraft? A million thoughts raced through her mind as the dazzling fireworks display danced outside her lander's viewports. Cortez said a brief prayer with her hands folded across her chest and her fingers crossed. *Hypocrite*, she thought to herself. You're an atheist.

As Aries' velocity dropped below six-hundred knots, its attack attitude changed. Now nose down in a shallow glide configuration with its wings extended, Aries became an aircraft. Cortez took control and banked the ship toward their ultimate destination, a small clearing west of Whoville.

Twenty minutes later, Aries was circling less than five hundred meters above the LZ (Landing Zone) while Stoner and Rodriguez used their night scopes to search for any heat signatures in the dark landscape below—indicators of life that might ruin their surprise party.

"All clear here," said Rodriguez.

"Same here," said Stoner.

"OK, let's take her in," said Cortez.

Cortez circled the small clearing once more before extending Aries' landing gear. As the LAV settled for a perfect landing, Stoner took a slow breath. "Nice job, Lieutenant."

"Thanks, sir. But I'll be happy when we get Aries hidden in those trees ahead."

Applying minimal power to the jet engines, Cortez eased the craft between two large and weirdly shaped trees at the edge of the dark forest surrounding the clearing. Finally satisfied with their hiding place, she cut the engines. Other than the creaking of the engines cooling in the night air, there was an eerie silence.

"Kind of spooky," said Cortez.

"I'd like to get out and perform a security sweep, Commander," announced Rodriguez.

"OK, just try not to shoot anyone," chided Stoner. "Oh, and don't forget to take your EPO pill. That goes for you too, Cortez."

Stoner was referring to the erythropoietin pills that sped up the formation of red blood cells, enabling each of the crew to operate more efficiently with the planet's lower oxygen levels.

"OK, Boss, anything you say," said Rodriguez.

After swallowing an EPO tablet, Rodriguez opened the forward hatch and hopped to the surface. Despite being a workout warrior, he immediately felt the effect of living on a low-gravity spaceship for the last two-and-a-half years.

"Oof," he grunted as he landed on the grassy surface. "That didn't feel good," he mumbled to himself.

After gaining his bearings, Rodriguez moved off to his left, circling the lander three times before he was confident no one was in the area. He then gave Cortez the all-clear signal.

Stoner reported to Endeavor before receiving the 'go' to proceed. Cortez then joined her crewmate on the planet's surface.

"I'll take the point, and you follow," said Rodriguez.

"OK, let's go," said Cortez.

With that last word, Cortez and Rodriguez headed toward the small hamlet and the alien Dualla's home.

The road to Whoville consisted of gravel pressed into a layer of clay, with shallow ditches bordering each side to collect runoff. Three shallow ruts straddled the center of the road, marking the frequent travel of three-wheeled vehicles. Thick vegetation choked the ditches, which might make it difficult for the two Earthlings to cross in an emergency.

"Looks like they've repaired the road since that torrential rainstorm Milo experienced," said Cortez.

"If you can call it a road," said Rodriguez.

"We still have roads that look just like this, Javi. Don't be so judgmental."

The night sky was free of clouds, unlike the storm clouds Bridges had experienced. Caerus and Erebus burned brightly in the night sky, while the ever-present aurora added a mesmerizing light show for the two explorers. The terrain was mostly flat as the road meandered toward the small hamlet. Three hours after they started, the Earthlings topped a slight rise and got their first view of Whoville—a cluster of dwellings and streetlights surrounding several two- and three-story buildings and a domed structure they guessed housed the telescope.

"Nice place to live," said Cortez.

"I like the big city," said Rodriguez. "More to do, lots of restaurants, clubs, you know, fun stuff."

"I will admit that it would be nice to be around more than thirteen people. However, I still like all the trees and the feeling of a small community."

"So, we start at the Doctor's house?" asked Rodriguez.

"That's the plan. Are you ready?"

"Ready as I can be. Wait, what's that?" said Rodriguez, pointing at a shiny object hidden under a pile of fallen branches and scrub. Moving close, Rodriguez lifted a tree branch lying atop the brush pile.

"Damn, look at that. It's Bridges' electro-cycle. What should we do with it, boss? Boss?"

Rodriguez looked in Cortez's direction, only to find her staring at a nearby tree. Walking over to her side, he quickly realized what had drawn her attention. "Well, would you look at that," he said.

There, carved into the tree was the inscription "Cat + Milo."

"Someone left a message for you, I see," said Rodriguez, grinning from ear to ear, to which Cortez answered, "Mind your own business."

# CHAPTER 58

*Cortez's Mission Continues*

Cortez turned and began walking toward the village, followed closely by a bemused Rodriguez. Together, they hoped to get to Whoville without drawing undue attention. They had already glimpsed a few inhabitants in the distance, though it was impossible to tell if the aliens had noticed them. If they had, the locals showed no sign of alarm or even curiosity, continuing with their routines as though nothing were out of the ordinary.

They hadn't gone far when a group of three aliens rounded a bend in the road, walking directly toward them. To Cortez, it looked like three males, each carrying a small bundle. Cortez could hear their voices, but couldn't quite understand what they were chatting about.

Rodriguez moved slightly ahead of Cortez, assuming a protective posture. She could see his hand move to the weapon he had concealed behind his back.

"Javi, don't overreact. Let's just play this out and see how it goes," she whispered.

The words were scarcely out of her mouth when one of the approaching sophonts hailed them.

"Welcome, strangers. Pray you slept well."

Cortez heard the English translation almost immediately in her earpiece and recognized it as one of the traditional hello messages used by the locals. Mouthing the alien's usual reply in English, she heard and felt the Heran words "On a bed of saszu grass" as they emanated from her vocalizer. A few friendly hand waves and the trio of sophonts were by them, chatting away and disappearing around a bend in the road.

"That was a rush," said Cortez. "How are you doing, Javi?"

Rodriguez re-engaged the safety on his firearm, looked at Cortez, and winked. "I wasn't worried," he said. "What did you say?"

"I told them you were armed," replied Cortez.

"You did not," said Rodriguez. "Really?"

As the two Earthlings neared the line of small dwellings at the edge of the hamlet, they turned left and slowly counted until they were near a small dwelling—the fifth in line.

"RHODA, distance to the alien Dualla's home," said Cortez.

"You are five meters away from the residence of the alien known as Dualla."

Cortez and Rodriguez slowly approached the structure. Following Rodriguez's lead, the pair circled the structure, examining it and the surrounding area, looking for any signs of danger or nearby sophonts. The alien's home, Cortez noted, was identical to its neighbors except perhaps somewhat larger. Semicircular, its one flat wall faced the center of the hamlet. The exterior was pale green with a stucco-like surface but somewhat smoother in texture.

Along the curved back wall were seven small windows plus one larger window measuring approximately three meters wide by two meters high. They obviously positioned the large window to afford those inside a view of the picturesque field and forest just one hundred meters away. Carefully, Cortez leaned toward the window and peered inside. The interior was shrouded in complete darkness, the kind that swallowed detail and shape alike. If there were sophonts within, they were hidden from sight, silent and invisible in the gloom.

Moving around to the front, Cortez and Rodriguez found several more windows, plus the only door to the building. "It looks like the builders were going for rustic, but you can tell they used modern construction techniques," said Cortez.

"I don't see any vehicles," she said. "The paths look too small for anything larger than a golf cart. My guess is some sort of planned community.

"I agree, a company town," said Rodriguez. "She must be one of the town's bigwigs," he added as he examined the front door of the alien's home.

Rodriguez signaled to Cortez that he would proceed her through the door, and she nodded in agreement. Rodriguez tried the door handle, finding it unlocked.

"They're not big on home security, are they?" he said.

"I'm sure that says something about their culture, like the lack of crime," Cortez replied.

"That will change if we keep breaking in," he said.

"You're probably right."

Rodriguez was about to enter, but Cortez stopped him.

"Let's try the old-fashioned and more neighborly approach," she said as she stepped between Rodriguez and the door. Raising her hand, she knocked four times and then stepped back.

After ten seconds of silence, she stepped forward and knocked again, this time more forcefully.

"Well, it might have worked," she said. "OK, let's try it your way." Cautiously, Rodriguez opened the door. He paused briefly, listening for anything that might suggest occupants. Hearing no one, he moved through the opening, followed closely by Cortez.

"Is there anyone here?" announced Cortez in the Heran language. "We come in peace," she said, instantly grimacing at the corny sci-fi character of her greeting.

"Anyone here?" she repeated.
Rodriguez stared at his crewmate in wonder at the strange sounds coming from her mouth. "That's just weird, Boss."

"You should have taken some lessons, Javi. Why didn't you wear a translator?"

"Didn't think I needed to, long as I'm with you. Besides, the damned thing caused blisters in my mouth."

Cortez had to remind herself to breathe. All she could think of was that she was on an alien planet and in the home of an intelligent being not of Earth. *This is surreal*, she thought.

She hoped that the alien sounds produced by Endeavor technology would be understandable by the natives. There was no way to test it. It was more a matter of faith.

Cortez wandered around slowly, looking at the home's furnishings and snapping photos with the camera feature on her communicator. The similarity of the things she saw and the alien nature of those same items amazed her. There was furniture—a chair, a table—identifiable, but unlike any table or chair Cortez had ever seen. The chair, if that's what it was, reminded her of the kneeling chairs she had seen in a museum of American history. She figured they would accommodate a species whose knees bent forward.
There were objects hanging on the walls—some familiar and some mysterious. A large basket in the corner of the main room held a collection of seashells, like one might find on any beach on Earth?

In another room—perhaps an office because it lacked a bed—Cortez found instruments, books, a drafting table, and other recognizable objects. She picked up and examined what could only be a microscope—primitive, maybe, but a microscope, definitely. On what was possibly a drafting table, Cortez found triangles, curves, and a weirdly designed compass. She also found a rather detailed drawing of a large telescope, complete with cut-outs and projections. She picked up and examined a rectangular device with a sliding mechanism. *I wonder what this is*, she thought. Then it came to her in a flash. *It's a slide rule*. She thought about putting it in her bag but resisted the temptation.

Rodriguez finished his security sweep of the structure and signaled to Cortez that no one was home.

"Maybe she went to work already," said Cortez, looking at her watch. "It is a bit earlier than her normal departure time, but maybe she had to go in early."

"And the child?"

"Maybe dropped her off with a babysitter or at school."

"Well, what's the next step, boss?"

"Let's try the telescope. If Dualla is not there, we'll try her office," said Cortez.

Cortez decided that first, she needed to check in with Stoner while her partner performed another security sweep around the dwelling. Stoner relayed the basics to Endeavor. A few minutes elapsed before Merriweather gave them the go-ahead to proceed to their new destination.

As Cortez walked through the tiny hamlet, she often exchanged glances with Rodriguez. Seeing the townlet from space through Endeavor's long-range optical sensors didn't do it justice. The occupants clearly took pride in their home. The dwellings were well-maintained, the grass well-groomed, and flowering plants grew everywhere. These people shared similar aesthetics with humans—that was clear.

A few adult sophonts were moving along the various pathways, and several adolescents were playing a game of sorts in one of the small, well-groomed grassy areas scattered here and there around the hamlet. Residents passed them by on the way to work or who knows where. Some greeted Cortez and Rodriguez with a smile and a wave, while others tried to avoid eye contact. *That's strange*, Cortez thought. Cortez was worried that as the sky brightened and the visibility improved, the Herans might notice something odd about their unknown visitors. Fortunately, they didn't seem to raise any suspicion from the aliens they passed.

After a fifteen-minute walk from Dakar Dualla's home, the Earthlings arrived at the large dome-like structure in the center of the hamlet.

"How are we going to play this?" asked Rodriguez.

"Well, we don't want to frighten them. If they are scientists and astronomers, then the idea of extraterrestrial life has probably occurred to them. So, let's try to keep it simple and play to their intelligence."

"Sounds good to me, boss."

"Here goes nothing," said Cortez, stepping inside the domed structure. Rodriguez followed closely behind, hand on the firearm hidden under his tunic. Cortez could tell immediately that the facility was occupied. The two Earthlings exchanged glances as they considered their next move.

# CHAPTER 59

*Road Trip*

Cortez and Rodriguez found themselves in a large circular room, dark except for the greenish glow from dozens of data displays. A low-pitched hum and the familiar scent of burned electronics reminded Cortez of an antique vacuum tube radio she had bought at a flea market years earlier. The semi-darkness offered some security—a fact they both appreciated. They could see several aliens milling about on the opposite side of the spacious dome, seemingly in an intense discussion about something. Three more aliens sat at consoles near the center of the structure beneath the powerful telescope that loomed above them.

"I don't see her," said Rodriguez, looking around. "Should we ask someone?"

"I have a more direct way." Cortez turned on her vocalizer with a press of her tongue and then silently mouthed the words, "Dakar Dualla, may we speak with you?"

A sensor attached to Cortez's head detected the signals from the part of her brain responsible for speech and relayed the signals to the neuralizer. The neuralizer then transmitted the information to the translator she carried in a pouch in her tunic, which then sent the translation back to the vocalizer pressed against Cortez's upper palate. The sentence, now translated into Heran, emanated from her mouth. All this in less than a millisecond.

A squeal and a string of clicks erupted from an unseen alien from somewhere in the semi-darkness. A heartbeat later, the translation sounded in Cortez's earpiece.

"Not here."

"Will she be here soon?" Cortez asked in response.

Cortez soon spotted the top of an alien's head bobbing on the far side of a row of instrument consoles and pointed it out to Rodriguez.

The sophont she had seen slowly stood, turned, and faced the Earthlings. "Who dares to inquire?"

"It's important we speak to her," said Cortez.

Cortez glanced at her partner, noting Javi's hand on his firearm, partially hidden under his tunic.

"You may speak to Glyvash," said the alien as he slowly walked over to confront the pair. "I am Glyvash. Do you have permission to be here?"

Cortez tensed as the alien drew closer. The two Earthlings stood in the light of the open door, where she was almost certain that their disguises would not withstand closer scrutiny. Cortez eased several paces to her right, to a darkened corner, motioning Rodriguez to do the same. She then leaned closer to her partner and, in a quiet voice, repeated what she had said and the alien's responses.

"When is she expected to return?" She asked in Heran.

"Who did you say you —?" The alien sophont abruptly stopped. Something was decidedly off with the two visitors standing before him. One stranger was female, but the second was, well, he couldn't tell. It wore typical male clothing, but something was different, and he couldn't quite put his finger on it. The female also had a childlike way of speaking. It took him a few seconds before a strange tingling sensation began crawling up his back.

"What did you desire of Dakar Dualla?" he asked pointedly.

Cortez paused for a moment as she heard the translation. She didn't want to frighten this alien, but she knew she would have to admit who they were if they had any hope of getting his cooperation. She also wanted to protect their secret from as many aliens as possible for the time being.

"Is there somewhere more private we can talk?"

Cortez was good at reading people, but trying to read an alien was something else entirely. She couldn't tell whether this one was about to flee or yell out for security. Fortunately, he did neither.

"Yes. There is an equipment room—there," he replied, pointing to a door on his left.

Slowly, the alien backed toward the door as the two strange visitors followed. After the three entered the equipment room, Rodriguez eased the door closed behind them. The alien noted that fact with some trepidation. Cortez raised her hands slowly in the universal—she hoped—gesture of peaceful intentions. Then she began her often-practiced introduction.

"My friend and I have traveled a great distance to meet Dakar Dualla," she began in Heran. "We understand she has some interest in where we come from."

The slight tingling Glyvash had felt was now screaming at him. He didn't know whether to flee or to bombard them with questions. He looked closely at each, then moved cautiously closer. Glyvash could now see that neither of the two figures that stood before him was completely normal. The male's head was devoid of frills, while the female's frills were not glowing green, the expected color for situations such as this, or any color for that matter.

"How far?" was all he could think to ask.

"Twenty-five light years," responded Cortez, leaving no doubt whatsoever of their identities.

Glyvash stared at the two. "Light…years," he mumbled. Slowly, he reached behind and pulled out a chair from a nearby equipment console.

"Glyvash must sit," he said as he almost fell into the chair.

Cortez and Rodriguez remained standing. "Can you help us contact Dakar Dualla?"

"Can you prove what you say? It seems…highly…unlikely."

Cortez and the crew of Endeavor had planned for this challenge. The easiest way to convince a wavering alien, they believed, was to show him or her technology unavailable on their planet.

Slowly, Cortez removed the bag she had slung over her shoulders.

The bag contained assorted items, among them a small portable holo-projector. Setting the bag carefully on the floor, Cortez removed the holo-projector and placed it down next to it.

"Don't be frightened," she said to Glyvash.

Glyvash stared at the two strangers with a look of amazement. "Frightened?"

Keeping her eyes locked on the alien, Cortez switched the projector on. Using the translator in command mode, Cortez thought,

*RHODA, display holo image of this planet's solar system, three meters in diameter.*

Instantly, a three-meter-wide 3D holo image of the Heran system blossomed into existence over their heads.

Cortez watched as the alien's mouth slowly opened in a very humanlike reaction. With apparent trepidation, Glyvash stood and approached the floating apparition. He raised his hand and hesitantly waved it through the ethereal image.

"How is this possible?" he exclaimed.

"We can help you understand later," said Cortez. "It's just science, not magic."

"Science," repeated Glyvash. "Yes, Glyvash understands science. Glyvash is a scientist."

Cortez looked at Rodriguez, who finally relaxed his death grip on his firearm.

*RHODA, show Endeavor's trajectory through the current system,* she thought

Immediately, a bright red line appeared in the holo image.

Cortez moved forward and 'into' the image now floating about her, and traced the red line with her finger.

"We were traveling through your system when we stopped 'here' to correlate our position with our star maps." Cortez thought it prudent not to divulge the accident that had crippled their ship. "Here, we detected electromagnetic transmissions coming from your planet. This is your planet 'here.' We are a scientific expedition seeking intelligent civilizations, so we changed course to your planet." Cortez's finger guided Glyvash's attention as she moved it along the red trajectory.

*RHODA, show the Heran planetary system—three meters in diameter*, she thought.

As Cortez, Javi, and the alien Glyvash watched, the holo image changed, zooming into the planet Hera and its two moons, Caerus, and Erebus. "Our ship is 'here' behind Erebus since the last orbital cycle of your planet," Cortez continued. "We wanted to learn your language before we made contact. We chose Dakar Dualla because of her interest in—well—us."

Cortez paused for a moment to let it all sink in. Then she continued.

"You are Supervisor Glyvash, correct?" Cortez used the name of a character she had remembered from an old TV show and assigned to this alien by the translation team aboard Endeavor. As she formed the sentence in her mind, RHODA converted the name Glyvash into the pattern of whistles and clicks associated with this alien.

Glyvash's expression suddenly changed.

"You know my position? How?"

Cortez continued. "We discovered your telescope during our study." She had decided against using words like surveillance and spying. Study seemed a more benign term. "We focused our attention on your small village and its residents. We believed fellow scientists like you would be less fearful of us than perhaps others might." Cortez hoped Glyvash would respond positively to a bit of flattery, and she was right.

"Yes, you are right. We scientists understand the importance of such an event. From what line do you descend?"

Cortez paused momentarily, trying to understand what Glyvash meant by 'line.' *Oh, he means genealogy*, she thought.

"My name is Catriana Cortez. My title is Lieutenant. This is fellow crew-member Javier Rodriguez. His title is also Lieutenant. You may call me Catriana."

"He wants to know your name and what to call you," Cortez whispered to her crewmate.

"Tell him he can call me anything he wants," said Rodriguez, the first words he had spoken since meeting the alien.

"My crewmate does not speak your language. He says you may call him Javi."

Glyvash considered this momentarily, then pointed at Cortez and said,

"Cah…tree…ana," carefully drawing out each syllable. He then pointed at Rodriguez and said, "Javee." Finally, he pointed at himself. "You may call me Glyvash."

"Thank you, Glyvash. Can you help us contact Dakar Dualla?"

Glyvash paused for a moment as if he were considering how to respond.

"I don't know where she is…exactly, that is. She traveled to Xanglora to petition for an audience with the Council of Eleven to make her case for… oh my, how should I say this…the existence of…you." Glyvash pointed to the sky. "I begged her not to go, but she can be so stubborn."

Glyvash's eyes went suddenly wide as he lowered his head.

"Ca…tree…ah…na, Glyvash begs forgiveness for my careless words. I meant no disrespect of your preeminence. Please grant kindness to an old fool."

"Glyvash, your words were not disrespectful. Our culture is not like yours. We do not elevate women over men or men over women. We have no royalty or privileged class. Where we come from, all are equal."

Glyvash slowly stood, looking back and forth between Cortez and Rodriguez.

"Is this so?" Glyvash replied, looking to Javi for verification.

Rodriguez looked at Cortez. "Is he talking to me?"

"Yes, he wants to know if men and women are equal on our planet."

"You're kidding me, right?" said Rodriguez.

"He says it is so," said Cortez, using her vocalizer.

"I would lose my position for even suggesting such a thing," said Glyvash.

"All is well, Glyvash," said Cortez. "Tell us more about Dakar Dualla's trip."

Glyvash thought for a moment before responding. He was speaking with…what exactly…beings from another planet? Could he trust them? A world where females and males were equal wasn't possible? Was it? Imagine a world where he would be just as important as any female.

"This was a dangerous trip for Dakar Dualla. She is female and of noble tutelage, but on Hera, the very idea of beings from the stars is heresy. Her status might not protect her. Should the Council of Eleven grant her an audience, and she presents evidence of such beings, the repercussions could be unthinkable. The Akan could publicly denounce her. She could lose her office and her authority. She could be confined or even—may the gods help her—expelled."

"What evidence does she have?" Cortez asked suddenly.

Glyvash pondered this for a moment before finally deciding to trust the strange visitors.

"Dakar Dualla and I witnessed your space machine between Caerus and Erebus. We have an image from our telescope. We also saw your flying machine to the west of Whoville. It flew over our heads."

Cortez smiled as RHODA's translation sounded in her earpiece. She briefly wondered what this alien would think if he knew the English translation of his city's name was a word from a children's book.

"Then I think we need to go there and help her make her case," said Cortez.

"Go there? Make her case?" said Glyvash. "I do not understand."

"I think we can make them accept the fact of our existence as we have you," she explained.

Cortez once again turned to her partner and translated into English the conversation of the last several minutes and her decision to travel to the Heran capital city.

"Lieutenant, maybe we should clear this with Endeavor," said Javi, leaning close to her ear.

"Yes, of course," she replied. Then, switching to Heran, said, "What do you say, Glyvash? Will you take us there?"

Glyvash knew he risked his position, reputation, and freedom by getting involved. The Council could be stubborn, and they might deny the obvious. What to do? Finally, Glyvash raised his head and looked straight ahead.

"Yes. I will guide you. Dakar Dualla has always treated me with respect— as a fellow scientist. I will help her."

"Great. Glyvash, we will need a few minutes to communicate with our ship."

"Of course, of course."

Cortez and Rodriguez moved a few meters away to gain a bit of privacy before contacting Endeavor. For fifteen minutes, Cortez laid out their options and her recommendations. She answered Merriweather's concerns and the XO's one by one. Finally, despite some reservations expressed by both Captain Merriweather and the XO, the plan was agreed to.

"OK, Glyvash, I have permission from my ship to proceed."

"You have a leader on your ship?" Glyvash asked.

"Yes, we do."

"Is she female?"

"He's male," said Cortez.

"Male?" Glyvash said. "He must be from a powerful family?"

"No, not at all. His parents were poor farmers. We choose our leaders based on experience, knowledge, and ability, and our captain has those qualities, so we follow his lead."

"Then I will help you, Catriana."

"Thank you, Glyvash. Our captain thinks flying to your capital city would be too dangerous. We would need a secluded area where we could hide our ship. So, the captain has given me permission to travel overland to—what did you call it—Xanglora?"

Cortez knew that Endeavor's AI had created the name Xanglora based on an algorithm and a frequency analysis of alien phonemes. The name appealed to Cortez because it sounded a bit like Shangri-La.

"Yes, Xanglora. It's our capital and sacred city. I will take you there in my motor carriage. It is very fast."

Glyvash looked at Javi before continuing.

"Catriana, my humble vehicle can carry a driver and only one passenger. This is a problem?"

Once more, Cortez and Rodriguez conferred with Captain Merriweather and the XO. Through the sheer force of her will and over Rodriguez's strenuous objection, Cortez convinced them to allow her to proceed on her own with the alien Glyvash.

"OK, Glyvash, Javi will return to our ship, and you and I will proceed to Xanglora."

"Very good. We should go right away."

"The sooner, the better," said Cortez.

"This is a bad move," said Rodriguez. "I should go with you. It's too dangerous for you to go alone."

"I know, Javi. I appreciate your concern. But this is a terrific opportunity to learn about these people."

"Still not convinced," he said.

"I'll be careful, Javi."

"Take my firearm," he said, reaching behind his back for the weapon he had hidden there.

"No," said Cortez, placing her hand on his arm. "I won't need it."

"Damn," said Javi. "You can be very stubborn."

"I'm ready to go as soon as we can," said Cortez, turning back to the alien and speaking in his language.

"Yes, I agree. We must go to my lodging to retrieve my vehicle. Your Ha… vee can stay there until it is dark."

"That sounds like a good plan, Glyvash," said Cortez.

"I hope he has something to eat," said Rodriguez after Cortez translated her conversation with the alien.

Thirty minutes later, Glyvash had retrieved his two-seat, three-wheeled personal conveyance from his residence, and the two were flying down a hard-packed dirt and gravel road at the fantastic speed of forty kilometers (24 miles) per hour.

Meanwhile, Captain Merriweather ordered the crew of Endeavor to make ready to leave L2 and its home behind Erebus for the last year plus. He intended to park Endeavor in a geosynchronous orbit directly above the alien city of Xanglora. He also ordered Stoner to lift off the planet in forty-eight hours and proceed to a rendezvous with Endeavor in orbit.

Cortez hoped she had made the right call.

# CHAPTER 60

*Be careful what you wish for*

Cortez wondered whether she had made the right decision when she agreed to take this trip with this alien. She really didn't know what dangers she was about to face. Was she up to the task?

*Of course I am*, she thought. ISA spent a lot of time and effort to train me, and I'm damn well prepared. I'm good at my job...or am I just fooling myself? OK, Cortez, knock off the self-doubt. You can do this.

Cortez took a long, hard look at her traveling companion, trying to commit to memory every detail for the report she would later write. Sitting beside her, just centimeters away from the alien species known as Heran, Cortez noticed details her briefing report had missed.

The most obvious missed detail was the alien's skin, or lack thereof. Instead of skin, the alien was covered in what appeared to be a hard, external shell. *An exoskeleton?* Cortez's first thought was that it looked like a greenish medieval suit of armor, suggesting that Herans might have evolved from crustaceans or perhaps from insects. This Heran was more grasshopper than human.

"Would you mind if I take a hologram of you, Glyvash?"

"A holo...gram?"

"A holographic image. I would like to record your image—for scientific purposes. This device will record and store your likeness," she explained, holding up her holo.

"An image recorder—we have that technology," said Glyvash.

"This device records a three-dimensional image," said Cortez.

"I would like to see that," said Glyvash. "You can show Glyvash this?" Cortez held her holo at arm's length and pointed the lens at herself.

"I press this button, and the device records what it sees."

After verifying that the holo had done its job correctly, Cortez activated its holographic projector.

Glyvash was so amazed by the hologram of Cortez now floating above her holo that he almost drove off the road.

"We do not have this technology," Glyvash said, steering his motorcar back to the center of the road. "Our recordings are...flat."

Cortez waited patiently while her traveling companion mulled over her question. Finally, Glyvash answered.

"Yes, you may take my...hologram."

Another detail lacking from the briefing report was that almost everything about the alien's physiology differed from first thought. The first surprising fact was that Herans bent backward at the hip, not forward. Cortez first noticed this when the alien boarded his motorcar and took his place behind the steering lever. Glyvash sat with his legs splayed out behind his seat, which had a 'seat-front' instead of a 'seat-back.' This created a problem. The seat's design would require Cortez to sit facing the rear throughout the entire trip. Fortunately for Cortez, Glyvash was not only a scientist but also good with tools. So, while Cortez waited, Glyvash unbolted the passenger seat from the floor of the vehicle, turned it one hundred and eighty degrees, and reattached it.

Cortez also noted in her report that Heran legs had two knee joints. The higher joint bent forward, the opposite of humans, while the lower bent backward.

"I have a question about your species, Glyvash. May I ask—as a scientist?"

"Yes. I will answer your questions—as a scientist."

"Thanks. Can you tell me how your species detect sound?"

There was no appendage or protuberance on her alien tour guide's head that Cortez could interpret as an ear.

"This is interesting," said Glyvash. "I assumed our species detected sound in the same manner."

"My species has tiny setae—here and here," he explained, brushing a hand across the small patches of fur on either side of his neck. "They vibrate in response to sound waves, allowing us to perceive them. Does your species not sense sound in the same way?"

While Glyvash listened intently, Cortez described the various parts of the human ear and their function.

"This is very interesting. I think our species has many differences," said Glyvash.

"And many similarities," said Cortez. "Do female Herans have setae?"

"Yes. It's the same. However, for females, it is below her frills."

Glyvash was full of questions, as one might expect, and Cortez was trying her best to answer. She was learning much about the culture of these aliens and growing more comfortable speaking the Heran language with the help of the translator and vocalizer.

"How long will it take to get to your capital?" she asked.

"Four days," said Glyvash, proudly. "It once took twice that before I acquired my vehicle. It has been such a welcome convenience."

*Four days? thought Cortez. What have I got myself into? OK, I've gotta get my mind around this. It couldn't possibly be more arduous than an archeological dig or a backpacking expedition in Asia, both of which I've done. Plus, think of the scientific papers I'll be able to write—if I don't die first, of course.*

Cortez had another thought that worried her. She had brought enough food for a week, but most of it was back on the Aries lander. She had only a snack in her bag. Could she make it last four or five days, or would she be able to eat indigenous food?

As if Glyvash was reading her mind, he suddenly asked.

"Caa...tree...ah...na, does your species require nutrients? I have not since this morning. A kujai just ahead makes a wonderful soup of saszu grass and corettle fish. Plus, we might get some ripe moke fruit."

Cortez didn't recognize the word kujai. It was likely a word RHODA constructed using Heran phonemes. She assumed from the context of Glyvash's sentence that it was a restaurant or cafe.

"That sounds delicious," said Cortez.

Glyvash gave Cortez a puzzled look. "How can sound be delicious?"

"It just means that your words make me expect a delicious meal," replied Cortez.

"Very good. I am very thirsty."

Twenty minutes later, Glyvash pulled his small three-wheeled vehicle behind a wooden structure that looked to Cortez like it might crumble at any moment.

"Do you think it's safe?" she asked.

Glyvash looked somewhat puzzled before he understood her concern.

"Oh, you are speaking about the appearance of the kujai. Yes, I think it should be safe to enter."

Glyvash's eyes appeared to grin. "It is humorous to me that you can fly between the stars and still be afraid of a simple kujai. Is flying between the stars so safe?"

"You have a point, Glyvash."

"A point? I do not understand."

"It means that you have made a brilliant observation."

"Thank you, yes, a point, I see," Glyvash replied, beaming.

As they entered the small structure, Glyvash checked out the current occupants.

"Caa…tree…ah…na, please sit there where it's more secluded," he said, pointing at a small table in a dark corner of the alien cafe. "I will bring the meal to you."

Cortez understood his wariness. She wasn't quite ready to announce herself to the cafe's customers, so Cortez seated herself at the table Glyvash had chosen. She hoped that here, hidden in the shadows, no one could make her out to be an alien. *I'm the alien here*, she realized with some amusement. Cortez slowly scanned the room. The establishment was not unlike a dozen other small inns or cafes she had wandered into while backpacking around the world during her gap year.

*Definitely a cafe*, thought Cortez.

*RHODA, translation correction. Reassign the word kujai to cafe.*

An adolescent male occasionally entered the room through an opening in the far corner of the inn, carrying a tray of food he would deliver to a patron. Sometimes he would stop to wipe a table or remove some empty dishes, tasks any Earthling would have recognized. Other times, he would appear to take the food order of a newly arrived customer. There was much laughter and conversation among the patrons sitting at nearby tables. It was clear to Cortez that this was a neighborhood hangout where everyone knew everyone. She also knew it was only a matter of time before someone would notice the strangers.

There were a dozen small wooden tables, each surrounded by precisely three chairs. However, some patrons had moved tables together to accommodate their larger gatherings. Paintings, both large and small, adorned the wooden walls. A large painting depicted what appeared to be a picturesque city over which floated a rainbow and a flock of white seabirds. Glyvash whispered that the large picture was of Xanglora. It was clear from his voice and mannerisms that he was quite proud of the city.

Ten minutes later, the server arrived carrying a large platter stacked precariously with various food items. Cortez watched nervously as he efficiently unloaded the platter, placing plates of food and two bowls in the center of the table. "Have I permission to serve others?" the server asked.

*This must be their version of 'will there be anything else?'*, thought Cortez. "Very efficient," she said.

"Still too slow," Glyvash complained. "I will tell the owner of this cafe."

"It is fine, Glyvash. We don't want to draw more attention."

"Yes, yes. You are right. Please consume."

Cortez retrieved her bag from the floor, placed it on the small table, then removed several items, with Glyvash watching with intense curiosity.

"I must test the food. You understand I've yet to eat any of your delicious-looking food."

"Test?"

"I am sure the food is tasty. I just need to ensure it's not toxic to my species."

Cortez again reached into her bag and retrieved her testing kit. On Endeavor, fully automated devices could have analyzed the samples and rendered their verdict in seconds. However, there were stringent weight restrictions on an LAV, and that meant lighter, more primitive tests were all she had available.

After scanning the room, she removed the Velcro strap and unrolled the kit, revealing a collection of vials, test tubes, and chemicals. After taking a quick inventory, she pulled a small eyedropper from her kit, carefully took a minute sample of the soup, and placed several drops into a test tube. Finally, she extended a probe from a small electronic device and dipped it into the test tube.

*RHODA, analyze the test sample for toxins, harmful biological agents, or viruses*, she thought.

"This device will inform Catriana if the food is bad for her species?"

"This device plus my ship's artificial intelligence," said Cortez.

Glyvash seemed confused.

Cortez removed her earpiece and showed it to Glyvash.

"This is a radio transceiver. It transmits and receives communications from my ship."

"Amazing, it is so small. You can communicate with your spaceship from anywhere?"

"Not from anywhere. It has a range of about five hundred kilometers, and I believe I'm still within range of my lander." Cortez assumed RHODA would accurately convert the range into the Heran equivalent.

"I understand. Tell Glyvash, what is artificial intelligence? How can intelligence be artificial?"

"This is a bit more difficult to explain. You have computers, right?"
"Computers?"

"Machines that think, that can perform mathematics, solve problems—calculate."

"Oh yes," Glyvash said, nodding. "Our scientists have built powerful machines capable of countless calculations."

"Good. We have also created computers that can mimic my species. They can understand when we speak and mimic our power of speech. We ask a question, and they can answer us. They also have access to all our accumulated knowledge."

"You have done this?" asked Glyvash, stunned by the implications of such technology.

"Yes. RHODA is the name we have given our artificial intelligence," said Cortez, reinserting her earpiece.

"But I saw you speak to no one but Glyvash," said Glyvash.

"I can communicate with RHODA just using my thoughts. I'm wearing a device on my head that can detect and interpret the electrical impulses in my brain."

"This is very exciting," said Glyvash.

"It's just technology."

"Yes, just technology," Glyvash repeated.

"RHODA says the soup is OK," said Cortez.

"This is good. You can eat now?" said Glyvash.

One by one, Cortez tested the various food items. Each one received the same answer from RHODA. "Test failed. No pathogens or toxins detected. Test failed. No biologics detected."

Cortez kept this information to herself, trusting that she would be OK.

"Let's dig in, Glyvash. I'm starving."

" Caa...tree...ah...na is starving?"

"It's just an expression we use. It means we are hungry. And please just call me Cat."

"Cat?"

"Yes, it's what we call a nickname."

"A nickname?"

"Yes. On my world, we can sometimes have more than one name. We might have a name that only our friends and family call us. Sometimes our formal name is hard to say, or maybe we don't like it. My nickname is 'Cat.' It's just a shortened form of Catriana. It is what I prefer my friends call me."

"And you want Glyvash to call you this?"

"Yes."

"It pleases Glyvash. You have honored me, nickname Cat."

"Just Cat, Glyvash."

"Ah, of course, let us dig in, just Cat."

Following Glyvash's lead, Cortez raised the bowl of soup to her lips and took a tentative sip. The flavor was similar to very salty and slightly sour milk. Glyvash watched her reaction like a father showing photos of his new baby.

Cortez smiled. "This is very good," she said, not wanting to insult her guest.

"Glyvash is pleased Cat likes it. Here, try the moke fruit. It is perfectly ripe."

Cortez carefully examined the strange fruit, turning it over in her hands. It reminded her of the Petaya or dragon fruit she had seen in the small *dai pai dongs* lining the streets of Hong Kong.

"How do I eat it? Do I peel it?"

"No. Just eat it, like this," said Glyvash before taking a big bite of the fruit.

Cortez brought the weird-looking fruit to her lips and took a small bite. Slowly, her eyes widened, and a big smile lit up her expression. "It's wonderful, Glyvash. I've tasted nothing quite like it. It's delicious."

Glyvash was beside himself with joy. "I am so glad, Cat. Glyvash does not want Cat to starve."

As Cortez and Glyvash prepared to leave the small cafe, Cortez searched her bag for the iron tablets Doc Lee had given her. After a minute of searching, she realized the bottle of pills was not there. For a moment, she searched her memory for the last time she had seen the bottle. Then she remembered. She had repacked her bag on Aries before she had departed the ship. Because she had expected her time on Hera would be short and that she would not have to stray far, she could leave some of her kit on Aries. That had turned out to be an unfortunate decision.

Forty-five minutes later, after a meal and several fermented beverages, Glyvash and the alien from Earth, Catriana 'Cat' Cortez, were back on the road, bumping along at the tiny vehicle's max speed of forty kilometers per hour. The once thick forest was now giving way to open countryside, cultivated crops, and grazing animals. *This could be Earth*, she thought, *if it were not for the two moons, the pinkish sun, and the ever-present aurora swirling overhead—in the daytime, no less*. Otherwise, the clouds floating overhead looked like ordinary Nebraska clouds. Farms were farms no matter where you were. She recognized farming machinery, grain storage buildings, and quaint farmhouses. Farm animals were harder to identify. Was that six-legged beast grazing in the field a source of milk, meat, or muscle? Glyvash provided answers to her inquiries, which often went against her first guess.

"This reminds me of where I grew up," said Cortez. "I was born in a small town called Stuart, in a state called Nebraska. We grew vegetables, mostly corn, but also some wheat and beans. We got our milk from our own cow." Cat expected to hear a string of Heran language whistles and clicks emanate from her vocalizer, but heard instead a message from RHODA in her earpiece.

"Translation lookup failure. The vocabulary does not contain STATE. The closest approximations are COLONY and DISTRICT."

Cortez frowned. After a moment's consideration, she gave the required silent command to the AI. "RHODA, substitute DISTRICT for STATE and translate." The corrected translation emanated from her vocalizer. When her road trip with Glyvash first began, there were many instances where Cat needed to substitute a word before the translator would produce the Heran equivalent. But these instances were getting less frequent as RHODA updated her vocabulary.

"Do you have countries like we do?" Glyvash asked.

"Do you want the long or short answer?"

"I don't understand."

"It's a complicated question, but I'll try to make it as simple as possible."

For the next hour and a half, Cortez tried to convey the idea of countries, geopolitical borders, ethnicity, nationalism, and governments, both national and local. She even touched on the concept of representative democracy and the choosing of leaders. Glyvash listened attentively, sometimes shaking his head affirmatively as if completely understanding a concept, yet sometimes tilting his head sideways like a golden retriever trying to make sense of the sounds coming from his master's mouth.

"Was that the long or short answer?" Glyvash asked.

"The short answer, very much the short answer," laughed Cortez.

"We have different regional governments as well. My country is called Xerelang. I am from the city of Be'longalora. It is far to the north and is much colder than here."

"Is that where your family is?"

"Family?"

"Your mother and father, brothers and sisters, your siblings. Who birthed you, Glyvash?"

"Cat's question confuses Glyvash," Glyvash replied as he searched for the words to answer. "The female who spawned Glyvash is the mother of thousands of hatchlings. I am one of many."

After a long pause, she asked, "OK, then tell me about the male who fertilized your mother's eggs," said Cortez. "Do you know him?"

"No, certainly not. All males of a certain age supply sperm to a local hatching center, where it is used to fertilize the female eggs. It would be impossible to know which male supplied the sperm that produced me."

"Doesn't Dakar Dualla's daughter live with her?"

Glyvash parsed the question in his mind before answering. "Cat is confused. Yuni is not a spawn of Dakar Dualla. One-in-a-hundred hatchlings are female. When they reach a certain age, the Ben`lei assigns a tal`shi (teacher) to guide them into adulthood. Dakar Dualla is Yuni's tal`shi."

"I see," said Cortez. "That is fascinating. What about the male hatchlings?"

"Males, they stay in hatching center until seven sols. Then, they are tested, to find what is true purpose. Some, if they show skill for higher learning, they go to school."

"I assume you received more schooling?"

"Yes, became a tal`su (student) at the Be'longalora School, a very prestigious assignment and very sought after."

"Dakar Dualla—isn't her last name taken from her birth father?" asked Cortez.

"Is this the way of your Earth?"

"Yes. My last name is Cortez, which was my father's last name."

"I see. This is interesting. On Hera, we receive our names from our teachers. Dakar Dualla's full name is Dakar Zaru, ninth tal`su of Dualla, first tal`su of Krei. Councilor Krei was her teacher. Dualla was first teacher in her line going back nine generations."

"Councilor Krei?" said Cortez.

"Yes, teacher of Dakar Dualla is on the Council of Ben`lei—the ruling council."

"You've given me a lot to think about, Glyvash."

"Cat, is this not the same on your world?"

Cortez didn't answer right away. She wondered how the alien would react to discovering she was a mammal. Glyvash was obviously not. She had suspected that the evolutionary history of this planet might differ from Earth's. Glyvash's features suggested as much. Was it possible that the dominant species on this planet was a fish or cephalopod? Humans evolved from the sea after all, so it was feasible that egg layers like the cephalopod would evolve to be the dominant species on this planet.

"Glyvash, let me ask a question first. Those animals grazing the field over to our right—the field beyond that small stream. How much do you know about how they reproduce?"

Cortez had noticed the cow-like behavior and appearance of the animals and was sure they were mammals.

"I'm not farmer, but know enough," said Glyvash. "The animals you speak of are called Domlans. The female Domlan carries her eggs inside. The male fertilizes the—" Glyvash's eyes opened wide. "Cat, you are saying that you—?" Glyvash turned away, obviously embarrassed. "Oh, this is very surprising, very surprising indeed." Turning back to Cortez, he asked. "You are dominant species on your planet?"

"Yes, we are."

Glyvash persisted.

"There are species like Glyvash on your world?"

"Yes, not as advanced, but yes, there are."

"Not as advanced? Please explain."

"We have many species where the mother produces eggs which are fertilized outside her body, but none have evolved as far as your species. Most still live in the sea, and their intelligence developed around hunting for food only. We have been unable to communicate with any. Most do not vocalize, and those that do are still a mystery to us."

Glyvash slowly shook his head.

"Cat, there are many on my planet who would be upset to hear this. Please be careful when you speak of this."

"Are you troubled, Glyvash?"

"No. I am scientist, Cat. I accept facts how they are. It is… interesting. You think my species—you think Glyvash—is interesting?"

"Yes, of course. I am more amazed by our similarities than our differences."

The two scientists were silent for a long time, each in their own thoughts. Several times Glyvash turned as if ready to ask a question, only to stop and return his attention to driving. Several times, Cortez did as well.

"Cat, have you spawned…?"

"…Children or hatchlings? No. I haven't spawned hatchlings." Cortez smiled to herself. *That's one question I've never been asked.*

"Why?"

"Humans are free to choose their partners, and if they wish, they can have offspring—what we call children. Parents raise their children until they reach adulthood. The number of male and female births is about the same. Most families have two or three children, though some may have none, and others many more. Males and females are raised together."

"So, a human hatchling—"

"—Child," Cortez corrected.

"—a human child knows both birth mother and birth father?"

"Yes," said Cortez, choosing not to get into the messy details of human relationships.

"And you have not found a mate?"

"No. Not yet. I just haven't found the right male," she lied.

"As scientist, I can see benefits of this. The child receives teaching and wisdom from the male and the female."

"This is true," Cortez replied.

The two traveling companions soon fell into a prolonged silence as the vehicle wove around the potholes of an apparently unmaintained roadway. Cat's thoughts turned to Bridges and their brief time together before she left. Was he the one? It certainly felt that way. *My God*, she thought. *I'm on an alien planet taking a road trip with someone who is more fish than human, and I'm thinking of my love life. Keep it together, girl.*

Soon, the furrowed fields and small farms gave way to lush forests. The variety of flora and fauna she witnessed speeding by in her alien friend's little vehicle amazed Cortez. She hoped she could return sometime and do some actual field research, but now was not the time.

There was already a lot on her plate. Cortez was learning a lot about the lives of these aliens—their language, culture, evolutionary history, scientific knowledge, and even their mythology. She was improving the quality of RHODA's language database, adding newly translated words to the vocabulary, and learning how these aliens think. She could write ten scientific papers and still have material for more.

"Do you plan on stopping for the night?" asked Cortez.

"Yes, Cat and Glyvash will stop to rest. There is small inn ahead, and they can provide resting chambers where we will stay tonight. They also offer food for tonight's meal. You will approve, Cat."

"Good. I am getting hungry, and I enjoyed your moke fruit very much. I hope it's on the menu."

"If not, I will insist they find some for their important guest, Cat of Earth."

Cortez smiled. *Cat of Earth sounds like a grade-B sci-fi movie title,* she thought to herself.

A little over an hour later, Glyvash's motorized buggy drove through a rustic stone archway into a cobblestone-paved courtyard bordered by a dozen small domed structures. The first thing that came to Cortez's mind was an old, animated TV show she had seen in a "History Through Pop Culture" course she had taken at her university. *Yabba dabba do,* she thought to herself.

Glyvash dismounted the vehicle and went searching for the proprietor, leaving Cortez behind. Noticing her labored breathing, Cortez popped another EPO pill and downed it with a gulp of water from her plastic bottle. She counted the remaining pills. *Twelve*, she thought. She hoped her body would adapt to the environment before she ran out.

The setting sun painted the horizon in shades of red and orange, casting a warm glow over everything around her and stirring memories of summers long ago in her hometown. From beyond the courtyard came the familiar sound of children laughing and playing. For a moment, it was hard to think of her surroundings as alien at all.

"Are you teacher (tal`shi)?"

"What?" Startled, Cortez turned quickly, looking for the source of the question. An adolescent alien had approached unnoticed and now stood less than a meter away.

"Are you teacher?" repeated the child.

Cortez's mind raced as she evaluated her options. Glyvash had not returned, so he could not help. Finally deciding the child posed no danger to her or the mission, Cortez let out a slow breath before answering.

"No, not yet," replied Cortez. "The Ben`lei has not yet honored me with a tal`su. Are you tal`shi?"

"Of course not. I am only seven. What a silly question."

"Well, in this light, you looked older," said Cortez.

"How old are you?" the child asked, stepping closer.

"I'm twenty-six."

"Then you should be teacher." The child was trying very hard to appear grown-up. "You look funny. What's wrong with your legs?"
Cortez glanced at her legs. "My legs?"

"Yes. You look different. Were you in an accident? I know a male who was in an accident, and he has scars. My teacher says he will look like that all his life."

"I am sorry your friend was hurt."

"He is not my friend. He is male. Male and female cannot be friends."

"Well, I think they can. My friend Glyvash is male. He will be back any minute."

The child tilted her head as if puzzling over an intractable problem.

"Why do you look different?"

"Well, where I come from, females look like me."

"I think you look funny. I have to go," declared the child, suddenly spinning around and dashing towards the distant sounds of children playing, nearly crashing into Glyvash.

"Don't worry, Glyvash. It was just a child. Do we have rooms—uh, I mean chambers?"

"Yes, Glyvash arranged for two, of course. Would Cat like to rest awhile before the evening meal?"

"Yes. I could use a quick nap. As I mentioned, your atmosphere has less oxygen than ours."

"Ah yes—your magic pills. There is your room, and mine is just there," he said, pointing to the structure on her left. "When you rest enough, you knock on my door, then we eat together. I speak with proprietor, and they have moke fruit, yes."

"Great. I look forward to it. I will not rest for very long. I'll knock on your door when I'm ready."

"Of course. Take the time you require."

Cortez opened the door to her chamber and entered. She noticed there was no lock. Inside, she found a small room with a mat on the floor meant for sleeping. Another door led to a small space—probably a bathroom? She surveyed the room, feeling both relieved and frustrated. There was a small shower, which was good, as well as a basin of sorts, but there was no western-style toilet. She thought that was a little too much to hope for on an alien planet. What they had was a hole in the floor. She could deal with that. Her time backpacking in Asia included three months in Japan. She figured that if she could squat over a Japanese toilet, she could do the same over a Heran one.

An hour later, Cortez and Glyvash sat at a small table in a dimly lit corner of the cafe, enjoying a meal of moke fruit and a mound of some sort of root vegetable. *So far, so good*, Cortez thought. *The food hasn't killed me yet*. She was also getting used to the exotic flavors. What she didn't know was whether her human physiology would accept them. She had read Dr. Graham's note regarding the chirality of life on the planet and the unlikelihood they could harvest the local flora and fauna to restock Endeavor's meager food stocks. Graham had summed up his report in the last sentence.

*Our DNA is laevo (L), so we can metabolize only L-amino acids and dextro (D) sugars. Based upon the chirality of life on this planet, I'm certain our metabolism would treat any locally harvested foods as inert contaminants. Thus, we would receive no nutritional value from anything we harvested from the planet.*

Cortez and Glyvash continued their discussions as the two enjoyed their meal together. Cortez wanted to press Glyvash on the evolution of his species and to see if there were also mythological stories that, in their culture, tried to explain their existence on this planet.

"Glyvash, has your species adapted to changing conditions on your planet?"

"You are speaking of transformation," said Glyvash.

"Well, we use the word evolution, but I think we're talking about the same natural process," said Cortez.

"Yes, I think it is so. Our scientist say we lived in sea billions years ago. Long time past, our far birth mothers want protect eggs from predators.

So they crawl from sea, lay eggs in sand. Stronger males follow, to fertilize eggs. With time, fins change to strong limbs. We learn to breathe air. We stay longer on land, to keep hatchlings safe from land predators. After billion years… here we are," Glyvash said with a smile.

"Did your species retain the ability to live in the sea?" asked Cortez.

"No, not to live, but to visit. We cannot breathe underwater, but we can cease our breathing for over an hour."

"Our story is very similar, Glyvash. We also emerged from the sea. Unfortunately, we retain less of our aquatic past than you do. It's a shame. Glyvash, are there alternative stories of your past, maybe unscientific stories?"

Glyvash thought for a minute before answering.

"Yes. The answer I give you is what our science say now, most accepted. But many on my world, they do not believe this. They believe old stories, sung in songs and poems, about great spirit Xenosta who come to our world thousands year ago. She find great cities, full of land creatures who worship knowledge and science, but they make air, ocean, and forests sick. She beg them change their ways, care for world that give them life. But they not listen. They chase her away, back to stars where she come from. Angry, she make moon fall on planet, destroy all that people build.

"Then she come again from sky, and go into sea, where she find our ancestors. Xenosta tell them come to land, and she change them quick into form you see now. She make female and male. She tell male they must follow female and do as female command. She also command they must care for land, sky, sea, or she come back and destroy them same way she destroy the evil builders before.

"Many of my people believe this is true story. Even Holy Akan, he believe."

"Some on my planet believe a similar story," said Cortez.

"We are more alike than I first imagined," said Glyvash. "Does your disguise hide other differences?"

"Maybe tomorrow I'll let you see me without my disguise. Right now, however, I am feeling fatigued. I would like to go to my chamber.

"Are you feeling ill, Cat?"

"I think I'm just tired."

"Then Cat must rest. We have another long day of travel tomorrow."

Glyvash escorted Cortez back to her chamber and wished her a restful sleep.

Cortez wished for the same thing.

# CHAPTER 61

*Chirality*

Forest Graham knocked softly on Jennifer Lee's door, hoping his colleague was not asleep, although, at 2:25 AM, he was sure she was. Still, this was important, and he was confident she wouldn't mind this late visit.

Graham leaned close to her door, listening for any signs that Lee was moving about, when suddenly the door opened.

"Forest! What are you up to? Why are you creeping about? What time is it? Is there something wrong?"

"No, there's nothing wrong. I'm sorry for waking you. You were asleep, yes?"

"Huh. And you call yourself a scientist."

"I found something," he said, ignoring the sarcasm. "I was doing some research using RHODA, and I found something that might help us."

"Help us what? Couldn't this have waited until tomorrow? I was right in the middle of a really pleasurable dream."

"Well, yes. I guess so. I was just so excited—I'm sorry. This can wait until tomorrow. I'll let you get back…"

Lee raised her hands to interrupt him.

"Forest, you're here now, and I'm awake, so what is it you've found?"

"I might have found an answer to our chirality problem."

"Might have?"

"Uh, yes, I, uh…probably."

"All right. I'll be there in a minute."

Thirty minutes later, Lee ambled into the galley dressed in a loosely fitting pair of sweatpants and a tee shirt emblazoned with the words "Sleep and Sex." She motioned Forest to wait while she fixed herself a cup of herbal tea and then, after taking a long slow sip, joined him where he sat, books and papers spread out before him.

"OK, show me what you got," she said. "And make quick. I have a dream to get back to."

"I've been doing some research," said Graham.

"I believe we've established that, Forest."

"Our chirality problem," he continued. "I found a paper written by Chinese geneticist Wei Zen Ho about seventy-five years ago, that might be the answer we've been looking for."

"Do you read Chinese, Forest?"

"Yes, indeed. I studied for a year at Tsinghua University in Beijing. They are very strong in molecular biology and genetics. I learned Mandarin while I was there."

"I didn't know that about you, Forest. I bet the coeds loved you, right?" Forest blushed. "Uh...well, I did know one young woman there, and we... uh...dated for a while."

"Dated is a euphemism in this story, right? And by a while, you mean..."

"A few times."

"What's a few times, stud?"

"OK, once. Happy?"

Lee smiled. "OK, stud, tell me about this paper you found."

"OK," began Graham. "Apparently, a student of this professor asked him a question in class about a hypothetical spaceship being stranded on a planet with opposite chirality. He asked the professor how those stranded might survive. The professor answered they wouldn't. They would all starve."

"That's very comforting, Forest. I'll see you in the morning."

"Wait. There's more."

"Sure-as-shit hope so," said Lee as she took another sip from her cup.

"The question got the professor thinking. How indeed could anyone survive on such a planet? So, for the next two years, he studied the problem. He spent months researching different approaches, eventually scrapping each as too impractical."

"I sense you're building to a big reveal, Forest," said Lee.

"Yes. Ho imagined modifying gut microbes so that they could convert opposite-chirality sugars to their mirror form. You see here—he's outlined the steps for converting each class of sugar," said Graham, pointing at diagrams the professor had provided.

"What about amino acids?" Lee asked, now more interested.
Graham leafed through the document before finding the answer to Lee's question.

"For those, he finally settled on creating a special enzyme that could force a sn2 nucleophilic substitution by an activated ammonia nucleophile on the opposite side of the alpha carbon atom from the amine function."

"That wasn't Mandarin, and it sounded a bit like English, so why didn't I understand a damned thing you just said?" Lee asked.

"Sorry," Graham replied. "Such an enzyme would convert all L-amino acids to D-amino acids or vice versa, and it's quite brilliant. Once converted, metabolism would proceed normally."

"So, did he tell us how to create this magic enzyme?" Lee asked.

"Well, no, but there are enough of his notes here to give us a head start. I was thinking about this while waiting for you and devised a plan."
Lee took another sip of her tea.

"Well, are you going to tell me, or do I have to beat it out of you?"

"Oh yes, of course. First, did you know scientists created the very first synthetic versions of DNA and RNA enzymes over two hundred years ago?"

"No, I didn't. Are you really giving me a history lesson at three o'clock in the morning?"

Ignoring Lee's sarcasm, Graham continued.

"From those basic building blocks, scientists could create other synthetic enzymes. I've asked RHODA to assemble and correlate anything written about the process. I've also directed RHODA to factor in Professor Ho's notes in the hopes she can give us at least a basic outline or procedure."

"Sounds like a reasonable plan, Forest. I'm impressed."

Lee turned as if to go, then paused and turned around to face Graham.

"Any ideas about how this planet got so screwed up?"

"You mean the opposite chirality? Well, there are several theories why we developed from L-form and not D-form. One would think the odds are fifty-fifty, but it seems our galaxy has its thumb on the scale a bit."

"I knew life wasn't fair," said Lee. "It's the galaxy's fault."

Once again, ignoring his colleague's comments, Graham continued.

"It has to do with our galaxy's spin and magnetic orientation. This spin causes cosmic dust particles to polarize starlight as circularly polarized in only one direction. This polarized starlight degrades D forms of amino acids more than L forms. We've witnessed this when analyzing the amino acids on comets and meteors. It would seem that in our galaxy, L forms are preferred."

"But this planet is in the same galaxy," said Lee.

"Not done yet," said Graham, holding up his hand. "There is also the role played by radioactive decay, AKA the weak nuclear force, which is also chiral. During beta decay, the emitted electrons favor one kind of spin. These chiral electrons degrade D-amino acids more than the L form."

"So, sunlight and nuclear radiation favor L-amino acids," said Lee.

"Seems so," said Graham.

"But that still doesn't answer the question. There is sunlight and the weak nuclear force on this planet."

"True," said Graham.

"So, how did this planet get so screwed up?"

"Don't have a clue," smiled Graham. "It may have something to do with having two suns."

"You can be really frustrating," said Lee, shaking her head. "Let's study this a bit more before we announce our findings to the captain. I don't want to give him false hope. Until then, I'm going back to bed. I'd suggest you get some rest yourself, Forest. You're going to need it."

*Sick*

Cortez slept fitfully, waking frequently with leg cramps. She felt like her heart was beating out of her chest. She felt more fatigued than she had when she went to bed. Something was wrong.

She tried to self-diagnose herself but found concentration difficult. Cortez didn't believe she had ingested anything that had poisoned her; she had tested everything she had eaten. Doc Lee and Dr. Graham had told her before she left that the chirality of life forms made it highly likely that she was immune to pathogens and biologics.

There was another possibility. Her body was not processing the alien foods she was eating, and she was starving. Her symptoms pointed to the inescapable conclusion that she was anemic.

She had to find some Earth food within the next few days, or she could die. Maybe she could last a week, but she was sure as hell in no condition to represent humanity to the alien rulers of this country.

She struggled to get up from her sleeping mat. Grabbing her bag, she dumped its contents onto the mat. Her eyes immediately focused on her last food packet, part of the standard emergency kit. She had been saving it for two days.

*Yummy—beef stroganoff, my favorite*, she thought, somewhat sarcastically.

*What else can I eat?* She thought, rummaging through the items piled on the mat. She found a small vial of breath mints. *Breath mints have sugar*, she thought. *Not much, but they were better than nothing.* "OK, do I eat now or later?" Holding the stroganoff packet in one hand and the breath mints in the other, she said, "To beef or not to beef, that is the question."

Cortez decided to keep the breath mints for later and eat the stroganoff now. If she were on Endeavor, she would insert the foil packet into the little warmer in the ship's galley. However, she was here, not there. Fortunately, this alien motel room—or chamber, as they referred to it—had hot and cold running water. She put the packet in the small basin, turned on the hot water, and waited for her dinner/breakfast to warm. A few minutes later, she squeezed the lumpy gravy and noodle mixture from the foil packet directly into her mouth.

"Damn, that's good," she said. "I can't believe how good that is."

After she licked every bit of the goopy mixture from the foil, she popped in a breath mint for dessert.

She still had a few hours before she was to meet Glyvash, so she lay down on the sleeping mat on the floor and immediately fell into a deep sleep.

Cortez awoke suddenly to a loud knocking. Forcing herself to her feet, she stumbled to the door.

"Hello, is that you, Glyvash?"

"Yes, Cat. I became worried when you didn't meet me in the cafe."

"I'm sorry, Glyvash. I wasn't feeling well. I slept longer than I had intended. Give me fifteen minutes, and I'll join you."

"Very well, I will order you some moke fruit."

"Uh, no moke fruit today, just something to drink. I'm not hungry this morning."

"Are you unwell, Cat?"

"I'm fine, Glyvash. I'm feeling much better than I was last night."

"I will meet you in the cafe, then."

After splashing some water in her face and checking her disguise in the tiny mirror in her field kit, Cortez checked in with RHODA.

"Any emergency messages from Endeavor, RHODA?"

"No, Lieutenant Cortez. There are no emergency messages. However, a newly updated version of the Heran translation has been downloaded to your translator."

"Any major changes, RHODA?"

"There is a greater usage of pronouns and articles."

"Thank you, RHODA."

*Well, that should make Glyvash sound more intelligent—and less like my newly immigrated uncle Mateus,* Cortez thought.

Twenty minutes later, Cortez entered through the front door of the small cafe. The cafe was more crowded than the day before, making Cortez super anxious. She could feel every female eye in the tiny cafe focused on her as she wound her way to the table.

"Good morning, Glyvash."

"Is that a traditional Earth greeting?"

"Yes," said Cortez.

"Glyvash approves. It is short and direct. Are you better?"

"Yes, I feel better, but still fatigued. It's possible my human physiology is not processing your foods properly, and I'm not receiving the nutrients I need."

Cortez had decided not to get into the whole chirality issue, and there were more important things to discuss. Notably, she wanted to focus on her future diplomatic contact with the leadership, including their culture, ceremony, symbolism, history, and everything else that could affect such meetings. Therefore, after quickly finishing the drink he had ordered for her and hinting that she wished to leave, the two traveling companions were back on the road.

# CHAPTER 63

*Chirality Breakthrough*

Captain Merriweather was getting worried. He had been agonizing over the wisdom of allowing Cortez to go on a four-day road trip with an alien—an alien he knew nothing about. That anxiety manifested itself in an increase in the acid reflux he suffered from every day this mission continued. Now that they had lost communications with Cortez, that acid reflux was burning a hole in his stomach.

*Dammit,* he thought, *I have no one to blame but myself. I didn't have to let Cortez talk me into this half-baked idea.* She could be persuasive, but he was the damn captain.

"Bridges," Merriweather called out as he stepped into the galley, "a minute."

"Yes, sir," said Bridges, jumping to his feet.

"I want to reposition the master drone," said Merriweather. "I want to get the drone as close to where we think Cortez might be. We can use the stronger transceiver on the drone to establish a link."

"Good idea," said Bridges.

"Of course, it's a good idea, Lieutenant. I'm the damn captain."

"Sorry, sir. I mean, yes, sir, of course," said Bridges.

"Damn. I'm sorry, Bridges. I didn't mean to bite your head off. I'm just mad at myself for putting Cat in danger."

"Cat is very resourceful, Captain. I'm sure she's OK."

Bridges seated himself at the nearest control station and commanded RHODA to display an image of the planet's surface centered on Whoville.

After a few adjustments and a command for RHODA to calculate Cortez's estimated position, Bridges began spinning up the master drone's propellers.

"RHODA, how far can the master drone fly on remaining battery life?"

"Approximately two hundred and fifty kilometers," she replied.

"RHODA, what is the distance between the drone's current position and Lieutenant Cortez's estimated position?"

"Approximately two hundred and twenty-five kilometers, Milo."

"RHODA, reposition the drone to Lieutenant Cortez's estimated location, then hover at one kilometer and broadcast contact protocol on channel one."

"Repositioning master drone. ETA thirty-five minutes," said RHODA.

"Let me know when you've made contact. I'll be in my quarters," said Merriweather as he quickly left.

Meanwhile, Doctors Lee and Graham hunched over an electron microscope as they examined their first attempt at creating a modified microbe using Professor Wei Zen Ho's notes. It was supposed to be gobbling up a biomolecule of glucose and producing its chiral cousin, but nothing of any consequence was happening.

"Give it another minute or two," said Lee.

"Damn, it's just not working. We're missing something," responded a visibly frustrated Graham.

One of the more valuable pieces of equipment in Doc Lee's medical bay was the BioSynth 200 system. The Bio 200 combined several functions commonly residing in separate devices: a PCR machine, DNA sequencer, incubator, etc. The Bio 200, combined with Endeavor's AI and an extensive scientific database, gave Endeavor's medical staff (Lee and Cortez) a powerful tool to combat any potentially hazardous alien pathogen or to create cures or vaccines. Lee and Graham were using it now to modify an existing microbe by following Professor Wei Zen Ho's notes.

"It could be frameshift errors in the sequencing," said Lee.

"OK, let's do a comparison sequence and combine the two sequences," said Graham. "Did you know that the first time DNA was sequenced in space was in 2016?" Graham said.

"I bet you're a whiz at trivia," said Lee.

"I am. I am very good at it. Would you care to play sometime?"

"I'd rather jump out of the airlock," replied Lee.

An hour later, Merriweather stopped by to check on their progress just as Lee and Graham were high-fiving each other.

"Can I take it you two have had some success?" Merriweather asked.

"Yes, Captain, we had a breakthrough," said Doc Lee.

Lee motioned Merriweather over to the BioSynth's video display. "Take a look," she said.

"What am I looking at?" asked Merriweather.

"You're looking at the world's first glucose biomolecule chirality reverser," said Lee.

"Which world are you referring to?" Merriweather asked as he watched one blob of color absorb a second.

"Oh yeah, there is that," said Lee. "OK, it's Earth's first…"

"I got it," said Merriweather. "That's good work. Keep at it. There is a lot of potential food down there, and I, for one, am tired of algae."

"Yes, Captain," said Lee and Graham in unison.

*That's one piece of good news*, thought Merriweather, as he hurried back to the ship's galley. Bridges was still waiting for the drone to arrive at the hover point two hundred and twenty-five kilometers east of Whoville when RHODA's voice sounded over the ship's speakers.

"The master drone has located Lieutenant Cortez twenty kilometers east of its current position."

"RHODA, reposition the drone to Lieutenant Cortez's coordinates," said Bridges. "Continue hailing Cortez on channel one every five minutes and report when you have contact."

"Cup of coffee or tea, Bridges?"

"I have one, sir. Can I fix you one?"

"Don't get up. I'll do it. No offense, but you don't know how to fix a decent cup of coffee."

Merriweather quickly rinsed out his cup in the galley's tiny kitchen sink and then placed the cup in a small recess in the CUBE. "RHODA, coffee, extra strong, black."

Merriweather waited patiently while the coffee dribbled into his cup. Thirty seconds later, he re-joined Bridges.

"So how is the coffee I make not as good? I give RHODA the same command." said Bridges.

"I don't know, it just isn't the same," said Merriweather. "Must be in the way you say it," said Merriweather, or maybe RHODA likes me more.

Merriweather could see the tension on Bridges' face.

"I know you're concerned about Cortez. I am too. Hell, we all are."

Bridges was hesitant to tell the captain about his feelings for Cortez.

"I know, sir. It's just that Cat and I…well, we…"

"Hell, Milo, everyone on the ship knows about you two. It's all anyone talks about."

Bridges glanced at his captain and then returned to the holoview, feeling somewhat chagrined.

"I suspected…" he replied.

RHODA's voice interrupted Bridges in mid-sentence.

"Contact established with Lieutenant Cortez."

On the planet below, Glyvash had pulled his tiny conveyance into a shady grove of tutu trees to give Cortez a chance to rest. It was clear to Glyvash that his alien friend was getting sicker, and he was extremely worried. He had broached the idea of taking her to a healer, but she had adamantly dismissed the idea.

"They won't be able to help because of my alien physiology," she had argued, "and it will only expose my identity before I'm ready. I just need to contact my ship, which means getting to Xanglora as soon as possible."

Glyvash excused himself, dismounted the vehicle, and disappeared into the dense forest, leaving Cortez alone to rest. Cortez tried to get comfortable in the motorcar's small seats, but was unsuccessful. Unable to sleep, she examined her surroundings.

The tutu trees soared above her head, appearing to converge near the top like a cathedral of ancient redwoods. Cortez lay back in her seat as far as possible and gazed upward. The noon sunlight streaming through the canopy of branches and greenery overhead produced ever-shifting patterns of light and shadows on her face. A cool breeze, moistened by a fine mist and illuminated by the red sun, created an almost ethereal glow that enveloped the grove and helped lift Cortez's spirits. The words of a poem she had recited as a child drifted into her consciousness.

> *Again, the woods are odorous, the lark*
> *Lifts on upsoaring wings the heaven gray*
> *That hung above the tree-tops, veiled and dark,*
> *Where branches bare disclosed the empty day.*[5]

The birds were different here—four wings instead of two. But they still flitted about like birds. Cortez estimated the ring of tutu trees surrounding the vehicle to be a hundred meters high and as much as five meters in diameter. The upper parts of the trees were resplendent, with short branches supporting long, slender ferns. Grasses and a few flowering plants, reminding Cortez of gladiolas, covered the ground like a luxurious garden. The effect gave the grove a spiritual feeling. She had been to a similar spot in Santa Cruz, California, when she traveled there with her parents. It seemed like eons ago.

As Cortez rested, RHODA's voice sounded in her earpiece.

"Endeavor to Lieutenant Cortez, do you copy over?"

Cortez responded immediately. "Endeavor, this is Cortez."

After alerting Endeavor that Cortez had made contact, RHODA completed the connection between Cortez's earpiece and Endeavor's com-screen.

"Cortez, this is Merriweather. How is the mission proceeding?"

Cat sighed with relief upon hearing Merriweather's voice.

"Good to hear from you, Captain. Very good. The mission is proceeding well. I am learning a great deal about the people on this planet. My alien friend, Supervisor Glyvash, has been extremely helpful."

"Very good, Lieutenant. We were getting worried up here. Do you need anything from us?"

"Well, now that you mention it, Captain, I think I could use some food."

"Understand. Be advised that Doc Lee and Doc Graham are hard at work trying to develop a long-term solution to that problem, but in the short term, we can get you something to improve your situation. It may take a day, however. Are you OK for that long?"

"Yes, Captain. I can hold out for that long, but try to expedite if you can?"

"Roger that. How far are you planning on driving today?"

"Maybe another fifty kilos. Glyvash knows of a quiet campsite not far from here."

"OK, sounds good. Stay at your campsite until we can get some food to you. There's a drone hovering over your head. I'll have it land at your location. Take it with you. It will extend the range of your earpiece."

"Sounds good, Captain. Is Bridges there?"

Merriweather gave an affirmative nod in Bridges' direction.

"Hi, Cat, this is Milo."

"Hi, Milo. I'm feeling guilty that you're not down here experiencing this. I know that this was your assignment."

"Cat, we've gone over this. You are absolutely the best person for this mission, and I'm completely on board with it. Plus, I've also noticed that you've been putting on a few pounds, so it's good that you're going on a diet down there."

"Watch it, buster," said Cortez in mock indignation.

"Too soon?"

"Damn straight," she replied.

"Just stay safe down there, and I'll see you in a few days."

"Hope so. This is me, over and out."

Glyvash had returned from the forest and waited patiently as the Earth alien spoke to her spaceship in her strange-sounding language.

"You have communicated with your ship?"

"Yes. I informed them of your plan to camp tonight, and they approved. They said we should stay there until they can deliver supplies."

"This sounds like a good plan, Cat. Will they be able to find us?"

"I hope so. I really hope so."

A few seconds later, the surveillance drone descended into the small clearing five meters from the alien vehicle. As Glyvash watched the new arrival, Cortez spoke.

"Could you grab that, Glyvash?"

Glyvash hesitated but a second or two before leaping from the motorcar to retrieve the drone.

"What is this?" Glyvash asked. "I found one just like this in Whoville."

"It has several functions, Glyvash. Right now, it is a communications relay. It will help me keep in touch with my ship," said Cortez, not mentioning the surveillance function.

"So, we will take it with us?"

"Yes. Just place it in the back and cover it with a blanket."

After covering the drone, the two were back on the road. Glyvash had opted for a secondary road to avoid closer examination by strangers they might encounter and because he felt this route was a bit more direct. The downside was that it was quite a bit rougher, and obstacles were to be expected. In fact, Glyvash had to stop and clear several downed trees since leaving the grove. However, the next obstacle they would meet would prove to be a bit more problematic.

The motorized buggy jerked, bounced, and skidded along the rutted and pockmarked dirt and gravel road, making for a most uncomfortable ride for the two disparate travelers. As the small vehicle crested a slight rise in the road, Glyvash suddenly and forcefully applied the brakes. His sudden movement and the vehicle's abrupt halt startled Cortez, arousing her from her hunger-induced trance.

"What's happening, Glyvash?"

Before Glyvash could respond, Cortez had already comprehended their situation. An enormous creature, no less than three meters in height, looking extremely displeased and exposing very long canines, was blocking the road. Nearby, four much smaller creatures cried out in alarm, seeing Glyvash's vehicle come out of nowhere. To Cortez, the creature looked like a giant grizzly, except that this monster was bigger. Like a grizzly, it was brown. However, that's where the similarities ended. This monster had yellow and red markings on its sides and face, a fin on its back like a freaking stegosaurus, and a glowing crest on its head. The thing looked like it came out of the prop room of a Japanese monster movie studio. Grizzly or not, she thought, this was not a friendly animal.

"Do not move, Cat."

"Don't worry, I couldn't run if I tried."

"We do not want to scare it."

"We what? *Scare it?*" Cortez said, emphasizing the word *it*.

"Do not worry, Cat. It will not harm us," said Glyvash. "Despite its physical appearance, the Xanglorian Kartusse is a very timid and harmless creature. Those fangs, for instance, are not teeth but long fleshy appendages. Those claws you think you see are illusions. They are just markings on its paws."

"So, we're in no danger?"

"No, not at all. In fact, if the Kartusse feels threatened by us, she will lose consciousness and fall to the ground as if dead."

"It, uh, *she* faints?"

"Yes. It can be quite humorous. However, we do not want to stress her out too much. There are few of her kind left. It is quite rare to see one. We are very fortunate."

"So, how do we get by?"

"We wait. Eventually, she will leave, and then we can go."

"OK, then, we wait. Let's talk about the royal court," said Cortez, closing her eyes.

# CHAPTER 64

*Drop-in visitors*

Lt. Milo Bridges slowly brought his Aries One LAV out of its steep dive before extending its wings and lighting off its two air-breathing jet engines. Putting his ship into a shallow glide and relying on his ship's night-vision capabilities, Bridges aimed for a spot three hundred meters above the forest canopy. Even with its wings extended and its engines throttled back and producing minimum power, Aries was still louder than Bridges would have liked. However, it would have to do

The plan was a simple one. First, Bridges would bring Aries down in the small clearing they had identified from surveillance imagery. Then he would double-time it on foot to Cortez's campsite. Once there, he would tend to Cortez until she recovered and assess the situation to determine whether her mission should proceed.

Night landings were always problematic. However, Bridges had received intense training for just such situations. It helped that he already had one night landing on this planet under his belt, but he couldn't afford to feel overconfident. Cat's health and well-being were too important.

Barely skimming the forest canopy, Bridges' small spacecraft rose and fell in synch with the rolling terrain below. Although RHODA would tell him when he was nearing his LZ (Landing Zone), his instincts focused on his instruments and the terrain below.

"The designated landing coordinates are three thousand meters directly ahead," announced RHODA.

Bridges leaned forward as if doing so would cause the light to reach his eyes a few heartbeats sooner. "There it is, that lighter area there," said Bridges to himself. "OK, RHODA, let's put this baby on the deck." At just the perfect moment, Bridges flared his ship, pulling the nose abruptly upward while simultaneously deploying and igniting the ship's four Artemis engines. Aries slowed quickly and began settling to the surface, cushioned by the thrust of his four downward-pointing engines. As the landing gear contacted the surface, Bridges killed the engines. The entire operation took less than four seconds.

"Damn, I'm good," Bridges said to himself, quickly unbuckling his safety harness.

Bridges, determined to minimize his time on the ground, wasted no time exiting and buttoning up his spacecraft. Popping an EPO pill, Bridges took his bearing and dashed off into the woods. He estimated it would take about an hour to cover the ten kilometers between his ship and his rendezvous with Cortez.

At Lee's urging, Bridges had opted for EPO pills, given his recent unpleasant experience using Oxy-Direc. He was in top shape due to his strenuous exercise regime, and the EPO pills should compensate for the planet's reduced oxygen level. His only worry was that he might run into wild animals or, worse, sophont aliens. He had forgone a disguise, relying on stealth and darkness to mask his presence.

The thick forest canopy blocked almost all the light from the planet's two moons. Thanks to his night-vision goggles, however, Bridges could see well enough to navigate the undulating forest floor at a pace somewhere between a jog and a sprint. He would have run faster, but he was concerned that in the darkness, he might run into a tree, step into a hole, or trip over a tree root. He had to think about Cortez. A sprained ankle, or worse, would be disastrous.

*I would eventually like to see what this planet looks like in the freaking daylight*, he thought a bit ruefully.

After covering four kilometers, Bridges slowed and then stopped. He could hear nothing except his ragged breathing and his heart pounding in his ears. He rechecked his bearing, using transmissions from the surveillance drone as a beacon. Bridges did a three-sixty while he waited for his breath to return to normal. The thing that concerned him the most was what he couldn't see. If there were any animals in the forest waiting to pounce on him, he might never see or hear them.

Bridges detached a water flask from his belt and took a swig. Then he took another. "Hang on, Cat," whispered Bridges. "Help is on the way." After another thirty seconds of rest, Bridges began jogging toward the campground. He felt strong, and at this pace, he thought he could cover the remaining distance in forty minutes.

The topology of the forest floor comprised a series of shallow channels and ridges, following one after another. Bridges wondered if an ancient flood might have formed this rippling of the forest floor. He had seen such rippling before in the Pacific Northwest and on a training mission to Gale Crater on Mars. With his mind temporarily distracted, Bridges began his climb up the next rise. He expected a gently declining slope on the other side. He didn't expect to collide with an immovable object and find himself lying flat on his back.

"What the hell?" Bridges groaned as he lay sprawled on the damp surface. He began taking stock of his situation. Nothing seemed to be broken, and he appeared to be OK. Slowly, Bridges got to his feet, anticipating a few aches and pains and staring into the gloom, wondering with what he had collided. Then he saw it. A ghostly apparition stood before him, menacing green eyes cutting through the darkness and staring directly at *him*.

Startled, Bridges let out a forceful yell and fell backward.

Whatever the thing was, it also produced a blood-curdling scream—a high-pitched, otherworldly sound that pierced the quiet night and sent chills up Bridges' spine.

Bridges wasn't the type to cower in any situation. However, he would later admit that he was afraid for his life.

Bridges' night-vision goggles painted the creature as a glowing, shapeless entity that seemed to float above him. He fumbled with his goggles to get a better idea of just what he was dealing with. Gradually, the true nature of the beast came into focus. If Bridges wasn't afraid before, he was now. The thing was at least three meters tall. Saliva dripped from an enormous mouth filled with very sharp-looking teeth. Massive canines hung from its upper jaw like a saber-toothed tiger. Rapier-like claws adorned its giant paws, and it was glaring at him with bad intentions.

Instinctively, Bridges grabbed the flashlight from his belt, pointed it at the creature, and flipped it on. The blinding light had more effect on Bridges than the monster. Bridges yelled in pain, grabbed his night-vision goggles, and pulled them from his face. Now unable to see, he continued to yell, swinging the flashlight like a baton, hoping to keep the creature at bay. If the thing attacked, he was dead meat. Fortunately and surprisingly, no attack came.

As his vision slowly returned, Bridges continued to yell while straining to locate the beast. Then he spotted it. The creature was no longer standing. Instead, it was lying flat on the ground, apparently dead.

"I killed it?" Bridges said to himself. He looked at his flashlight, then at the creature, and again at his flashlight. Did he do this? How? *Maybe the flashlight blinded it. Maybe it stroked out*, he thought. Perhaps it was a human virus. Could a virus have acted that quickly? Bridges approached slowly; flashlight trained upon the prone creature. The thing was huge, ugly, and "ugh," smelly. The animal's pungent scent assaulted his nose. *What the hell is it? Wait*, he thought. Bridges noticed the slight rise and fall of the animal's chest. A wisp of vapor spurted from its nostrils. *The damned thing is still breathing*. Milo took a step back. It must have fainted. "Well, I'll be damned," he said. On the other hand, it could be playing dead. Was it more afraid of him than he of it?

Bridges looked around, hoping no more of these creatures were out there. Seeing nothing, Bridges decided it was time to make as much distance as he could between the monster and himself. Warily, he clicked off the flashlight and returned his night-vision goggles to his face. Once he could see, he began running toward his destination as fast as he could, trees be damned.

Thirty minutes later, Bridges arrived at the spot RHODA had directed him to. He tried to control his breathing, fearful that his ragged breath might betray his presence to whomever or whatever was nearby. He crouched in the darkness motionless until his breathing returned to normal. Only then would he risk moving forward.

He didn't see the alien or Cortez, but he sensed they were close. As he scanned the surrounding forest, Bridges remained hidden in pitch-blackness. He could feel his heart racing, and not just from the physical exertion of his effort to reach the spot. The alien was close by, and Bridges could feel it. Suddenly, there he was, just ten meters from Bridges' position. The alien was tending a small fire and apparently had not detected Bridges. Near the fire was a small tent. Beside it, he could see a strange-looking three-wheeled vehicle.

"RHODA, distance to the surveillance drone?" Bridges whispered.

"The surveillance drone is approximately ten meters from your location, Lieutenant Bridges."

Bridges scanned the area again. There was nothing else close other than trees. This had to be it.

He watched the alien toss a small log onto the fire, producing a shower of sparks rising in the fire's heat.

Bridges clicked on the translator clipped to his belt. Keeping a close eye on the alien, Bridges placed the transceiver behind his ear and pressed a vocalizer onto the roof of his mouth.

*Well, here goes nothing*, thought Bridges, switching the prosthetic on with his tongue. Then, he mouthed the words "Supervisor Glyvash." Instantly, a stream of dolphin-like noises emerged from Bridges' mouth.

Startled, Glyvash jumped to his feet. "Who calls me?" he cried.

*Wonder of wonders, the damn thing works*, thought Bridges.

"Are you Supervisor Glyvash?" Bridges mouthed.

The alien backed away from the voice in the shadows, almost tripping over the fire pit.

"Yes, yes, I am. Who calls out to me?"

"I am Lieutenant Bridges. I am a colleague of Lieutenant Cortez."

Glyvash peered into the darkness, trying to glimpse the voice's owner. "Why do you hide yourself? Come into the light. It is safe."

"I don't want to frighten you," said Bridges. "I'm not wearing a disguise."

"Glyvash is not afraid. You may show yourself."

"OK. Here I come."

Bridges slowly rose to his feet, trying to keep his movements as non-threatening as possible. He was now clearly visible to the alien.

"I come in peace," said Bridges, instantly regretting his choice of words.

Bridges walked forward until he was two meters from the alien. The Earthling and the Heran examined each other across the blazing campfire for several minutes.

"How is Lieutenant Cortez?" Bridges asked, breaking the awkward silence.

"Lieutenant Cat is resting."

Suddenly, a voice from the tent interrupted their conversation.

"Is that you, Milo?"

Bridges moved quickly to the tent, knelt, and crawled inside.

"Cat, are you OK?"

"Weak—I've been better. I think it's just a lack of food. Speaking of food, what have you brought me?"

Bridges opened the pack he was carrying and removed several items. "Doc Lee whipped together something special just for you. I can't vouch for the taste, however."

Cortez took the bottle from Bridges' hand and took a slow sip. "Tastes awful," she said.

"Doc says you should drink the whole thing. Then rest. I'll have a yummy breakfast for you in a few hours."

"Do I have to?"

"Doctor's orders," he replied.

"She also gave me another bottle of iron pills. She said you lost yours?"

"Yeah, I did. I feel so stupid."

"Don't beat yourself up. Shit happens."

"Milo?"

"Yes?"

"I'm glad you came."

"Go to sleep. We'll talk later."

Bridges tended his patient for thirty minutes before she dropped off into a sound sleep. He then crawled out of the tent to make a more formal introduction to his crewmate's traveling companion.

# CHAPTER 65

*Second Contact*

After reporting to Endeavor, Bridges moved toward the fire, cautiously taking a seat on a large rock across from the alien. *Hell, I'm the alien,* thought Bridges. *What's the other guy thinking? One day he's happily working at his desk; the next, he's camping with two space travelers. His mind must be racing.*

The two studied each other intently, each waiting for the other to speak. It was Glyvash who was first to break the silence.

"Is Cat your superior?" Glyvash said, speaking in his own language.

Bridges heard the translation in his earpiece but could make out the gist of what the alien had asked, even without RHODA's help.

"No. We are equals. We have the same rank in our chain of command and are friends," said Bridges.

"So, it is true that females do not rule over males?"

"Yes. That is true."

"This is interesting."

"Can I ask you a question?" Bridges asked.

"Yes, of course."

"Will Lieutenant Cortez be in danger when her existence becomes known to your government?"

Glyvash had been thinking about this very thing from the beginning of this journey. He had tried to organize his thoughts, thinking through every conceivable scenario, so he was ready with an answer.

"Yes, Lieutenant Bridges, I'm afraid there is some danger. The head of the Council of Eleven, the Akan, would think your existence dangerous, even blasphemy. Others on the council are more tolerant and would be more receptive to the idea of people from the stars. But not the Akan."

"Thank you for being honest. It's not what I wanted to hear, but thank you anyway. How can we reduce that danger?"

"Yes, of course. The danger to Lieutenant Cat must be reduced, Lieutenant Bridges."

"Call me Milo," interrupted Bridges.

"Is *Milo* your nickname?"

"You know about nicknames?"

"Yes, I do. Cat…tree…ah…na gave me the great honor of allowing me to call her Cat."

"Then you can call me Milo."

"I am honored. Please call me Glyvash."

Bridges smiled.

"I will, Glyvash. So, you were about to discuss ways to reduce the danger."

"I was? Oh yes, of course. If we can introduce Cat to two or three of the more receptive members of the Council before we meet with the full Council, they may help protect Cat."

"That sounds like a plan, Glyvash. I recommend you proceed alone to your capital to find your Dakar Dualla. Tell her about your meeting with Cat and me. Use Dualla to put together a meeting with the more progressive members of the Council. Cat and I will appear at that meeting."

"How will I contact you?"

Bridges opened his bag, removed a small handheld communicator, and handed it to Glyvash.

"When you are ready, just push this button and talk—like this," said Bridges, holding the communicator to his lips. "I'll be able to locate you by tracking your transmission."

Glyvash turned the small device over in his hand, examining it from every angle. "I can contact you from anywhere with this small device? Amazing. I approve of your plan, Milo. I will start at first light."

"Before you leave, I want you to return Cat and me to my ship. It's not far—about fifteen kilometers. But let's let her sleep a few more hours."

"Yes, that is a good idea. Glyvash too will sleep."

Three hours later and several hours before sunrise, Cortez, Bridges, and Glyvash were motoring carefully through the dark alien forest. Cortez and Glyvash occupied the only two seats while Bridges clung to the rear of the bouncing alien vehicle, hoping not to get bucked off. The buggy's solitary light, considerably less powerful than Bridges' flashlight, barely illuminated their path. Bridges, still a bit freaked out from his earlier encounter with the narcoleptic creature from Hell, kept a careful watch for danger. Despite the rough ride, Cortez somehow slept, while Glyvash, lost in thought, anticipated his first close look at an actual spacecraft.

Less than an hour later, the tiny vehicle emerged from the forest at the edge of a small stream. Bridges recognized it instantly.

"Head upstream," said Bridges, showing the direction with his arm extended.

Slowly, the vehicle entered the stream and then turned northward. A few hundred meters later, the stream widened, and the stream's depth decreased. Suddenly, there it was, Bridges' spacecraft, sitting in the middle of the stream and almost filling the entire clearing. Its long wings folded upward and backward like the wings of a housefly. Glyvash pulled his vehicle alongside, switched off the small motor, and slowly exited the motorcar, staring at the otherworldly machine.

"Your space vehicle is much larger than I expected. How can such a thing fly?" Glyvash asked.

"Very well, those are its wings," said Bridges, pointing out Aries' long folded wings.

For the next five minutes, Bridges proudly described the LAV, going over the basics of flight aerodynamics and rocketry in great detail.

"He sounds like a new father, Glyvash," said Cortez, before realizing the comparison didn't fit the alien's experience.

"Would you like to see the inside?" Bridges asked.

"Yes. That would be most agreeable."

An hour later, having given Glyvash the grand tour, the two stood outside, preparing for Glyvash's departure.

"OK, we'll need somewhere to land my ship near the city. An early morning landing before your citizens are up and about would be preferable. Perhaps somewhere enclosed where the ship could remain hidden until we're ready to introduce ourselves to the public."

Glyvash nodded in agreement and then walked around the ship to better understand its size.

"I will do my best," said Glyvash.

"How long will it take to get to the city, Glyvash?" Cortez asked.

"I can get there by this time tomorrow if I do not stop tonight."

Cortez was silent, glancing first at Bridges and then at Glyvash as if trying to decide something.

"I'm going with you," she said finally.

"What? You're in no condition to go," said Bridges. "We have a plan. Glyvash goes and sets up the meeting, and then we go."

"Look, Milo. I can learn more about their culture in the hours it will take us to drive there than I can just lying about here."

"What about your condition?"

"I'll be fine. I'm already eighty or ninety percent. If I keep eating normal food, I'll keep getting stronger. I'll be a hundred percent before we get there."

"Damn, you're stubborn," said Bridges.

"That's why you love me," Cortez replied.

After getting Merriweather's reluctant OK and stuffing as much food as possible in the alien's tiny machine, Glyvash and Cortez resumed their trek to the capital city of Xanglora.

"Endeavor, out."

Jake Merriweather ended the connection and scowled. He had just received a report from Lieutenant Bridges, and although he had ultimate confidence in the abilities of his officers, he couldn't help worrying about their situation. It didn't help to hear that the alien, Glyvash, thought Cortez might be in danger if she continued with the planned mission. He was considering calling it off, but he wanted to hear what his second in command, Don Stoner, thought about it.

"RHODA, please locate Dr. Martin, the XO, and Lieutenant Rodriguez and ask them to meet me in my quarters."

"Yes, Captain," said the ship's AI.

Ten minutes later, a firm knock on the door signaled the arrival of Endeavor's XO, Don Stoner, followed two minutes later by Lieutenant Rodriguez and Mike Martin.

"Come," said Merriweather.

The three crewmates crowded into Merriweather's quarters. Martin and Rodriguez sat on the bunk while Stoner stood.

"I want your assessments of the security situation on the ground," said Merriweather.

Martin began. "Captain, I think the danger is minimal. We've been watching the planet for over a year, and thanks to Bridges, we've got a shitload of their documents. In addition, now that we understand their language, we've been able to follow radio transmissions that amount to what we might describe as news broadcasts. There's no sign of conflict, no wars, no reports of criminal activity, etc. It seems like a very peaceful society. Who knows what the alien meant when he said she was in danger—danger from a good tongue-lashing?"

"What about you, Stone?"

"Captain, we didn't come all this way just to observe, and our trip here wasn't exactly risk-free. I don't see that we have any other option but to proceed."

"Shouldn't I be down there, Captain?" said Rodriguez. "She needs some kind of security?"

"What's your arsenal look like, Javi — a handgun and a rifle?" Stoner asked.

"A handgun and two rifles," corrected Rodriguez.

"Exactly. We don't know what they have, but you won't be able to defend Cortez if they really want to harm her," said Stoner.

Merriweather understood how narrow his options were. First contact was always understood to be dangerous—they had trained for it, prepared for it, and each of them accepted the risks. Still, the memory of his fallen friend, Dutch Swenson, surged unexpectedly into his thoughts, tightening his chest with grief. The idea of losing Cortez or Bridges in the same way was unbearable. Yet the mission demanded action, and he knew he had no choice.

Would it make sense to risk as much as they had already and shy away at the last minute?

"Let's make sure Aries Two is prepped and ready to go. Bridges is down there already, but I want a second option if things go to hell," said Merriweather. "I want updates every hour."

Merriweather dismissed the meeting and made his way to the medical bay. He had last spoken with Doctors Lee and Graham eight hours earlier and wanted to get an update. Merriweather found the two huddled together in front of a holoview in an animated discussion. On the holoview was a molecular diagram of their latest efforts to create a solution to the chirality problem.

"Jennifer, Forest, how's it going? You're making progress, I hope."

"Yes, sir," said Lee. "Forest and I just may have had a breakthrough. Forest, the stage is yours."

"Thanks, Jen. We've made rapid progress creating a variety of synthetic enzymes that convert the various amino acids to the correct chirality by nucleophilic attack. They work fine in a Petri dish but not so much in an environment like the human gastrointestinal system. We needed to make a few changes to the molecular structure of each so that they could survive long enough to do the job," explained Graham.

"So, it's ready to go?" asked Merriweather.

"We still need to test it on a real, live human," said Lee.

"Do we have food to test?" Merriweather asked.

"Fortunately, yes. Javi collected some samples after he left Cortez down on the planet. That, plus the small sample I collected, and we should have enough for some basic testing," said Lee.

"Who's going to be the guinea pig?" Merriweather asked.

"I wish we had guinea pigs, or lab rats or rabbits or any damn thing, but we don't," said Graham.

"If we had, we'd have eaten them already," said Lee.

"So, to answer your question, I am," said Graham.

"Can you do any testing before Forest risks his life?" Merriweather asked.

"We've done all we can to minimize the risk," Graham said.

"When are you going to—to try it?"

"We have to categorize the food samples we have first before we can put together a proper testing procedure to generate formal results. Maybe tomorrow," said Lee.

"Let me know before you start. I want to observe," said Merriweather.

"OK. Will do," said Lee.

"Captain," Lee said, placing her hand on his shoulder. "Cat will be fine. Bridges won't let anything bad happen to her."

"I know. And I'm sure she won't let anything bad happen to him," said Merriweather.

Before Merriweather turned to leave, RHODA's voice got his attention.

"Captain Merriweather, Dr. Mann has asked to meet with you. He states that it's important."

"Tell him to meet me in my quarters," said Merriweather.

# CHAPTER 66

*The City of Xanglora*

Glyvash drove back through the woods in silence, his mind racing. He had now met three beings from the stars he trusted, and he considered them his friends. Glyvash was now entrusted with the most important mission of his life. His role in the historic meeting between the two civilizations was crucial. His place in history was assured, and he, a mere male. The thought both thrilled and humbled him. Beings from another planet, where males and females were equal, had entrusted him, Glyvash, with this critical mission.

He then thought about his superior, Dakar Dualla, whose safety was in his hands. Then there was the well-being of the alien named Cat, now asleep in his vehicle. He knew he must put aside all thoughts of his place in history and focus instead on Dakar Dualla and the alien. Nothing else mattered. He would let nothing happen to either of them.

Glyvash followed the tracks his vehicle's wheels had previously carved into the forest floor until he emerged back at the site where he and Cortez had first camped. From there, he followed the unpaved and unmaintained secondary road northward for another twenty kilometers until finally arriving at the great Narwa River and the road that ran along its southern bank.

The Narwa River was the widest and longest river on the continent, flowing from the Croto mountain ranges three thousand kilometers to the west before plunging into the great eastern ocean. The Narwa varied from a few hundred meters wide at the great Posha narrows, a thousand kilometers westward, to fully eight kilometers at its mouth, supplying a critically important artery for commerce and travel. Vessels, private and commercial, plied the great river nineteen hours a day.

At the mouth of the Narwa, where the river was widest, and its waters merged with the eastern ocean, sat the holy island city of Salalamba. The "Island City," as it was called, was a favorite of tourists and vacationers. The island was relatively small, just three kilometers in diameter. Still, it was overflowing with bleached white dwellings built chaotically on top of one another, as if cascading down from the highlands that dominated the island's interior. Travelers loved exploring the tiny alleyways, large enough only for foot traffic, enjoying the wide variety of small shops and restaurants.

It was toward the island city that Glyvash and the alien named Cat now sped, following the scenic roadway that hugged the banks of the Narwa. Glyvash did a rough calculation and figured reaching the fabled city would take another six hours. He had the stamina to drive for another six hours, but that was only half the distance they needed to go. The city of Xanglora lay on the coast another six hours to the north, and Glyvash had doubts he could drive that far. It had always taken him two days to cover the distance he was trying to cover today.

Fifty thousand kilometers directly over Xanglora, ISA's Starship Endeavor maintained an orbit synchronized with the planet's rotation. From Hera, Endeavor looked like any star, albeit one that did not move with the other stars but stayed fixed at the same point in the sky. This did not go unnoticed by some on the ground. In fact, the strange star that didn't move was soon a matter of much discussion in the capital city of Xanglora.

Meanwhile, on Endeavor, Merriweather had asked everyone on board to sit in on his call to Bridges and Cortez because he knew everyone was worried about their health and safety. The crew was also keenly aware of the importance of the mission. They had all gathered in the ship's galley. With mugs of coffee, tea, or their beverage of choice, they all listened to the report firsthand.

To their relief, Cortez dispelled concerns about her health by giving a report that lasted a good forty-five minutes and that covered everything she had learned from her discussions with the alien, Glyvash, her insights, and her analysis. Included in the information were the following facts:

- There were seven major countries on the planet Hera, of which the country of Xerelang was the largest and most technologically advanced, with a population of approximately five million.
- The second largest country was Belore, with a population of four and a half million. There had not been a war on Hera for centuries.
- The ruling government of Xerelang was called the Council of Ben`lei (Council of Eleven). Members of the Council were called Xenorians and were all female, as were the heads of every other government

department or agency. The head of the Council and, thus, the country's leader was the Akan.

"OK, gentlemen, we are a go on the ground. However, we have a lot to learn about these people. For example, I'm curious about why there are so few beings down there. This planet should be big enough to support a much larger population. Mike, do you have any thoughts about that?"

"Captain, I noticed that too. Just judging by where Earth was at this stage of technological development, we would expect a population of between one and two billion. However, this could be normal for their species. We're saying they're not mammals, right?"

"Lieutenant Cortez believes they are closer to reptilian or ichthyoidian," said Merriweather.

"Is that a word?" asked Mills.

"What word, ichthyoidian?" Merriweather asked.

"Yes, that word."

"Of course, it's a word. I'm the captain."

"Copy that, Cap'n," said Mills to a scattering of laughs.

"Maybe they're recovering from some near-extinction event," said Dr. Mann. "The geography of their capital city suggests an impact crater."

"Let's take a look," said Merriweather. "RHODA, display a two-meter holo-image of the planet's surface. Center it on the alien city Xanglora and show an area approximately fifteen kilometers in diameter."

As the captain and crew of Endeavor watched, a two-meter holo-image appeared instantly above their heads. The image showed a large city surrounding a near-circular bay approximately eight kilometers in diameter.

"I see what you mean, Herbert," said Merriweather. "It looks like an impact crater."

"As you can see," continued Mann, "the western edge of the crater has either collapsed or been worn away by erosion, while the eastern edge extends out into the ocean and forms a natural barrier for the bay. This side of the crater rises over three hundred meters above sea level. The inner wall slopes inward toward the bay, while the ocean-facing side forms an almost vertical escarpment. The city proper lies on the bay's western and southern sides, while its government sits on this eastern crescent."

"That's what the natives call it—Crescent City," said Girard. "That's an approximate translation, of course."

"So, you think an impact here might have been a near-extinction event they're just recovering from?" said Merriweather.

"It's within the realm of possibility," said Mann. "Cortez mentioned that their religious tradition speaks of their moon crashing into the planet."

"That's an interesting thought, Herbert. Perhaps you and Mike could investigate that," said Merriweather.

"Will do," said Mann. "You up for it, Mike?"

"I'm in," answered Martin.

"But before you get too deep into that," interrupted Merriweather, "I'd like you to see what you can uncover about the workings of the Council and anything you can find out about their leader, the Akan."

"Yes, sir."

Meanwhile, on the planet below, Glyvash had made a decision. He and the alien "Cat" would travel to the Island City and board one of the many river barges that plied the northern fork of the great Narwa from Salalamba to Xanglora. The trip by boat would add two hours to the six it typically took him to drive. However, it would allow him and Cat to recover from their arduous journey before reaching Xanglora.

He prayed they would reach Xanglora before something terrible happened to Dakar Dualla.

# CHAPTER 67

*Councilor Krei, Eighth of Dualla, Tal`su of Bentar, Tal`shi of Zaru*

Dakar (Zaru of) Dualla had been in her teacher's personal chambers before, but she still marveled at the opulence and grandeur afforded members of the ruling Council. The floor, made of polished vistmantu, was the color of doree flowers. The cerulean color of the polished stone gave visitors the feeling of walking on water.

Eleven bleached-white columns supported a grand vaulted ceiling, conferring upon the room the feeling of a holy temple. Delicate arches spanning each pair of columns drew the visitor's eyes to the intricately gilded grand ceiling. Paintings of sea creatures and heroic scenes reflecting the history of Hera adorned each column. Other scenes depicted the governing Council and the importance of the Council in Heran culture.

Dualla's teacher had chosen a grand carpet woven from domlan wool and designed by local artisans to complement the expansive polished stone floor. Diaphanous curtains, suspended from the high ceiling, enclosed her doku, or sleeping mat. The sheer curtains, made of the finest fibers, edged with silver embroidery, and beaded with tiny seashells, gave the chamber an elegance that befitted someone of great stature.

However, Dualla was not here to admire the architecture. She was on a mission.

Councilor Krei Dualla, who was Zaru's tal`shi (teacher/mentor), was taking her daily ablution in a shallow indoor pool filled with brackish river water, covered with blue-green algae, a practice she believed contributed to her continued good health.

Zaru sat on a nearby bench made of polished fancha wood, carved with mythical figures, and upholstered with lavaleen, a fabric only afforded to royalty.

"I forbid you to speak of this," said Krei Dualla in a voice that carried the weight of a royal command.

The Dualla line was, in fact, royalty. Krei was the eighth in a succession of the Duallas honored with membership on the Council of Eleven and first in line to be the next Akan when the current leader of the Council either died or retired.

"But, teacher, how can we deny what is so clearly obvious?" Zaru implored.

"Do you want to be censured? I cannot save you if the Akan chooses to shun you or, even worse. Your ideas are heresy. You know this, Zaru."

"But what if I'm right, teacher? What if an alien species is on the verge of invading? Shouldn't someone tell the Council? Should not we prepare?"

Krei Dualla pondered this for a moment before responding.

"The risk is just too great," she said finally. "I forbid you from speaking of this again. Do you understand?"

"Yes, teacher, I understand and will do as you wish."

"Then go back to your chamber. We will speak no more of this."

Zaru's neck frills glowed yellow, signaling her hopelessness as she left her teacher's chambers.

<h1 style="text-align:center">CHAPTER 68</h1>

Glyvash had booked separate sleeping compartments for himself and his alien traveling companion. His compartment was barely large enough for a typical Heran male, let alone a taller female from Earth. Nevertheless, he hoped she would find it comfortable enough to sleep. He, unfortunately, did not. Thoughts of aliens and spaceships swirled around in his mind. One moment he was contemplating awards and grand parades in his honor or leading a renaissance of male equality, while in the next moment, he imagined spending the rest of his miserable life locked away in some dark, cold dungeon.

Shaking himself awake, Glyvash pushed away all thoughts but the successful completion of his mission. A steaming mug of corettle-fish tea is what he needed. Therefore, off he went in search of a crew kitchen and, hopefully, a delicious, healing brew.

Cortez was up much earlier, unable to sleep herself. Although she felt fully recovered from her anemia, she was anxious about her mission's chance of success. Given the stories Glyvash had shared with her of the Akan's religiosity and intolerance of science, Cortez understood the difficulty she faced. She knew that the most challenging part of the trip was ahead of her. A successful first contact would depend on her focus and clarity of thought. Was she up to it?

Cortez retrieved the drone from her bag and checked its batteries. She was glad she had remembered removing the drone from the rear of Glyvash's vehicle and bringing it with her. Without the communications range provided by the drone, she would be out of contact with her ship.

After replaying the previous day's events in her mind, Cortez contacted Endeavor and Aries and briefed them. Despite her concerns, speaking with her crewmates made her feel better. When she ended the link, her concerns were gone.

Cortez stared out of the small, round porthole of her sleeping compartment and marveled at the bustling harbor scene before her. Small boats of every description, coming and going in large numbers, passed alongside the ferry as the river widened into a spectacular bay. Cortez could just make out the edges of the ancient impact crater that formed the boundaries of the bay. Only the far wall of the crater still stood, a magnificent edifice reaching high into the sky and dominating the city below. A blanket of early morning fog was just dissipating. Rays of sunlight bathed the upper floors of the city's taller buildings. Cortez was impressed by her first glimpse of the Holy City of Xanglora. The city defied easy definition. A jumble of randomly arranged irregularly shaped buildings and green-domed roofs gave the fabled city the appearance of an organism consuming the crater's far slope. If it weren't for the color of the domed roofs—green instead of blue—it could be the Greek city of Santorini Cortez visited as a nineteen-year-old, or it could be any of several similar coastal towns that lay within the Cycladic islands archipelago. The beauty of the city warmed Cat's spirits and buoyed her confidence. How could she fear a species that could build something so beautiful?

The ferry's engines throttled back as it slowly approached a stone pier that stretched out into the bay almost a hundred meters. Cortez watched the harbor workers moving about the dock, handling mooring lines, loading and unloading the vessels currently tied up along its length on both sides. Workers waiting for the ferry expertly caught the fore and aft lines heaved by the ferry's deck seamen. In a dance performed countless times during any given day, the dockworkers pulled in the mooring lines and tied them to bollards, not unlike those found at any pier in any sea town on Earth.

Thirty minutes later, Glyvash and Cortez cautiously descended the ferry's loading and offloading ramp onto the marina district's large cobblestone wharf.

The size of the crowd filling the huge bay side common astonished Cortez. *This must be a primary social gathering spot*, she thought. Cortez estimated five to ten thousand aliens, primarily male, packed into the open plaza, taking part in a celebration.

"Today is an important day for us, Cat," shouted Glyvash over the din of thousands of aliens dancing and singing about them. "We call it the *Festival of Xenosta's Gift*. We celebrate the day Xenosta came to our world to teach us how to protect our planet. It is said she paints the sky every day to remind us of her words."

Cortez glanced upward at the ever-present aurora dancing faintly in the sky.

"That's why it's so crowded, I'm guessing."

"You are guessing, Cat?" said Glyvash.

"It's just an expression we use to mean we aren't positive. We are speculating."

"I understand," said Glyvash, tilting his head like a family dog as he pondered the Earthling's words. "Guessing is unnecessary. I can provide you with the information you require."

"Thank you, Glyvash. Your knowledge has been immensely helpful to me—to my mission."

"I am happy," he beamed.

"How are we going to get through—this?" Cortez said, pointing at the vast crowd.

"It will not be that difficult, Cat. We should go toward that tower," said Glyvash, indicating a large structure in the distance.

"OK, if you say so."

"You are mistaken, Cat. I did not say *so*. I said—."

"I know, Glyvash. I just meant I agree," said Cortez.

"Your language is—"

"I know. So confusing, right?" said Cortez, interrupting her Heran guide. Cortez tentatively moved toward the crowd, expecting that she and Glyvash would have to push their way through the throngs of revelers. However, an opening suddenly appeared in the crowd as if created by some unseen force. Cortez cautiously stepped into the void, followed by her alien companion.

"What's going on, Glyvash?"

"You are female, Cat. They are showing respect."

"Cool."

"Are you sensing a decrease in the temperature, Cat?"

Cortez laughed. "No. It means *good* in some circumstances."

"You have words that change meaning? Your language is very confusing," said Glyvash.

Cortez moved through the crowd with her head down and avoided eye contact as much as possible. Glyvash followed close behind. Cortez was initially concerned that her disguise would not hold up under the gaze of thousands of aliens, but her fears eased when she noticed they weren't looking at her. In fact, they seemed to be actively avoiding looking at her.

"Are they trying to not look at me?" asked Cortez.

"Yes, of course. It would show disrespect if any Heran males stared at you."

"Works for me," said a clearly relieved Cortez.

Eventually, the two reached the structure on the far side of the commons and entered a small alleyway. Food stalls, quaint shops, and cafés, packed with hundreds of Herans, all brightly adorned with every color imaginable, lined the narrow corridor. As they did in the commons, the crowds parted for the unlikely companions as they hurried down the narrow passageway.

"So, what's the plan, Glyvash? How do we find Dakar Dualla?"

"I have a plan, Lieutenant Cat," said Glyvash. "I believe Dakar Dualla will be in the holy Temple. That is the glorious structure at the top of the eastern rim. Her teacher keeps her royal residence there, and Dualla would stay with her whenever she came to the visit."

"Will they let us in? Will they let *me* in?" said Cortez.

"I do not know. With all the visitors to the city this week, there will be many requests to enter the Temple. They may not allow everyone."

"And if they won't?"

"I will attempt to get a message to her. If that does not work, we will have to take more direct action."

"I don't think I like the sound of that, Glyvash."

Glyvash looked confused. "Were you not able to understand my speech? Why was it unpleasant?"

Cortez laughed. "No, I mean that taking more direct action worries me."

"I understand," said Glyvash with a slight shake of his head. "It would be very dangerous."

"Dangerous? I definitely don't like the sound of that."

The two traveling companions walked the next thirty minutes in complete silence as they contemplated the risk they were prepared to take, and although they were different species, the feeling of excitement mixed with a sense of foreboding they each felt was uncannily similar.

Cortez tried to ease her apprehension by focusing on her surroundings. That was her job, after all. She marveled at the alien architecture—strange and unique, yet oddly familiar. Rectangular buildings were rare. Instead, there were wedges, octagons, pentagons, and ellipses—structures of every imaginable shape. Some buildings defied description—formless, chaotic, unorganized blobs that were still appealing. The most prevalent form seemed to be circular buildings with one flat side, the same design used in Dualla's residence in Whoville.

Despite the plethora of architectural designs represented in Xanglora, one color was prevalent—white. Xanglora was a sea of white. *Was there a law that mandated white?* thought Cortez.

Topping many of the white hexagonal and circular buildings were domes of pale green, the color of the locally mined mineral known as vistmantu. The combination of white and green was aesthetically pleasing to the eye. Cortez couldn't shake the image of the sun-bleached cities dotting the Greek islands. *I wouldn't mind living here*, she thought.

After the prolonged silence, Cortez began asking questions in rapid fire:

"What is that building?"

"I believe it's a trade school."

"Is that an office tower?"

"Yes, I believe it is."

"What kinds of industries or businesses exist in Xanglora?"

"Many. I acquired these clothes on my last trip here."

"That looks like an outdoor eating establishment."

"Yes, it is. Are you hungry, Lieutenant Cat?"

"No, thank you, Glyvash. Do you have the concept of fast food?"

"Fast food?"

"Yes, simple meals delivered quickly."

"Yes, we do. You have this on your Earth?"

"Yes, it's extremely popular on Earth. Is this a pedestrian city, or do they have public transportation?"

"We walk in the holy city. Motorized vehicles are not permitted. We have self-powered two-wheeled vehicles for those who dislike walking."

"Is that a church?"

"No. It's the residence of a prominent official," answered Glyvash.

"Do you have churches or temples?"

"Yes, we do. Many of the domed structures are temples."

Cortez wondered what it would be like to live in this city—at least vacation here. Maybe she and Milo could—*Stop it. Girl, keep your mind focused on your responsibility*, thought Cortez.

"Glyvash, are there areas of the city that are—how should I say—poorer or economically disadvantaged?" Cortez asked.

"I don't understand, Cat."

"Are there areas in the city where poor people live?"

"Poor people? I don't understand."

"Poor people...peasants...the homeless...people who make less money or are unemployed."

"What is money? What is unemployed?"

Cortez's memory flashed back to the little alien café Glyvash had taken her to on the first day of their road trip. *Did he not pay for the meal?* She couldn't remember.

Cortez mouthed her response and listened to the series of alien sounds emanating from the prosthesis in her mouth.

"It's difficult to explain, but here goes. Money is a symbolic representation of value that we use to facilitate the exchange of goods and services among the inhabitants of my planet. It works like this. We trade our work for credits. The more you work, the more credits you accumulate. We trade those credits for food, lodging, clothing, etc."

Glyvash seemed puzzled. He tilted his head one way, then the other, in that same puppy dog mannerism Cortez had previously noticed.

"I do not understand the need to trade something for food or clothing. It is the purpose of many to provide those things to anyone who needs them. Is it not so on your planet?"

"Don't you earn credits for the work you do at the Science Center in

Whoville?" Cortez responded, not directly answering his question.

"I receive nothing for my work, Lieutenant Cat. It is my purpose."

"And the owner of the café we ate at on the first day of our trip—that is his purpose?"

"Yes. A purpose to one is a benefit to all."

"You've given me much to think about, Glyvash."

After a few minutes of silence, Glyvash turned to Cortez and asked: "Are there people without homes on your world?"

Cortez was hoping Glyvash had not noticed her reference earlier.

"Unfortunately, there are, Glyvash. I wish it were otherwise."

"You have given me much to think about, Lieutenant Cat."

Cortez also had much to think about. She thought about her life aboard Endeavor. Did she trade her work for money? Didn't Endeavor's albeit small society function perfectly well without the need for compensation? What if a society relied solely on robots to perform all tasks? How would someone earn a paycheck? Had the Herans developed a better way? It seemed to work for them.

Glyvash's route through the old city seemed random as he steered Cortez down one narrow corridor after the next. Some were barely wide enough for two aliens to pass by each other. Cortez recalled the New Testament quote—*It is easier for a camel to go through the eye of a needle than for a rich man to enter the kingdom of God*. She wondered if their holy book referred to a Domlan and an alley in Xanglora.

"We are almost at our destination, Cat."

"I'm thankful, Glyvash," said Cortez, and she was. Glyvash's mad dash through the city had made her tired. She had taken an EPO and an iron pill that morning, but this had been the most active she had been since landing on the planet.

Less than a minute later, the traveling companions emerged from the shadows of a narrow alleyway and into the bright glare of an open courtyard crowded with more aliens. These aliens seemed quieter and more respectful, undoubtedly out of respect for the location—the Temple of Xenosta.

The fabled Temple of Xenosta loomed over the far side of the stone commons, stretching a good hundred meters in both directions. An imposing structure, its front-facing façade featured a row of slender stone columns spaced every dozen meters, and spanning the length of the ornate design. A series of pale green domes topped the brilliantly white Temple.

A narrow channel filled with water flowed between the Temple and the commons area. An arched stone bridge about thirty meters long connected the Temple to the commons and was apparently the only entrance. At the near end of the bridge, two guards stood at attention next to an ornate stone guardhouse. The guards wore uniforms that would have made the Vatican's Italian Guardia Svizzera look drab. A short queue of Herans patiently waited their turn to cross the bridge.

Separating the guardhouse, the bridge, and the Temple from Cortez and Glyvash, was a procession of Herans, primarily male, moving briskly across the commons.

"I will approach the guards alone," said Glyvash. "Cat will wait here, yes?"

"Yes," she answered. "Cat will wait here."

Cortez was doubtful that her quickly deteriorating disguise would fool what she presumed were highly trained security guards. Therefore, she was more than happy to wait some distance away and watch Glyvash approach the guardhouse.

The guards were unusually tall for Heran males. Each towered over Glyvash by at least half a meter. Cortez couldn't make out their conversation amidst the noise of the busy commons, but she could see that it was animated. Glyvash turned and pointed at Cortez several times as if to explain that an important female needed to gain access to the Holy Temple. After several minutes, Glyvash turned from the guards and slowly walked back to Cortez.

"I have failed. The guards will not permit us to enter."

"You said it would be difficult. So, what's your next plan?" Cortez asked.

Glyvash turned and looked at the two guards, who returned his gaze with menacing stares of their own. Then he turned to his left and then to his right, as if looking for something. Finally, he pointed at something in the distance.

"We need a boat."

# CHAPTER 69

*The Eastern Sea and the Secret Entrance*

Cortez closed her eyes and let her mind wander. The sound of the water slapping against the side of the boat, the sound of the sails flapping in the wind, and her face wet from salt spray all brought back memories of days spent on Chesapeake Bay during breaks in her Academy courses. The sounds of the strange four-winged seabirds squawking overhead evoked memories of the gulls, terns, and skimmers that populated the Severn estuary. Despite the ever-present aurora swirling overhead and the alien sitting behind her in the cockpit, this could be Earth, she thought. *This could be home.*

Cortez realized that the thought of being stranded here no longer filled her with the same dread she had felt just a few days earlier. Neither did it cause her much anxiety either . She was feeling more comfortable in this strange new world. She now saw things differently than when Endeavor first arrived and took position behind Erebus. Cortez saw more similarities than differences. She had resigned herself to the thought that if no ship arrived from Earth to rescue them, this would be her home for the rest of her life—maybe with Milo. She now felt comfortable with that thought.

 Cortez felt the tension in her body slip away with each breath. A pleasant thought occurred to her.

"We shall not cease from exploration," she began, "and the end of all our exploring will be to arrive where we started and know the place for the first time."

The stream of alien sounds emanating from her lips surprised her. She had not really intended her words to be translated.

"I don't understand, Lieutenant Cat."

"Oh, I'm sorry. I was just thinking aloud, meaning it was a private thought. I spoke aloud unintentionally."

She saw the look of confusion accompanied by the puppy-dog tilt of his head.

"It's like having a conversation with oneself. It's hard to explain. Anyway, I remembered something an Earth poet wrote hundreds of years ago."

"What do the words mean?"

"Interpretation of poetry is always personal—words can carry different meanings for different people. I can't claim to know exactly what the author intended, but for me, it speaks to seeing things in a new way. As I look at your planet, I find myself thinking that I could belong here. It stirs echoes of where I come from—memories of moments that once brought me joy." Glyvash smiled. He was happy that this alien found his world appealing.

"What is poetry?" he asked.

Cortez rolled her eyes and gave a slight shake of her head.

"It's a complicated subject. Maybe we can discuss it later when we can focus on it."

"We will discuss poetry tomorrow. Do you have boats like this on your world?" Glyvash said, changing the subject.

"It's an intriguing design. We may not have boats precisely like this one, but the basic ideas are similar."

"Maybe we will have time later to discuss boats ... and poetry," said Glyvash.

"Sure," Cortez answered.

The boat was unlike anything she had ever seen. The craft had an enclosed ovoid shape, about six or seven meters long and five meters wide. *It looks like an eggplant*, thought Cortez. It had two round openings at the top, one near the bow where Cortez now sat and one near the stern where Glyvash sat and operated the rudder. Two triangular sails made of a transparent fabric extended horizontally from the vessel's sides. A pontoon on either side near the waterline kept the craft stable. The overall effect was that of a winged bug, which for this species made perfect sense, thought Cortez.

Cortez watched with fascination as Glyvash worked the rigging lines, making subtle adjustments to the position and shaping of the sails.

"You've sailed a boat before. I'm impressed."

"Yes, of course," beamed Glyvash. "The last time I was in the capital for the festival, I enjoyed several days' sailing."

"I feel perfectly safe in your expert hands. So, what's the plan?"

"I remember the speech Dakar Dualla gave at the science center when she was first appointed Chief Astronomer. She spoke of her childhood here at the Temple, learning under her teacher's guidance. One moment from that speech has always stayed with me. She said that as a curious child, she loved to wander the Temple's corridors and once discovered a secret entrance—known only to the Council—that opened onto a beach along the eastern wall. Even the guards, she said, did not know of it."

Cortez lifted her gaze to the towering escarpment above. Nearly three hundred meters high, the sheer rock face marked the eastern rim of the vast impact crater. Beyond that barrier lay the Holy Temple and the royal residences.

"Dakar Dualla spoke of a tunnel that leads from a narrow beach on the ocean side. She used to sneak out at night to swim and gaze at the night sky."

"Do you know where the tunnel is or where it leads?"

"No, Her Eminence provided no other details."

"Hell of a way to introduce humans," said Cortez. "Sneaking in the back door."

"What is—hell?" Glyvash asked.

"A topic for another day," said Cortez. *I need to watch what I say*, she thought to herself.

For almost two hours, Glyvash steered the strange craft parallel to the rock wall, looking for anything that might be a tunnel opening onto a beach. Several times, he shouted he had found it, only to be disappointed.

*This is a fool's errand*, Cortez thought to herself. "Let's give it another hour, and if we don't find it, we should turn back," said Cortez.

"Not a good plan," said Glyvash.

"No? Why is it not a good plan?"

"Because I have found it."

Cortez immediately turned toward the rock wall, trying to see what Glyvash had found.

Glyvash swung the vessel hard to port and steered it toward the towering crater wall. It took a few seconds before Cortez could make out the tiny strip of sand at its base.

Minutes later, Glyvash grounded the eggplant-shaped craft onto the ribbon-thin stretch of sandy beach. With an agility that surprised Cortez, the alien hopped out of the boat and into the shallow surf. Directly in front of them was a small dark opening in the rock face, looking like the entrance to a tunnel.

"I believe this is Dakar Dualla's secret tunnel," said Glyvash.

"Did you bring a flashlight?" Cortez asked as she waded through the surf and onto the beach.

"What is—flashlight?"

"It's probably very dark in there, and we'll need illumination."

"Oh yes. You are referring to a glow reed, and there should be one or more in the locker below."

Glyvash suddenly disappeared into the interior of the eggplant boat, reappearing a minute later, holding several objects in his hand.

"These are glow reeds, Cat. They will provide the illumination we need."

Glyvash handed one of the devices to Cortez, demonstrating its operation with another. "A simple twist turns it on or off."

Cortez followed suit, admiring the device's clever design but not its underwhelming output.

"OK then, lead on, Macduff," said Cortez.

"What is, Macduff?" Glyvash asked, a questioning look on his face.

"It just means you go first, and I'll follow," said Cortez.

"I am a scientist, but I cannot see the logic in your language."

Cortez laughed. "A topic for another day, Glyvash."

"We have many topics for another day," said Glyvash.

Cortez nodded in agreement as she turned toward the tunnel opening.

*It's smaller than I expected*, she thought.

It measured less than a meter high and three-quarters of a meter wide, with barely enough room for the two to enter. Cortez rarely suffered from claustrophobia, but the thought of crawling through a pitch-black tunnel of unknown length on an alien planet did not give her warm and fuzzy feelings. However, she saw no other option. So, she slowly lowered herself to her knees and followed her alien guide into the unknown.

"Any idea how long this tunnel is?" Cortez asked after crawling for only thirty seconds.

"I do not know. Dualla did not speak of this."

"Pity," mumbled Cortez.

After a few more meters of crawling, the tunnel suddenly opened into an enormous cavern, allowing Glyvash and Cortez to stand.

"My knees will never be the same," said Cortez, slipping the strap from her bag over her head.

"Your species' body covering—what you call skin—is more fragile than ours," said Glyvash.

"True, but it's self-repairing," said Cortez defensively.

"That is very interesting," said Glyvash. "We should also speak of this another day."

Cortez laughed. "The list is getting long, isn't it?"

Glyvash and Cortez silently contemplated their new surroundings. The cavern yawned around them, devouring the faint light of their glow reeds until only pitch-black darkness remained beyond reach. Every distant crash of surf on the hidden shore thundered through the hollow chamber, echoes rippling through the stone like a relentless, ominous drumbeat. A vile miasma of rotting fish and brine clung to the air, curling into her nostrils and twisting her stomach with its rank intensity. Thin wisps of cold mist drifted through the tunnel, clinging to the stone in a slick, icy film that made the walls feel slimy and unforgiving under her fingers. In the hush between wave-crashes, the silence deepened oppressively—as if something unseen were stirring just beyond the edge of her flickering light, waiting in the darkness.

"Can you see how far this space goes, Glyvash?"

"No, I cannot. I suggest we stay close to the cave walls."

"Agreed," said Cortez. "You go around to the right, and I'll follow the wall to the left. Call out if you find a door or stairway that might lead to the Temple."

"Yes, it's an excellent plan," said Glyvash.

Cortez's thoughts flashed back to her Academy training. She remembered taking part in night navigation drills that many in her class struggled with. One session required trainees to navigate a cave with little or no light. Instructors had escorted her cadet class to a cave system in Garrett County called Crabtree Cave. From a location deep inside the cave and armed with a single penlight for illumination, the cadets had to find their way out, leaving no one behind.

That's what this felt like. Except on an alien planet, she had no way of knowing what kinds of animal life existed inside this cave, and the thought only added to her unease.

Cortez slowly traversed the dark cavern, her hand brushing nervously against the cold and slimy cave wall, hoping not to get stung or grabbed by some alien creature. The two intrepid explorers inched through the pitch blackness around the cavern's perimeter for what seemed like an eternity, but was only about five minutes.

"Cat, I have found something," shouted Glyvash, his excited utterance echoing off the cavern's stone surfaces.

"I'll be there as fast as I can," said Cortez.

As quickly as she safely could, Cortez retraced her steps around the cave's perimeter, then followed the path taken by her fellow spelunker. She was excited to be closer to her objective, but careful not to step into a hole as she felt her way along the cavern's walls. The cavern floor was uneven, worn smooth by time, and made slippery by the salt spray drifting in from the entrance. She slipped several times, almost falling, but managed to stay upright. After calling Glyvash several times, she eventually found her Heran guide.

"What have you found, Glyvash?"

"I found an opening," he said, pointing at a gash in the cave wall.

Cortez held her glow reed near the fissure and looked in. The fissure extended from the cavern floor, reaching into the gloom far above their heads. It was barely wide enough for Cortez to squeeze through, which she did before Glyvash could volunteer.

"It looks like someone's carved stairs into the rock here, Glyvash. I'm going up."

"You are Macduff," said Glyvash.

Cortez laughed. "Yes, I am. Are you coming?"

"Yes, yes. I will follow Macduff."

Milo was getting anxious. Cortez had radioed before disembarking the Narwa riverboat when she and Glyvash reached the capital. She had also radioed him from the beach below the ancient city's sea-facing cliffs—but nothing since. This was the most dangerous part of her mission, and here he was, unable to help if something went terribly wrong. Sure, Cortez was very capable and all that, but despite that, he couldn't help but worry about her safety.

In the meantime, Milo continued to ready Aries for imminent departure. He wanted to ensure he could respond in seconds if she needed him. He wanted to be over the capital city within twenty minutes or fewer.

Over the last few days, since Cortez and Glyvash had left Aries, Bridges had busied himself doing some basic science for Doc Graham and Doc Lee. He hoped that the plants he loaded, almost a quarter of a ton, would be edible with the new chirality reversal drug developed by Docs Graham and Lee. Cortez had collected water and soil samples from the streambed and surrounding forests, and he had performed many physical activities while Doc Lee monitored his vitals. He had even set up the PEME (Proton Membrane Exchange) unit in the flowing stream and filled Aries' LOH and LOX fuel tanks.

He was running out of things to do to keep busy. Now, it was mostly waiting and worrying.

Bridges had received some good news and couldn't wait to share it with Cortez. Merriweather had informed him that RHODA had finished deciphering the language of the Belorians, the second largest country on Hera. Fortunately, the Belorian language was similar to Xerelang's, which made the task far more straightforward. However, it was still a significant milestone. Since then, Mills had been listening to Belorian radio transmissions and using RHODA's new translation to catalog Belorian culture, governmental structure, politics, and, more importantly, the names of Belorian scientists. Merriweather had instructed Bridges to be ready to travel to Belore as soon as Cortez had contacted Dakar Dualla and was safely back aboard Aries.

However, here he was, still waiting for a call from Cortez, and he wasn't good at waiting.

# CHAPTER 70

*We have a problem*

Merriweather stared at the hologram floating over the small table in the ship's galley and slowly shook his head.

"Are you absolutely positive?" Merriweather asked.

"RHODA gives it an eighty-seven percent probability," said Mann.

Mann paused as Zoe Bishop walked into the galley and took her place at the small table. Her hair was wrapped in a towel as if she had just washed it.

"Hi, guys. You all look too damn serious. What's an eighty-seven percent probability?" Bishop asked. "Or was I not invited for a reason?"

She had a reporter's instinct and always seemed to show up when critical issues were being discussed. Mann glanced at Merriweather, who nodded in the affirmative.

"OK. You remember our close flyby of the planet Ulysses?" Mann asked.

"Of course, we used its gravity to slingshot us toward Hera," answered Bishop.

"Right, we expected Ulysses to continue out of the system as it's done for thousands of years."

Mann pointed at the red line in the hologram that represented Ulysses' path through the system.

"Our calculations showed its trajectory crossed the orbits of Hera and the large gas giant Hypatia-f."

"Colossus?" said Bishop.

"Yes. In fact, my report then mentioned that it would come very close to Hypatia-f but not impact it. I didn't foresee, however, the possibility of a collision with one of Hypatia-f's many moons."

"Ouch, a direct hit?" Bishop asked.

"Pretty much," said Mann. "What we're seeing now is a ring of debris around the planet that wasn't there before."

"I'm guessing, given the sour faces, that there's more to the story," said Bishop, glancing at Merriweather.

"Unfortunately, you are correct," said Mann. Pointing at a red dotted line in the hologram, he continued. "This dotted line coming from behind Hypatia-f is a kilometer-wide piece of what's left of either Ulysses or one of Hypatia-f's moons. As you can see, it is heading approximately in our direction."

"Crap. Pardon my French. Is it going to hit us—uh, I mean them?" she said, referring to the Herans.

"Not right away. We expect it to miss the planet strike by a safe margin. However..."

"Here it comes," said Bishop.

"However," continued Dr. Mann, "it continues along this trajectory toward the red dwarf where RHODA shows it swinging around the star and back toward Hera's orbit. RHODA predicts a planet strike in about eighteen months and gives it an eighty-seven percent probability."

Bishop glanced at Merriweather, hoping the captain would say something reassuring, like Dr. Mann and RHODA were wrong or that he had a plan that would prevent the death of millions on the planet below, but there was just silence.

"Captain?" said Bishop.

"Herbert, I need you to run the numbers again. Refine the estimates until you can tell me—without a shred of doubt—if, when, and where it's going to strike."

Merriweather turned to look at Bishop.

"This stays here," said Merriweather. "There's no reason to add to the stress level of those on the surface. We will inform Bridges, Cortez, and the rest of the crew at the proper time. Right now, we all have work to do. So, get back to it, and keep your damn mouths shut."

Zaru Dualla was despondent. Her life was coming apart, and she felt powerless to stop it. She had gone to see the Akan, against her teacher's expressed wishes, to inform the leader of her scientific findings and her concerns about beings from the stars coming to Hera. She was confident that with all the evidence she possessed, she could convince the Akan. However, it had not gone as she had hoped. Instead, the Akan had erupted in rage, accusing Dualla of heresy. She threatened to expel Dualla from the Royal Order and to denounce her publicly. Zaru would be exiled, shunned, and never allowed to return to the Temple.

Dualla knew these actions would ruin her family name. Her teacher, Krei, would never attain the position of Akan. Eventually, Krei would lose her seat on the Council and face a bleak future.

Dualla begged the Akan to reconsider. She told the Akan of her teacher's words, expressly forbidding Dualla from speaking to the Akan about such things. She beseeched Her Holiness to hold her teacher blameless.

After much pleading, Dualla succeeded only in getting the Akan to delay her actions. Out of respect for Dualla's teacher, the Akan would call a meeting of the full council to seek their advice. In the meantime, she ordered Dualla detained at the Akan's offshore residence, a secluded retreat on a small island in the eastern ocean, a few kilometers east of the Holy City.

"You only have yourself to blame," said the Akan as her guards dragged Dualla from the Royal Temple chamber.

# CHAPTER 71

*The Secret Stairway*

Cortez let her fingers trace the rough edge of a step as she studied the ancient stairway. The passage vanished into the darkness above, swallowing her gaze no matter how she strained to follow it. Was this the secret entrance Dualla had spoken of? It seemed likely. Someone—an inspired soul, perhaps centuries ago—had carved this ascent from the bones of the cavern itself. The builder had seized upon a natural fissure, wedging rough stones into notches hacked out of the walls with primitive tools. Each piece, hand-sized and clumsy, bore the marks of effort rather than craft. The steps rose unevenly, their jagged placement betraying not the work of a mason but of some desperate laborer, driven less by skill than by necessity.

"Did Dakar Dualla tell you where the stairway leads?"

"No, she did not tell me this," said Glyvash. "Do you not believe it leads to the Temple?"

"You're asking me? All right. From what you've told me, yes, I think it leads to the Temple. Either way, we have no choice but to follow it—wherever it leads."

Cortez held her glow reed above her head and took one long look at the gap, twisting its way into the depths of the rock face far above. Then she took a tentative first step, hopping on the lowest stone step to test its strength. Feeling no hint of wobbling or instability in the stone, she took another step.

"It seems to be sturdy enough," said Cortez. "I'm going up."

This was not a typical stairway. It was much steeper, and with haphazardly spaced steps. Cortez found it more comfortable to traverse it as she would a ladder, placing her free hand on the next higher step as she began the climb. Glyvash followed suit, and the two slowly and carefully ascended the ancient stone steps.

"What's the plan if we run into some of those scary-looking guards?" Cortez asked.

"I do not believe anyone will confront you, Lieutenant Cat. You are female and will receive the respect all females receive. Males in the Temple will only look directly at you if you speak with them. Females will be curious, but assume you have the right to be there."

"Hope you're right, Glyvash."

"Yes, I hope I am right."

The two continued their climb, carefully testing each step before transferring their full weight. Centuries of use had worn smooth the stones, and ocean mist now made them slippery. The replica alien footwear she wore supplied little traction. She struggled to keep her footing and several times came perilously close to falling.

Her footwear was but one of her problems. Still feeling the effects of the planet's stronger gravity, Cortez had to stop often to catch her breath. In addition, her legs were cramping. When was the last time she had water to drink? She wondered. She was also feeling a bit claustrophobic. Cortez pushed all negative thoughts aside as she continued her climb. She briefly wondered what Milo was doing now. *Wish he were here*, she thought.

Cortez felt the pain in her fingers. She had been holding her glow reed in one hand while using the other to steady herself and to take the strain off her cramping legs. Instinctively, she began transferring the light to her climbing hand, only to feel it slip from her fingers and fall into the darkness.

"Hell," she exclaimed. "Sorry about that, Glyvash. I lost my grip."

"What is hell?"

"Not now, Glyvash," she said.

"Can you continue?" he asked.

"Not sure," she replied. "Give me a moment."

"Do you want me to lead?"

"The fissure isn't wide enough for you to pass me."

"I can give you my glow reed."

Cortez considered the suggestion for a few seconds before responding.

"You hold on to it. The way my hands feel, I might drop it too. I'll just have to do without."

"Cat should be watchful," said Glyvash.

"Cat will try," she replied.

Cortez took a deep breath. The claustrophobia she had earlier pushed to the back of her consciousness returned stronger than before. She could feel her heart racing, her pulse pounding in her ears. *It can't be that much farther*, she thought to herself, *but I can't be sure.*

Cortez noticed the fissure getting narrower as the stairs curved to the right. She could no longer navigate the stairs without twisting her body sideways. The rock walls now pressing in on both sides added to her anxiety.

"How are you doing down there, Glyvash?" she said, trying to keep the panic from her voice.

"I am doing well," he replied, seemingly unconcerned with their predicament.

With trepidation, Cortez resumed her slow ascent, now in almost total darkness. One step at a time, fingers cramping, legs throbbing in pain, fear welling up from within, she crawled up the stone edifice, squeezing her body between the walls of the ancient fissure.

Cortez was struggling. She needed an EPO pill but couldn't retrieve it from her bag. She was finding it more difficult to breathe. Unless they found the entrance to the Temple soon, she...

Cortez remained motionless for a few minutes, trying to catch her breath. Then she took another step, reaching into the darkness above for the next stone step. Instead of a step, however, her hand hit solid rock—a ceiling.

"I think...we've reached...the end...Glyvash," she said, trying to breathe.

"The end! What do you see?" he replied.

"Not sure. It's too dark...to see much...of anything."

Cortez struggled in the narrow crevice to twist her body around.

"Wait. There's an opening...in the rock...behind me...a horizontal shaft... maybe."

Cortez struggled to make out any details of the opening in the cave wall. To Cortez's right was a tunnel cut into the rock and disappearing into the darkness. Carefully, she extricated herself from the stone stairway and squeezed into the tunnel.

Cortez took a deep breath. Reaching into her bag, she retrieved the EPO pills and a small water bottle. After taking a pill and a swig of water, she answered Glyvash.

"Bring your light. I can't make out a damn thing."

Glyvash joined her inside the tunnel. His glow reed's meager light revealed a horizontal shaft large enough for Glyvash and Cortez to stand side by side.

"It doesn't look natural. It looks like someone chiseled it from the rock," said Cortez.

"I believe we have found Dakar Dualla's secret entrance," said Glyvash, smiling.

"Hope so. I don't know about you, but when it's time to go, I'm leaving by the front door," said Cortez.

"I'll go first. You follow, Cat."

"Lead on," she replied.

His glow reed held high over his head, Glyvash moved carefully along the tunnel, his friend, Lieutenant Cat of Earth, not far behind.

# CHAPTER 72

*The Akan*

The Holy leader of the Ben`lei, Daughter of Xenosta, Goddess of the Sea, Protector of the Faith, Defender of the Planet, the Great Akan, nervously paced her royal chamber, replaying in her mind her conversation with Councilor Krei Dualla's tal`su, Zaru Dualla. On the one hand, she couldn't allow a challenge to a primary tenant of Heran belief—that Herans were the center of the Universe and were the protectors of Hera and the Universe, made so by the great God Xenosta Herself. *If there were others…up there…able to fly between the stars, it would…*she couldn't bear to finish the thought.

However, what truly worried the Akan was the possibility that Dualla was right. Could she ignore the possibility? Was there an imminent invasion of monsters from the sky?

"Nonsense," she said aloud. "I will deal with Zaru Dualla tonight."

Knock, knock.

Startled from her thoughts, the Akan turned quickly, glided to her chamber door, and flung it open. Still agitated by her earlier meeting with Zaru Dualla, she was prepared to admonish whoever dared intrude on her privacy. However, upon seeing two of her guards and two strangers, she withdrew into her apartment a few paces. "What is this?"

"Sorry, Your Primacy. We found these two wandering about the Temple. We would have put them out, but one is female."

At first, Cortez and Glyvash had gone unnoticed. Their goal had been to find the apartment of Zaru Dualla's teacher, Krei. They had hoped she could tell them the location of her young tal`su. However, after wandering the labyrinthine halls without success, they had no recourse but to stop those they encountered and ask for help. This strategy soon attracted the Temple guards' attention, who quickly confronted them. Unable to persuade the guards that Councilor Krei herself had authorized their presence, Cortez and Glyvash were quickly escorted to the Akan's royal chamber.

*I've totally mucked this up*, thought Cortez, as she contemplated her fate. Then again, this could be a good thing. Having spent the last four days with Glyvash, she had received a crash course in Heran culture and geopolitics. Of course, what she had learned was from a Heran male's perspective. How much more could Zaru Dualla have taught her? However, there was nothing she could do about it now. She was about to make first contact with the leader of the most powerful country on this planet, which made her the ideal person, didn't it?

Cortez and Glyvash stood silently as the Akan scrutinized her two new guests. Simultaneously, Cortez tried to take the measure of the ruler of Xerelang. Standing a good one and three-quarter meters, the Akan was taller than most Heran females Cortez had seen. Her skin markings were more elaborate, making Cortez wonder if they were all natural. *Maybe they add markings in the same way Earth females use hair extensions*, she thought. The Heran's neck frills were glowing, a color Cortez hadn't seen before. *Was that a good thing, or a terrible thing?*

The Akan wore a long flowing robe imprinted with what appeared to be flowers—*maybe doree flowers*, thought Cortez. There were also symbols Cortez had seen on her trip through the city. She hadn't the foggiest what they meant, however. Cortez wondered if she could get a robe like that when this was all over. Did the Temple have a gift shop? The thought made her smile to herself and eased her apprehension.

Suddenly, her friend Glyvash took a halting step forward and tried to explain their presence in the Temple.

"Your Primacy, we were looking for—"

"Silence!"

The Akan glared menacingly at Glyvash.

"I know you. You are Zaru Dualla's underling. I suppose she has infected you with her delusions of creatures from other worlds."

The Akan slowly circled Glyvash like a predator circling its next meal. After a few seconds of silence that seemed like an eternity to Glyvash, the Akan spoke again.

"Well, has she? Has your master infected you?"

Cortez saw the anguish and fear on her friend's face. She couldn't let this attack go on. So, throwing caution and protocol to the wind, she stepped forward.

"You are the Akan? You're the leader of this country?

The Akan shifted her withering gaze to Cortez.

"Do I know you?" she asked. "You do not look familiar. Who are you?"

"I am an envoy," began Cortez. "My name is Catriana Cortez. I come from another world."

"Stop right there! I will not allow this perversion in the Holy Temple," shouted the Akan.

Pivoting to her guards, the Akan pointed toward Glyvash and Cortez.

"Take these—these perversions—to my island. I will deal with them tonight. I don't want them in my city."

Cortez stepped toward the Akan, desperation rising in her voice, but the guards seized her arms and wrenched her back, dragging her away before she could speak.

*Where had it all gone wrong?* Cortez thought. Perhaps a better approach would have been to land Aries on the Temple steps and announce to everyone that life for their species would never be the same. She knew the answer to that. ISA had game-planned many scenarios, and the shock approach was quickly ruled out.

Maybe they shouldn't have come through the back door uninvited. However, if she was to speak to the Akan, Cortez would have to force the issue. She couldn't simply send her a flash-com or thumb her up on her communicator. One thing she was positive of, however, was that the Akan knew the truth. Cortez saw it in her alien eyes. But could she accept the reality of visitors from another world? Could she bring herself to announce to her people the existence of aliens? That was the question and Cortez's challenge. The Guards had force-marched Glyvash and Cortez out of the Temple through a side entrance and to the royal barge docked in the Akan's private slip. There was a positive side to all of this, thought Cortez. At least she wouldn't have to climb down that damned secret stairway.

As the royal barge departed the calm waters of the protected inner harbor and into the choppy, windswept waters of the eastern ocean, Cortez was clearly worried.

"How much trouble are we in? Glyvash. How worried should I be?"

"Do not worry, Cat," he replied. "You are female. It is possible the Akan will banish you from Xerelang, but you will not be harmed."

"And you," said Cortez.

"I do not know. I-I don't even want to think about it," he replied.

"I've seen no evidence that your species is prone to physical violence," said Cortez.

"Silence!" shouted a guard.

Cortez returned the guard's stare with a menacing one of her own, which seemed to have no effect whatsoever. Leaning back against the gunnel, she turned and smiled at her friend Glyvash, hoping to buoy his spirits. Whatever happened, Cortez could depend on Milo if things really got bad.

# CHAPTER 73

*Informing the Crew*

Merriweather felt he couldn't wait any longer. The crew deserved to know what he knew. Therefore, he assembled everyone in the galley. Lieutenant Bridges, currently cooling his heels on the planet, joined the meeting via holoview.

"Bridges, give me some good news. What's the latest on Cortez?"

"I don't have any, Cap'n. She missed her 1600 check-in, which is unlike her. However, I have her tracker signal. She's moving east from her last position, and it appears she's in a seacraft of some sort. I've attempted to reach her via the translator, but so far, no response."

Bridges was referring to one of the more notable features of the translator. Bridges could send a transmission using RHODA's connection to the language translator Cortez carried in her tunic. The translator would relay the message to Cortez's earpiece, and Cortez could respond just by mouthing silently. It was the same process used to speak the alien's language, albeit with the vocalizer mouth prosthetic switched off.

"Does she still have the relay drone with her?"

"It doesn't look like it. It appears to be at her last known location. However, she should still be within range. Her tracker signal is being relayed through the drone. She's about two kilometers to the east. She will be in range out to five kilometers thereabouts."

"RHODA, are there any islands or structures on Lieutenant Cortez's current trajectory?" Merriweather asked.

"There is an island 2.7 kilometers east of her current position, Captain

Merriweather."

"That must be where she's heading. Keep transmitting and let me know the moment you reach her. Also, get ready to go get her at the first sign that she's in danger."

"Aye, aye, Cap'n."

"Right now, we have something else to discuss," continued Merriweather. "Dr. Mann, can you tell the crew what you've discovered?"

Dr. Mann slowly stood and flipped on the holo-projector. A few commands later, the pertinent section of the Heran planetary system floated above the crew.

"As most of you know, I was tasked with mapping this system using probes and the Endeavor's onboard sensors." Mann took a deep breath before continuing. "Four days ago, we detected a large asteroid we've designated Alpha-one, coming in from the vicinity of the gas giant, Hypatia-f, or Colossus. My preliminary calculations predicted that, while coming uncomfortably close to Hera, it would miss the planet by about seventy thousand kilometers. I had RHODA rerun the numbers, and she concurred.

"I then looked at where this rock was heading. RHODA, show the predicted trajectory of Alpha-one."

Instantly, a red line showing the asteroid's trajectory appeared in the hologram floating over their heads.

"As you can see, Alpha-one continues on toward the red dwarf, Hypatia-Proxima, circles it, and impacts Hera—here—several months later," said Mann, pointing to the point of impact. "RHODA has upgraded its prediction to a 97.3 percent certainty."

After a few seconds of stony silence, Merriweather stood. "Does anyone have a question?"

"Do we tell them? Are they better not knowing?" asked Mills."

"Tell them what? Do we even know how damaging the impact will be? Is it a mass extinction event?" asked Zoe Bishop.

"RHODA is still modeling the after-impact damage, but the loss of life will be significant," said Mann.

"Should we offer to take some of them on board?" asked Dr. Girard.

"And do what with them?" said Merriweather. "How would we even go about choosing who to ask? We don't know how their species would react to microgravity. I think we should focus our efforts on figuring out how to stop this catastrophe from happening in the first place. Any ideas?"

"How big is the asteroid?" asked Bishop.

"It's about two kilometers wide," said Mann.

"Not as big as Chicxulub," said Mills.

"Chicxulub?" asked Bishop.

"Wiped out the dinosaurs," said Mills.

"Ah, gotcha. I knew that."

"Where will it strike?" said Doc Lee.

"I'll know in a few hours. RHODA is crunching the numbers," said Mann.

"Is there any possibility of deflecting it?" asked Lee.

"Deflect it! With what? It would take a nuke, which we don't have," said the ordinarily reticent Javier Rodriguez.

"You're right, Javi. We don't have a nuke. Maybe we'll bring one on the next trip," said Merriweather. "But we have one thing we could use—Endeavor."

"Endeavor—how?" said Bishop.

"I asked Dr. Mann to compute the energy needed to deflect the asteroid just enough to miss the planet. I also asked him whether a collision with Endeavor would be enough. Herbert?"

"At the captain's direction, I've calculated several scenarios to see if any are workable," said Mann.

Once again, Mann turned to the holo-image floating over their heads.

"RHODA, display *Mann three-one*. As you can see, I've created a collision with Endeavor here when the asteroid is still four months from Hera. Using our main engines and the TAMARAKS, we could attain a velocity of about 65,000 km/h if we left within the next five to seven days.

"Given a successful impact, Alpha one would still miss the planet on its initial flyby, but it would pass by a lot closer. It continues toward Hypatia-Proxima, the red dwarf star, circles it, and intersects Hera's orbit here. However, as you can see, it misses Hera by over twenty thousand kilometers."

"How sure are we?" asked Girard.

"Well, we don't know the surface composition of the asteroid. The calculations assume that it's solid rock, more or less. If it's not—if it's not as dense as we believe—we might not get the deflection we want, meaning we still get a planet impact."

"Where does the crew go—down to the surface?" asked Bishop.

"Right. We would need three volunteers to pilot Endeavor while everyone else remains on Hera," said Merriweather. "The crew would ensure Endeavor is targeting the best impact zone on the asteroid before transferring to the Aries lander. They would then continue in Aries, swing around the gas giant Hypatia-f, and head back to Hera. The trip would take eighteen months."

"Eighteen months! That's a long time in a small lander," said Bishop.

"Is what it is," said Merriweather.

"I'd like to volunteer," said Bridges, speaking through the holoview.

"I thought you might," said Merriweather. "However, before we decide to go through with this plan, everyone must agree, including Cortez. More problematic, we would need to get agreement from the Herans.

"If we go ahead with this, we will leave satellite beacons in orbit around their sun, any rescue spacecraft from Earth could detect. I still expect that ISA will mount a search-and-rescue mission, and they *will* find us."

"You'd sacrifice Endeavor to save them? I thought a captain's job was to protect his or her ship," said Bishop.

Merriweather smiled. "To quote Thomas Aquinas, 'If the highest aim of a captain was to preserve his ship, he would keep it in port forever."

*The Akan's Secluded Island Retreat*

Cortez hadn't known what to expect, but it certainly wasn't this.

The trip to the Akan's secluded island retreat had taken an hour and a half, by Cortez's estimation, and had delivered them to a small, densely forested island about five kilometers from Xanglora. The only evidence of any construction on the island was an ancient stone pier that jutted from the shoreline almost thirty meters into the eastern ocean. Cortez counted a dozen small boats tied up along the dock. To Cortez, these boats looked like pleasure craft. They weren't the fishing and work boats she had seen along the pier where she and Glyvash had disembarked from the Narwa ferry. These boats obviously belonged to important people.

After securing their vessel to the pier, the guards physically escorted Cortez and Glyvash out of the boat and up a stone stairway. Cortez didn't rattle easily, but being shoved along by aliens was not a pleasant experience. They didn't appear to have weapons, but they were surprisingly strong.

While she waited for who knows what, Cortez took inventory of their situation. The guards hadn't harmed her, and she still had her translator, which meant she had a lifeline. She thought about contacting Aries—Milo had tried several times to raise her on her translator—but she was afraid Merriweather intended to pull the plug on her mission, and she didn't want that. However, she couldn't keep ignoring his calls and wanted one more crack at getting through to the Akan. Then, if her mission failed, she promised herself she would contact Milo to come to her rescue.

From her vantage point on the pier, the Akan's island appeared undeveloped. Other than the pier, Cortez could see no artificial structures at all. At the very least, Cortez had expected something grand—some Greek-style columns; an altar; or something that looked like an upscale dwelling. Surely, the all-powerful leader of the planet's largest country could demand something palatial. However, Cortez could see nothing but dense, impenetrable jungle.

"Why does the Akan come here?" whispered Cortez.

"The Council of Eleven and the Akan come here often to conduct official business," said Glyvash. "I also believe that being the Akan is stressful. Do you not think she would come here to rest and meditate?"

"I don't know," said Cortez. "Is the island completely overgrown in jungle?"

"It is said that the island's center is more open, filled with wetlands. I have also heard that the Akan takes her ablution in marsh ponds found on the island."

"Interesting," said Cortez, as her thoughts flashed back to a weekend she had spent in Napa Valley with a few girlfriends. She had reluctantly agreed to a mud bath at one of the hot springs there, but found the experience less than appealing.

"Any idea who belongs to these other boats?"

Glyvash tilted his head as he deciphered Cortez's question.

"Do you wish to know who the other boats belong to?" asked Glyvash.

"Yes," said Cortez. "That."

"I do not know," said Glyvash.

"Where are they taking us?" Cortez asked.

"There must be a temple, a sanctum or other structure deep within the island's heart. Cat, I doubt any Heran male has been here before. I am humbled."

"I'm glad you see something positive in all of this, my friend."

"Stop talking," commanded one of the bigger guards as he motioned Cortez and Glyvash toward a path that disappeared into the dense jungle.

"I guess he wants us to go that way," said Cortez. "After you."

"I am Macduff," whispered Glyvash.

Cortez and her alien friend, bracketed by three palace guards, proceeded single file into the jungle under a darkening sky.

"All we need is the sound of jungle drums beating in the distance," mused Cortez.

"I do not understand," said Glyvash.

"It's nothing," said Cortez. "I…"

Before she could finish the thought, she heard the voice of Milo Bridges in her earpiece.

"Cat, this is Milo. You need to respond if you can. I am under orders to come and get you. If you can hear this, give me some sign."

*Damn*, thought Cortez. Her translator picked up her thought, converted it to the alien's language, and sent it to her vocalizer mouthpiece.

"What does *damn* mean?" asked Glyvash.

"It's nothing. I'll explain later," Cortez said before switching off the vocalizer.

Cortez wasn't ready to report in—nor was she prepared for Bridges to come charging to the rescue on his fiery chariot..

"RHODA, comm-link mode. Aries, this is Cortez. Sorry to keep you in the dark, Milo, but I'm fine, and the mission is proceeding."

With the vocalizer switched off and the system in comm-link mode, Cortez's thoughts were transmitted to the relay drone, which relayed the message to Aries and Milo Bridges.

"Cat, where in the hell are you? Why haven't you reported in?"

"I'm fine, Milo. I'm with Glyvash, and we are on the Akan's private island, approximately five kilometers from the crater's eastern rim. We are meeting with the Akan later this evening."

"Something tells me there's more to the story," said Bridges. "Why have you missed your scheduled reports?"

"I'll fill you in later, Milo. Right now, the important thing is my meeting with the Akan."

"It's not me you'll have to fill in, Cat. Merriweather is not happy. I had to talk him out of launching a rescue mission."

"And I do appreciate that, Milo. I'll smooth things over with the captain once this is finished. But for now, I need you to stay put—if you arrive before I've won the Akan's trust, the entire mission could be at risk."

"All right. I don't like it, but I'll defer. I'll inform the captain. You owe me—big time. Please stay safe."

"I will," said Cortez. "One more thing."

"What's that?" asked Bridges.

"Fire up, Aries. I may need you to come and get me if things go wrong. Cortez out."

# CHAPTER 75

*Intruders*

"What the hell!" Bridges exclaimed.

Cortez could be exasperating. Obviously, she was in the critical phase of her first contact mission, and he had to rely on her assessment of the situation—didn't he? He was worried Cortez would be overconfident. Should he fire up the engines and ride in on a fiery white horse to rescue the damsel in distress and probably piss her off royally, or should he cool his jets and wait for her call?

Suddenly, the ship's AI interrupted Bridges' thoughts.

"Milo, sensors have detected alien life forms approaching approximately fifty meters south."

Bridges' attention immediately pivoted to the com-screen.

"Hmm. Let's see who's paying us a visit," he mumbled.

Bridges toggled on Aries' rear-facing cameras, giving him a clear view of the stream where the ship currently rested. He scanned the display for any unusual movement in the trees lining the shoreline of the shallow stream. However, everything seemed normal. There had been a few close encounters with sophonts since Cortez and Glyvash left for the holy city, but fortunately, none had gotten this close.

"How many, RHODA?"

"There are four sophonts approximately forty-five meters south."

Milo continued to stare at the display. He had gotten somewhat familiar with the area, having explored it for four days straight. The stream where Aries had landed was only ankle deep, making it too shallow to navigate by boat, but relatively easy to walk. It wasn't surprising that locals or hunters would use it as a pathway through the forest. He was fortunate that more sophonts had yet to stumble upon his presence.

Bridges had tried his hand at catching fish from the shallow stream—anything to supplement the bland ready-to-eat rations from Aries' emergency stores—but his efforts ended in miserable failure.

Bridges' thoughts briefly returned to his last conversation with Cortez. While she had tried to exude confidence and calmness, Bridges could also sense a seriousness in her demeanor that told a different story. This weighed on his mind as movement on the com-screen pulled his attention back to his situation.

Suddenly, a party of four aliens rounded the slight bend in the shallow stream about twenty meters south of the ship. To Bridges, it appeared to be three adults and one child, although the child could have been just a very short alien. Given their typical male clothing, Bridges assumed they were male.

"A hunting party, maybe? I don't see any weapons—weapons I recognize, anyway," mumbled Bridges.

As soon as Bridges turned on the ship's external microphones, a cacophony of dolphin-like sounds flooded his headphones. He looked for the bag holding the language translator kit, finally finding it beside his boots. Then suddenly, as if someone had toggled a switch, the squeaking stopped, as did the four aliens.

Bridges flipped on the translator and inserted the earpiece, hoping to eavesdrop on his new Heran visitors. However, they were now completely silent. The aliens stared silently at the strange alien machine blocking their path. To Milo, it seemed they intended to stand there staring forever. Finally, after about 10 seconds, the short one laughed and started running toward Aries, only to be yelled at by another member of the party.

"Stop, Amorack! Do not approach that...that...that thing. It could be dangerous."

Little Amorack did as told and reluctantly returned to the small band of aliens standing in the stream.

One of the taller aliens walked slowly toward the spacecraft, the others following a step behind. They exchanged glances, as they all seemed to be fearful of the strange object. One of the Herans bent down, picked up a rock from the stream bed, then stood and threw it at the spacecraft. The rock bounced off Aries with a muted metallic sound. Another Heran bravely approached the spacecraft, reached out, and touched it.

Bridges had prepared for just such an encounter. Plan "A" was to convince them he was just some eccentric hermit living in some bizarre dwelling he had built. If that didn't work, his plan "B" was to tell them he had quarantined himself because of a highly contagious disease. His last recourse was to fire up the engines and head for another secluded area to hide.

"Who goes there? What do you want? You are intruding on my privacy?" said Bridges through his translator.

Bridges' alien voice booming through Aries' external speakers startled the Heran visitors, causing one to fall backward in the stream and another to turn and run away from the strange object. The four Herans quickly regrouped about ten meters upstream from Aries. The rock thrower picked up another stone from the stream bed and drew back his arm to throw it.

"Why do you attack my home?" shouted Bridges.

"Who is speaking? I do not see you. What is this thing?" shouted back the rock thrower.

"Who I am is my business. This is my home. I built it myself. I do not want visitors. Go away."

"It is a strange home," said the rock thrower.

"It is my home, nonetheless."

"I've never seen a home like this," said the Heran.

"I was an architect," responded Bridges. "People rejected my designs as too strange. They ridiculed me."

The four Herans considered what Bridges had told them, discussing his words quietly between them. Finally, one spoke.

"We will leave you in peace."

Satisfied with Bridges' explanation, the four Herans skirted the strange hermit's home and continued northward away from Aries. Bridges smiled at himself. His plan had worked perfectly. However, he was under no illusions that the scam would always work. The longer he stayed here, the more likely someone would chance upon his spacecraft and the next intruders might not be so easily convinced.

# CHAPTER 76

*Convincing the Akan*

After a forced thirty-minute slog, Cortez, her friend Glyvash, and their three Heran guards emerged from the darkness of the island's junglelike forest into a broad, tree-less interior. The party was at the edge of a sweeping boggy marshland under a slate gray sky and setting red sun. Cortez estimated the bog at a half to three-quarters kilometer across, with large swathes of reed-like grasses waving in the moderate sea breeze, interspersed with wetlands and lakes, teeming with strange four-winged birds. Thousands filled the sky, soaring and diving in unison as if one amorphous organism. A cacophony of squawks and shrieks from the murmuration filled the air, making it difficult to hear.

Did the birds, she wondered, lift their eyes to the aurora as it danced across the heavens? Or were they weaving an aurora of their own in answer? The spectacle was otherworldly, a tapestry of light and wings that stole her breath. In its glow, she heard again the lilt of her mother's voice, reciting a poem from long ago, as if the memory itself had taken flight.

> *In the darkening sky, a dazzling hue,*
> *The aurora dances, a shape-shifting view,*
> *As birds in unison, gracefully slew,*
> *A murmuration's choreography, me, and you.*[7]

In the distance, Cortez could see a strange structure roughly resembling a pile of bubble wrap. Cortez had seen some peculiar building designs before, especially during a working trip to Beijing three years earlier. However, a bubble wrap building was beyond strange.

Surrounding the pile of bubble wrap was a ring of stone columns topped with sculpted female figures.

"I suppose those are statues of Xenosta," said Cortez. She had intended to whisper, forgetting that the vocalizer had but one setting. The volume of sound emanating from the prosthetic startled her. She made a mental note to ask Jonathan Mills to explore the possibility of a new volume feature.

"I believe you are correct, Lieutenant Cat."

"What's the inspiration for the design of the structure?"

"The exterior? I have not seen it before, but I believe it's meant to re-semble the egg mass a Heran female produces. It may be the designer's attempt to represent Xenosta's eggs," said Glyvash. "It is very inspiring. I will remember this moment until my last day."

Cortez could see that Glyvash was emotional.

"Hopefully, that won't be today, my friend," said Cortez, as she placed her hand on his shoulder.

"Quiet!" shouted a guard, prodding Cortez to keep walking.

As the party neared the bubble-wrap temple, Cortez could see a small group of female Herans standing near what appeared to be an entrance. Suddenly Glyvash shouted, "Your Primacy, Your Primacy. Cat, see there? It is my supervisor and my friend, Dakar Dualla."

"Be silent," shouted the nearest guard as he shoved Glyvash to the ground.

Cortez quickly helped her friend to his feet, giving the guard a menac-ing glare. The guard ignored Cortez's stare, gesturing for the group to keep moving. Together, Cortez and Glyvash proceeded as directed toward the group of Heran females.

As they approached the group, one of the Heran females walked forward to meet them. "Glyvash, what are you doing here?"

"We have come to find you, Your Primacy. Are you well?"

"No, I am not, Glyvash. I told her about the flying machine and the object we saw through our telescope. I thought I could convince her, but she was angry. I'm afraid of what she might do. She's coming here tonight."

Then she added as an afterthought. "You came to find me?"

Dualla's eyes flicked from the guard who had thrown Glyvash to the ground, back to her friend. Her voice trembled between shock and relief. "How are you here?"

"Cat and I entered the temple without permission. We found your secret entrance and…"

"Cat? Who is Cat?" asked Dualla.

Glyvash smiled at his boss.

"Your Primacy, I am honored to introduce you to Lieutenant Cat from Earth."

With that simple introduction, Cortez stepped forward and extended her hand.

Of course, handshaking was not the custom for Herans. Dualla simply stared at this new peculiar-looking female.

"My name is Lieutenant Cortez, and I've come a very, very long way to meet you, Dakar Dualla."

Dualla was confused. First, she had not expected to see Glyvash here, on the Akan's private estate no less. Second, it was unheard of for a male to introduce a female, and usually, females took the lead.

"Cortez? I do not recognize that family name. Where is—Earth?"

Cortez smiled at Dualla. It was time for the big reveal. Slowly, Cortez lowered her garment's hood. Next, she peeled off the latex skullcap she had worn for the last four days. The cool air felt good on her recently shorn head as she rubbed the four-day growth of stubble.

Watching Dualla's reaction, Cortez carefully peeled off the nasal prosthetic Doc Lee had applied four days earlier.

"What is this?" Dualla asked, taking a step backward. "Who—what are you?"

"She's proof that you were correct," said Glyvash, grinning from ear to ear.

Dualla looked at Glyvash and then back to Cortez. She opened her mouth, but no sound emerged.

Cortez slowly peeled the fake frills attached to the sides of her neck.

"I have traveled a long way to meet you, Dakar Dualla. My friend Glyvash said you saw my ship with your new telescope. That's why you are here, correct—to convince your Akan of the existence of visitors from the stars?"

Dualla again looked at Glyvash. "Is she—?"

"Yes," replied Glyvash. "I have been inside her vessel. She calls it a 'space ship.' It is the same flying machine that flew over our heads when we were trying to discover its—her—landing place."

"And you have been inside it?"

"Yes, your Primacy."

"Glyvash has been my guide ever since I arrived on your planet," said Cortez. "I am from a planet we call Earth. I am traveling with a small scientific team, searching for other intelligent species."

Dualla stared at Cortez, seemingly unable to speak. Finally, she said, "There are others?"

"Yes. Most of them are in a ship in orbit around your planet."

Dualla glanced at the sky and then back to Cortez.

"Orbit ... most of them?"

"One of my crewmates is nearby in our lander—the flying machine you saw."

Dualla looked up, still in shock. However, she still managed to smile at Cortez.

Suddenly, as if she had just remembered where she was, Dualla turned to look at the other Heran females who had respected her privacy and kept their distance.

"Councilors, please come greet our new visitor," she said as she excitedly waved the others over. "This is our new friend, Loo…"

"Cat," interrupted Cortez. "Call me 'Cat.'"

"Cat from Earth—the planet Earth," said Glyvash, beaming.

"Yes, Cat from the planet Earth," said Dualla smiling broadly.

#  CHAPTER 77

*Confrontation*

*Thank God the Guards didn't search me*, thought Cortez.

As the Heran guards turned their attention toward the approaching councilors, Cortez used their distraction to retrieve the portable holo-projector from the hidden pocket of her robe. She needed to persuade the Akan and her councilors that she was who she claimed to be. She would have to rely on Earth technology if she couldn't convince the Akan with her words.

The female Heran scientist, Dakar Zaru Dualla, enthusiastically accepted the idea of alien species from other worlds. However, the Heran councilors were more skeptical.

*It's show and tell time*, thought Cortez, as she switched on the projector.

Cortez watched the reaction of the doubting Herans as a four-meter hologram of their solar system popped into existence and was now floating all around them. Several cried out, and all of them quickly retreated in fear. Even the Heran guards moved away from the floating illusion.

"Don't be afraid," said Cortez. "There's nothing to be afraid of. It won't harm you." Cortez waved her arm through the image. "See, it's perfectly safe."

The Akan's councilors were unconvinced. Then Zaru Dualla slowly moved toward Cortez, raised her arms above her head, and waved them through the hologram as Cortez had done.

"It is, as she says. It is like smoke. See, it does not harm me," said Dualla, looking at the other Herans.

"It is technology," added Glyvash. "The Earth female has technology we do not have."

"Dualla and Glyvash are correct," said Cortez. "It is just technology."

Turning again to the hologram.

"This is Hera," began Cortez, pointing at the blue-green dot floating over her head. "This is your red sun, and here is your yellow sun. The red line is my ship's trajectory through your system. We were here when we detected your planet's media transmissions. The small dot here is our ship's current position."

Cortez saw their doubts slip away. Some looked worried, while others seemed excited. Dualla was downright giddy as she peppered Cortez with questions.

"There will be time to answer all your questions later, Dakar Dualla. As I've said, we are scientists seeking other civilizations and would like to…" Cortez stopped mid-sentence. Something had changed. The excitement and sense of wonder she had seen in the faces of Zaru Dualla and the Council members were gone, replaced by something else. Reading the expressions of these Herans wasn't easy, she thought. Was it anger—fear? Cortez also felt like someone or something else was watching her. Slowly, Cortez turned.

Standing less than three meters away from Cortez was the Akan herself, with a phalanx of her palace guards surrounding her. In all the excitement, Cortez had been unaware of the Akan's arrival.

Slowly, the holy leader of Xerelang glided forward and circled Cortez like a predator stalking its prey. Glyvash, Dualla, and the councilors timidly backed away, leaving Cortez alone to face the Akan's wrath.

"I will not have you telling lies to my councilors."

Cortez might have been more frightened by the alien's words if the Akan's eyes focused on her. Instead, the Akan was glaring at the hologram floating above her Councilors.

"What is this sorcery?" exclaimed the Akan. "Who are you, and what do you want?"

*Is that fear?* thought Cortez. The last thing Cortez wanted was to instill fear in the Akan. The next few minutes would decide the success or failure of her mission.

"Your Holiness," Cortez bowed her head slightly in deference. "I am but a traveler, a visitor to your beautiful planet, and a scientist like your Dakar Dualla. I am traveling with a small group of scientists from a planet we call Earth. We are explorers looking for other intelligent lifeforms with whom we can communicate. We are no threat to you."

"No threat? Of course, you are a threat," hissed the Akan. "You are a threat to everything we believe. You would pollute our culture, blaspheme our religion. I do not believe you. What you say is impossible. Xenosta gave us dominion over all the stars in the sky. You are just a mutant seeking attention. What you speak is blasphemy."

Turning to her guards, she commanded, "Take that device."

"Your Holiness, I am not alone," said Cortez. "Look there, in the eastern sky."

Cortez pointed toward the east, just above the horizon. A pinpoint of light, visible against the background of stars, was moving toward the west.

"That is one of our starships. More of my fellow scientists are there. There is also a starship nearby. That is how I landed on your planet. I can prove who I say I am."

The Akan watched the strange light for several minutes before speaking.

"That is most likely a sign from Xenosta warning us of your lies. However, if you are..."

The Akan paused and turned her gaze once again toward the light in the sky moving against the background of stars. She then turned toward the hologram, still floating in the air as if by magic. Finally, she turned to face Cortez. "We do not want you here."

"We ask for nothing, Your Holiness. We want only to meet you—to learn about your people."

"Your Holiness," interjected Zaru Dualla, "their visit is of immense scientific importance. We could learn so much."

"Quiet, child. I've heard enough from you."

The Akan glared at Cortez, who no longer saw fear in the Akan's eyes. Instead, the fear had turned to hate—or maybe sadness. It was difficult to decipher their facial expressions.

"You say you are no threat," said the Akan. "What if I tell you we want no contact with you?"

"No!" shouted Dualla.

"Quiet child," said the Akan, with a voice now softer and more forgiving.

"What if we tell you to leave?" She repeated.

"Then we will leave," said a disappointed Cortez.

"We want you to leave. That is what we want."

Cortez nodded her head.

"As you wish. I will have to call my ship to retrieve me."

Cortez turned off her vocalizer with her tongue and silently mouthed the words, "RHODA, transmit the following; emergency channel, Cortez to Aries. Come and get me, Milo."

Milo Bridges was of two minds about his prolonged stay on Hera. He was happy to be free of the relatively cramped spaces of the Endeavor spacecraft, his home for the last two-plus years. In addition, he couldn't imagine a more idyllic location than the one where he now found himself: a beautiful stream flowing through a dense sub-tropical-like forest; beautiful summer weather; stunning aurorae putting on a light show the likes of which few people on Earth had ever seen.

Waiting gnawed at him. Ever since Cortez had motored off with that little alien, Glyvash, Bridges had been on edge, expecting a message—any message—telling him to come fetch her. But the silence dragged on, and he hated every moment.

Bridges tried to put it out of his mind as he performed other tasks on-planet, but the feeling of impending doom kept invading his thoughts. *Was she OK? Was she safe? Was she too stubborn to ask for help?* Bridges already knew the answer. A resounding *YES!* And that worried him.

The only antidote for his rising anxiety was time spent outside doing every physical chore he could think of. Bridges occupied most of his time preparing for departure. He set up the PEME unit, which split water from the shallow stream flowing under Aries into hydrogen and oxygen gases. The cryogenic unit lowered the temperature of the gases to produce the liquids needed to fill the spacecraft's fuel tanks. The Sabatier unit was creating fuel for Aries' air-breathing engines. He installed four solid-fuel booster rockets, additional power the lander would need to climb out of Hera's deep gravity well and into orbit. He spent the last few days loading the cargo bay with various possible food stocks and other biological samples for Doc Graham and Doc Lee to analyze. Bridges had even bathed in the cold mountain stream—his first bath in two years. He was running out of things to keep himself busy. He hated waiting.

Therefore, when Cortez's call came in, Bridges was more than happy. He was ecstatic. The problem was that he was far from Aries when he received her call.

Earlier in the day, while foraging for biological samples, he discovered a fruit-laden bush about five hundred meters west of the lander. It was the first bush with this strange-looking fruit he had seen, and this was just the type of biological sample he was looking for. Therefore, he had picked three or four of the coral-colored fruit to include with all the other samples he had collected over the last four days.

However, after returning to Aries, his stomach rumbling and in much need of filling, Bridges had sampled one of the alien fruit samples he would later learn were called *moke*. He had been eating only MREs (Meals Ready to Eat) for the last four days and was frankly sick of them. So, despite the warning from Doc Lee to avoid eating any indigenous flora or fauna before she could test them, Bridges decided to chance it.

Twenty minutes later, having polished off all four mokies, Bridges returned to the forest to find the moke bush and collect more of its delicious fruit.

He had just finished picking the moke bush clean when Cortez's call came in.

"Cortez to Aries One. Come and get me, Milo."

Milo dropped his sack of samples and pumped his fist, yelling, "YES!"

"RHODA, transmit the following to Lieutenant Cortez's neural interface. Aries to Cortez. I'm on my way. Are you OK?"

A few seconds later...

"I'm fine, Milo. There's a dry spot just to the north of my location. Land there, lower the ramp, and wait inside Aries."

"Wait inside? Why?"

"Just wait inside. I'll explain later."

"I'll be there as soon as I can, Cat. It's good to hear from you."

*I guess I don't get to meet the Akan*, Bridges thought. *But if Cat says wait inside, I'll wait inside.*

Bridges tied off the bag of moke fruit, slung it over his shoulder and headed back toward the Aries.

Bridges had gone only about a hundred meters when suddenly, a distant sound caught his attention, causing him to freeze in his tracks. It was a sound he had heard before. "RHODA, scan the area for Herans or any sophont lifeforms."

A second later, RHODA replied, "There are four Heran lifeforms four hundred meters east of your location."

"How close to Aries?" asked Bridges.

"The four Herans are within ten meters of Aries One."

"Damn," Bridges exclaimed.

Bridges doubled his pace, careful not to step in a hole or trip over a tree root, of which there were many. The narrow forest footpath meandered through the forest, branching off in countless directions. It would be easy to follow the wrong fork and get lost, or at the very least, delayed.

Bridges constantly referred to his handheld communicator as he followed Aries' tracker beacon. He was glad he had remembered to enable the beacon before venturing away from his spacecraft.

After covering three hundred of the four hundred meters, Bridges stopped again and asked RHODA for another update. Unfortunately, the aliens were still there.

The yellow sun had already slipped below the horizon, leaving only the dim red sun and the aurora's ghostly shimmer to light the sky. Bridges killed his flashlight, the darkness closing in around him—better unseen than discovered. He stood perfectly still, forcing himself to wait while his eyes strained to adjust to the gloom.

After a few minutes, with night vision restored, Bridges again moved toward the wide spot in the stream where Aries was resting. The thickness of the ground cover and the forest's darkness gave Bridges some sense of security as he approached the clearing. Ten meters from the stream, he froze. Through a gap in the dense ground cover, he spotted a Heran, who, fortunately, was not facing in his direction. Instead, the alien had his hands pressed against the side of the Aries lander. He was saying something, but Bridges had not taken his translator kit with him on his foray to the moke bush. He couldn't communicate with the aliens even if he wanted to.

Keeping low to the ground, Bridges inched ever closer to the edge of the clearing until he had an unobstructed view of all four aliens. One alien seemed determined to get the attention of any spacecraft occupants by screeching and banging on the side of the ship. Another had climbed to the top of the LAV and was looking for a way inside. The third and fourth aliens seemed content to stand back and watch the other two. A constant stream of dolphin-like sounds filled the air.

*Those are the same aliens that were here before*, thought Bridges. *They didn't buy my story after all*.

Bridges lay flat on the forest floor, peering out through a small gap in the ground cover. He assumed they wouldn't be able to see him, but that was a big assumption, given that he knew nothing about their visual acuity. There was nothing Bridges could do now but try to wait them out. They had to leave sometime, right?

Thirty minutes later, the aliens were still there, and Bridges was still waiting. His anxiety level and probably his heart rate were through the roof. Bridges' thoughts focused on Cortez's last transmission. *Come and get me, Milo?* That sounded like things could have gone better. It sounds as if something is terribly wrong. "Stay in the lander? That sounds like I'm her getaway driver, and she's just bungled a bank heist," said Bridges. "Damn. She needs me, and I'm stuck here. I've gotta do something."

# CHAPTER 78

*Where the hell was Bridges?*

Cortez was in trouble. She had tried her best to convince the Akan of her peaceful intentions—that Hera had nothing to fear from the Earthlings—but the Akan was having none of it. Cortez hadn't given up, but she thought an orderly retreat was advisable. Maybe when the Akan had time to think about it, she would change her mind. Therefore, Cortez had no choice but to send for help.

There was now nothing to do but wait. *Where is he?* She thought. Milo sure is taking his own sweet time in getting here.

Cortez believed at first that the Akan was going to let her go. Now, however, she wasn't so sure. It appeared to Cortez that the more the Akan considered what to do about her and the other invaders from space, the angrier she got. Dualla and her teacher, Councilor Krei Dualla, had spoken to the Akan, urging her to let the unknown visitors stay, calling attention to all the advanced technology they could introduce to Xerelang and the answers to the big scientific questions they could provide.

However, the Akan was immovable. "The knowledge these invaders have could decimate Heran culture," she argued. "Beings from an advanced civilization from space could prove an existential threat to Heran religious belief," something the Akan could not and would not risk.

Reluctantly, Cortez understood the Akan's concern. What if the situation were reversed? What if advanced beings from space showed up on Earth's doorstep? How would Earth respond? How would ET's (extraterrestrials) arrival impact the various religions of Earth? It wasn't a totally irrational fear.

Cortez's mind flickered back to one of her "first contact" courses at the Academy that covered that possibility.

Her instructors taught that the shock of another intelligent species would negatively affect a society with a state religion or lack of religious diversity, such as found on Hera, more than it would on Earth. Her class had studied Lucian of Samosata, who wrote about first contact in the second century in his novel *True History*. Lucian's novel recounts his trip to the moon, where he discovers beings on the moon who are at war with beings of the sun.

She had also read H.G. Wells' 1896 novel *War of the Worlds* and British author Arthur C. Clarke's 1968 novel 2001: *A Space Odyssey*, which foretold an advanced species that had mastered space and time and had directed human evolution.

There was consensus in her Academy class that many religions on Earth could incorporate the discovery of *others* into their belief systems. Some, for example, the Church of Jesus Christ of Latter-day Saints, had already done so.

The counterargument would seem to buttress the Akan's worst fears. Thomas Paine wrote in his 1794 Age of Reason that multiple worlds render Christianity at once little and ridiculous and scatters it in the mind like feathers in the air.

*All of that is academic, of course*, thought Cortez, and none of that was evidence that the same applied to Hera. Endeavor had yet to identify religions other than the one that seemed to dominate Xerelang. There appeared little evidence that they would tolerate such flexibility in their beliefs.

Cortez's friend, Glyvash and the female Dakar Dualla, seemed to accept the idea, but then again, they were scientists. From Cortez's vantage point, half the Council members favored human visitation, while half did not. None of that mattered, of course, since it was the Akan's decision, and she was openly hostile to the idea.

*Where in the hell is Bridges?* She thought.

Bridges had hoped the aliens would quickly tire of their investigation of the Aries lander and leave the area, but that was not the case. In fact, two of the aliens had busied themselves collecting firewood and had built a small campfire. The other two were erecting tents next to the stream. It appeared the aliens were here to stay, at least overnight.

*This is a disaster. I can't wait any longer. Cat could be in serious trouble. Desperate times call for desperate measures*, thought Bridges.

"RHODA," he whispered. "Broadcast an ultrasonic sound wave through the ship's exterior speakers. Set the frequency at twenty-five kilohertz and the decibel level at a hundred and fifty."

Bridges waited for any response from the aliens, but there didn't seem to be any. He heard nothing, but he didn't expect to. Humans couldn't hear frequencies over about twenty kilohertz.

Bridges recalled reading one of Cortez's reports about how Herans detected sound using small patches of hair on the sides of their necks, and that reminded him of the way some insects detected sound. Then he remembered how his grandpa used radio-frequency sound emitters to discourage termites and other insects that might want to chomp on his farmhouse. *Why not employ the same strategy here*, Bridges thought?

"RHODA, are you broadcasting over the ship's speakers?

"Affirmative, Lieutenant Bridges."

"OK, increase the frequency to thirty kilohertz and the decibel level to one seventy-five."

Almost instantly, Bridges noticed a difference in the activity around the campfire.

*That got their attention*, thought Bridges. The aliens had all stood and looked around as if confused about something.

"RHODA, increase the frequency to forty kilohertz."

Something was agitating the four Herans. One even picked up a stone and hurled it angrily at the spaceship, watching it clank harmlessly off the ship into the stream. The sound was obviously affecting the aliens, and not in a good way. Bridges could see that they were experiencing a bit of discomfort, holding their necks like humans might cover their ears. He didn't want to harm them, but he wanted them to vacate the area. After a few more minutes of agitated movements, the four Herans put more distance between themselves and the injurious noise from the spacecraft.

"Damn. It's working," whispered Bridges.

Once Bridges determined the intruders were far enough away, he sprang from his hiding place and sprinted to the spacecraft.

"RHODA, open the pilot hatch."

The small cockpit hatch on the forward bulkhead swung open just as Bridges reached the craft. Grasping the exterior handles on either side of the hatch, Bridges pulled himself up and into Aries.

"RHODA, close the hatch and discontinue the ultrasonic broadcast." He didn't want to risk causing the aliens more damage from the high-pitched sound.

"Can't believe that worked," said Bridges. "Let's get this show on the road."

Aries' four engine pods erupted minutes later with a deafening roar. The lander, engulfed in a cloud of steam from the boiling water flowing beneath the spacecraft, slowly lifted off from its home for the last four days.

"That should give them something to tell their hunting buddies about," said Bridges as he piloted Aries toward the east and Cat Cortez.

# CHAPTER 79

*Goodbye and Troubling News*

Glyvash was the first to see the lights of Aries' jet engines approaching from the west, while Dakar Dualla, her teacher Councilor Krei Dualla, and the other councilors, focused their attention on the drama unfolding ten meters away. The Earthling Cortez was pleading her case while the Akan was, for the most part, ignoring her. The Akan's complement of palace guards had surrounded the Earth female, and it looked like they were about to take her away to face an unknown fate.

Glyvash was also watching fretfully and very worried for his new Earth friend. He knew that her fate might hinge on her fellow space traveler, Lieutenant Bridges. So Glyvash kept one eye fixed toward the quickly darkening skies to the west, looking for signs of the Earthlings' spaceship.
Suddenly, there it was—a bright point of light just over the western horizon, rising quickly and moving eastward. Glyvash knew at once it was the Earth ship.

"Look!" Glyvash shouted, trying to get Dualla's attention. "Up there—just above the horizon—a flying vessel."

"Where?" said an excited Dualla, now looking skyward at the fast-approaching object.

"Your Holiness," shouted Dualla, excitedly pointing toward the western sky. "The alien's space vehicle is coming—there—that bright light.

The Akan jerked her head toward Dualla with a menacing scowl, obviously displeased and surprised that anyone would have the audacity to shout at her. However, once the meaning of Dualla's words registered, she turned to the western sky, where she quickly located the bright object speeding toward them. Almost instantly, the roar of Aries' engines reached her ears.

"Guards!" she shouted. The Akan's guards quickly responded by surrounding their leader, leaving Cortez unguarded.

"There's no danger, Your Holiness," said Cortez, once again painfully aware that her mouth vocalizer had no volume control. "My colleague has come because I summoned him. I told him I was unharmed. He will do you and your guards no harm. He is a scientist like me," she added as if that might allay the Akan's concern.

The Akan did not respond, and Cortez wasn't even sure she had heard her. However, to Cortez, the sight and sound of a flying machine spitting fire appeared almost too much for the Heran leader.

Dualla leaned toward her friend Glyvash and spoke loud enough to be heard over the roar.

"Is that the flying machine we saw near our observatory?"

"The very one that flew over our heads—yes, it is," answered Glyvash. "I have been inside," he added, beaming with pride.

"I—I am envious, Glyvash."

"The Earthlings will show you their vehicle, if you desire it so," he replied.

"I desire it."

Then Dualla added.

"Glyvash, you were fearless to travel alone with the Earthling."

Glyvash beamed. "I am a scientist. We risk all for science?"

"Yes, my friend. Yes, we do."

Glyvash beamed with pride. His employer, Dakar Dualla, had called him *friend*.

As Aries approached the patch of dry, level grassland Cortez had described when she radioed for help, Bridges flared the ship, swiveled the landing pods downward, and fired the four rockets. The spaceship slowed and then, for a moment, hovered motionless ten meters above the surface. The assembled crowd watched in awe as the alien craft settled to the ground, producing a cloud of dust and steam.

As the ship touched down, its wings folded backward like a grasshopper, and its engines shut down. Finally, as requested—more like ordered—Milo lowered the cargo bay ramp and waited for Cortez's next move.

Cortez was still trying to salvage her diplomatic mission, and a bit of deference never hurt. However, she wasn't going to wait for the Akan to sic her guards on her. Walking briskly, Cortez covered the fifty meters between herself and Aries in less than a minute.

Arriving at the Aries lander, Cortez glanced back over her shoulder at the crowd of onlookers before climbing the cargo bay ramp and entering the ship.

No one knew what to expect next. Were the aliens leaving? Were they coming back?

Councilor Krei Dualla approached the Akan. "Your Holiness, have you thought about what the aliens might do if they leave?"

"What do you mean?"

"If Your Holiness tells them to go—that they are not welcomed—"

"The Earth female said they would leave," said the Akan, admitting for the first time the truth of Cortez's claim.

"True, but the Belorians could welcome them," said Councilor Dualla. "Belore would benefit from all the advanced technology the visitors possess."

The Akan was quiet for almost a full minute before responding.

"The people would panic if I let them stay, and they would begin to question the wisdom of Xenosta."

"Maybe not, Your Holiness. Look around. Your councilors are not panicking, and this male, Glyvash, is not panicking. Your subjects may accept this as part of Xenosta's offering to us if you present it to them in this way."

The Akan turned to Glyvash, who was watching a few yards away. "You... come!" She commanded.

Glyvash meekly approached. "Yes, Your Holiness."

"You were with the alien female in the temple."

"Yes, I traveled with her from the Science Center in Whoville. She came to the observatory looking for Dakar Dualla. We spent four days together, traveling to Xanglora."

The Akan looked up. "There's another space vessel—up there?"

"Yes. We saw it through our new telescope, Your Holiness."

For a moment, the Akan seemed lost in thought.

"I will hear what the Earthlings have to say," she said, dismissing Glyvash with a wave of her hand.

It was fifteen minutes before the female Earthling reappeared from the space vessel and walked down the cargo ramp, followed closely by another, somewhat taller Earthling. They were both dressed in strange clothing. Wearing their dress uniforms and now devoid of any alien disguise, Lieutenants Cortez and Bridges walked toward the gathering of Herans and their leader, the Holy Akan.

"How do you want to play this, Cat?"

"We tell them," Cortez replied. "They either believe it or they don't, but they deserve to know the truth."

Reaching the cluster of Herans, Cortez stopped in front of the Heran leader. For the first time, the Akan could see how alien this Earth female was. Cortez had removed the skullcap she had worn for the last four and a half days and was now wearing one of the fake wigs Lee had given her. She also wore her ISA cap adorned with her lieutenant's insignia. The long tunic was gone, as were the markings on her neck. She had also removed the contact lenses that had mimicked Heran eyes.

"Your Holiness, this is fellow officer Lieutenant Milo Bridges."

The Akan barely acknowledged Bridges, keeping her eyes fixed on Cortez.

"We will leave as you ask," continued Cortez. "However, first, I must inform you of some troubling information we have uncovered."

Two weeks later on Hera, Captain Merriweather and his crew gathered in the captain's tent to watch Endeavor's departure on the holoview display. High above Xanglora, the ship hung in geosynchronous orbit, a skeleton crew aboard. Their mission was simple in concept but brutal in execution—intercept and, if possible, deflect the massive asteroid racing toward the planet. The odds were slim. Failure meant millions of Herans would die.

Those remaining behind on Hera said their farewells to Stoner, Bridges, and Lee, and watched in silence as Endeavor slipped out of orbit for the last time.

Merriweather had wanted to go himself, but his duty was clear: he had to remain on the surface to establish the outpost. Choosing who would fly the perilous mission had been agonizing. He could have sent Endeavor unmanned—RHODA was more than capable of flying the ship—but in the event of mechanical failure, only human hands could replace parts or swap out modules. And a one-person crew was out of the question. Health, both medical and psychological, had to be monitored.

That was why he chose Lee over Cortez. Cat had already forged trust with the Herans, especially their leader, the Akan. Pulling her away from that fragile relationship could jeopardize the entire first-contact effort.

Merriweather refused to dwell on the possibility of failure. None of them did. The team on Hera had to keep working as though their friends on Endeavor would succeed. "We have a mission of our own," Merriweather reminded them. "First contact. Earth's future on Hera depends on us, asteroid or no asteroid."

After a week of delicate negotiations, the Akan finally granted permission for the Earth crew to transfer down—but only to her island. She was still wary of how knowledge of the newcomers might affect her people.

It took half a dozen shuttle trips to ferry personnel and supplies from Endeavor, but at last the camp was established. By unanimous vote, the crew named it Outpost Swenson, in honor of their fallen comrade, Dutch Swenson.

Three months later, the settlement still looked more like a high-tech tent city than a colony, dominated by rows of mylar shelters. But Jonathan Mills was determined to change that. Using a massive 3D printer of his own design, he began fabricating permanent structures from crushed regolith hauled up from the beaches. The crew shifted equipment into the first completed building while Mills, tireless, pressed on with construction of a larger one.

# CHAPTER 80

*Four Months Later—Onboard Endeavor*

On Endeavor, time was swiftly dwindling before the anticipated collision that could mean salvation for an entire planet.

"Our target has a few satellites of its own," said Stoner. "I count upwards of fourteen objects."

Stoner shifted his gaze from the holoview to his young acting first officer as if expecting a reply.

"That's interesting," said Bridges, looking up from his console's holoview "Um. You know, that gives me an idea."

Bridges turned to face his commander. "We could use those objects to measure the target's density."

Stoner nodded thoughtfully. "A gravity map?"

"Yep," Bridges replied. "We could do a gravity study based on the motion of those satellites."

"Great minds think alike, Lieutenant. I've never done a gravity study. What do you need?"

"Just a few hours of RHODA's time," said Bridges. "I'll get started on it and let you know as soon as I have results."

"We only have a few hours, so make them count, Lieutenant."

"We have a message coming in," interrupted Doc Lee.

"They're a bit early," said Stoner. "OK, Doc, let's hear what they've got."

Lee activated the communication system using a series of hand gestures. A few seconds later, Captain Merriweather's voice boomed over the ship's speakers.

"Stone, Jennifer, Milo, I'm a bit early, but with the clock counting down, I wanted to touch on a few things. First, I just got a request from the Akan for an update on our progress."

"That'd be a first," said Stoner.

Stoner's reply was not intended for Merriweather. The speed of light limitation meant that communications from Hera took about four minutes one way, given their current distance. Any response would also take four minutes. Knowing it would take eight minutes plus to get an answer to a question, protocol called for Endeavor to wait for Merriweather's entire transmission before responding.

Merriweather continued. "The Akan traveled down to the Whoville observatory for the first time and got to see our uninvited guest firsthand. Seeing that massive rock through their telescope finally removed any doubt she might have had. She's now feeling a sense of urgency.

"Her Holiness has requested, and I've agreed, for herself and the entire council to watch a video feed of the impact. So, make sure you've got everything set up and checked out. There are no do-overs, so no technical glitches—understood.

"On a diplomatic front, the Akan has reluctantly agreed to let us leave the island on brief excursions but always accompanied by one of her councilors. We're also not allowed to have one-on-one conversations with the locals and no talking about religious issues. She's paranoid about that.

"Of course, we insisted that we be allowed to warn other countries about the asteroid, so Cortez and Rodriguez are currently in Belore. Their mission is going so well that they've delayed their return by a few weeks. They are following your progress from there.

"The Belorian government, unlike Xerelang, has been highly transparent with its citizens and has told them about our arrival and the threat posed by the asteroid. Their leader has been much more open to our presence than the Akan. They're already beginning to build shelters in their population centers, just in case our mission fails. In contrast to the restrictions placed on the media here, the Belorian media has received a full briefing and is even broadcasting your progress.

"Cortez is also negotiating future visits for Mann, Girard, and Graham. Belorian scientists are eager to meet them. Bishop also wants to go check the country out. I've agreed to let her go. Of course, that may depend on what happens today.

"Oh, before I forget, have you made any progress estimating the object's density? I was thinking about our last communication. Have you thought about a gravity study? Of course, that depends on whether the object has any satellites. Check it out.

"And Stone, everyone down here is rooting for you, so good luck. Over and out," said Merriweather, ending the transmission.

Stoner paused for a moment before speaking. "RHODA, begin transmission."

"Aries to Camp Swenson. Stoner here.

"Your transmission received and acknowledged, Captain. Mission status remains nominal. Currently, Endeavor is 1.4 million kilometers from Alpha One with an estimated time to impact just over fifteen hours. Our last course correction was six hours ago, refining the projected impact zone to an area less than fifty meters.

"We plan to evacuate Endeavor at approximately 23:00 hours, about twelve hours from now.

"Aries One has undergone thorough diagnostics over the past two weeks, and all systems are operational. She's fully fueled and stocked and will be ready when it's time, Captain.

"We like your gravity study idea. We'll get right on that," said Stoner, grinning at Bridges.

"Suck up," said Bridges, smiling that big toothy grin of his.

Stoner smiled at his young lieutenant before continuing.

"RHODA predicts a velocity change post-impact of approximately eight to ten meters per second. We only need a little over four, so anything over five would be great. However, as you know, it all depends on the object's density. If it's just an enormous pile of sand, it could absorb the energy of the impact and not change velocity at all. So, we're hoping for a big ole chunk of solid rock. But you know all of that.

"We'll commence video transmission about twenty minutes before impact. Wish us luck. Over and out.

"RHODA, end transmission.

"Well, guys, it's going to be a hectic day tomorrow. If you want to grab a quick siesta, you have my permission. I'll take the first watch."

Twelve hours later, with the three crewmembers buckled into their seats, Lieutenant Bridges slowly backed the Aries lander away from its docking port on Endeavor's starboard side for the last time.

"Anyone else feeling a little sad?" asked Bridges.

"Think of the lives she'll save if this works, Milo," said Stoner. "Can't think of a more fitting epitaph for that venerable old spacecraft."

"I'm sad that I'm going to be crammed into this sardine can for the next year and a half with you two idiots," chimed in Doc Lee.

"Well, this idiot has work to do," said Bridges. With a final glance back at Endeavor, Bridges fired Aries' rear thrusters, moving the spacecraft, with the EX-23 booster attached, away from Endeavor, their home for the last three years.

"Move us out to about ten thousand kilometers, Lieutenant," said Stoner. "We should be able to get a good look at the impact from that distance without putting ourselves at risk."

"I'm not sure I want to watch," said Lee. "It's like watching a tornado blow up your home."

"I hear you, Jen. However, you need to watch," said Stoner. "The captain will probably ask each of us for a report."

"Well, I might close my eyes," she replied.

An hour and a half later, Don Stoner, Milo Bridges and Jennifer Lee stared transfixed at their holoviews, and waited silently for the impending collision.

"Thirty seconds to impact," said Bridges.

Each crew member's holoview displayed the feed from Aries' long-range optical telescope and Endeavor's forward-facing camera video.

"Twenty seconds," said Bridges.

"Are we transmitting the feed to Hera?" Lee asked.

"For the last twenty minutes, Jen," said Stoner.

"Ten seconds," said Bridges.

The video from Endeavor's forward cameras showed the fast-approaching asteroid growing quickly in its field of view. As the crew watched, counting down silently to zero, the video feed from Endeavor abruptly stopped as a bright flash of light and a cloud of dust rose over the impact area on the asteroid.

"It's a lot less dramatic without sound," said Lee.

"I still have a lump in my throat," said Bridges.

"She was my first command," said Stoner, "as short as it was. How do you think I feel?"

"She certainly lived up to her reputation," said Bridges.

"Agreed. And then some," said Stoner. "However, our mission isn't over. We still have to get back to Hera. How sure are you of our new trajectory and delta-v requirements?"

"I did the calculations in my head," said Bridges.

"You what?"

"Just kidding, Stone. RHODA blessed the numbers," said a grinning Bridges.

Lee let out a hearty laugh.

"Very well, you have my permission to get us to hell out of here."

"Aye, aye, Cap'n. Everyone strapped in?"

Bridges received a nod from both his crewmates before giving RHODA the command to fire the EX-23 Booster rocket.

"RHODA, execute mission-plan Hypatia-f."

# CHAPTER 81

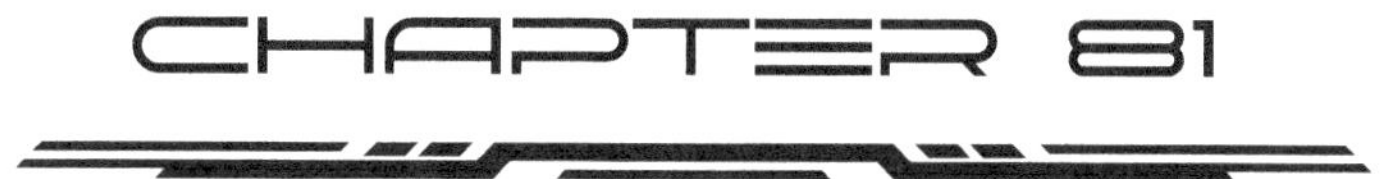

*Diplomacy*

Merriweather emerged from his tent and made his way toward the mess, craving his morning caffeine. Hera's higher gravity weighed on his fifty-six-year-old bones, and the Heran sleeping mat beneath him each night was no substitute for his bunk aboard Endeavor. Only Zoe Bishop's companionship made the arrangements bearable.

Jonathan Mills had begun to make progress with his improvised 3D printer, but Merriweather doubted permanent quarters would be ready for at least two months. Until then, he endured.

Four months earlier, the Akan had reluctantly permitted Cortez and Bridges to remain on Hera until Heran scientists confirmed the asteroid threat. Only after that did she allow Bridges to return to Endeavor and bring Merriweather down to the surface. Since then, the captain had been locked in near-constant negotiation with the Akan and her Council of Eleven.

It hadn't taken him long to realize the Heran leader's deepest concern: the effect knowledge of space travelers might have on her people's beliefs. A devout follower of Xenosta, she held fast to the teaching that Herans were the chosen children of her god. The arrival of Earthlings threatened that truth.

The Council, however, was divided. Some members argued the strangers had been sent by Xenosta herself to save Hera. Merriweather, careful not to undermine that interpretation, let the argument carry. Eventually, the Akan bowed to her Council's advice, though she confined the Earthlings to her private island retreat.

Since Endeavor's success, her stance had softened. She had grown more accepting of Merriweather's role, though she still preferred speaking with Cortez or Bishop. Recently, she had become curious about his relationship with Bishop, whom she frequently saw at his side.

Merriweather was about to step into the mess tent when the Akan herself appeared.

"Your female, Bishop," she said. "Tell me of her family. Is she of royal lineage?"

"No. I don't believe so. She comes from a poor family," Merriweather answered.

The Akan frowned. "Is she submissive to you?"

"Definitely not."

"That is good. And you are submissive to her?"

Merriweather chuckled. "It's... complicated."

"In your society, each person has a function?"

"I suppose so."

"What is the female Bishop's function?"

"She's a reporter."

The Akan tilted her head. "What is a reporter?"

"She's a writer—she chronicles our journey."

The Akan's frills turned a bright magenta, a color Merriweather had learned meant she was frustrated with his answers.

"Chronicles?" she said.

"She tells stories," Merriweather explained. "When we return to Earth, many will want to know what happened here. Bishop's skill is in telling that story so people will understand."

"Ah. We too have storytellers. Xenosta herself blessed me with that gift."

"I believe it," Merriweather said sincerely.

The Akan studied him. "I see you with Bishop often. Does she provide... another function for you?"

Merriweather hesitated, weighing how much to reveal. "Humans often bond in pairs—typically a male and female."

"And you and Bishop have bonded?"

"Well... yes."

"This is for reproduction, yes? The male Glyvash tells me your kind reproduces like Domlans." She spat the word *Domlans* as though it were distasteful.

Merriweather laughed. "I don't know about your Domlans, but yes, reproduction is one reason. Not the only one. Sometimes bonding is simply for companionship."

"Will you reproduce with Bishop?"

"No," Merriweather said, flushing. "At least... we haven't planned it. The situation here makes such things complicated."

The Akan smiled knowingly at his discomfort and shook her head. Merriweather could almost hear her thinking: *males*.

"Good. There are enough of your species on my planet as it is."

He took it as humor—a welcome sign.

"When will the other Earthlings return?" she asked.

"In about a year."

"Yet it took them only four months to reach the asteroid."

"That's true," Merriweather said carefully. "But they're traveling too fast to simply turn around. Space travel is more complicated than that."

"Explain," she commanded.

He caught himself—her tone was not a request but a warning: *Do not patronize me*.

"Our ships can carry only so much fuel. Aries doesn't have enough to fly straight back. Instead, when it nears Hypatia-f—what we also call Colossus—the planet's gravity will bend its course toward Hera. From there, the return will take about eight months."

"This is dangerous?"

"Very dangerous, Your Holiness."

The Akan considered his words, then nodded. "Your science is impressive. If you can fly from your world to mine, I believe your Aries can fly around this... Hypatia-f."

She turned to go, then paused.

"I place great value on what you and your Earthlings have done to save my world. It is difficult for me to say this to a—"

"A male," Merriweather offered.

"Yes. A male," she confirmed. "A male alien."

She took a step, then glanced back. "Tell your Lieutenant Mills he is using too much sand from my beach."

Merriweather smiled as she walked away, feeling for the first time that there might be real hope for peace between their peoples.

# CHAPTER 82

*Around Colossus*

Four months after the collision between Endeavor and the giant space rock, the tiny Aries lander, and its crew of three Earthlings sped through the Stygian blackness of space toward a rendezvous with Colossus, the gas giant that marked the outermost boundary of this alien solar system. Although well-trained and psychologically suited for the rigors of long-duration space missions, the three space travelers were feeling the effects of their arduous journey. The crew kept to a strict schedule, designed in part to combat the loneliness, the cramped conditions, and the absence of personal space. Surrounded by perpetual night, they established a diurnal environment, using subdued lighting and reduced temperatures in the evening, eight-hour daytime work schedules and fixed dining hours. They also encouraged each other to maintain a positive attitude and to remember that what they had accomplished was monumental and well worth any sacrifice they had to make.

Encouraged by Doc Lee, they established daily exercise routines as a key to their mental and physical well-being.

Lieutenant Bridges, face glistening with sweat, disconnected the bungee cords and the shoulder harness and stepped off the treadmill. He had just finished his daily exercise regimen when Doc Lee floated into the cargo bay. Aries had three pieces of exercise equipment crammed into the small space: a treadmill, a stationary bike, and a weight machine that used vacuum cylinders to mimic traditional weights, each designed for microgravity environments.

"You need a shower," she said, wrinkling her nose. "How far today?"

"Ten on the bike and ten on the treadmill," he replied.

"Slacking off a bit, aren't we? Didn't you do twenty yesterday?"

"Didn't know you were keeping score," said Bridges. "Just didn't feel like it today. I'm thinking about going back to bed."

"I don't think so," she said. "I need to run a battery of tests on you. It's time."

Bridges sighed. "I'm not in the mood, Doc. Can we do it later?"

"Like hell you will. You know the schedule. Captain's orders. Besides, you know very well what space travel does to the body, and what would Cortez say when we get back and you're a jellyfish? Sorry honey, I can't tonight," said Lee, doing her best Milo Bridges impression.

"All right, all right. I'll do another rep. Then I'll do your damned tests." Bridges mounted the stationary bike, activated the foot restraints, and began pedaling.

"That's my boy," said Lee. "Keep at it. I'm going up front to check in on our captain—and don't forget your shower. You stink."

A minute later, Lee floated into the cockpit where Captain Stoner was using RHODA to calculate their position relative to the enormous gas giant planet dominating the view from the cockpit holoview. Stoner was deep into his work and didn't notice Lee. However, that was common. Aries was a relatively small spacecraft, especially compared to Endeavor. It was impossible to be anywhere in Aries without rubbing elbows with one of your crewmates. One quickly learned to tune out everyone around them.

"Damn, that's bright," exclaimed Lee, shielding her eyes from the glare of the massive planet looming ahead.

"There are some sunglasses under the copilot seat," said Stoner, not looking up from his work.

"It's warm in here, too," said Lee as she retrieved the glasses.

"Sorry, nothing I can do about that right now," said Stoner.

"I have to run some tests on you and Milo today, Captain—Captain?"

"Fine," answered Stoner, hunched over his holoview, and not really hearing what Lee had said.

Lee waited a few seconds for Stoner to say something else. However, when nothing was forthcoming, she continued.

"Milo said that he's going to take a walk outside the ship to get some air, and he wanted to know if you want to join him."

"Fine," Stoner replied, "anything he wants."

"STONE," shouted Lee.

"What!" Stone abruptly turned to face the source of the shout.

"You and Bridges drive me bonkers. It's like talking to the bulkhead," Lee replied. "I said I have to do some scheduled medical tests on you and Bridges today."

"We may have to put those off a day or two," said Stoner, returning his attention to the holoview. "RHODA has finished our trajectory calculations."

"Still," she insisted," it's on the schedule, and the schedule is the schedule. Your orders."

"Can't help it, Doc. We're going to have our hands full."

Stoner tapped the actuator on his communicator.

"Bridges, can you come to the cockpit?"

"I don't see why we can't keep to the schedule," continued Lee.

"We have to…Oh, morning Milo. We've got our trajectory, and RHODA predicts we're within the window."

"How far off?" asked Bridges.

"Less than a tenth of a percent," said Stoner. "We'll likely have to make a minor adjustment in our trajectory after we clear the planet, but we definitely have enough velocity to escape orbit."

"So, we're home free," said Lee.

"There's still the issue of reentry," said Bridges.

"How bad is it?" said Lee.

"Colossus will bleed some of our velocity when we escape from its gravity, but not enough. We'll need to get our velocity down to about twenty-five K before reentry."

"We'll fire the EX23 when we get close to Hera in eight months," added Bridges.

"Any chance we'll get trapped in orbit around that thing?" Lee said, pointing at the gas giant hanging over Aries.

"We're OK there, Doc," said Bridges. "We're going too fast for that."

"Well, looky here," said Stoner. "Milo, I think I've found the Phoenix."

"Really? The Phoenix? Where? Let me see."

"RHODA, center the display around the following coordinates, maximum magnification," commanded Stoner. "I've already entered the coordinates," he added for Bridges' benefit.

Bridges examined the image now filling the holoview.

"There it is. Beautiful, isn't it? Too bad we don't have FTL on this rig. We might have been able to use the antimatter she's collected. How far away is it?" asked Bridges.

"About fifty thousand klicks," said Stoner. "It's pretty close to our current trajectory."

"How close?"

"We'll make our closest approach in about an hour—about two thousand klicks."

"That close? Great! We should be able to get some excellent images at that distance," said Bridges.

"How close are going to get to that damned thing?" Asked Lee, referring to Colossus.

Stoner scrolled down his holoview before answering.

"At perigee, we'll be about two hundred and twenty thousand klicks from the planet's photosphere. We'll have to wear our radiation suits."

"Damn. It's already too hot in here," said Lee.

"Can't be helped," said Stoner. "Jennifer, can you break them out?"

"How come you always use my first name when you want me to do something?" Lee asked.

"I wasn't aware," said Stoner, smiling.

"Captain, just for grins, can we see how much antimatter the Phoenix has collected?" asked Bridges.

"Want to check on your handiwork?" asked Stoner.

"Yeah. Mills and I worked damned hard on the design and construction. I'm sure he would want to know, too."

"OK. It's all yours."

"Thanks. OK, RHODA, put the containment vessel on Phoenix in transport mode."

"The vessel is in transport mode," RHODA replied.

"What's that all about? We're not planning to retrieve it, are we?" asked Lee.

"It was a shortcut," said Bridges. "The containment vessel supports direct communications with RHODA already. However, its com port address is disabled when the vessel is powered by the reactor. Which means we have to place the vessel..."

"Yeah, yeah, I got it," said Lee.

"RHODA, give me a readout of the current antimatter in the vessel."

"There are approximately five point three grams of antimatter in containment," she replied.

"Wow. That's a hell of a lot more than we expected. Colossus can be a future refueling station," said Bridges. "That would have given us enough to make it home."

"If only," said Lee.

"Yep, if only," repeated Bridges.

Suddenly, a loud siren sounded in the cockpit.

"What the hell," said Stoner. "RHODA report."

"Collision imminent—multiple objects—collision imminent."

"Shit!" Stoner exclaimed.

Stoner glanced at his crewmates, trying hard to remain calm. It wouldn't be the first time Stoner was involved in a collision with space debris; however, it was never something to take lightly.

"RHODA, take evasive action. Display the objects on the main holoview. Milo, Doc, get your suits on."

Bridges and Lee helped each other into their spacesuits while Stoner tried to find the inbound objects on the holoview.

"RHODA, highlight the incoming—"

Before Stoner could complete his request, a second audible alert sounded.

oooowaaaa oooowaaaa oooowaaaa.

"That's a cabin breach," said Bridges.

"Damn. RHODA, locate any cabin pressure leaks," said Stoner.

After getting no reply from the ship's AI, Stoner repeated the command.

"RHODA, report status."

Stoner, Bridges and Lee waited for RHODA's reply. There was none.

"Milo, get RHODA back online while Lee and I patch the leaks. Jennifer, grab the patch kit under the copilot seat. And turn off that damned alarm!" Bridges floated to the electronics bay and quickly found the damage: the same object that had punctured the hull had also shredded several computer modules.

Meanwhile, Stoner and Lee used the ULD to trace the hiss of escaping air to a hole in the forward bulkhead. They were already working the patch into place when Bridges shouted from across the cabin.

"I found the problem with RHODA—and it's bad."

"Can you fix it?" Stoner asked.

Bridges shook his head. "Not without spares for the modules. They're gone."

"Damn."

For a long moment, the three of them floated in silence. They were alive. That alone was no small thing. Experience told them the odds of being struck by anything catastrophic were vanishingly small; the odds of a second strike were slimmer still. RHODA's loss was serious—they had come to depend on her—but they were trained to survive without constant AI guidance. They had each other, and their own skills.

Bridges finally broke the silence.

"We have a big problem."

"No shit," Stoner muttered.

Bridges' face was grim. "No—I mean a bigger problem. We left the Phoenix containment vessel…"

"…in transport mode," said Stoner, finishing Bridges' sentence. "Holy crap."

"What?" asked Lee.

"The containment vessel is being powered by a battery, which will run out in about fifty minutes from now," said Bridges.

"Just about the same time, we'll be at our closest approach to the Phoenix," added Stoner.

"So, five grams of antimatter will come in contact with the vessel's walls and…"

Lee didn't have to finish her sentence. They all knew that if the explosion didn't kill them, the massive blast of radiation most certainly would.

"We could fire our engines and try to put more distance between us and it," said Lee.

"And then what?" Bridges asked. "We would be going in the wrong direction with no chance of getting home. We'd live longer, but our supplies won't last forever."

"If we're dead, there's zero chance we'll get home, Milo," said Lee.

"Bridges, can we even fire our engines without RHODA?" Stoner asked.

"I'll run a quick diagnostic to see if we can," answered Bridges.

It didn't take long for an answer, one they didn't want to hear.

"Are you sure, Milo? There must be a way," said Stoner.

"Maybe, if I had several hours and all the documentation, however, to save space and weight, we left much of it on Endeavor," said Bridges.

"Well, keep working on it. Jennifer, can we create a cocoon back in the cargo bay that could afford us more protection?"

Lee knew in her heart it was a fool's errand. However, she had no other option.

"We have some water and fuel bags back there. We could get between those."

"All right. Let's also get into our radiation suits and our EVA suits."

For the next forty minutes, the crew of Aries worked to improve their chances, each knowing it was probably in vain. The cramped cargo bay made it difficult to reposition the auxiliary fuel and water bladders Aries needed for this long-distance mission.

"RHODA, report the status of the Phoenix's containment vessel," said Stoner.

As before, there was no response from the ship's AI.

"Still dead," said Stoner dejectedly.

"Whatever happens, I've really enjoyed serving with you guys," said Bridges.

"Same here," said Lee.

"Maybe they'll name a city after us back on Hera," said Stoner.

Bridges was the first to hear it.

"Did you hear that?" said Bridges.

"Hear what?" said Lee.

"That noise on the emergency channel—there's a voice in there—in the noise," said Bridges.

"I don't hear anything," said Stoner.

With a forceful kick, Bridges propelled himself toward the ship's cockpit.

"Milo, there's no time," shouted Stoner.

Bridges reached the ship's communications panel and began fiddling with the signal filters, trying to suppress the noise caused by the proximity of the gas giant below them. Suddenly, a voice sounded through the panel's speakers.

"Aries spacecraft, this is ISA Starship Discovery, Captain Tyler speaking. Do you read?"

# EPILOGUE

*Aftermath*

The Phoenix didn't explode as feared. The artificial intelligence on ISA's Starship Discovery restored reactor power to the Phoenix's antimatter containment vessel with thirty-seven seconds to spare. Much to their gratitude, Captain Stoner, Lieutenant Milo Bridges, and Dr. Jennifer Lee were rescued from their crippled ship. Their disabled Aries One spacecraft was recovered and later restored to full readiness.

The voyage back to Hera took a little over seven minutes using the Starship's FTL drives.

The Discovery Starship, sent from Earth on a rescue mission, had followed the breadcrumb trail of marker buoys dropped by Endeavor during its two-year voyage to Hera and had immediately established contact with Outpost Swenson and Captain Merriweather. Merriweather informed Discovery's Captain Tyler of Endeavor's mission to deflect the incoming asteroid and asked him to intercept the Aries crew and bring them home.

Both Earthlings and Herans, including the Akan, welcomed the rescued crew as heroes.

A year later, in a ceremony attended by the Akan and her Council of Eleven, Merriweather raised ISA's flag over the first Earth Embassy, located not on the Akan's island retreat but in the city of Xanglora, less than a half kilometer from the Akan's Holy Temple.

Jake Merriweather had resigned his commission and accepted the position of ambassador to Hera—a first of its kind.

Don Stoner and newly promoted Lieutenant Commander Milo Bridges returned to Earth on Discovery to assume the duties of captain and first officer on the newly commissioned Starship Plank.

Newly promoted Lieutenant Commander Catriana Cortez assumed the duties of chief pilot and first contact officer on the starship Discovery.

Although Bridges and Cortez decided to pursue their careers in ISA, they were able to stay in daily contact using the perfected quantum communication technology. Two years later, they reunited on the newly discovered inhabited planet of Ba`ku.

Lieutenant Javier Rodriguez also transferred to Discovery as its senior mining officer.

Doctors Mann, Girard, and Graham established a new Earth University on Hera, the first institute of higher learning on the planet, to accept male and female students.

Zoe Bishop returned to Earth on Discovery. Her book, *My Life Among the Stars*, was number one on the Chronicle's best-seller list for over a year. A year later, she returned to Hera, where she married Ambassador Merriweather—the first marriage on the planet, human or Heran. Dakar Zaru of Dualla was her maid of honor. It was also the first ever broadcast on the new Heran Television Network, produced by Zoe Bishop.

Doc Jennifer Lee created a medical facility for those crewmembers of Endeavor and Discovery that stayed on Hera. She planned to extend her practice to all Heran patients as well.

Exoplanetologist Dr. Herbert Mann continued studying the Heran solar system, especially Hypatia-f, the gas giant known as Colossus. After much calculation, he and RHODA determined that the rogue planet Ulysses had not collided with one of the gas giant's moons as he had first thought. In fact, the lone moon circling Ulysses had collided with a Hypatian moon, hurling the asteroid Alpha One toward Hera.

Ulysses remained unscathed as it sailed past Colossus on its highly elliptical orbit and would return to Hera's vicinity in seventeen years.

The newly commissioned ISA Starship Plank would later embark on a multi-year mission to investigate an earth-sized water planet circling a binary star system 150 light years from Earth. The Heran male, Glyvash, was a member of his crew.

[1]William Stanley Braithwaite, "Distances" Lyrics of Life & Love, 1904, (1978-19620)

[2]Rudyard Kipling, "If", 1895, (1865-1936)

[3]D.H Lawrence, "Aware", 1913, (1885-1930)

[4]Emily Dickinson, "Ah Moon — and Star", ca 1860, (1830-1886)

[5]Rainer Maria Rilke, " In April ", 1918, (1875-1926)

[6]T.S. Eliot, "Little Gidding", 1943, (1888-1965)

[7]Victoria Tyler, "Murmuration", 2023, (1946-2023)